The SUGAR PALACE

Fiona McIntosh is an internationally bestselling author of novels for adults and children. She co-founded an award-winning travel magazine with her husband, which they ran for fifteen years while raising their twin sons before she became a full-time author. Fiona roams the world researching and drawing inspiration for her novels, and runs a series of highly respected fiction masterclasses. She calls South Australia home.

BOOKS BY FIONA McINTOSH
AVAILABLE FROM PENGUIN RANDOM HOUSE

Fields of Gold
The Lavender Keeper
The French Promise
Nightingale
The Tailor's Girl
The Last Dance
The Perfumer's Secret
The Chocolate Tin
The Tea Gardens
The Pearl Thief
The Diamond Hunter
The Champagne War
The Spy's Wife
The Orphans

In the DCI Jack Hawksworth series:

Bye Bye Baby
Beautiful Death
Mirror Man
Dead Tide
Foul Play

FIONA McINTOSH

The SUGAR PALACE

PENGUIN BOOKS

PENGUIN BOOKS

UK | USA | Canada | Ireland | Australia
India | New Zealand | South Africa | China

Penguin Books is part of the Penguin Random House group of companies
whose addresses can be found at global.penguinrandomhouse.com.

Penguin
Random House
Australia

First published by Michael Joseph, 2023
This edition published by Penguin Books, 2024

Copyright © Fiona McIntosh, 2023

Cover photography by Richard Jenkins Photography
Inside cover image by Rachel Kelli/Unsplash
Cover design by Louisa Maggio Design © Penguin Random House Australia Pty Ltd
Typeset in 11/16 pt Sabon LT Pro by Midland Typesetters, Australia

Printed and bound in Australia by Griffin Press, an accredited
ISO AS/NZS 14001 Environmental Management Systems printer

A catalogue record for this
book is available from the
National Library of Australia

ISBN 978 1 76104 702 2

penguin.com.au

MIX
Paper | Supporting
responsible forestry
FSC® C018684

We at Penguin Random House Australia acknowledge that Aboriginal and Torres Strait Islander
peoples are the Traditional Custodians and the first storytellers of the lands on which we live
and work. We honour Aboriginal and Torres Strait Islander peoples' continuous connection
to Country, waters, skies and communities. We celebrate Aboriginal and Torres Strait Islander
stories, traditions and living cultures; and we pay our respects to Elders past and present.

For Mum, who at age 95 adores confectionery in all shapes and sizes, has never stopped taking two sugars in her tea and whose eyes light up when I've baked something sweet.

PROLOGUE

LONDON

1913

The tailored gentleman stepped out slightly from the shadows and unfolded a cut-throat razor. It was the casualness of his movement – almost lazy – that sent a thrill of threat coursing through the younger man quaking before him. That and the benign smile, now partly illuminated. Only seeing half his face made him look even more dangerous, not that sixteen-year-old Alfie needed reminding of the fact. Right now, he was all too aware that he needed to explain himself to arguably the most dangerous person in London.

This man might be one of the new breed, but Alfie knew the North London gangster's reputation. He leaned especially into racketeering around racecourses, but he was up for most criminal sport, from bootlegging and drug trading to fixing football matches. Born to an Italian father and English mother, he sported a wholly London accent and lived in Clerkenwell, known as Little Italy – and he behaved like the famed Cosa Nostra that even Alfie had heard whispers about.

Just one candle had been lit, although thin lamplight from outside was bleeding into the deserted warehouse through dirty windows and cracks in the wall. Alfie wasn't sure where he'd been brought; the couple of burly men had captured, hooded and tied him before throwing him in the back of a van. The odour of old vegetation suggested he was in one of the grocery storehouses, or perhaps a depot where the continental flowers were brought for immediate storage after unloading. He was definitely down by the docks; he knew that much from the sound of water and the smell of oily ships.

From the intimidating, lengthening silence, Alfie decided they were waiting for him to speak first. 'Mr Sabini, sir, I'm Alfred Sweeting – er, Alfie – if you didn't know.' It was highly likely that his captor knew exactly who stood before him, but Alfie was aiming for respect by introducing himself politely.

'Go ahead, lad, I'm listening,' the shadowed man urged.

Alfie's hands shook as the two thugs on either side of him let go of his arms. He regarded what he could see of the gangster boss in his dark suit and waistcoat with his instantly recognisable collarless shirt. Even in the low light, there was no doubting the shape and certainly no mistaking the gritty voice of Charles 'Darby' Sabini.

Nevertheless, Alfie loosened his shoulders, shaking off the pain from being held so tightly, and tried unsuccessfully for a nonchalant expression, acutely aware that the man with the blade was not to be treated with even a hint of carelessness.

'Thank you, Mr Sabini,' he said. There was no point in playing dumb or innocent; these men didn't trouble themselves unless a point needed to be made. *Take responsibility for your losses*, he told himself as his late father had instructed. *Always make good*. He found his best manners and leaned into his well-developed lexicon. For a poorly – barely – educated child of the East End, he amused his elders with his champagne vocabulary and manner. 'I'm sorry to put you to this trouble. There was no need for you to take time from your busy life on my account. I want to assure you that I will pay what is owed, plus interest, by this time next week.' His words were courteous with just the right amount of subordination, he felt, to win him some extra time on his debt.

Alfie already knew that Sabini was a notorious stickler for the ways of the mob. He had learned about the hierarchy; that family was everything. And yet, even family was not immune, and the needs and rules of the mob came first; the flow of power must be adhered to.

Money flowed up and everyone answered to someone higher.

Except Sabini.

The money and power arrived at its zenith to reside with him. He was the boss of this family. His word was law.

Despite his control, Alfie found himself justifiably terrified that Sabini was here. If the young gambler was simply to be knocked around, left beaten and bleeding, perhaps, the order would have been given from a comfortable armchair while he smoked a cigar, and the dirty work would have fallen to one of his gang, known as the Sabinis.

The man gave a nod and refocused Alfie's thoughts keenly on the blade in his hand and its intentions. The features on Sabini's thinnish face rearranged themselves into a more serious expression that seemed contemplative. 'You see, Sweeting, I've already been waiting two weeks. And now you want me to wait longer still?'

Alfie dipped his gaze. The track had not been good to him; both horses and dogs had refused to win on his behalf. 'I made some bad calls, Mr Sabini. I've learned my lesson.' It sounded pathetic and hollow to him, and he could only imagine how empty it sounded to the gangster, who surely couldn't care less about a squit like him.

Sabini sighed. 'How old are you now, boy?'

'Fifteen, sir,' Alfie lied. He could get away with the fib due to his still-boyish looks; he didn't yet have to shave frequently and he hoped that fifteen just didn't sound old enough to be treated as a man.

He couldn't tell if Sabini was fully smiling or half scowling with part of his face shadowed. 'You don't have family left, do you, son?'

'No, sir. I'm all alone now.' Alfie hoped that might help.

'Shame. Family is important and you might not be in this pickle if you had some wisdom around you, especially with all the troubles in the world right now.'

'Yes, sir. I do know you're right.' He hoped he didn't sound oily and immediately began to fret that he had.

'I knew your old man,' Sabini said, now sucking on a cigar. In his fear Alfie hadn't noticed the cigar silently glowing in the man's other hand; his eyes had been fixed on the razor. Sabini lifted his chin and slowly blew out the smoke. 'He was a gambler too,' he continued, 'but your mother kept him in line and he knew when to quit. I fail to see what excuse you have for taking the risk the second time. You see, I understand you losing your money on the gee-gees a couple of weeks back. But you didn't cut your losses, son; instead you asked for grace from my boys.' Sabini pointed the blade, allowing it to catch the meagre light seeping around them. It spoke only menace. 'Now, I'm a generous man,' he added conversationally, 'and I granted you that grace, but you used your wages this week to bet some more instead of paying me what was owed. That's right, isn't it?'

'Yes, sir,' Alfie said, looking down. What else could he do but be honest now and show contrition?

After taking another puff on his cigar that glowed an angry orange as he sucked on it, Sabini spoke again. 'You were no longer gambling with your money, lad, but mine. You should have paid me first, like your mother would have made your father do. Unlike you, I have mouths to feed,' he said with a nod, sounding altogether amiable. 'I have three daughters and my boy is growing big; he eats as much as me already. His mother can't keep up with how much

4

food he needs.' Sabini's expression broke into a sorrowful smile and his prey nodded, dejected. 'I want that boy to play for one of the top football teams. He's got the goods, you know. Ambition too.'

Alfie nodded again, trying to sound interested, but his gaze was helplessly fixed to the blade. Was it destined for his throat?

'Do you have ambition, Sweeting?'

He snapped his attention back to the half face. 'I do, Mr Sabini, sir. I have many ideas for making money. I just don't have the money to get started.'

'Perhaps if you saved rather than gambled . . . just a thought?' It was dryly said, meant to make a cutting point. 'You're young, not much older than my kid, so I'm going to allow you some slack here.'

Alfie's fearful expression relaxed, his eyes widening with the joy of pleasurable disbelief . . . but only for a heartbeat.

'I'm only going to take a finger.'

And the hope was dashed as quickly as it rose. Alfie's trembling returned, now more intense. 'A finger?' he stammered, horror arriving with an acid taste at his throat.

'Yeah, lad. You understand I've gotta be fair. I can't have fellows like you running amok or everyone will. They'll think I've gone soft.' He chuckled kindly. 'Now, it may be my failing, but I like you. You're not a bad kid so much as unlucky. But you also have a problem, and I think what I do tonight will help you to focus on it. I'm doing you a good deed with this. Consider it a lesson.'

'Mr Sabini, please, I—'

'Don't beg, son.' He gave a tutting sound. 'Where's your dignity?'

Alfie felt his dignity leaving as his bladder emptied. The thugs smelled it before they pinpointed the source and stepped away, smirking. 'I'm frightened,' he admitted unnecessarily but it was something to say into the silence.

'That's normal. Everyone is when they must pay their dues in kind. Tell you what,' Sabini said, almost conspiratorially, and blew out a lungful of smoke. 'Call me an old softie, but I'll let you choose.'

'Choose what?' Alfie wondered aloud, looking between the boss and his men, and then understood, his terror deepening. 'You mean which finger?'

'There, you see.' Sabini smiled at his minions. 'He's a bright boy, what did I tell you?' He gave a nod. 'Right, lads, I must be somewhere. Let's get this done. Make it clean and quick. We'll get you something to bite on, boy, as an extra kindness.' Sabini nodded towards an old fruit carton and Alfie watched as one of the men broke off a piece and offered it.

1

'Where've you been?' Mary Fairweather asked her daughter, Grace, lips stitching themselves into a line of dismay.

Grace busied herself with retying her apron, catching her breath. 'I've just had to work my way around another riot in the Domain. There are hundreds, probably thousands, of people there.'

Her father, Hugh, handed out change and thanked a customer before strolling up. 'What's going on?'

'Grace is saying there's more of that socialist rioting going on in the city.'

'They were burning a red flag when I was passing,' she added.

'Well, Grace, you're safe, that's what matters,' he replied, straightening his own apron. 'And you've always got Norm to protect you.' The bell over the door tinkled twice in rapid succession as new customers walked in. 'It's like Clapham Junction in here,' he admitted.

Grace didn't know where Clapham Junction was, but it sounded busy. Probably a place in the old country, which her father and his own often became nostalgic about. 'I imagine Norm's in the thick of it,' she remarked to her mother, who predictably gave an indulgent smile. Grace knew how much her mother approved of Norman Jenkins, who'd risen from the ranks of the Ragged School at The Rocks to make something of himself. He was now a senior sergeant in the local police, working around Circular Quay.

'I thought I'd make some toffee apples.' She looked between her parents as her mother drifted off to serve the customers. 'We could sell them for a penny each as the weather is cooling. Also, Dad,' she said, before realising her father was busy sorting tins on shelves, engrossed in his task. 'Dad, listen to me,' she pleaded softly.

He turned, unable to hide the pride in his voice despite his words. 'So my slip of a daughter is now going to tell me something about the grocery business, is she?'

Grace smiled; her father's tongue was never truly sharp. He found a way to communicate everything from vexation to fury in the most accommodating manner. 'I've been thinking about the boxes of chocolate we have on sale.'

'Have you now,' he remarked absently.

'Dad, please,' she said, a hint of frustration in her tone. She looked at her mother, who was fully engaged with a customer.

Hugh Fairweather sighed and turned to face Grace so she might continue.

'I pay close attention to what our customers say, and I've noticed that the most popular choice in the box of Hoadley's Violet Milk selection is the little chunk of honeycomb. Can you believe that?'

'I see. Should I be impressed with this observation?'

Grace sighed audibly to show him his lack of interest was frustrating.

He shrugged. 'And?'

'Let me make some honeycomb that we can sell as our own product in separate blocks. If it's that popular, we can take advantage of the preference and give our customers what they want.'

Her mother returned to the conversation. It seemed to Grace that even out of earshot she somehow was able to eavesdrop. 'Now, how would you offer them, Grace? Honeycomb is notoriously sticky and then it liquefies and oozes.'

'Well, that's just it – I've solved the problem or I wouldn't be suggesting it.' She tried to keep impertinence from her tone.

'Oh, go on with you,' her mother said. 'Your head is full of lollies and chocolates when it should be full of lace and wedding bells.'

Grace sighed loudly. 'I'm in no hurry for that.'

'Well, you should be,' her mother admonished. 'A lovely man like Norm. They don't come along that often, my girl. He'll do you proud.'

'I'd like to think you'll both be proud of *me* one day for more than who I marry – when I have my own confectionery store. I'll remind you of this day when Hoadley's catches on and starts producing blocks of chocolate-covered honeycomb that it sells separately for a huge profit. Time is of the essence, don't you see?'

'I'm sure we will, my love, but right now, I want you to stack the new delivery of eggs. The fellow is unloading them now. Hurry along.'

Grace sighed. 'I'll be out the back, then,' she said, scowling at the sound of hammering on metal, a regular part of their life now that the famed Sydney Harbour Bridge was under construction. It had been noisy enough when the building works began on the two approaches that would allow a bridge to span the harbour, but now it felt overwhelming – like a loud concert that relentlessly accompanied their lives. The wireless and the newspaper reports were full of its excitement daily, but for those who lived nearby or beneath it, the new bridge was a cacophony.

Moving away from the counter, Grace went through a small doorway to the storeroom and then to the back door that led out into a tiny alley. There she noted a man, not too far off her own age of twenty-six, she guessed; he was carrying trays of eggs with great care, whistling as he walked.

'Hello, gorgeous,' he said in something that wasn't an Australian accent.

She gusted a laugh at his forwardness. 'You're new. Where's old Bert?'

'Oh, he had a fall. I'll be doing the deliveries for a while.' He grinned. 'Now, I think I'll look forward to them.' He gave a cheeky wink, his face settling into an expression that spoke of endless mischief.

'I see. So what's your name?'

'I'm Alfie,' he said.

'I'm Grace.'

'And you work here, do you? Amongst all this terrible noise?' he asked.

'Oh, you get used to it.' She sighed. 'We try not to complain about the bridge. It will change Sydney forever.'

He grinned. 'You know it's an English firm that won the international competition to design it, don't you?'

'Yes, I do,' she said. So he was English then, that made sense. She was highly aware of the difference in their accents now she'd heard more than his hello. She hadn't thought of herself as having one before, but he certainly did – there was no doubting the cockney in him. What did she sound like to him?

He didn't seem in a hurry to leave. 'Do you live around here, then?'

She pointed up. 'Above the store. Er, my parents own this grocery.'

'Oh? You're a shopkeeper, eh?' His voice took on a lofty tone.

'Not exactly.' Secretly, that was precisely what she planned to be. 'It's Dad's place. I've worked here since I was in school.'

'You going to inherit it, then?'

'I don't know. I don't really want to think of that time.'

'I don't have anyone, so I can think like that.'

'Like what?'

'You know . . . a bit selfish,' he said, shrugging.

'Cynical too.'

'I don't know what that means. You must have stayed at school with your clever language.'

Grace nodded. 'You didn't?'

'No. Not where I was brought up.'

She couldn't help enjoying his London lilt. 'How long have you been in Australia?'

'Ooh, probably a couple of years now. I have to be honest, Gracie, I didn't expect to survive the war in Europe. But when I got back from the Front I couldn't settle. So I took myself off on a ship to the other side of the world, like a grand explorer.'

Gracie. A nickname already? 'Gosh, how adventurous,' she said, impressed, wishing she could do something as exciting as that. 'So, are you enjoying Sydney?'

'Course! Who wouldn't love this place and its sun and warmth? I've been doing all sorts of odd jobs, but I've got plans.'

'What sort of plans?'

He tapped his nose to say they were plans for only him to know. 'I'll tell you when they're feeling ripe.'

She laughed. 'I'll look forward to it. So the boy who didn't finish school is ambitious?'

'Aren't you? Or are you one of those with your head full of marriage and tin lids?'

'Tin lids?'

'Kids . . . babies.'

She found she was helplessly drawn to the way he spoke, with his dropped consonants and his cocky manner, but she bristled at the presumption. 'Oh, I have plans too.'

'Good. Be a waste to marry the wrong fellow,' he said, casting her a dimpled grin. 'Leave these here, shall I?' He pointed to a counter just in the doorway. It came out as 'ear', and she wanted to keep listening to him forever.

'Yes, that's fine. And how would you know who is right or not right for me?'

'I dunno, I must have the gypsy in me and can foresee these things.' He winked.

She grinned at this assuredness. 'Wouldn't school have made it easier for your *plans*?' she asked, leaning on the final word.

'Nah, I left school as soon as I could. I was rubbish at everything, except adding and taking away, multiplying. You know, numbers.'

'Arithmetic,' she said.

'That's what they called it, yes. I used to annoy the teachers because I knew the answers before they'd hardly set the question.'

'You're a fibber, Alfie.'

He looked wounded, and touched his heart. 'Would I lie to a beautiful girl like you? No, sir. Go on, test me.'

She laughed. 'Pardon?'

'Test me. Throw some numbers at me.'

Grace leaned her head to one side, considering. 'All right.' She reeled off the first numbers that came into mind. 'Nine plus four, minus six, add three, and times it by five.'

'That would be a nice round fifty.' The answer was a second short of instant.

'Wait, what?' She couldn't help sounding shocked. 'I haven't worked it out for myself yet. Hang on.'

'You don't have to, Gracie, darlin'. I'm right.'

He was. She gave him a slit-eyed look of disbelief.

'I'll do it again if you don't trust me.'

'Right, well, this time I'm going to know the answer first.'

She removed a tiny stub of pencil from behind her ear – just as her dad had worn his for as long as she could recall – and pulled some paper from her apron pocket. She took a couple of moments to calculate. Distantly her mother's voice sounded. 'Coming!' she called over her shoulder. 'Are you ready?'

'Yep, but this time it will cost you a kiss.'

'Pardon?' She looked astonished.

'Just on the cheek. Don't be naughty now and suggest anything more.'

She found him helplessly amusing; his turn of phrase was addictive and his eyes were like polished glass buttons of grey that won their shine from the endless humour in them. Grace couldn't deny he had a lovely open face, full of amusement and daring. His features were a bit ragged, like his clothes, and he had an unshaven chin, unkempt eyebrows and the hint of a wispy moustache. His hair was untidy, its unruly edge like an untrimmed hedge, falling haphazardly over a grimy collar. There were smudges on his skin and his fingernails were grubby too but despite it all, there was something powerfully attractive about him and his lean, long-legged presence. She felt drawn like a child to a proffered sweetie. And he was fun. Given the understandable gloom of so many of the men who had returned from the war, it was like a gift to have a man with a sense of joy in her midst.

'Fine,' she agreed, trying not to think of Norman as Alfie grinned at her, putting a hand behind his ear to add drama to the moment as he feigned listening with extra care. 'Ready?'

'Whenever you are, darlin'.'

'Twenty-seven divided by nine, times eleven, minus fourteen.'

'Nineteen,' he said within two beats of her heart.

She opened her mouth in part awe, part vexation that he'd solved it so fast, and watched him tap his cheek with a finger. 'Oooh,' she grumbled. 'Are you cheating somehow?'

'No. I told you. Just good at numbers,' he repeated, tapping his cheek again. 'You'd better hurry, that lady's calling again.'

She nodded. 'That lady is my mother.' She stepped into the alley to pay her dues and as she leaned to kiss his cheek, he whipped his head around and instead kissed her on the lips.

Grace gaped at him, as Alfie exploded into delighted laughter. 'You walked right into that,' he explained.

'How wicked of you! I'll have you know I'm engaged.'

That didn't seem to give him pause. 'I see no ring. Hope he's not a tightarse as well?'

'As well as what?'

'Boring,' he said.

'Bor . . . You know nothing about him!'

'I know he's got good taste but that's about all. What's his name?'

'Norman Jenkins, Norm, if you must know.'

'Well, that's a dull enough name, darlin'. What's he keeping you waiting for? Doesn't he know someone will snap you up?'

She looked back at him, her mouth gaping at his mockery. 'Well, it's not official yet,' was all she could manage to mumble.

He shrugged. 'Actually, don't be hasty, Gracie.' He winked. 'I told you, I've got the sight in me and the right bloke hasn't asked you yet.'

'And he is *not* boring.'

'Isn't he? See you, beautiful Grace,' and as he gave a little bow, his hand at his waist as he bent, she saw he had only four whole fingers. The little finger was a stump. He must have lost it during the war, she thought sadly.

Grace watched as Alfie strode away, his gait cocky, his whistle jolly. He seemed to know she was watching him and turned back to blow her a kiss. He hadn't needed to. The touch of his lips on hers was still strong in her memory, and despite him being rough around the edges, he tasted of peppermint, while Norm tasted of tobacco.

2

It was a few days later that her father properly introduced Grace to the new delivery lad. It was nearing nine-thirty in the morning and she had emerged from their rooms above the store where she had just finished testing a recipe for marshmallow. Standing at the counter, looking every bit as cocksure as she recalled was the young man who'd stolen a kiss.

'This is Alfie Sweeting. Alfie, this is our daughter—'

'—Grace,' he finished for her father. 'Yes, we've met.' He nodded politely in greeting.

'Ah, the eggs?' her father asked.

'Yes, Mr Fairweather.'

'Right, well, Grace, I've hired Alfie as our new delivery boy.' He didn't notice her surprised expression as he turned to Alfie. 'Grace will show you how we do things around here. Can you start tomorrow?' Alfie nodded eagerly. 'Good. We'll provide a bicycle, but my wife will want you looking neat. Have a bath, clean your fingernails.' He grinned before turning back to Grace. 'I've got some business to attend to. Your mother should be here shortly. Watch the shop, Grace.'

She nodded and made sure she saw her father leave before she let her gaze land back on Alfie, who was now giving a low whistle at all the goods behind the counter. 'Imagine being you and just being able to take down a tin of something and eat what you feel like.'

'And where's the profit in that?'

He chuckled. 'You've been trained well.'

'I've grown up as a shopkeeper's daughter. What do you expect? You will clean up properly, won't you?'

'Is your mother that scary?'

Grace shrugged with a smile. 'Don't say my father and I haven't warned you,' she replied. 'Do you like looking grubby?'

'Not at all. I'd like to look all clean and beautiful like you, Grace. But the sort of work that comes my way isn't pleasant. It's grubby work.'

'So wash.'

'I do, whenever I can.'

She laughed. 'What does that mean?'

It was Alfie's turn to shrug. 'I don't always know where I'll be kipping.'

Grace stared at him, embarrassed and now with concern in her expression. 'Why?'

'Don't you worry about me.'

'But if you're going to work for Fairweather's, they'll expect you tidy every morning.'

He clearly didn't know how to respond to that, so he turned on his heel and began exploring the shop.

'I'll ask my father if he knows of anyone who might have some room at the back of their shop,' Grace continued. 'We use ours for storage but others might—'

'Would you?' Alfie looked hopeful. 'I'll be no trouble. In fact I'll earn it, how's that? Odd jobs, help around the place.'

She smiled. 'I'll ask.'

16

He returned to stand in front of her. 'Listen, about the other day. I was just being cheeky and—'

The bell sounded and they both looked over at the door. Grace felt a brush at her sleeve and when she looked back, Alfie was no longer there. She blinked in consternation but turned back to the customer. A well-dressed man who had his back to her was holding the door out politely for a woman entering with a small child.

'Thank you,' the woman said.

'You're welcome,' the fellow said, raising his hat before closing the door.

Grace stepped out from behind the counter and smiled at them both welcomingly. 'Perhaps you'd like to serve the gentleman first,' the woman said. 'I promised my little one a sweetie and I know she'll take an age choosing.'

'All right, Mrs Phillips.' Grace smiled at the woman and then bent down to be level with the child. 'And welcome, Lucy. We've got some new lollipops over there.' Grace pointed to where she had insisted to her parents they put the sweets, all at a lower level for children to be able to see easily. They'd fought her on broadening into confectionery, believing barley sugars or butterscotch more than sufficient, but she'd remained determined that the stocking of sweets was her domain and they were to trust her on this. It hadn't taken long before she could grin at them and say, 'Next to cigarettes and bread, our confectionery outsells everything else.' At her mother's raised eyebrow, she'd qualified her statement. 'If we compare by number of units sold.'

Grace moved behind the counter to serve the newcomer and to her astonishment found Alfie cringing with his back against the big bench's shelves and his knees hugged close. He put a finger to his lips and his keen expression pleaded that she say nothing.

'Er,' she stammered, looking back at the customer. 'Er, yes, sir, how can I help you?'

The dapper man in a pinstripe suit removed his hat and as he raised his eyes to meet hers, she saw a vicious scar that ran vertically the length of one cheek. He was a bit too well-dressed to be from around The Rocks area but that scar spoke of the eastern side of the city where all the crooks tended to lurk.

The man nodded towards a shelf behind her. 'I'll take a tin of Dixson's flake cut, love.' Nervously she pointed to one of the tins. 'No, the Yankee Doodle.' He gestured further over.

She put the right tin on the counter and forced her gaze from the scar to meet his hard look. 'Do you need some papers?' she asked, sticking to her personal creed of always trying to sell one more item to each customer than they perhaps came in for.

'Er, yes. Good idea, I'd better get some.' As she fetched the tiny packet, he frowned. 'Listen, love, you didn't see a young fella in here a few minutes ago, did you?'

Grace was sure her attempt at appearing innocent only made her look vacant. 'A young man?' She shook her head.

'I don't have change.' He put a florin on the counter.

'That's all right. We have plenty,' she said, managing to dredge up a tone that sounded impossibly bright as she rang up the sale on the till. 'You were saying?'

'What?'

'About the young man.'

Scarface nodded thoughtfully. 'He's a scruffy-looking fellow, about yay high,' he said, gesturing just above his shoulders. 'Probably bought nothing as he hasn't got a couple of ha'pennies to rub together. More likely to steal from you.'

Grace was aware of Alfie shaking his head vehemently below the counter. 'Your change,' she said, counting out the heavy coins into his palm. 'No, sir, I didn't see him and I've been here all morning, but perhaps—'

'Never mind. I could swear he came in here.' He placed the

coins into his pocket in a jaunty motion and gathered up his tobacco and papers.

'Is he in trouble?' Grace chanced.

'When I get hold of him, he is.' The man smirked, walking towards the door.

'And why's that?'

Scarface tapped his nose. 'Don't you worry your pretty little head. He knows he's got what's coming.'

'You make me feel scared for him,' she admitted, not daring to look at Alfie.

'You should be, love, because when I catch him, I plan to kick him into next week.'

She shrugged, hands open. 'Then I can't help but hope you don't catch him. I don't like aggression in any shape or form.'

The man chuckled but not kindly. 'For a girl at The Rocks you have a high opinion of yourself, love.'

'Not everyone around The Rocks is uneducated or illiterate, sir.' She didn't care that she was challenging Scarface; she did not anticipate he'd ever be around this way again, so he wasn't a regular customer she needed to develop or pander to.

He laughed at her. 'I like your attitude. Listen, I'll tell you what, my beauty. If you see a scrawny fellow as I've described, with hard-to-miss pale grey eyes, can you tell him that George is looking for him?' Scarface put a penny back on the counter. 'Here, get yourself some nice ribbon for that pretty hair of yours.'

Grace hated him in that instant, not just for the aggression that seemed to simmer beneath his innocuous words, but for the condescending way he talked to her . . . It was dismissive. Norm did that sometimes and she didn't enjoy it much from him either. She noticed a wedding ring on the man's finger and immediately felt sorry for his wife.

A tiny voice whispered, *You could be her someday if you're not careful.* It vexed her that the voice spoke in Alfie's cockney accent.

'George,' she repeated carefully.

He nodded. 'Good girl. You do that or I might have to be back.' He tipped his hat and gave a wink and then annoyed her further, although she hadn't thought it was possible in this moment, by tapping his fingernail near the coppers that sat on the counter. His grin pulled his scar at his cheek towards his eyes, and it looked even more fearsome as a result. She watched him leave, the sound of the bell jangling her already twitching nerves.

She swung around to scowl at Alfie, still seated on the floor behind the counter. His hand was on his chest as though trying to slow his breathing.

'Cor, that was close,' he said but looked amused rather than fearful.

'I'm to tell you that George is looking for you,' she hissed with a low breath, her voice hard and clipped, filled with enough sarcasm to drown him.

He laughed. 'Yeah, I got that.'

'Alfie, I don't know what you're playing at but if either of my parents—'

'They won't.'

'Won't what?'

'Whatever you were about to say,' he said, giving her such a bright smile that she found it hard to remain angry.

Mrs Phillips arrived at the counter, with Lucy clutching her sweets. 'Musk sticks,' her customer said with sigh. 'I can't imagine she'll love the flavour.'

'It's the colour,' Grace replied, letting go of her held breath. 'Little girls can't resist the bright pink. Two?' she offered. 'And what about you – no treats for you today, Mrs Phillips? Or perhaps some necessities? Tea, coffee, bread, biscuits?'

The woman smiled. 'Are biscuits a necessity?'

'I think they are on a Thursday, especially these lovely fresh Marie biscuits. We've been waiting on these for a few months.'

'Is that so?'

Grace had taught herself all sorts of sales techniques but had discovered that a short story, nothing too complex, always helped to get a positive answer from a customer. She moved into story-telling mode now. 'Yes, they're so fresh – at their best – and directly from Peek Freans in Bermondsey, England.' She gave a grin. 'I don't know if you are aware of this, but Bermondsey is known as Biscuit Town because the plant is so huge and the whole town always smells of sugar and baking biscuits.' She knew this would make her customer smile. 'Wouldn't that be delicious? I learned that Mr Peek is a tea importer, and he and his sons set up a biscuit manufac-turing business that complimented the tea, but when one of his sons died and the other went to America, Mr Peek encouraged his niece, Hannah, to run the biscuit factory with her new husband George Frean.'

Mrs Phillips chuckled. 'And a new business began?'

'Exactly!' Grace praised. 'Anyway, I suspect these will be gone by next week; we only have a couple of tins at the ready.' It wasn't strictly a lie. What she should have said was, *We only have two tins on the floor. The rest are still in the boxes ready to be unpacked.* 'I also have some Pat-a-Cake shortbreads and some Golden Puffs.'

'Oh, all right then, you've twisted my arm. I'll take half-a-dozen of the Maries and two Golden Puffs. My John will enjoy them with his tea.'

'The Maries are great for dunking,' Grace said, mimicking the motion of dipping a biscuit into the tea.

The woman smiled. After she'd paid and left, Grace turned from the till but before she could land another rebuke, Alfie grinned and stood up from his hiding spot. 'You're some saleswoman,

Grace,' he said, straightening his clothes. 'I bet if I fell asleep and you removed them, you could sell me back my own shoes.'

'Now why would I want to do that?'

He shrugged but didn't lose the amusement from his expression. 'It was praise for your sales skills.'

She ignored the compliment. 'What about that nasty man?'

Alfie's features straightened but his eyes seemed to sparkle with mischief. 'Thank you for not shopping on me.'

Her frown deepened in confusion. 'Shopping?'

'Shopper, grasshopper . . . grass.'

'You're making no sense to me.'

'Us cockney lads rarely do.' He put on a posher voice. 'But I'll speak the King's English for you. I am grateful you didn't tell him anything.'

'Well, I'm not a dobber,' she assured him. 'Besides, I didn't like him. I didn't like his tone or his manner or the way he spoke down to me. I don't answer to him.'

'Good for you. Don't let any man push you around.' Alfie lifted his cloth cap in respect. 'Now, about that bed for tonight . . .'

'Wait. Why is he looking for you?'

'I don't know,' he tried.

She held his gaze far more directly than he could hold hers, and he shifted guiltily.

'Right, look, I might owe him some money.'

'Might?'

'I do owe him,' he admitted, sounding resigned to her interrogation.

'So now you've made me complicit.'

'Have I? Not sure what that means, darlin'.'

'It means you've dragged me into your problem and if he sees you here, he'll leap to the wrong conclusion that we're friends and I—'

'Aren't we friends?'

'Alfie, my father is your new employer.'

He stepped closer, trying to disarm her. 'But the two of us are friends, right? We've kissed.'

'No.' She stepped back. 'That was a trick. I'm engaged.'

'No, you're not,' he said, waggling a finger.

She took a visible breath to show him how hard it was to stay calm. 'Let's be clear. You kissed me. There is a stark difference to what you're inferring. I didn't invite you to.'

He laughed. 'Oh, Grace. Just the mere sight of you is an invitation. There's no hot-blooded chap on this continent who wouldn't want to kiss you.'

'His words made her blush. 'I don't know what to say to that.'

'Say you'll let me take you out sometime.'

She dismissed his invitation with a sigh. 'How much do you owe, Alfie? Don't lie to me. I want the truth or we will never be friends.'

'I owe him ten shillings.'

She looked mortified. The Australian pound had been returned to its gold standard only that year, but it had catapulted in worth since the Great War. 'That would feed a family around here for weeks. How did you accrue such a debt?'

'I was trying to win money to pay rent, food and to look after a family.'

'You have a family?' Grace's voice became small, less high-handed and she sounded chastened.

'They might as well be my own. Four youngsters, father dead, mother very ill and can't work.'

'Are you lying to me, Alfie?'

'I swear I'm not. I was gambling, that's the truth,' Alfie said with earnest, his hand covering his heart. 'But I had my reasons.'

Her whole demeanour changed to one of empathy. 'Does he mean it? He'll hurt you if he catches you?'

'At the very least, yes. But I've faced worse.'

She blew out her cheeks, worried. The bell sounded again. 'Wait here,' she said. 'I must serve a customer.'

Alfie amused himself looking through some of the hardware items for sale. When she returned, she handed him a half sovereign note.

'There. Go find that nasty George, who dresses like a gentleman but acts like a thug, and pay him,' she instructed. 'And then come back tomorrow and begin your workday.'

'Did you take this out of the till?' he asked, astonished.

'You're very fortunate that someone had to settle up their bill not long before you arrived. Otherwise we'd never have such a big note on hand. I'll return it before my father cashes up for the day.'

'How?'

'From my private savings, Alfie. That's how.'

He blinked, looking momentarily stunned. 'Why would you do that?'

'Who else is going to help you? I want to know that you will turn up tomorrow to hold down this steady job, so that you can continue helping the family you mentioned.'

He looked ashamed and she presumed his pride was getting in the way.

'Take it. I want to help them too.'

'I'll pay you back.'

'Yes, you will. In fact, I'll put interest on it. As of today, you owe me ten shillings and a penny. And just like George, I suspect, I shall keep adding interest for as long as you keep me waiting.'

'You're tough.'

'This is a business transaction. My charity is to the needy family. But we need you to work here.'

24

'Oh.' He grinned. 'Come on, that's not the only reason. You like me, I think.'

'You presume too much, Alfie Sweeting.'

'What's your gentleman's name again?'

Grace blushed. 'Norman Jenkins. He works for the city now.'

'Ooh, pride is a sin, my old granny used to say.'

'I am proud of him.'

'You're not in love with him though, Gracie.'

She gave a soft gasp. 'How would you know? And don't give me the gypsy excuse.'

He grinned. 'Because if you were, you'd have slapped my face the other day when I chanced a kiss.'

Grace blinked, feeling trapped. It was true, she hadn't felt offended. If anything, she'd felt flattered. 'I'm not the violent type.'

'Good, because before another week's out, I would love to kiss you again and prove to you how much you don't love boring Norm.'

'You owe me money, Alfie.' She offered a hand for him to shake.

Alfie smiled. 'All right.' He shook.

'Your word had better be your bond.'

'It is. Tell me, what are you saving for?'

'When I know you better and I trust you more, I'll share,' she said. 'Now go. I don't want to see that man in here again, and you certainly wouldn't want my mother catching wind of any debt collectors. Be here for seven-thirty or you'll answer to my parents. And before you ask, I will try to find a place for you to sleep. You can wash up in our storage room each morning before work. We have a sink there.'

He gave her a salute and hurried to the door, before turning to blow her a kiss. 'You're a lifesaver, Grace Fairweather, and don't go saying yes to that Norman bloke, all right? Give me a chance.'

After he'd gone, she realised her cheeks felt hot; it was not from his flattery, but from her guilt. Perhaps Alfie did have the gypsy sight, because he was reading her doubts about her relationship with Norman.

3

Alfie whistled as he weaved his way jauntily around The Rocks, dodging barrows, horses, children playing around the street, the laundry women and the sailors strolling around the neighbourhood, newly off the latest ship to dock and looking for beer, food and women. One of the launderers suddenly gave a warning before tipping out a large tin basin of sudsy water and several people, including Alfie, skipped ahead or aside to avoid the slush.

For the first time in a long time, Alfie's grin felt real and his heart felt full. Finally, aged twenty-eight, he felt like he had something to aim for. His mind was full of Grace. Girls couldn't resist him, it seemed. Even his old ma used to say his looks could return soured milk to sweet again.

'You mind my words, though, Alfie,' she said, waggling a finger in between terrible bouts of coughing. 'Those looks will only carry you so far.' She'd died just a few months later.

He'd been a magnet for girls; luring them had never been an issue. At first it was fun, knowing he only had to cast a glance at the right time and a pretty girl would notice him. The trouble, though, was that most of the girls he met were not ambitious. They wouldn't match his aspirations to improve their lot and were often perplexed by his big plans. To Alfie these girls seemed happy to be moving around in the same familiar circle that their mother had before them and her mother before that, and he could sense their resignation that living hand to mouth with a troupe of children to worry about was their future. They needed to marry and they were hunting for husbands who were young, strong and capable of working for years. The fact that women found Alfie pleasing to the eye was the bonus – not a prerequisite, he gathered, not even a basic desire once they'd moved past the dreamy early teen years. By the time the girls of his neighbourhood had hit seventeen and eighteen, their outlook had become pragmatic; their aim was to marry and get out from under their parents' roofs and rules . . . if they were fortunate enough to have two parents and a roof over their heads.

The Great War had taken too many fathers. When Alfie had joined up – mostly to escape his creditors – he'd fully expected not to return and he'd made his peace with that. But luck had followed him; there had been plenty of near misses, and a couple of injuries but none so serious that he couldn't return to his fellow soldiers, who seemed to be dropping with alarming speed. By his second year he'd stopped making friendships because of the trauma of losing them almost as soon as they were made. He'd spent 1918 as a loner and had then volunteered to be part of the clean-up corps in France, which sapped another eighteen months of his life. By 1920 he was back in civvies in England and feeling lost. Everything seemed so different. He'd tried lots of normal jobs and failed, mostly because he was bored. Loud noises in warehouses and around the docks tended to make him jump, but if he was being honest, he was coping better than most. He heard many stories of men unable to fit back into life in England, men who felt like strangers to their families or were simply unable to set the memories of war and its traumas aside.

Alfie had once admitted to someone – he couldn't remember who – that he tended to seek danger, even though he didn't mean to. At war, he'd put his hand up for the most lethal of tasks and once back in quiet England he realised he was missing that danger . . . certainly the feeling of adventure. He'd hoped sailing to the other side of the world would reset his life, giving him something to work hard for.

Was his luck running out now though? It had to be. Two years almost in Sydney and not only a new job but a crisp note in his pocket. Best of all, there was Grace in his life. *I don't care if you're promised*, he thought. *You're the love of my life. I feel it in every bone.*

'Oi, whistler!' Alfie snapped out of his thoughts as he saw weedy Ron Dyer in front of him. Ever since they'd met as new rat-catchers in this area, Ron had reminded him of the creature they hunted, both in looks and manner. Alfie knew not to trust him entirely, but they had become friends of sorts and helped each other out to get good numbers of the rats. It was Alfie who had advised Ron on the difference between a ship rat and a sewer rat.

'They tear each other to pieces,' Alfie had explained.

'What does it matter? We kill 'em anyway.'

'I'm educating you, Ron. You see, we can also make money if we sell a few alive to Big John Locke.'

'Who's he when he's at home?'

'Big John runs a ratting circus.' At Ron's puzzlement Alfie explained. 'People bet on small dogs that kill rats in a pit. So he needs a constant supply of fighting rats to fling into the pen – it's about six feet long and has a high timber rim. Ha'pence a bet.'

Ron still looked confused. 'So why does the type of rat make a difference?'

'Because, you oaf, someone has to handle them and the bite of a sewer or water ditch rat is bad for the dogs and especially for us – it leads to infection and possibly death, whereas a rat that's grown up in a warehouse is less dangerous. Sewer rats fight better, of course.'

Ron's eyes lit with understanding.

Now Alfie smiled at his friend, pleased to see him. 'So what are you up to, Ron?'

'I've got a day's work with one of the alehouses.'

'Good for you. I've just landed myself a proper job.' Alfie told Ron about the grocery store.

'You've always had the luck, Alfie,' Ron moaned.

'It's not forever. Something to keep me liquid.' He rubbed his fingers together in the universal sign of money. 'But perhaps you're right and I do have the luck, because on this one day I've not only got myself a respectable job, but I met the girl I'm going to marry.'

Ron gave a snort of derision. 'Whatever you say, mate.'

Alfie's features straightened. 'I mean it – you watch me. Grace Fairweather will become Grace Sweeting.'

'*That* Grace? From the grocers?' Ron sounded full of ridicule. 'Well, you're punching way beyond your weight there, Alfie boy.'

Alfie hated being called boy by anyone, least of all Ron Dyer. But he kept his emotions in check and gave one of his trademark grins instead. He knew how that alone could infuriate someone.

'You know she's going to be married, right?'

'Yeah, to some geezer called Norman. Even his name is boring. I even told her so.'

'Well, that may be, but Norman Jenkins is the local copper around here.'

That caught his attention.

'I see you don't know everything, Alfie. Anyway, you don't want to tread on his toes.'

'I have no intention of doing so. It will be Grace who makes her own decision. I'm just offering a better option.'

Ron gave another snort. 'And how do you match up against a policeman, with his reputation and smart uniform and prospects?'

Alfie, seemingly unfazed, winked. 'You just see.'

The public scavenger's cart hauled by. 'Oi, watch out, lad,' the bloke yelled, interrupting his loud call for rubbish.

Alfie sidestepped out of the way and tipped a finger from his forehead in thanks. He hadn't realised he'd moved into the path of traffic. The smell of what he considered the rag 'n' bone man wafted past. He remembered there being poverty-stricken men, similar to this fellow, all over London, walking their horses as they pulled carts down the streets and accepting people's old rags and furniture. Alfie seemed to remember hearing that back in early Victorian times they collected rats just like he and Ron had. This fellow, though he was dressed in filthy clothes, seemed to be faring better, walking tall, looking fed.

Ron was giving his rat-faced giggle. 'Nearly got yourself run over before you made it to the altar,' he quipped.

'You watch me make that beautiful girl my wife.'

'Yeah, well, in the meantime, apart from the policeman fiancé, you'd better watch out for George Dooley. He's looking for you and he's got a mean glint in his eye.'

'I'm not scared of Dooley,' Alfie lied, remembering himself cringing at Grace's feet.

'Well, you should be. He said your debt is up to ten shillings now.' Ron shook his head. 'I'd be frightened if I were you.'

Alfie couldn't resist it. He pulled out the crisp brown-grey note and waggled it briefly before Ron the Rat's gaze. 'And I shall pay him. I have nothing to be scared about.'

It was Ron's turn to give a whistle. It came out low and impressed. 'Did you steal that?'

Alfie grabbed Ron's thin shirtfront. 'I'm no thief. Those days are long behind me. I told you, I'm working. This is an advance on my earnings,' he lied. It sounded good, and it seemed to impress Ron even further, going by the way his eyes widened.

Ron pushed away Alfie's hands. 'Well, go pay him then. I don't want him bailing me up, looking for you again.'

Alfie had every intention of paying George, because the consequences of ignoring the warning tingled in the little finger he no longer possessed. Phantom sensation, the hospital had told him when they patched him up. It had been a clean cut; Sabini had made sure of it.

'Can't have you bleeding to death in this warehouse, Alfie boy. Now make this an important lesson in your life. Always pay your debts.'

And he would.

Except he wanted to see if he could make up the money quickly to repay Grace. He wanted to impress her. No, it was more than that. He wanted to convince her he was reliable and trustworthy, someone she could count on. And he wanted to believe that about himself too – it was time for him to stop gadding about in odd jobs and living hand to mouth. Time to make something of himself.

After leaving Dyer, Alfie made for the east of the city. The ten-shilling note was burning a hole in his pocket and he realised he needed to break it up. He called into Hillier's Soda Fountain in Pitt Street and purchased the smallest tin of chocolates he could that were being made on the premises. They would be a gift to Grace as thanks for lending him the cash. He'd give her the tin of chocolates with the ten shillings.

'That will be four shillings, sir.'

'Four sh—' Alfie felt his throat constrict. Nearly half of all he had in the world.

The man gave a smile that really didn't get much past a sneer of pity. 'Shall I put it back, sir?' the man asked, trying to sound helpful.

His mock servility irritated Alfie. He was sick of people looking down upon him, judging him by his clothes, his accent, his impoverished presence. 'No, I'll take that tin. Wrap it, please.' He tossed Grace's ten-shilling note onto the counter, still warm from his hand that had been clutched around it to keep it safe.

The man's oily smile widened a fraction. 'Let me just fetch your change . . . sir.' He looked ridiculous in a white coat, more like a doctor than a chocolatier. Except he wasn't, was he? Alfie thought. He was just a shop assistant. Nothing lofty about that.

The assistant was back. 'Your change . . . and one shilling makes five, plus five and that's ten. Enjoy your chocolates, sir. They're some of our finest.'

Prat! Alfie thought, pocketing the change and taking the bag that held the red tin. Well, at least he had a proper surprise for Grace, but now he was down to six shillings with an account now amounting to one pound owed between Grace and George Dooley. How did he always manage to do this? He shook his head at his own stupidity. Couldn't he have just bought a box of matches to achieve what he'd needed? Then he'd have nine shillings and a lot of coins jangling. But no one bought matches with a ten-shilling note, did they? That would get him noticed by the wrong sort, particularly if they followed him into the seedy part of Sydney where he was headed.

Ah well, at least the money in his pocket was a whole lot more than he had yesterday.

His destination was King's Cross, Sydney's underworld heartland. He had no idea why it was called that, something to do with a statue of King George IV that had been demolished not that many years after it was erected, but he knew nothing more than that.

Nor did Alfie care. The King of England and his lot had never done anything to improve Alfie's life or that of his family. He was not a royal lover – all that pomp and ceremony – and he just felt lucky that he'd made it far away from his place of birth without having a prison sentence behind him or the label of convict. He was a free man in a country that believed in freedom for all, even though it paid homage to a royal head on the other side of the world. He didn't mind that. It was too far away to bother him. What he admired was that anyone could make something of themselves in this young nation. He wanted to be remembered for achieving something positive.

Blimey, but he was in an ambitious mood. He blamed Grace. She must never know he had gambled part of the money she lent him in such good faith, trusting his word. He must learn to live up to his word, make it impenetrable. A fortress. But how could he do that when he was so poor? He needed to begin from a better base . . . just a few shillings would be a start and could set him up to feel brighter for his future.

At Surry Hills, still with an intention to reach the Cross, his eye was caught by a familiar doorway: the illegal two-up school. It was mid-morning; plenty of gamblers would be around. A man with a face like a hatchet stood outside.

'What are you hanging around for?' the bloke growled, his square jaw barely moving.

Alfie smirked and flashed his fiver, not that he planned to break it. 'I'm going in.'

'Get on with it then,' the man said, flicking his thumb past his shoulder with irritation. 'We don't like punters hanging about on the street.'

Alfie entered the gloomy atmosphere, walking down a narrow flight of stairs to what was little more than a cellar. He inhaled the old breath of at least twenty sweaty men blowing out smoke from cigarettes burning in their hands. The police turned a blind eye around here. Harmless enough, they probably thought, now that the racetrack and sport was where their attention was focused. Perhaps it felt wrong to even tackle the two-up schools given the game had been such a stalwart piece of entertainment – what little there was – for the men in the trenches during the war. Too many of these guys in here had survived those trenches too.

A cheer went up, urged by the boxer, the man in charge of the overall game of chance and the money exchanging hands. The applause, Alfie noted, was because a new spinner had entered the ring. He cast a glance towards another fellow, the ringkeeper, who was responsible for making sure the coins were tossed in a valid manner and taking care of the coins in between tosses so there was no tampering; he was probably fifty or so, wearing a waistcoat with a fob watch. It made him look respectable around a bunch of desperate gamblers.

A younger man sidled up to Alfie, standing a bit too close, he thought.

'First time?' the newcomer asked.

Alfie snorted. 'No. I'm a regular.'

'D' you mind explaining it?'

'What? How did they let you in?' Alfie gave a laugh.

'Came with a mate but he's the guy in the middle and I've got no idea what's going on. What's the spinner?'

Alfie blinked, feeling sorry for the fellow, recalling his first visit to a two-up school. It was an alien game to him at the time, having never seen it played in London, but he'd slipped in under the guise of being a delivery boy and watched. His sharp mind had taken in the game quickly. And even now he observed the room – would so for a while – taking a measure of the mood, the spinner, even the way the coins were falling.

'Look,' Alfie began, sounding resigned. 'Your mate is the spinner, right? See that piece of wood in his man's hand?'

He watched the wide-eyed fellow nod. 'That's called the kip. Watch now, the fellow in the waistcoat – he's the ringer or the ringie, and he's in charge of the two coppers. Those pennies will be slotted into the kip by him only. Watch.' They did. 'Right, so now he's satisfied it's all been properly done, and he'll wait to get all the betting finished. Then he'll hand over to that guy'—Alfie pointed to a man in shirtsleeves with a thick moustache—'that's the boxer and he'll now take charge of the betting. Are you going to bet?'

'Not yet,' the man said, jangling coins nervously in his hand.

'Wise. What's your name?'

'Johnno.'

'So, Johnno, once the betting is placed, the boxer will give the signal and your mate . . .?'

'Bill.'

Alfie smiled. 'Yeah, Bill – well, he'll toss those coins as high as he dares and the ringie will call the toss valid or not.'

'What's the point to the toss?'

Alfie laughed. 'Are you sure you should be here?'

'I want to learn,' Johnno said.

'Think of the ways the coins can fall.'

'Er . . . what do you mean? Oh no, wait, I see. So two heads, two tails, or one of each.'

'Exactly. So that's what you're betting on – how they'll land. Heads, tails or odds – that's one of each. A good gambler works out his odds.'

'I don't understand.'

'No, well, you have to study the game and then you'll see how many times it falls one way or the other but you also have to know – this is chance. There aren't rules for how those coins will land. Now we all know the rough odds – it's roughly half the time each.' Johnno nodded but Alfie could see he was losing him. 'That's the average chance, but coins don't obey averages. They fall how they fall. Sometimes you win following the odds and sometimes you lose, but you win big if you defy the odds.'

'Meaning?' Johnno looked like his head was beginning to hurt.

'Well, let's say Bill here throws two tails. The chances of him throwing another two tails feels less likely than a heads and tails, right?'

'Is it?'

Alfie laughed. 'I think you should keep watching.'

'No, you've convinced me. I think I'll bet now or I'll never do it.'

'Hurry, then. You can cover your mate – he needs someone to cover his bet, which is likely heads so you need to bet heads. They'll close in a sec.'

'Wait. You can't win with tails?'

'No, mate. Only heads if you're covering him. If you want to bet against others and win their money, then you go tails.'

Johnno looked completely confused but rushed off anyway and Alfie stood back. He looked at Bill. He was rangy, with long arms. He'd be tossing those coins high. They'd bounce hard, probably flip over from first landing.

Johnno was back. 'Just in time,' he said, looking nervous. 'I'm going for two heads with Bill.'

'Brave.'

'Come in, spinner!' went the cry from the boxer in a voice that sounded trained for vaudeville theatre. It was met with a huge cheer and then a quietening as Bill lurched to the centre of the ring wearing a toothy grin.

The atmosphere was thick with nicotine smoke and anticipation.

Odds, Alfie thought, finally deciding what Bill would toss. It was the beginning of his calculation . . . a one in four chance. If he was right, the bets would be frozen and Bill would throw again.

Bill stopped just short of jumping as his long arms ripped the kip into the air and he let go of the pennies. They spun well, which impressed Alfie, and hit their apex in the tight silence, men pressing in on all sides to watch. On the coins' journey down, murmurs of 'Come on, heads!' or 'Come on, tails!' could be heard.

The coppers landed almost simultaneously and one flopped onto one side, while another bounced. A roar went up and the boxer stepped in.

'Odds it is!' he yelled.

Alfie cast a glance in Johnno's direction, feeling his chest loosen. His journey towards paying Grace back had begun. 'Never mind,' he said, his tone casual. 'Odds means the bets are frozen. No one wins and he'll go again.'

'I don't mind. I didn't bet a lot. Just showing my mate I'm barracking for him, that's all.'

'Good. Save your money, learn by watching.'

Alfie moved away but Johnno followed. 'Are you betting?'

He sighed. 'Not yet.'

'Why?'

'Because I want to be sure. I'm going with heads in my mind.'

Johnno looked baffled and Alfie couldn't blame him.

Right enough, Bill threw heads and a massive cheer went up.

'There, you win,' Alfie said. 'He'll keep tossing now until he throws tails – then he's out.'

'Do you think he will?'

'Eventually everyone will, Johnno. That's plain arithmetic.'

Johnno couldn't have looked more confused if he'd tried. 'You mean it can be plotted?'

Alfie shook his head. 'No,' he said, just short of exasperation. 'This is chance. One throw doesn't affect the next, I promise.'

Johnno's eyes were wide with excitement. 'He's looking confident.'

'He is. Makes no difference. He'll throw what he'll throw.'

'What will he throw?'

'I reckon heads again.'

Bill did just that to uproarious applause. Johnno looked fit to burst. 'But you keep getting it right. Why aren't you betting?'

'I will.' Alfie decided it was time. He flipped a silver shilling and deftly caught it. 'The only one I have,' he said, telling the truth. 'I needed to be sure that I was feeling confident. Wait here.' Alfie's instincts were telling him that the ringie, who was placing both coins heads up in the kip, and the length, speed and spin of Bill's throws was going to give them heads or odds again. Either way Alfie wouldn't lose his money.

With a sudden heat to his brain, and feeling lucky, determined to win favour with Grace, Alfie held up his five-shilling note and called out his bet. 'Heads!' he yelled over other excited voices, waiting to catch the eye of someone who thought him a lunatic.

It only took a heartbeat. 'Hey, idiot. I'll take that. There's no way he's tossing heads again,' one of the side betters called back. He moved closer, holding a beer; it clearly wasn't his first but he wasn't swaying or slurring. He looked like a man with a thirst.

'You're on,' Alfie said. 'Five shillings on heads.'

'All right, mate. I'm going to enjoy taking your riches because that is a losing bet if ever I heard it. He'll toss odds, I'm telling yer.'

Alfie smiled. 'I enjoy risk.'

'I'll say! You don't look like you've got a cracker to your name.'

'You can see my money,' Alfie said, rustling the five-shilling note and hoping the man didn't see him swallowing hard. 'You just make sure you can match it.'

'Oh, I've got you covered, lad,' he said. 'I'm just up from a gold haul in Victoria. I'm flush while you look homeless.'

'I'm not. Just down on my luck,' Alfie said, hoping to lure the guy into further confidence.

'Good. Keep it that way.'

'No more bets,' the boxer roared and they watched the ringie load the kip.

'Come in, spinner!' the ringie called again to wild applause.

Bill took the little holder of wood and a deep breath.

Not too deep, Billy boy, Alfie cautioned in his mind. *Toss the same.*

Bill threw, leaping slightly in that curious way of his, and everyone watched the pennies ascend from the pit, spinning to reach their summit before they came plummeting down again. Both bounced this time.

'Odds!' the boxer said. 'All bets frozen.'

The man who'd covered Alfie's bet laughed aloud. 'What did I tell yer, idiot?' He swigged his beer. 'And he won't toss heads again. He'll go out on two tails next toss.'

Alfie winked at his rival. 'He'll go heads, all right.'

The man pointed at him. 'My name's Don and I'm gonna break your legs if he throws heads.' He grinned but it was crooked and looked unnerving.

Alfie laughed though, unthreatened. 'Break his,' he said, nodding towards Bill, 'not mine. I'm just laying a simple bet. I didn't ask you to cover it.'

'You a friend of his?'

'Never met him in my life.'

'Why are you standing with his pal, then?'

'Stupid luck, I guess. Like me winning your money . . . *mate*.'

The boxer had them in his sights. 'Oi! You want to argue, take it outside.'

Alfie put his hands up. 'No problem here.'

The gold-digger shook his head like he didn't have a care in the world.

'Come in, spinner!'

Bill tossed the kip and the coins leapt away from their snug holder. The pennies caught the light of the dingy lamps and glinted, just for a moment, before raining down on the pit's earthy floor.

'Heads!' the boxer yelled, stepping forward.

The cheering was tumultuous, and Alfie gave his rival another wink. 'I win,' he said quietly over the noise, knowing full well the man could lip-read that much.

4

Alfie made a dash for the surface even though he was feeling lucky. It was a rare moment for him to quit while he was winning. He'd never had something so important to quit for, though, and suddenly Grace was worth everything: she gave him something to strive for and was someone to work hard to impress and win her admiration.

At some point during all the cheering and the exchange of monies, he'd decided he would allow nothing to stand in the way of him marrying Grace. He'd found all the reasons in the world to be optimistic through that smile of hers. So much promise in her kindness to him. He would make her love him, no matter her reservation, or her parents' – no doubt they would be thinking he was beneath her. But he'd seen something in her eyes that told him she wasn't so sure about marrying the policeman. She wouldn't admit it – not yet, not openly – but it was there; he sensed it. And she knew he was right.

Clutching the tin of chocolates, he burst out into the autumn sunshine and was immediately grabbed by the scruff of his shirt.

'Alfie Sweeting. I thought I'd find you, you little cock-a-roach.'

'Mr Dooley,' Alfie said brightly, defying how instantly scared he felt. He'd learned from a young age, around Sabini in London, never to show fear; you won more respect if you faced your foe and feigned calm.

George Dooley swung him round, still holding him firmly at the back of his neck. 'Where's my money?'

'I have it for you.'

'Don't say tomorrow. Don't even say this afternoon, you little bastard. I want it now.'

'I have it now,' Alfie said eagerly, squirming out of the man's clutch. 'If you'll let me . . .'

Dooley let go and Alfie took a moment to straighten his clothes. 'No need to get physical, Mr Dooley.'

'Hand it over, then.'

Alfie had taken the precaution of putting most of his notes in his sock and his coins in a tiny bag he had always worn hanging inside his trousers, tied to his waist: a necessary precaution for a man used to the world of gangsters and thugs. His winnings had been paid in two ten-shilling notes, four pound notes and five florins, along with a scowl from the goldminer, who didn't follow through on his threat. He knew when he was beaten and, besides, the ringie was watching carefully.

'Get home, lad,' the ringie advised Alfie. 'Get that money safe.'

Alfie didn't need any further encouragement. He knew at least one of the half sovereign notes was crispy; the rest, including the pounds, were limp and well used. Keeping Dooley diverted, muttering about having just had a small win in the two-up school, he casually felt around in his pocket and took a chance on one that felt the newest.

He withdrew a rusty-coloured ten-shilling note and inwardly sighed with relief. 'There you are, Mr Dooley. That's all I have. But it's yours. I know I owe you ten shillings.'

'There's a matter of interest, Alfie lad.'

'Interest?' he repeated, buying time. 'But that includes the inter—'

'No, well, you've cost me more money trailing you, don't you see? I've spent a whole morning having to find you, wait for you. If you'd paid me back as promised, you'd not have had to pay the extra I'm now insisting upon.'

'How much extra?'

'Another shilling.'

'A shilling?' Alfie repeated, unable to hide his astonishment. 'That's robbery, Mr Dooley.'

Dooley shrugged. 'Never borrow, lad. That's the key.'

Alfie thought about his money. He didn't want Dooley seeing the other notes, or even knowing he had pounds to his name. He didn't trust Dooley not to have him fleeced somehow by one of his marauding thugs.

'Mr Dooley, can I bring the interest to you this week?'

'No, Alfie. Your word is not your bond – this I've learned the hard way.'

'I mean it. I will bring it to you tomorrow if you could just give me some time.'

'What the heck are you going to do between now and tomorrow that earns you a spare shilling?'

'I have work.'

'What work?' Dooley sneered. His breath smelt fishy.

Alfie would have to lie. He didn't want to incriminate the Fairweathers, especially since Grace had denied seeing him this morning. 'I start this afternoon as a rat catcher, Mr Dooley,' he said, impressed by his own artfulness. 'Do you know Ron Dyer?'

'I know that weasel, yes.'

'Well, he got me a job. I'll have your shilling for you by tomorrow. I intend to catch plenty of rats tonight.'

The tension went out of Dooley; he was going to let him go. 'You're something of a rat yourself, Alfie. You're cunning. What's in here then?' He snatched the bag that Alfie had been protecting.

'That's mine,' Alfie said, feeling stupid for saying the obvious. 'Can I have it back, Mr Dooley? It's a gift.'

'A gift. Who are you giving gifts to?'

'A girl,' Alfie said as vaguely as he dared.

'What girl? A slag, you mean. Who else would look at you, Alfie boy?'

Alfie refused to defend Grace to this piece of nastiness.

Dooley looked inside. 'Phew . . . These look pricey, lad. You don't give sluts this kind of gift. Where did you get the lolly to pay for these? Or did you st—'

'I didn't steal them. I have a receipt.'

'You bought them? How? That's a lot of money for a some-time rat catcher and lowlife.'

Alfie was, for a rare moment, lost for a clever reply.

Dooley laughed. 'I'll tell you what, Alfie. Forget the shilling you owe. I'll take these instead. Mrs Dooley is very partial to choco-late and always complaining that I never bring her any treats. Might even put me on a promise for these.' He gave Alfie a hideously sly wink and licked his lips. 'We can call it quits until the next time, eh?'

'No, Mr Dooley, those were four shillings and—'

'Shut your mouth, lad, and bugger off now. You're getting away lucky. Don't think I didn't see you go into that grocery store down by the quay, and don't kid yourself for a moment that I didn't take note of the pretty young thing behind the counter. Maybe these are for her. Maybe not. Either way, you don't want me making a visit to her again.'

Alfie slumped, hating how helpless he felt.

'Good boy.' Dooley slapped him twice, playfully, on the cheek but to Alfie it was a condescending dismissal, as though he was worthless. Dooley walked away casually, the tin tucked under his arm, whistling tunelessly as though he had no care in the world.

Moments later, with Alfie still in the same spot, bemoaning his ill timing, the goldminer came blinking out into the sunshine, another man with him.

'Still here, mate? Waiting for me to break your legs?'

Alfie grinned. 'I don't suppose you'd like to make some of your money back?'

'No more gambling for me. I need beers, a good meal and a warm woman. Prepared to pay honestly for all.'

'Well, let me pay for those beers.'

'Oh yeah?'

Alfie pointed. 'You see that bloke chatting to someone there – the one with the bag under his arm?'

'I see him.'

'Can you get that bag from him?'

'Why would I do that?'

'Because it's mine. He stole it.'

'Why?' Don was too sharp to be hoodwinked.

Alfie told the truth. 'I owed him money.'

The miner blinked. 'So why didn't you pay him with your winnings?'

'I did pay him, but I owe others as well,' Alfie explained. 'I want to settle those debts too. But he decided to charge extra for having to wait for me to win at two-up.'

'Bastard. I do remember you holding that parcel.'

'He took it from me even though I offered to settle up by tomorrow.'

The miner seemed to lose interest in the why and wherefore. 'How much?'

'How about a shilling to lift it?'

'And where will you be?'

'Not here, that's for sure. I'm presuming you're headed for the Cross?'

'Yep.'

'If you bring it to Minton House at the main King's Cross intersection, I'll be there.'

'What's in the bag, son? Nothing dangerous or that's going to come back and bite me?'

Alfie laughed. 'Nothing like that, I promise. It's chocolates for my sweetheart.'

'They must be good or she must be perfect.'

'Both,' Alfie admitted. 'He took them instead of the shilling he decided to add to my debt. Will you do it?'

'For a florin, I will.'

'Done,' Alfie said with an inward sigh. These chocolates had now cost him six shillings, but he wanted Grace to have them, not ugly Dooley who it seemed would be using them to have sex with his wife. Made sense that the brute would have to buy it. Who would give Dooley anything that intimate willingly?

'You'd better keep your word, lad, or me and my friend here really will hunt you down and break your legs.'

'I'll be there, Don, with your florin and my thanks.'

———

Grace was busy making a counter display of her newly made toffee apples on a tray. She'd only made eighteen, which was all the fruit her mother would spare.

'Those had better sell, Grace, so help me, or I'll have Norm arrest you!'

'I promise they will,' Grace assured her, carefully balancing the last of the glassy baubles on its heavy, flattened end. 'Don't they look superb?'

Her mother sighed and Grace knew not to take it to heart. She and her father were dreamers and her mother was the practical one – 'the ogre', she called herself, which wasn't true. But she did always take the more pessimistic view of life, claiming that someone had to. This sounded like an excuse to Grace, but neither she nor her father were very good at managing a budget. Fortunately for them, her mother was frugal and carefully worked within the plan she had for running the grocery store at a small profit.

A small profit, however, was never in Grace's mind. She dreamed big and wanted to be involved in an enterprise that was capable of large earnings.

'Mum, I am going to sell these at tuppence ha'penny each,' Grace had announced earlier.

Her mother had given a soft snort. 'You realise how much that is all up, don't you?'

'Yes, I added it up,' Grace said. 'It's five shillings.'

Mary Fairweather shook her head. 'Grace, each of those apples cost us a ha'penny to buy. We can sell them for a penny each. And you're telling me that with a little bit of sugar you're going to make tuppence per apple?'

'No, Mum.' Grace grinned. 'I'm going to return more than that. You see, this isn't just a little bit of sugar. This is toffee that I've perfected so it's like glass. I've dipped each apple once and then once again to get this shimmering appearance that no child will be able to resist. And the toffee has been cooked to perfection, so it's sweet but with that delicious and ever so slightly bitter hum that contrasts with the sugary juices of your sweet Cox's Pippins. And—'

Her mother gave a huffing sound. 'They've come all the way from Tasmania, and I'll be damned if you've wasted them with your toffee larking.'

'I was going to say that more than the immediate profit, these toffee apples will drive in new business. I'm so convinced about this recipe, you'll want these on the counter every day.'

'Will I indeed?' her mother said, sounding resigned. Grace knew her mother was simply thinking about the one and six shillings she knew she could, with luck, have in her till by the end of the day, instead of being excited by the potential of three shilling and sixpence pure profit. *Oh, wait*, she thought: calculate the sugar and it's probably a little less, not considering her time. But her time was freely given and she'd made these outside of shop hours. 'I've even got gloves to wear while handling them that make these treats seem more special.'

'For the life of me, I don't know where you come up with these things.'

Now her father breezed in from the back, blowing on his hands. 'Getting chilly out there, girls.'

'Yes, I'd noticed. You'd better start wearing those socks I've knitted and your gloves, Hugh. I don't want you with chilblains this winter.'

'What would I do without you?' Hugh said and kissed his wife's cheek.

She pretended to shake him off but Grace smiled at the affection that her mother obviously enjoyed.

'Go on with you,' Mary said. 'Has that new lad turned up?'

'Yes, he's out the back,' Hugh said.

'Alfie's here?' Grace reined in her enthusiasm immediately so her mother's ears didn't prick up. 'It's just that I need him to lift some fruit for me.'

'I've told him to start rearranging the dry stores how you want them, Mary, and then when you're ready, we'll get him away on some deliveries. Oh my, Grace, look at those toffee apples!' Her father beamed. 'Can't imagine those will last long.' He gave her a wink and Grace looked to her mother in triumph, but Mary simply shook her head.

'I'll get onto the delivery orders . . . not many this morning. Right, I'm opening up.' Mary moved to the door to unlock it and turn the sign to open. Hugh had already wandered off to wash his hands and put on his apron.

Alfie took that moment to step inside the shop from the back, already smiling at Grace. 'Morning, beautiful,' he said, removing his hat.

'Hush,' she warned, nodding towards her mother.

Alfie caught sight of the glistening apples. 'Blimey! I'll bet those taste brilliant.'

Mary arrived back behind the counter.

'Good morning, Mrs Fairweather.' Alfie nodded, half bowing, nearly making Grace laugh.

'Alfie, we don't eat the stock, in case you were wondering,' her mother cautioned him, and Grace was reminded of how sharp her hearing was.

'But has anyone tasted them to know how scrumptious they are?' he asked.

Grace felt crestfallen. How right he was. 'No. They were ripe apples on arrival and I know that's a beautiful toffee . . .' She gave a shrug that she knew didn't explain anything. 'I just assumed . . .'

Alfie shook his head. 'They look superb. Don't you worry, Miss Fairweather.'

'But you're right. I should always do a taste test.' Grace snatched one off the counter and, before her mother could protest, bit into it.

A shard of toffee broke away and Alfie caught it. 'Well, we know the toffee's got a snap to it.' He sounded delighted.

'Here, Alfie. You taste,' Grace said, much to her mother's dismay.

He gladly took a bite and just before the bell sounded the arrival of the day's first customer, they all heard the appealing crunching sound of thin sugar. Apple juice ran down his hand and he looked at Grace in wonder. 'You'd better get cooking on the next batch,' he warned. 'These are even tastier than they appear . . . and they look like jewelled treats.'

Grace beamed and her mother gestured with a flick of her hand that they should both get rid of the evidence of the sampling. They ducked out the back, grinning as they heard her welcome a familiar customer. It was one of the wealthy ladies from North Sydney who volunteered at the schools for the impoverished and raised funds to buy food for widows and their families. Grace knew her as a generous woman, a mother and wife of one of the Sydney councillors.

Mary greeted her warmly. 'Good morning, Mrs Chalmers.'

'Hello, Mrs Fairweather. It's certainly brisk today.'

'The crossing must have been a little choppy.'

'Choppy and cold,' Mrs Chalmers agreed. 'Those ferries aren't built for comfort, I'll say. Just practical craft to get us from one side of the harbour to the other.' She chuckled. 'But this Harbour Bridge is so exciting.'

'Exciting – and noisy,' Mary admitted. 'And we've been promised years of it.'

'Yes, I imagine that is going to be a symphony that accompanies your life for a long time,' Mrs Chalmers said, and Grace could tell she was trying to shine a pretty light on the situation. It was, at times, hugely inconvenient as well as deafening. Add to that the dust, the sheer volume of people and animals moving around at either end of the pylons being built, the high-pitched sound of welders and loud reports from the riveters . . . Grace figured Mrs Chalmers probably didn't really understand how overwhelming the building of the new Sydney Harbour Bridge was for the families of The Rocks. She was brightened, though, by the woman's next comment.

'Oh my goodness, Mrs Fairweather! I spot toffee apples.'

'Freshly made today by my daughter. Just tuppence ha'penny each and they won't last long.'

Grace and Alfie shared an open-mouthed stare behind the shop, thrilled her mother was so vigorously promoting her new product.

'Get out there,' Alfie said, grabbing the remains of the shared toffee apple. 'Go sell! This is delicious – so be confident.' He gave her a light shove and Grace was back in the shop smiling at the customer.

'They're so shiny – makes you want to eat one immediately,' Mrs Chalmers remarked, moving to where Grace stood, where she inhaled audibly. 'Oh, and they smell delicious, Grace! Well done.'

'Grace made these as a trial to see if customers enjoy them.'

Grace was thrilled that her mother was giving her the praise and the opening she needed. With an encouraging nod from Alfie, whom she glimpsed listening through the doorway, she shifted effortlessly into her sales parlay.

'Good morning, Mrs Chalmers. Yes, we thought we'd make them as a special treat for autumn when the apples are at their freshest and most delicious. These came in from Tasmania and are right off the ship. They've got a lovely ripe crunch to the fruit beneath the thin shield of toffee.'

'Gosh, I remember eating toffee apples as a tiny child on bonfire night. We don't do that here in Australia, but I remember it fondly. A toffee apple is the flavour of an English late autumn, I'll grant you.'

'Well, I hope to make them an Australian treat for early autumn too,' Grace said. 'These are not inferior apples either, Mrs Chalmers,' Grace continued, warming to her task. 'Nothing less than the finest Cox's Orange Pippins. Are you familiar with them?'

'I am, yes.'

Grace beamed. 'Then you'll know that complex flavour of the Pippin dessert apple, with its tang and sweetness of so many other fruits – pear, melon, even orange juice. But that's not why they call them Orange Pippins – no – that comes from its beautiful warm blush of orange glowing to red, which shows through this magnificently rich toffee. I've spun it from the best cane sugar into the thinnest of crusts, and I've dipped them twice so there's a double crunch of sugary deliciousness.'

Mrs Chalmers let out her breath of amazement. 'Well, Grace, I don't need any further convincing. I think I shall have to buy one for each of my children as a special treat.'

'Three, is that correct?' Mary asked, knowing full well how many children her customer had.

'And one for you too, Mrs Chalmers,' Alfie mouthed, nodding at the customer while hidden from her line of sight. Grace glanced once at Mrs Chalmers and back at Alfie, who nodded vigorously.

'And one for yourself, surely?' Grace suggested, hopefully.

'Ooh, I shouldn't but yes, why not? Make that four, Mrs Fairweather.'

'Grace, dear, will you pack those carefully for Mrs Chalmers, while I serve her for whatever else she needs?' Mary nodded at her customer before looking back at Grace. 'Don't forget to put your gloves on, dear.'

She didn't mind her mother remarking in the way she had; it helped draw attention to the effort, as had been her intention. 'Yes, of course,' she replied.

'Mrs Chalmers, I've got your regular order here too, if you'd like to follow me to the till? Unless there's anything else we might fetch for you?' Mary looked attentively at her customer.

'Thank you, Grace,' the woman said over her shoulder, following Mary. 'How's that lovely young man of yours?'

'He's fine, thank you,' Grace said, clearing her throat of the immediate clog of guilt.

'We're thinking of a very early spring wedding, Mrs Chalmers, perhaps September first,' Mary remarked.

'Oh, how lovely. I'll have some gorgeous freesias, jonquils and violets in my garden if you'd like me to gather some up for your bouquet, Grace?'

'I'm not really—'

'You're too kind, Mrs Chalmers,' Mary jumped in. 'We'll be making our own, of course, so any spring blooms will be most welcome. Norman's sorting out the local hall now – we just have to encourage our Grace to settle on a date.'

Both women turned to beam at Grace with matching indulgent smiles.

'And then it will be grandchildren for you, Mrs Fairweather,' her customer warned with a knowing finger in the air.

Grace shook her head, feeling both impatient and vexed at being discussed like she wasn't there. 'When you come next week, Mrs Chalmers, I hope to have something new to tempt you with as a treat for the family.'

'You're a wicked girl,' she said, waggling the same finger.

'Anything else?' Mary asked.

'No, that's all, thank you, Mrs Fairweather.'

'. . . and with the additional ten pence for the toffee apples, that makes it six and ten,' Mary said, sounding pleased as she rang up the amount.

Grace had carefully packed the toffee apples into a box lined with waxed paper and came around the counter to hand them to her customer. 'Thank you for trying them. I hope you enjoy. They'll keep well for the rest of the day but best eaten today, of course.'

'Grace, my children will not be able to resist these from the moment they arrive home from school. And I shall have to hide them from the children at the Ragged School where I volunteer.'

'Maybe I can slice up a couple of apples and dip them in some leftover toffee I have for the Ragged School children?' she offered, instantly feeling guilty she hadn't considered them.

'Oh dear, Grace, would you? I'm happy to contribute . . . perhaps—'

'No, no, Fairweathers will gladly donate a treat. How many, do you think?'

'You'll need at least twenty-five pieces for the one on Harrington Street,' Mrs Chalmers warned.

'Oh, that's only a couple of apples. Alfie, our new delivery boy, can bring them up later today.'

'You have an angel for a daughter, Mrs Fairweather – thank you, Grace. See you all next week.'

When the door closed, Mary Fairweather gave her daughter a look of exasperation. 'Why don't you give all those toffee apples away, Grace? There'll be no profit at all once you send another pile up the road.'

'Mum, I don't plan to use Cox's Pippins. Dad's got some old McIntosh apples going a bit wrinkly in storage, but the flesh is still sweet, if not as juicy. He was talking about turning them into puree anyway, and wanted me to think of how to use that. It won't hurt us to give a donation to the Ragged School and, if anything, it spreads very good word about our store. It's just some extra sugar and effort, Mum . . . no cost and no dint to our profit, but very good publicity.'

'Publicity? These modern words and notions of yours, Grace.' Mary sighed. 'Right, well, only fourteen toffee apples to sell.'

'If the first customer of the day takes four, I promise I'll have all of those sold by midday. Ah, here comes someone or three.' Grace nodded towards the front window. Her mother turned and saw a trio of new customers arriving at the same time, all telling the others to go ahead.

'Grace, I'd like you to sound a bit more interested in your own wedding, by the way. Everyone's excited for you.'

'Everyone but me,' she muttered beneath her breath.

'I've asked Norm to share a meal with us this evening – perhaps we can get this wedding date sorted out once and for all,' her mother said, almost dismissively. 'Now, will you get Alfie moving on those deliveries?'

Not wishing to argue, Grace nodded and ducked out the back.

'Well done!' he said.

'Four sold!' she exclaimed, as pleased as she could remember being in a long time. It was exciting to have not just had the idea, but to have executed it well.

'Grace, you know when I said she should take four?'

Grace nodded.

'I meant for you to give her the fourth.'

'Why?'

'Well, I guess for the same reason you're giving away slices of toffee apples to the needy kids.'

'I'm doing that out of charity.'

'That may be, but deep down,' he said, pointing a finger towards her chest, 'you're being smart and broadening the reach of your product and your name.'

'Am I?'

'Well, yes, even if you don't realise it.' He grinned. 'You said it . . . publicity. It's why companies advertise their wares on posters and signs.'

'And in newspapers . . .' She frowned, realising the notion was exactly that. 'You think I should advertise?'

'No. No need to pay for it yet, darlin'. Word of mouth is the best and cheapest way of all.'

Grace heard 'mouf' instead of 'mouth' and smiled; she really did enjoy the way Alfie spoke. 'We need to get the deliveries going. I'll show you how—'

'I can see them lined up. Nothing hard about it, Gracie.'

Gracie again. She had to smile. 'Yes, but Mum wants paperwork, signed and returned. You have to be diligent.'

'No problem at all,' he assured her. 'Deliver, get a signature, return the document to Mrs Fairweather, do the next delivery.'

Grace nodded. 'There's a temptation to do a few at once and sometimes it would make sense to, but don't take on too much – you're on a bicycle and that could mean breaking the eggs or squashing biscuits, that sort of thing. Then you'll have customer wrath at one end and Fairweather wrath at the other.'

'Who has stuff delivered anyway?'

'Oh, the accommodation places where all the sailors stay, some of the pubs. The maritime offices and the warehouse managers have tea, biscuits, coffee, cocoa and dry goods delivered for their staff breaks. We even deliver to the General Postmaster's office.'

'Easy,' he said. 'Er, listen, Grace . . .' He pulled her towards the back door.

She frowned. 'I have to get back . . .' She gestured with her thumb over her shoulder, but he insisted, taking her hand. 'What's going on?'

They were outside now, and Alfie carefully looked around to see there was no one else in the back lane. 'I wanted to give you something. Two things, actually. This first.' Out of his pocket he pulled a ten-shilling note; it was crisp and hadn't been in circulation long. 'Thank you for the loan.'

'Already?'

He nodded. 'Paid my debt to Dooley, so he won't be back, I promise. Plus, I want to pay you back.'

'Alfie, how did you manage to do both?' She frowned. Had he done something illegal?

He shook his head, communicating to her, *What does it matter?*

'Tell me.'

'Why?'

'Because I can look out for you.'

That seemed to touch him. She watched his eyes flare with understanding and then narrow as he made the decision to be honest – perhaps something he wasn't terribly good at being. 'I played two-up and won.'

She nodded. 'Right. I figured as much. Well, no more gambling now, Alfie. Honest wages.'

'That's the plan,' he said, sounding cocky again.

She didn't wholly trust his bravado, but she felt happy for him that he was rid of Dooley.

'And now the other thing I wanted to give you.'

'Hurry up, my mother—'

'I know.'

Grace watched him reach beneath a crate and pull out a red tin. She didn't even need to see its label to know what that tin contained. 'Hillier's?' she whispered, wondering if she'd gone pale.

'Wow, you're good,' he said and whistled. 'The real deal, Grace.'

She stared at the tin, her expression reluctant.

'Go on. Take them,' Alfie urged.

'I don't understand.' She'd only ever dreamed of buying Hillier's. The most she could do was walk into the store and stare at the products before a sneering look from one of the assistants, realising she was only a voyeur, sent her scuttling off. She'd wanted to tell them that she could afford to buy something, she just chose not to part with so much money for something that would be consumed in a blink.

'Alfie. Only rich people buy Hillier's Chocolates!'

'Who says I'm not rich?'

She looked back at him with fresh exasperation and breathed out audibly.

'All right, all right. Look, I know you're interested in sweet things. And this is thanks for your kindness and because . . . well, because you're my friend.' He pushed them into her hands. 'Please.'

'You didn't steal these, did you?' She hated seeing how much offence she caused as his expression darkened and became wounded. 'Oh, I'm so sorry to even think that, let alone ask it. Forgive me, Alfie,' she pleaded, squeezing his arm. 'It's just . . . how do I explain these to my parents? Do you think they don't know how much these cost?'

He shrugged. 'Tell them four shillings. I'm not embarrassed.'

Her eyes narrowed. 'They won't want a gambler in their midst. And they'll just presume you're up to no good.'

'Tell them someone owed me and paid me in kind.' He winked. 'Now, stop holding me up! I've got deliveries to make.'

She had to chuckle at him. 'All right. We'll share them.'

He grinned. 'Call it research.'

'For what?'

'For the confectionery shop I'm going to help you open.'

5

Norman Jenkins was laughing at his own jest. It hadn't really been that funny, but her parents were chortling along with him. Perhaps it was the uniform he wore that impressed them, or maybe the fact that he'd pulled himself up from his childhood in The Rocks, away from slum life, even with the responsibility of caring for his host of siblings. She did like that about Norman – he would be a good father, and he was still very caring towards his brothers and sisters. They were now all grown and working, but while they lived hand to mouth, Norman had done better; he'd become a policeman. He had shown talent in the role, was trusted by those in the neighbour-hood and had quickly risen to the position of senior sergeant with his eye on becoming a detective this year.

Given Norman was not yet thirty, it was a meteoric rise – even she could acknowledge that – and his forthcoming move from the headquarters at the Quay to the new police headquarters on the corner of Phillip and Hunter streets, suggested his trajectory was still ascending sharply.

Grace wore a fixed smile as she sat patiently at the dinner table with Norman and her parents, but behind it she was scrutinising the man, trying to balance in her mind her assured future as a potential senior policeman's wife, with all the convenient trappings his salary would bring, against the boredom that was surely ahead of her. They'd met as children and were friendly all that time ago. Her parents knew his parents, but then everyone knew everyone in The Rocks . . . as well as each other's business. They'd lost the daily contact as they'd grown and she'd gone to a school on the North Shore. However, when some stock had been pilfered from their small shed at the back of the store five years earlier, it was Norm, now all grown up and a policeman on the rise, who had come to investigate, taking statements and making a report. Grace had been the one to discover the missing tins of biscuits and so he'd interviewed her.

Back then, Grace too had been impressed with the smart uniform and shiny buttons, his sober and impressive presence. And he'd noticed her. It had begun with joining her family on a picnic, and then he'd taken Grace and her parents on a ferry ride and a visit to the newly opened Taronga Zoo. Then he'd been allowed to accompany Grace to a local dance, and then a weekly trip to the cinema and suddenly she was in a seemingly durable relationship that, if she really examined it, she'd not really had an active role in pursuing. Norman had done all the asking and her mother had done all the accepting.

Grace liked Norm but couldn't say she loved him because she had never been in love; she didn't know what it felt like, only what she'd observed between her parents. She didn't think she shared that special bond with Norm, where a look could say so much. But there was no denying he was a good man . . . a good catch. It hadn't taken much time in his presence to work out that he was a traditionalist, however, and would not want his wife working. Grace didn't think she would be able to handle that. And now she had met Alfie, who she had to admit she felt instantly drawn to, and who had given her the impression that he could think of nothing more exciting than to work alongside her in a shared endeavour to build an enterprise . . . her enterprise. The only quality that Alfie shared with Norman was ambition. Except, Grace rationalised, Alfie was ambitious for her and her dreams rather than his own. Norman would say he was ambitious for both of them, but his ambition was for status, wealth and having the beautiful adornment of a wife and children to match. He had his eye on being Inspector General by his mid-forties; he'd already admitted as much to her, no doubt hoping it would impress her.

Grace focused on the conversation for fear that her mother would note her drift in interest.

Norman was leaning back, smoking and espousing as usual. 'Well, Mary, I was thinking of somewhere around Kirribilli.'

'Isn't that mostly a wool warehouse area, though?' her mother asked.

'That's true but there are some nice homes dotted about.'

'Mansions, you mean,' Grace qualified.

'No, Grace, my darling,' he said, sliding her a patient smile that she didn't feel was altogether genuine. 'We're not quite ready for that. There are a few other smaller homes scattered about and they have lovely fresh air, nice gardens, a view of the harbour. We can watch the new bridge being built from our verandah, and we can catch the ferry to work together, until you have our first child and then you can wave me off at the dock and look out for Daddy's return each evening.' He sat forward and squeezed her hand across the table.

'First child,' she murmured.

'I'd like a host of children to come home to,' he said, smiling at her parents.

'What if I want to keep working, though?'

He glanced at her parents sharply with a mildly quizzical expression. 'We've talked about this, haven't we?'

'Well, actually, Norm, *you've* talked about it, but you haven't discussed it with me.'

He looked at her, feigning a deeper puzzlement with a benign smile, waiting for her to explain.

She continued. 'There's a difference between you telling me something to us exploring it, weighing up options together.'

'Weighing up options,' her mother repeated with a nervous laugh. 'I'm sorry, Norman. You'll have to get used to Grace's ways. She's always been a wilful child.'

'Oh, I'll sort her out, Mary,' he assured her. He said it lightly but it landed like a blow on Grace's senses.

She cut her father a hard look and quickly turned back to Norman, who was still chuckling with her mother.

'Norm, we haven't properly discussed this, but my parents are aware that I plan to set up a new enterprise. It's already begun, truth be told.'

'A new enterprise?' Norman frowned.

'A new business,' she clarified. 'In sweets.'

'Whatever are you talking about, Grace?'

'If you'd only pay attention, you'd know that I have aspirations too. I want to open a new shop – one that I own myself – that offers confectionery of all shapes and sorts to the public.'

Norman gave all of them a look of befuddlement now. 'I know you like making toffee apples and marshmallow for the grocery store, Grace, but—'

'Indeed,' she interjected. 'And now I'm scaling up.' She was aware of her mother looking down at her lap and her father removing his glasses to give them a polish. Neither chimed in.

'Scaling what? I don't understand. We're to be married. And when you are Mrs Jenkins, wife of the Detective Norman Jenkins, you will—'

'No, you see this is where you've gone wrong with me, Norm.

You cannot tell me what I will have to do . . . ever. I am Grace Fairweather, not your wife yet, and possibly not your wife ever.'

'What the hell . . .?' Norman blinked angrily. 'I'm sorry, Mary. Forgive my language.'

'More pudding, anyone?' Mary said, standing, looking embarrassed. With narrowed eyes, she slid her daughter a look that promised retribution.

Everyone mumbled they'd had enough food.

'Grace, I won't permit this aggressive talk,' Norm continued.

'Won't permit?' She had to laugh. 'See, this is exactly what I'm talking about. I make my own decisions, Norm.'

Norman seemed to take a steadying breath as he squared himself on his chair and sat upright. Grace watched him open his hands palms facing down, as though pushing away whatever this conversation was. He found a smile and looked back up, taking in all three of them around the table, his thin moustache forming a line of dark strokes above his top lip. 'Let's set that date, shall we? Mary, you were talking about an early spring wedding. The hall is available on the first Saturday or Sunday in September. I'm happy to book the church, and then Grace and I can speak with the vicar. Of course, if you'd prefer to hold the ceremony on the North Shore away from the noise and dust, I'm only too happy to—'

'Norman.' Grace took her own steadying breath. 'I don't think I'm ready for a wedding. I think setting a date in the next few months is premature and asking for disappointment. I don't want to let you, my parents or our friends down.' She tried to smile but it departed within a heartbeat of breaking; she couldn't sustain any brightness as she looked at the falling expressions of the people around her. 'May we just hold off, please?'

'Hold off? I thought this was all—'

Grace shrugged lightly. 'I know you did. You feel it was all settled, but as I just told you, it was settled only in your mind. I don't feel ready.'

Her mother turned away with a groan and her father decided to re-polish his glasses.

'What do you mean not ready?' Norman demanded, his features giving up their control and falling into what looked like anger.

'I don't feel ready to be married, to give up work, to relinquish my dreams, or my daily duties here.'

'Don't you want a secure life, Grace? Don't you want a home of your own and a family?'

'I do . . . just not yet and . . .'

The silence that followed was so thick that Grace felt she could have sliced through it like rich fudge. Her father cleared his throat awkwardly and her mother, for once, had nothing to say.

'And what?' Norman asked, impaling her with a stare that definitely felt angry.

'And I'm not sure whether I want that future with you.'

Her mother gasped and put a hand to her mouth in despair. Grace watched her father put his glasses slowly back on his face, carefully looping the thin gold wire around his ears, before trying to restore calm to the escalating tension of the atmosphere. 'Norman, on behalf of our fam—'

Hugh Fairweather got no further, startled into silence by the sound of Norman's hand slapping down hard on the table, his eyes squinting slightly to make his angry point.

'Hugh, Mary, this is unacceptable. Do you mock me, Grace?'

Having flinched along with her father, Grace now opened her hands in a sort of plea. 'That is not my intention, truly.' But inside she knew she was making the right decision; his reaction had only confirmed her fears.

'Forgive our daughter, Norman,' Mary began but it was Grace's turn to take exception and show it.

'No! Wait! Mum, Dad, this is the twentieth century. Women can have their say. I will not have you apologise to anyone for my behaviour, especially when all I am doing is being honest about my feelings. Only I know how I feel and right now, what I feel is not love for you, Norman. I like you. I respect you. We're good friends. I feel proud of all you've achieved. I know how popular you are. And I also know, Norm, that despite our differences of opinion, you are a good man. But even though I have never been in love – so, frankly, I can't tell you how it should feel – I just do not think it's this.'

Her father stood and joined her mother. 'Why don't you both have a private moment?' Against her wishes, he began ushering his wife from the kitchen.

'There's no need. I don't mind you both hearing what I have to say – you'll have to hear it eventually anyway,' Grace said. She waited for Norm's astonishment to settle and for his attention to return to her. 'I think it's best you know now that I will not be ordered around by a man. I will not simply follow my husband's instructions and have him tell me how my life will now be shaped, precisely to his whim. I will not stay at home as the good wife, cooking, cleaning, raising children and being satisfied with my lot.'

Norman and her mother, who was leaning forward, desperate to prevent Grace from making a damaging decision, both took a breath to speak but she stood, with a shake of her head and a hand in the air.

'No, it's my turn to speak and to be heard. I am no longer a child,' she said, addressing her parents, eyeing each of them in turn. 'And Norman, I am not some mouthless, spineless, adoring woman who is blinded by the shine of the brass on your uniform, or impressed simply by your status. Like all the people around here, we're proud of one of our own doing so well – congratulations to you. But that doesn't give you the right to feel you own me, or to tell me – not ask me – what my future is.' She relaxed her shoulders and put appeal in her voice. 'We used to run around The Rocks together as youngsters. Back then we were equals, the best of friends. And I'm sure you'll remember I had dreams, even all that time ago. You used to call me bossy, do you remember?' She knew he did. 'Why do you think I've changed? I haven't. You may have but I always said you'd go far, Norm. You have already. And it's obvious you're not done yet and that you have a glittering future. But I don't think it has me in it as anything more than a friend.'

'I don't want a friend, Grace. I want a wife.'

'I know you do, Norman. But that's it. It's not me you want, it's a wife. Another symbol of your growing status. There are dozens of women out there who would marry you in a heartbeat and not give you half the grief I would.'

'That's where you're wrong, though. I do want you, Grace.'

She couldn't deny hearing the authenticity in his word and she was touched by it, but she shook her head sadly. 'Well, I'm sorry.' She took in the three of them with a sweep of her gaze. 'I'm sorry to each of you for letting you down. But I am not ready to marry and when I do feel ready, I'm not sure it will be to you, Norm.'

Now he stood and his chair squealed on the floorboards. 'But why, Grace?' He banged the table again, with fists this time.

She could feel her own anger rising now. 'Because of that, Norm,' she said, nodding towards his clenched hands. 'One day that table could be me. You have a temper and it flares when you don't get what you want. I can't and won't promise to give you what you want. You want a wife – go and choose one. But I will not be that lifeless, voiceless table, or an adornment to parade in front of your colleagues. I don't need a husband. I don't need my own house or a family right now to feel important or successful.'

'What do you need, Grace?' her mother asked, her tone as hard as the steel girders they could hear being riveted and hammered into place on the bridge nearby.

'I need to follow my own path,' Grace said, not really knowing how else to answer that question.

Norman pointed a finger towards her, but mercifully his anger had calmed. Now he sounded cold. 'You'll regret this, Grace. Marriage offers will not be as plentiful as you think. I'm offering the kind of security that most women from this neighbourhood would leap at.'

'Then offer it to them, Norm!' Grace snapped. 'And stop hoping I might change my mind because you threaten me. I will marry who I choose, when I choose, and for my own reasons – not because it pleases my parents, pleases our neighbours or even society.'

Norman's expression rearranged itself to neutral, although Grace sensed scorn coming and wasn't disappointed. He ignored her now, addressing her parents instead. 'Your daughter's just made a mistake. I won't ask again. It will be the other way around if there's a next time.' He moved to the sideboard and fetched his military-style peaked cap. 'Good day, Mr and Mrs Fairweather.' He blinked. 'Grace.'

'Norman?' Grace said softly.

He regarded her without expression.

'There won't be a next time, but perhaps we might remain friends?'

He smiled without affection. 'Perhaps.' He departed.

There was a terrible silence until they heard the back door close.

'Grace, what have you done?' her mother murmured in disbelief.

'I've done us all a favour,' Grace replied.

6

Grace was alone with her father. Her mother was avoiding them both and Grace thought that was wise; she had felt the simmering resentment coming off her mother in waves, ever since Norman had left their home two days earlier.

'She won't forgive me, will she?'

'Your mother only wants what's best for you, Grace,' Hugh said, peering down at her from a small stepladder, where he was busy rearranging some tins on the shelves behind the counter.

Grace grimaced. 'Then she might like to think about how I feel . . . that I suspect I might have been dreadfully unhappy as Mrs Jenkins.'

Her father looked down at her through his glasses. 'Which is why I haven't said anything against your decision.'

'I noticed. Thank you for trusting me.'

He shook his head. 'No, you're right. You're not a child. And you should be making these sorts of decisions for yourself. I didn't appreciate Norm's attitude, but I can imagine he was feeling humiliated and hurt, as well as angry. You know he's a good man.'

'I do. We're just not suited. I didn't want to hurt him, but I also knew I needed to be direct – with him and with you and Mum as well. I didn't plan it, but I realise now it has been nagging at me for weeks.'

'Since Alfie Sweeting came into our lives?' Her father fixed Grace with a gaze she squirmed beneath. He could read her better than anyone.

'No . . . but . . .'

'But what, my darling girl? He may try but that fellow can't hide how he feels about you. And Grace, if you think I of all people can't see how your gaze follows him whenever he's around, then you don't know me at all.'

'Is it that obvious?'

He nodded with a sad grin. 'To me anyway. Is it real?'

'I don't know, Dad. I do like him. I like that we just talk – as equals – sharing ideas. Norm never did that. Norm was always telling me things, telling me what was going to occur and it was always about him and his life and how that would look with me in it.'

'People have different ways of expressing themselves, of course.'

'Yes, but I didn't enjoy Norm's way. We were headed for calamity, Dad. Imagine children in that mix, with us at logger-heads. I can't bear even thinking about what that would have done to them, to me.'

'I can't either. I'm impressed by your courage, but your mother is obviously deeply upset.'

Grace gave a short laugh. 'Upset that she doesn't get to show off at a big wedding.'

Her father gave her another firm look. 'Don't be unfair.'

'I'm sorry. I just want her to consider my feelings rather than making it about her.'

'She doesn't mean to. She just wants to see you settled, safe.'

'But she surely doesn't want me settled, safe and desperately miserable, does she? Because I know that's how I would be if I was Mrs Norman Jenkins.'

'Perhaps we're at fault for encouraging him.'

Unable to help herself, she gave her father an accusatory nod. 'Do you remember when Norm first got it into his head that I might be the one for him?'

'Yes, Grace, I do. You said he wasn't your type.'

'And I've been trying to find ways to convey that ever since. But his determination and Mum's idea that he was the right person for me took on speed. It was as though I had no say, and I felt like I was drowning under the weight of expectation. I tried, Dad, but I hoped it might just run its course and he'd tire of my indecision about setting a date. But Mum wanted it so badly. I began to believe I should just be less absorbed with my own dreams and try my best to make it work . . . I'd almost convinced myself that I was the problem, not him. But it took meeting Alfie for me to realise that Norm is not good for me, nor I for him. He doesn't even understand me, Dad. He just wants his ideal wife – there's no room for me to be an individual.'

'Some men are struggling to get used to modern society's attitudes,' her father replied.

She nodded sadly. 'Yes, I think you're right. Thanks for not being disappointed in me.'

Her father stepped down off the ladder to hug her. 'Never,' he said, kissing the top of her head.

The bell rang and it was Alfie with his head around the door. 'Sorry to use the front door, Mr Fairweather.'

Hugh glanced at Grace with a speak-of-the-devil smile. 'That's all right, Alfie. I don't mind at all. Are you off?'

'Yes, sir. Final delivery for the day. Morning, Grace.' He smiled.

'Hello, Alfie, I have an errand to run in George Street. I might come with you. Do you mind?'

'Mind? No, are you mad? We'll walk up together.'

———————

Alfie's final delivery of tea, biscuits and sugar was to a local office midway up George Street. Thrilled to have Grace at his side, he left his bike behind and they made their way on foot.

As they walked, Grace greeted many of the people they passed by name.

'It's amazing that you know everyone.' Alfie gave a small whistle.

'Only around here. Once we head past Bridge Street, I only know our regular clients.'

'Even so, it's a skill to remember everyone's names. Where are you going for your errand?'

'I told a fib. There's something I just want to see.'

'Can I come with you?'

'No.'

Alfie grinned, liking the intrigue. 'This sounds like a mystery. Are you sure I can't come?'

'You have jobs to do,' Grace insisted.

'This is my last delivery,' he reminded her. 'And then I'll finish up in the storeroom. I spoke to your father, by the way – thank you for asking him. He said I could sleep in the backroom of one of the laundries he's spoken to, until I can find some lodgings. I should be able to afford that by next week, so just a few days at the laundry.' He felt proud that he was making progress towards a life that might be good enough to win Grace's heart.

'Oh, good. I'll warn you now, keep it tidy or it will come back to them.'

Alfie nodded obediently. He wouldn't mess this up.

'Listen, Alfie . . . what you said to me about the store . . .' Grace trailed off.

Alfie glanced at her sideways. 'If you'll let me take you out, I'll explain fully what I meant.'

'Take me out?'

He hesitated, not wishing to make a misstep with her but then, a bit like in the two-up game, he knew he had to commit to taking a risk, even if she laughed in his face. 'Listen, I know you're engaged and all that but—'

'I'm not,' she cut in.

'What? I thought—'

'I know. I was. I'm not any more. Can we leave it at that?' Grace looked down at her feet.

He gave her a wide grin. 'Yes, that would be my pleasure. In that case, if you're not attached, may I take you out for an afternoon?'

She didn't laugh. She looked concerned. 'I . . . What will . . .'

If Alfie had one skill, it was the ability to read people, and he could tell that Grace was not against going out with him, but anxious about how her mother and father might react. 'When did you break off your engagement?'

'Two days ago.'

He nodded. 'And how old are you, Grace?'

She stopped walking. He did as well, annoying the two people behind him.

'Watch it!' One of them scowled over a shoulder.

'Sorry, mate,' Alfie said.

'I'm twenty-six. Why is that important?' She frowned, but he could see she knew where he was headed.

He gave a shrug, knowing he should tread with care. 'Grace, you're a third of the way through your life, near enough. How long are you going to let your parents make your decisions?'

She bristled. 'Just because you have no one doesn't mean—'

He pulled her to one side of the street, put his parcels down and his hands up. 'I'm sorry. You're right, I've been living on my own terms for years because I've had to. And what wouldn't I give for a couple of loving parents? But Grace, I know you have big ideas. When are you going to act on them, and not let them just be something you dream about?'

He watched her blush and knew his words had hit true. 'I . . . well, I do have plans.' She sounded almost frightened to have been found out. 'But I can't just leap in, Alfie.'

'Why not?'

'I need a proper path, I need to budget, I need to consider how to do what I want to do. And as for going out with you . . . I've just let Norman down and deeply disappointed my mother in the process, to the point where she's finding it hard to look at me. It's a bit soon for me to be stepping out.'

He shrugged. 'All right, let's have a meeting instead. We can talk about what you want to do in your life. It's pretty obvious to me – and I've only been around you a short while – that your interest isn't in tea or flour, Mrs Packer's monthly biscuit order or the fact that Mrs Gunn wanted a proper pail and not what she termed a bucket.'

A grin twitched at the side of Grace's mouth.

He grinned back. 'Tell me I've got it wrong. Tell me you don't want to make confectionery and have your own shop?'

She blinked once. 'You're not wrong. That's exactly what I want. And Norm would never have let me have it. I have so many aspirations for it.'

Alfie was glad she'd admitted it to him. He nodded, smiling broadly. 'Then we'll make your dream happen.'

'We?'

'I want to help. I want to be part of it.'

'That's kind,' she said with a sigh. It didn't sound defeatist, more like she was glad to be daydreaming but she still believed it was just that, a dream.

'I'm not just being kind, Grace. I'd like to be a fellow investor.' As she looked ready to protest, he shook his head. 'Look, let me take you somewhere lovely on Saturday afternoon when the shop closes . . . somewhere your parents might approve of, so we can just talk.'

'Like the Tea House?' Her tone sounded lofty, almost scornful.

Alfie didn't get it. 'If that's what you'd like.'

'Don't be daft,' she spluttered, bending to pick up his packages.

He helped, balancing them comfortably again in his arms. 'Why not?'

'I don't want you spending your money on somewhere fancy.'

'Grace Fairweather, you promise me that you'll put on your prettiest dress and coat and I'll take you to the Teapot or whatever the hell it's called, this Saturday afternoon.'

She gave a snort of laughter. 'They'll see you coming, Alfie. We'll need to be dressed right and have plenty of money.'

'Do I look like I care? That joker back at Hillier's thought he'd come over all snooty with me too until I showed him my money. I'm not worried about what people think of me, Grace. My money's the same as anyone else's. I promise, you will walk among the ladies of town with your head held high.'

'The thing is, I don't know that I want to. I'll tell you what, we'll go for afternoon tea – it will impress my parents that it's all above board and innocent – and we'll share the cost and I'll share with you what I see in my imagination and how I know I can make it work.'

Alfie's expression brightened as though the sun had just

emerged from the clouds on this cool April day to warm him. 'This Saturday, then. Are you sure I can't come with you on your fib?'

'No.' She smiled at him, softening the refusal. 'Get on with your delivery and I'll tell you more on Saturday.'

'You're on.'

'Don't follow me,' she warned, with a glint in her eye to make him smile.

Alfie made a cross sign over where his heart used to be, because Grace Fairweather now owned it.

———————

The rest of the week passed without incident and Mary Fairweather's chill began to thaw gradually. Grace even managed to engage her mother in a conversation about her future with an apology for the disappointment.

'Grace, it's your happiness I want. I thought marriage is what every girl looks forward to.'

'I know. And I do. But with Norm it would have been problematic.'

Grace was pleased to see her mother nod. 'I didn't take kindly to his attitude, I must admit. All that banging on the table,' her mother recalled.

'I couldn't help but think that might be my ribs or face one day.' At her mother's gasp, Grace shrugged. 'Well, there was violence there, wasn't there? I don't want to live around that or for my children to be raised in a house of fear. I want them to have the kind of upbringing I've had.'

That made her mother's smile arrive at last. 'I'm sorry I've been—'

'Don't apologise, Mum. It was a shock to you, I know. I could have handled it better, but I had to tell you – and Norman – that I didn't want to marry him.'

'Your father tells me you are close to Alfie Sweeting.'

And there it was. Grace needed to be honest with her mother. 'I do like him. He's hard not to like,' she said.

Her mother nodded. 'That's true, but be careful, darling.'

'Why do you say that?'

'He comes from an entirely different background to ours, Grace . . . a shadowy one, I'm guessing. And you need to beware of people who move in shadows.'

Her mother's words sounded a soft note of alarm, reminding her of George Dooley. 'I think Alfie has shaken off what you refer to,' Grace replied. 'He's got this job now and he's got plans. He has steadied his life.'

'Darling, Alfie sleeps on the floor of a laundry.' At her daughter's intake of breath, Mary shook her head. 'I accept you've changed your mind about Norm Jenkins, but I'm just pointing out – as a mother is allowed to – that Norm was offering you a future . . . a house, a regular income, respect. Alfie can offer you very little in that way.'

Grace nodded, knowing her mother's heart was in the right place. 'But Norm would have suffocated me, Mum, while Alfie makes me laugh, walk with a bounce in my step.'

'All right. You're old enough to make your own decisions, as you said. Just don't say I haven't warned you.'

Over the next few days Grace noted that Alfie was diligent in his timekeeping, his work and especially his living, careful not to draw anything but compliments from his new employer. He also began to chat to customers using his helplessly friendly manner that charmed even Mary. Grace even heard her say to her father, 'Well, I think young Alfie is working out splendidly for us. Everyone seems to like him.'

When Grace was helping her father count stock as she usually did on a Saturday before they closed, with Alfie out running errands, she made her approach.

'Where's Mum?'

'She's taken the ferry across to Manly to see that Aunt Cora of hers – the one who doesn't like me. Bit of a last-minute thing. Sorry, I forgot to tell you.'

'That's all right. Everything fine?'

'I encouraged her to go visit. She hasn't seen the old witch in a while, and I think your mother's looking weighed down by book-work, so some fresh sea air and family time will be good for her.' He frowned. 'How many tins of those did you count?'

'Five,' she repeated. 'Dad, Alfie and I might take the afternoon together.'

'Five of those, correct,' he muttered. 'Pardon, my love? Did you say you and Alfie?' He looked up from the clipboard where he was ticking off products as they counted.

'We're going to the Tea House at the Queen Victoria Markets.'

Her father raised his eyebrows. 'That sounds posh.'

'We thought we'd treat ourselves to a new experience.'

'Something going on I should know about?' He looked over his glasses at her.

She gave a soft shrug. 'We're just talking. We're friends.'

'He's a good lad . . . a larrikin at times.' Her father nodded. 'Bit of a dreamer.'

'It's the larrikin and dreamer that I like about him.'

'And precisely what your mother won't appreciate. You know she's going to tell you that you need to aim higher.'

'Dad. I'm going to marry who I want.'

'Marriage now,' he remarked without changing his gentle tone.

She gave a short laugh, nervous. 'I didn't mean that. What I meant—'

'I know what you meant, Grace. And I'm all for my daughter's happiness, truly – it's all that I want for you – but be ready for your mother's objections. Steady and reliable is her mantra. She only has your safe future in mind.'

Grace nodded. 'I know. Alfie wouldn't be on her list of suitable husbands.'

'Definitely not. But if he's on yours, I think that's all that matters. You might like to remind her that her folk were dead against me at the time; her aunt still is. Bit of a larrikin and a dreamer, they said.' He grinned.

Grace burst out laughing. 'You, a larrikin?'

'In my day, young lady,' he said archly. 'But your mother tamed that instinct in me, and I rather enjoyed having someone set up a sort of . . .' He trailed off, giving a shrug.

'A sort of what, Dad?'

'Well, a foundation.' His eyes widened as a thought occurred. 'You know our famous bridge out there?'

Grace nodded.

'What they're planning isn't going to work without those brilliant piers at either end.'

'So Mum's a pier?' She laughed again.

He put his hands together in a soft clap. 'That's right. Both of them. It gave me the stability I needed for the architecture of the life you share now.'

Grace smiled. 'That's poetic.'

Her father smiled back at her. 'All right, you go on. We're all square here. And I'll be closing up in ten minutes anyway,' he said, glancing at his fob watch that he pulled from his waistcoat pocket.

'Thanks, Dad.'

'Have fun.'

'Wait,' he said, opening the till. 'Here's a florin to spend on yourself.'

'No, Dad, you give me wages. I've got—'

'Can't a father treat his daughter?'

'Of course. Thank you!' She took the coin, kissed his cheek and turned for the stairs that led to their house.

'Grace?'

She looked back, pausing at the doorway.

Her father gave a soft smile. 'Don't let him break your heart.'

———

Feeling conspicuous in a floaty, flapper dress of chiffon, fashioned in a pale colour straight out of the arctic, Grace looked for Alfie, who was late. It was still warm enough in temperate Sydney not to need a coat, but she carried a thin cape over her arm. Her cloche hat matched her outfit and she hoped there would be no breeze off the water to lift it off her especially bouncy hair, freshly washed that morning. She heard a whistle and turned to see Alfie standing by a hansom cab, waving at her from across the street.

He said something to the coach driver and ran back towards her. 'Sorry, only place he could stop. I thought we'd go in style.' Alfie blinked at her. 'Blimey, Grace! You look so gorgeous, you're like a dream.'

She gave a nod, smiling at him. 'Thank you. You've scrubbed up well yourself, Alfie Sweeting. Where did you get that suit?'

'I rented it,' he said proudly. 'But looking at you, now I know I'm going to have to get myself one.'

'You should. You cut a fine figure,' she admitted.

He took her gloved hand and led her towards the waiting cab.

'I thought we were going on the tram.'

'No,' he said. 'We're doing this day top-notch.' He looked up to meet the waiting man's eye. 'Thank you, driver.' After seeing Grace to her seat, he closed the door and just managed to sit alongside her before the cab lurched forward. 'I've paid for just us. No one else is allowed to join us.'

'Alfie, you're spending too—'

He stopped her with a finger to his lips. 'It's my pleasure and I want to spoil you. Truly, Grace, I always thought you were beautiful but you've taken my breath away today. You look like a summer sky in that colour.'

She gurgled a laugh of pleasure. 'It was made for a wedding. Actually, my mother's visiting that family today. Mum's cousin married rather well and now has this sort of snooty attitude towards everyone. I've heard her say to Mum that she should have aspired higher than being a shopkeeper's wife. Can you imagine that?' Grace shrugged. 'Mum didn't want me wearing the label of a shopkeeper's daughter, so she had this made for that woman's daughter's wedding. I never have occasion to wear it, to be honest, as I quite like being a shopkeeper and the daughter of one.'

Alfie laughed. 'Let's face it, you'd look good in a rice sack. I'm guessing you haven't told your mother we're having the afternoon together?'

'No,' she admitted. 'But I've told Dad and he'll pass on the news.'

'I respect your mother. But today is about us. We're not going to worry about what anyone else thinks.'

Grace nodded once and firmly. 'I agree and thank you, Alfie, this is exciting. It would never occur to me to do something like this.'

'You must indulge yourself sometimes . . . good for the mind and all that.'

She laughed. 'I like your attitude to life.'

Alfie shrugged. 'We only get one, so we might as well enjoy it. Can't be all duty and responsibility, can it?'

Shaking her head, she nodded out of the window. 'You're right, but there never seems to me to be enough time for all that I do. I spend most evenings trying out new recipes.'

'I know, I get the smell of cooked sugar when I come in.'

'Powerful, isn't it?'

'Brings back memories of England. Only good ones.' He grinned.

'Given all the tea we sell, it's rather fun to be taking high tea in the city.'

'What are the bestsellers?' he asked, and his question sounded genuine.

'Tea, definitely. Sugar. Flour. Biscuits. The staples.'

'Does tea outsell coffee?'

'Oh, by miles! Dad reckons Australians drink more tea than the British.'

'I can't believe that!' He laughed.

'Dad does. He has long conversations with his suppliers about it, and he told me that someone's done some sort of study on it and apparently . . .' She frowned. 'Now, let me get this right. I don't know if these figures are current, but the average Australian drinks in excess of eight pounds of tea per person each year.'

Alfie blinked. He cupped his arms, seemingly trying to guess what eight pounds felt like. 'You're joking.'

She shook her head with a wry smile. 'And he also told me that even a decade before the turn of this century, we drank our way through more chests of tea than all of continental Europe bundled together.'

'Someone's pulling someone's plonker,' Alfie said, denying the fact with a shake of his head.

Grace found this statement highly amusing, laughing into the warm atmosphere of the coach as they clip-clopped slowly up George Street. Trams rattled by and voices yelled in the distance, but she was already having a splendid afternoon. 'I should add that my confectionery shelves are beginning to be one of the most visited in the shop . . . especially if children are present.'

'Hold that thought, Grace – we're here. Come on,' Alfie said, taking her gloved hand and helping her down from the cab. She could feel the warmth of his hand through the lace of her gloves and felt the same trill of excitement as she had the first time they'd touched. In his mid-grey three-piece suit, with his hair newly cut and slicked down, his face neatly shaven and his broad grin on display, there was no doubting they made a handsome couple. When he slid her a quick look and wink of courage, Grace, for the first time in her life, felt a stirring of something new and deep that caught in her throat. She had never been drawn to any man as she was to Alfie. He was so confident in himself; even when he was cowering behind the shop counter, he'd been grinning with amusement at his own cunning. Having never lived a dangerous moment in her life, there was something splendidly dangerous about Alfie and his risks.

It was only now that Grace realised her entire life had been predictable, reliable and wholly orchestrated by her parents, particularly her mother. Even when she was speaking her mind, it all came from within the relative safety of her home and all its reliability. Well, things were going to change from now on; she'd make sure of it.

Alfie nodded thanks to the driver, whom he'd clearly already negotiated with and paid. 'Now, Grace, I want you to remember, you belong here, all right? Don't look down – look everyone straight in the eye.'

7

The wintry colour of Grace's chiffon seemed even more pale and ethereal beneath the Tea House's cascading chandelier, which cast a theatre-like glow about the vast dining hall. It was full of mainly ladies, busy chattering, but there were also plenty of gentleman, suited and paying attention to the women they had escorted into this palatial room.

'Table for two?' the man in the frock coat enquired as Grace and Alfie approached. 'We're rather busy today, as you can . . .' He was craning to see. 'Ah yes, we do have one available. The girls are just preparing it with a fresh tablecloth.' He looked back at them, allowing his smile to fall on Grace. 'I hope you've brought your appetite, Miss. Our afternoon teas are legendary for their generosity.'

'I'm starving,' she quipped.

'Oh, excellent.' He put a long finger to the side of his mouth. 'I fear too many of you gorgeous ladies worry about your figures and so you forget to eat all the wonderful food that Chef and his team work so hard to prepare.'

'I was taught to eat everything on my plate,' Grace replied with a cheeky grin.

'And don't you look very beautiful on that creed.'

Alfie's expression looked lost, which only made Grace's smile widen. She'd explain in a minute.

'Lily?' the maître d' called. 'If you'd show this lovely couple to table nineteen, please.'

'This way, please.' The woman called Lily gestured. She was an exquisitely pretty Chinese woman, dressed in a dark day dress overlaid with a crisp, stiffly starched apron of white voile and a tiny bonnet.

The chiffon floated about Grace as, nervous, she allowed herself to glide across the room, gently holding Alfie's elbow, which he had expertly crooked for the purpose.

'Everyone's staring at you, Gracie. No, no, darlin', don't you look down. You accept their stares because they're all wishing they were you,' he whispered, touching her glove with his free hand.

'Why, because I'm on the arm of such a handsome gent?'

He gave a chuckle. 'No, darlin'. It's all you. Those candles on the candelabra are shining all on you.'

She didn't correct him but graciously accepted the compliment and smiled when the waitress gestured to their table, in full view of the other diners. As she sat, she noticed several women quickly avert their gazes. She hadn't expected to be regarded in this fashion, but she did note envy in their glances; Alfie was right.

Lily gave them each a tall menu. 'Shall I give you a few moments to consider?'

'Thank you,' Grace said.

'I'll be back shortly,' the waitress said, looking over at another diner, who was trying to catch her attention.

The room glittered with light, jewels and the glint of gold leaf from crockery. Around its twinkling space people exchanged conversation and tinkling laughter like a cluster of sparrows chittering on a sparkling morning. Everyone was engaged in their own dialogue but highly aware of each other, sitting close enough to just overhear a neighbour's gust of laughter or gentle clearing of the throat. The dining room was as vast as it was tall, interspersed with classical columns and ornamental arches, over which narrow windows reached the room's crown, the decorative, gilded ceiling. Artificial light from the chandeliers bounced off the gold and bathed the scene below in a warm hue.

Grace swallowed, smoothing her dress over her lap, and watched Alfie unconsciously copy her, running his palms across the fabric of his smart trousers. 'I can't believe we're really here. Do you know that back in 1884, the Sydney School of Arts actually ran a cooking course that focused on the preparation of an afternoon tea? It's been part of the fabric of our society since way before our time.'

'Blimey, Grace, I'm a simple boy. I drink tea because I like it. That's it. End of story. I don't study why.'

'But the whole ritual of tea is so intriguing. Look at everyone here. They're not here because they're thirsty.'

'They're here to be seen,' he said.

'Precisely. But it's more complex, I suspect. Not just to be seen, but to be in an environment where conversation feels easy. It's got such an atmosphere of social splendour . . . and even though it's a public place, I can imagine that the most private admissions are made here. It's a place where secrets are shared.' She chuckled. 'Everyone is noting each other but spaced out enough so that they cannot eavesdrop. Look at that couple there.' She inclined her head gently in their direction and was pleased that Alfie didn't whip his head around, but pretended to straighten and glance about the room, looking for a waitress. 'Surely you sense a tryst right there.' She realised he didn't know the word and seamlessly followed up as though she wasn't trying to explain. 'What do you see? Forbidden love, perhaps?'

He surprised her by reaching across and covering her gloved

hand with his own slightly calloused palm. 'I think I see a tryst right here, and if it means what I think it might, then yes, I think they're just like us.'

She focused on her companion more seriously. 'Alfie,' she began.

'Don't spoil it,' he said, with a tiny shake of his head. 'Don't decide anything. Give me a chance, Grace. We think the same, you and I, about a lot of things, I'm convinced of it.'

She wasn't ready for all of this, she knew that. 'Let's just enjoy today.' She returned her attention to the menu.

'All right.' He smiled. 'But I'm not done with that subject.'

They both regarded the menu in a brief silence, Grace relieved for the respite from Alfie's attention. She was impressed at the scripted handwriting on each menu in a royal blue ink. The offerings were vast, including seafood and oysters. The scent in the room lacked the salty aroma, however, and she suspected today was not the day for fruits of the sea. Rice pudding and rhubarb was the featured dessert. She was no fan of it, though. Just as she thought that, she heard Alfie give a low whistle.

'Rice pudding. Oh, delicious!'

It made her laugh. 'Ugh!' she declared softly for his hearing only. 'I'll faint if you order that.'

'You don't like rice pudding?'

She shook her head definitively. 'I do not.'

'Hmm,' he said, scratching his chin. 'What does this word mean?' He pointed at the menu.

'Entremets,' she read aloud gently. 'It means afterwards ... dessert.'

'Well, why don't they just write "pudding"?'

'Then the whole elegance of this experience is lost. Why have a simple English word when a confusing French one works so much better at being pretentious.'

'Pretentious? I'm guessing that means snooty.'

'You would be right. Alfie, shall we just have tea and cake? I don't really need a big meal.'

'Splendid,' he said in a posh voice, pretending to twirl a make-believe moustache.

'Behave,' she said, amused nonetheless.

The waitress returned. 'Now, can I fetch you some afternoon tea?' Her voice was soft, her smile pretty.

'Yes, please,' Alfie said over Grace's more demure response of, 'You may.'

An elegant hand gestured towards Grace's menu. 'Have you chosen, Miss?'

'Yes, thank you. I'll have a pot of black tea and your famous scones, please, with jam and cream.'

'Certainly. How about some dainties?'

'What's that?' Alfie asked.

'Sandwiches, savoury pastries, and then of course a range of our beautiful little cakes.'

'Oh yes, all of that, please.' At Grace's surprised expression, he added, 'I'm hungry.'

It made the waitress chuckle. 'Well, we shan't let you leave hungry, sir. Tea for you?'

'Yes, please. I'm not fussy, so long as it tastes like regular tea.'

'And another pot of black tea,' she said, scribbling on her notepad. 'It won't be long.' She disappeared to place their order.

'Go on, Grace, give me more of your lecture.'

She feigned a scowl at his choice of word but obliged. 'We sell a lot of tea, as I've said. I take an interest in the products on our shelves that never stop selling. You know, in rural Australia, tea is considered to be extremely masculine. It's connected with the bush and hardworking men living in rough conditions, whereas in the cities it has a feminine connotation; it's about domestic life and situations such as this.'

Alfie pulled a face that suggested she was testing him. It didn't bother her; she was having fun.

She smiled. 'Sorry, I find that sort of information intriguing, not that I've ever travelled beyond Sydney. But the idea of men in far-flung places, sitting around a small fire and boiling the billy is fascinating to me. But more to the point, I like learning about what people like and why.'

'For instance, confectionery,' Alfie said, leaning in with a knowing grin.

Lily returned with a tray and their pots of tea. 'I'll be back with your food. Please feel free to allow that a couple of minutes,' she said, nodding at the tea. 'People tend to pour it too soon.'

Grace thanked her, then turned back to Alfie as the waitress left. 'While we wait for our tea to brew, tell me what you wanted to discuss,' she said.

'You tasted the Hillier's chocolates?' he asked.

'I did.' She shook her head. 'I'd like to have offered for you to share them but you've been elusive this week.'

'They were for you. I wouldn't understand them, Grace. I've told you, I have simple tastes.'

'I know you said that, but that's why I would have liked you to try one or two. Hillier chocolates are only appealing to certain strata in society.'

Alfie looked wounded. 'You didn't enjoy them?'

'They were exquisite.'

He frowned. 'I don't understand.'

'Well, there isn't a soul around The Rocks who wouldn't enjoy them, but who can afford four shillings for a tin of those? I'll tell you – only the rich . . . and perhaps the silly but generous young man who wants to give a girl a lovely gift.' She watched his smile break. 'The everyday person loves chocolates and sweets too, but they can't afford to buy what is on offer. And the poor are simply trying to survive – they can barely fit a cake or a treat into their budget, even if they would love to give their child or loved one that pleasure.'

Alfie nodded. 'And so?' he urged.

Grace paused as their food arrived. In front of Alfie, the waitress presented a china cake stand with a small array of sandwich triangles on the bottom layer, some tiny pastry savouries on the next and, glimmering on the top layer in various jewel-like colours, the sweet treats she had mentioned featuring small jelly cakes, chocolate eclairs and a square of coffee and hazelnut macaroon cake.

Grace's two scones were put down before her, wrapped in a delicate napkin, and she was thrilled to note they were warm. Whipped cream was billowed into a small dish and another held a shiny, generous serve of what looked to be raspberry jam.

'Enjoy your afternoon tea,' Lily said and left them with a wide smile and a copy of the bill placed neatly beneath the sugar bowl.

'Let's pour,' Grace said, excited to look at the range of scrumptious treats on Alfie's pyramid.

He was yet to say anything but now exhaled excitedly. 'Where to begin,' he said, all but licking his lips.

'The sandwiches,' she suggested, smiling.

'Well, you can share. Come on, don't be shy. Let's share everything.'

Grinning, she took a sandwich and a small bite from it. Alfie's first sandwich was gone in two bites, but she suspected only because he was being polite.

'In between delicious mouthfuls, we talk, Alfie. Tell me why we're here.'

He swallowed what he'd been chewing. 'That was so good,' he said pointing to his mouth. 'Anyway, apart from me being here because I can't think of anywhere I'd rather be than with you . . .'

He paused to look her in the eye meaningfully, then continued. '. . . I wanted to show you that people enjoy treating themselves and each other. How would you describe this place? I mean, it's just a room in a building but it makes everyone here feel good, doesn't it?'

'Alfie, it's like stepping into a storybook. Outside is Sydney, with all of its dust and grime, its hard work and everyday problems that people face. But this is a different world people can enter. It's a fairytale palace.' She laughed.

'Exactly! Everything you just said. And yet all of that . . . that . . . escape,' he said, grinning as he landed on the right word, 'that is wrapped up in this room doesn't have to be expensive to be a treat.' He held a hand up as she made to interrupt, and gestured to her teapot. Grace nodded and he poured her tea, passing her the jug of milk when he'd finished. He busied himself doing the same with his own. 'Now, I know you already have this feeling that affordable treats are an area that is being ignored. Or you wouldn't be toiling so hard with your toffee apples and marshmallows.'

'Honeycomb is next,' she said, taking a sip of her tea.

'Everyone has a different level, though. Most of the folk in here would consider this a pleasurable treat but an affordable one. But the blokes I know down at The Rocks would no more be caught in here than fly and, more to the point, they couldn't afford to be in here. They couldn't afford the clean clothes, let alone the pot of tea or the dainties, as the waitress called them.' He put a burnished pastry into his mouth and shook his head. 'Oh my. You must taste this. I don't even know what it is.'

Laughing, she took one and pondered as she chewed. 'Creamy chicken, I think.'

'I could eat a mountain of them.'

'Why are you telling me what I already know, Alfie?'

'Because you need to trust your instincts, darlin'. I realise you already feel what I'm saying in your bones, but you're keeping your dream too small. Selling out your toffee apples in your father's grocery shop is brilliant, but why not have toffee apples on the floor every day, along with all those other amazing treats you have in mind?'

Grace took a breath and realised she was hesitating because she was weighing up whether to trust him with the full scope of her dream. She sipped her tea and sighed. She'd not shared this with anyone, but then she'd never felt as close to someone as she did right now, with Alfie.

'I have been thinking bigger than that,' she began. 'My idea is simple. A shop of sugar treats that not only can anyone afford, but everyone – no matter their status – feels drawn towards. I want to sell sweets that trigger the child inside *all* shoppers: young or old, rich or poor, from the city or country. Toffee apples don't carry status or labels – they're delicious no matter who you are, and I'm betting Mrs Chalmers enjoyed her own toffee apple as much as her children enjoyed theirs.'

'I think that's a safe bet,' Alfie agreed through a mouthful of pastry. 'But I'd take your idea even further, Grace. With no disrespect to your line-up of sweets on offer, I think the shop itself needs to attract attention.'

At this she frowned. 'The shop itself? How?'

'Easy!' he said, too loud and excited.

She put a finger to her lips, looking around at the other patrons. A few had glanced up and over to their table.

Alfie couldn't be less concerned, going by his laughing expression. But he demurred. 'Easy,' he repeated, murmuring this time. 'You make the shop the destination and part of the whole treat experience.'

She blinked in wonder. 'Tell me how.'

'Let your imagination go, Grace. Colour, posters, your products, the windows of the shop, and then within it – from the uniforms of the people behind the counter, to the bags you send your sweeties away in. All of it has to be a treat.'

'An experience,' she breathed.

'Exactly! Now you're talking, Grace darlin'. From the moment they walk into the shop, it's all fun and sugar and smiles.'

'For everyone, young or old, rich or poor,' she qualified, her mind racing at his words.

'That's it. Costs nothing to walk in and as they do they get to inhale the glorious smell of sugar in all of its forms.'

'And we give away samples as you suggested,' she added, filled with excitement at the possibilities. She took a scone and absent-mindedly broke it open, the top half coming away from the bottom with precision.

'Yes! It's easy enough, I'm sure, to build that cost in.'

'It's not to be feared . . . the extra is minuscule,' she said, deep in thought.

'Well, there you are, Gracie. It costs so little to let a customer sample the goods, but one free taste and you've got them! Chances are they'll not only buy what you're offering the sample of, but other products too. Better still, they'll return and it's return business that makes money.' He was nodding vigorously at her.

'I've found the shop,' Grace suddenly blurted out. She hadn't meant to but she'd become so excited to be talking about all that she'd had imprisoned in her imagination for so long.

'What?' Alfie shook his head. 'Where?'

'That was the fib.' She covered her mouth with her hands.

He opened his mouth in wonder. 'Oh, I see,' he said, chewing on the final pastry, while she began to spoon cream onto her scone, already brimming with jam. 'Go on, taste it.'

Grace bit into it. 'Mmm. My mother makes lovely scones, but

we don't ever have cream, just jam. Here – you have the other one and then we can attack those cakes.'

He laughed, helped himself and followed how she'd dressed her scone, making a sound of soft pleasure at his first bite. 'Where's the shop you've found?' he asked, swallowing.

She took a hesitant breath before grinning. 'Not too far away, actually. It's downstairs.'

His features dropped into surprise. 'This building?'

She nodded. 'A lovely double window too. It looks onto George Street.'

'Grace,' he breathed, sounding awed. 'You can't just dream this, you have to do it!'

She laughed. 'Oh, I dream about it all the time and of course I want to but . . .' She sighed and shrugged.

'Don't say your parents. Don't say the grocery store. This is your life, your passion. You must follow this dream or you'll regret it.'

'How, though? How am I supposed to raise the money to open my own shop?'

'You'll do it. *We'll* do it. Together. Will you let me be part of this, let me help you? I've got so many ideas.'

Grace nodded slowly, realising that she believed him, even though she already sensed that Alfie might be unreliable because of his larrikin nature. Despite that reservation, she could see a kindred spirit opposite her, and she knew none of his enthusiasm was faked. She could imagine him shaking her by the shoulders, imploring her to follow her heart. Added to this, Alfie's vision of making the shop itself a type of treat for anyone to visit was not something she'd considered previously. But now, suddenly, her mind was igniting with colours and smells, all manner of visuals to tempt – and thrill – shoppers, for their enjoyment but also to open their purses and wallets. That was Alfie's doing. He did think big, but he also thought broadly and, some might say, with more cunning than Grace. Perhaps that was an ingredient she could benefit from.

She smiled. 'Partners then.'

His face lit with fresh pleasure, while his eyes flickered with astonishment. 'You mean that?'

She nodded. 'Yes,' she replied, sounding resolute. 'I can't do it all alone.'

'To partnership,' he said, raising his china cup.

She repeated his toast and smiled, gently clinking the porcelain of her cup against his, enjoying the satisfying chime. 'So Fairweather and Sweeting?'

'No, no,' he said, shaking his head. 'That makes us sound like Foy's. We're not a department store.'

'Then what shall we call our shop?'

'*Shops*, Grace . . . think big. And shop is too common.'

She laughed but he gave her look of soft admonition.

'It has to be an experience, remember? What about "salon"?'

'No, that word sounds exclusive,' Grace said. 'It wouldn't be welcoming to all. We need a name that conjures magic in the mind and feels irresistible – especially to children.'

'Oh, well, that's easy, darlin'. You used the word not so long ago – "palace". How about we call it the Sugar Palace? And when people enter, we'll make sure it feels like a colourful fairytale spun from sugar.'

'The Sugar Palace,' she murmured, testing it, loving it immediately. 'Oh, yes . . . yes, that's perfect, Alfie.'

8

When they'd finished their afternoon tea, Alfie imagined Grace had wondered how he had afforded this treat. He had insisted on paying the bill and deliberately didn't flinch as he looked at it; she must have thought it wise to let him have this moment, despite her offer to share the cost. And he was sure that she could sense how chuffed he was to have spoiled her. He followed her down to the ground floor past the dingy end shop; it looked like a sad bookshop, Alfie thought, and said as much out loud.

'That's not a bookshop,' Grace corrected him. He loved her stern expression. 'That's our city library, although it's hardly welcoming.'

'Well, you won't find me in any bookshop.'

'You need to see Angus & Robertson Bookshop in Castlereagh Street. I go in there and never want to leave.'

'That's because you can read,' he said, wishing he hadn't admitted this.

She paused and cut him a look. 'Then I'll teach you.'

'I can do the basics, signs and letters and things.' He shrugged. 'It's just books with lots of words that scare me.'

Grace nodded. 'Your ability to talk the talk belies that you can't read.'

'I've been accused of being a "champagne talker",' he said with a grin.

'You are that. But we'll work on your reading. I'll find you a book you'll think is so irresistible you'll want to read it with me.'

He gave a softer smile now. 'I enjoy everything with you,' he said, and risked leaning in to kiss her cheek. 'You know I'm in love with you, don't you?'

Grace looked down. 'Alfie . . . you promised.'

'Did I? All I can promise you is myself. Marry me, Grace.'

'What?' She pulled his sleeve, dragging him into the shadows. 'Are you mad?'

'Yes. Mad for you.' He suddenly strode into the centre of the highly decorated tiled floor, raised his hands and his voice, startling the shoppers around them. 'Madly in love. Maddened that you're not already my bride.'

People laughed, looking towards Grace.

'*Shhh!*' she hissed urgently, pulling at his hand.

Alfie allowed himself to be dragged back near the library, where he took both her hands in his. 'Grace, we were meant to meet. Meant to be together. I feel it fizzing through my blood. We'll be business partners and partners in life.' He meant every word, though he couldn't quite believe he was saying them out loud.

'What am I going to do with you, Alfie?' she said, looking both exasperated but helplessly flattered at once. 'You definitely do talk like champagne must taste.'

'Marry me and you'll only drink champagne,' he promised.

She took a deep breath. 'If we pull this mad idea off and we open a confectionery store, I'll marry you.'

He grinned, thrilled. 'Why the condition?'

'Because I've only just got to know you! I'm not reckless like you – I don't live dangerously – but I do see myself as adventurous, so I'm not saying no . . . I'm saying let's wait until we feel more secure . . .' She held a finger in the air before he could leap in and corrected herself, saying firmly, 'Until *I* feel secure.'

'When will that be?'

'When we open.'

Alfie nodded; he could live with that. 'Deal. Will you wear a ring?'

'Not yet. It's too soon after my rejection of Norman. I need you to be patient. Now, come on, I want to show you the premises.'

Alfie was more than aware of how carefully she was watching his reaction as she led him around to the shop frontage in busy George Street.

'Here,' she said, sweeping her hand across the span of the large window, doorway and second window. There was stained glass in deep pink and green. Meanwhile the ornate ironwork surrounding the entrance added a pretty welcome in its dark green, almost charcoal, colour.

Alfie's mind was already racing towards how they might fit out the shop. 'Home of the Sugar Palace,' he breathed. 'It's perfect, Grace.'

'It is, isn't it?' she said excitedly, clinging to him, squeezing his arm. 'It's hard to see in because the windows have been painted over for privacy while awaiting new tenants, but I've been inside. As our customers leave, they'll walk back through this stained-glass entrance, and it dazzles like jewels.'

'How much is the rent?' Alfie asked, all but holding his breath.

'It's not cheap,' she admitted, 'not up this end of town, but they're keen to keep the space filled, so I think we could probably negotiate.'

'How much?'

She told him.

He closed his eyes and made a rapid calculation. 'That's a frightening amount, and that's before we sell a single lollipop.'

Grace shook her head faintly at him. 'You're amazing how you do that.'

'Would you let me do the bartering?'

She nodded silently, eyes wide and worried. 'I can sell a lot of lollipops, I promise.' It sounded like a plea.

'I trust you, darlin'.' He grinned. 'We've got to think about setting up inside, finding staff, kitting them out. Advertising and promotions. There will be a lot of upfront costs. Maybe we should get a licence to set up a barrow in the laneway at Martin Place with the flower sellers so we can raise some capital. You could start selling some things there.'

'Oh, Alfie, that's a clever idea.'

'Told you, Grace, I'll never be short of ideas. You leave that with me. The barrow will get people used to the product, looking for it, getting to know the name. Meanwhile, you think about what stock we can sell easily from a barrow for a month or two while we save madly.'

'It feels like a mountain to climb.'

'Now you're adopting your mother's attitude,' he warned. 'Don't start thinking like that. If you want something badly enough, Grace, you go after it. Picture it. Picture yourself in here, surrounded by lovely girls selling your product in their new, smart uniforms. Picture in your mind's eye all the colours, the smell of the products, the lure of chocolate and licorice, marshmallow and cinder toffee.'

'Cinder toffee?' she asked, breaking the spell he was trying to cast.

'Honeycomb,' he corrected himself. 'Cinder toffee is what the sweet sellers have in London – same thing. Anyway, can you see it?

Can you taste the sugar and smell the sweetness in the air of the shop on entry?'

He watched her smile, close her eyes and inhale. Blimey, she was beautiful.

'Yes . . . yes, I can,' she confirmed.

'Good. Because I want this very badly for you. For us. I'm all in.'

She opened her eyes grinning. 'Me too.'

Alfie, enchanted by both her sparkling beauty and trust in him, suddenly jumped into the air and clicked his heels together on one side. He wanted to yell that he couldn't believe it was him, Alfie Sweeting, who had got so lucky as to deliver eggs that day to the Fairweather's grocery store.

His leap was so unexpected, so suddenly comical, that Grace guffawed. So he did it again, on the other side, longing to hear that genuine explosion of laughter. It felt special to know that laugh was only for him.

Alfie was in love. And now he knew everything he did, he was doing for Grace.

———————

Alfie's words of affection were like tiny, hot shocks, similar to the ones Grace felt when she was testing the iron. But these didn't scald . . . *Mad for you, madly in love, maddened that you're not already my bride* – well, no, but they burned invisibly through her defences and pierced a place in her heart that had never been broken or damaged. Her whole body responded to the pleasurable wounds of his sweet, funny declarations. No one had ever spoken to her like this before. Certainly not Norm.

Grace had grown up in such a sheltered environment of home, the school her mother had insisted on sending her to across the harbour – well away from The Rocks – and then serving at her parents' grocery store. She'd stepped out with two young men that Mary had approved of – Grace was sure her mother had been in the background then, too, organising it with their mothers – but while they were pleasant enough, neither had set her thoughts afire as Alfie did. It wasn't just his talk of love. Alfie thought like her. He wanted to succeed, to achieve some goals in life that weren't about being safe or steady. Inwardly, Grace could hear herself debating this very situation with her mother.

'He's adventurous, Mum. He has ideas and he's prepared to risk failure for success.'

'We call those people dreamers, Grace. They're the people who build hot air balloons with grand plans to fly across the world and—'

'But Mum, where would the world be without adventurers? We wouldn't be in Australia if your folk hadn't risked the great voyage and Dad's people hadn't done the same. They were pioneers. Surely . . .'

'It's not the same, Grace, and you know it. Our families had to make a new life for themselves or risk starvation or poverty – they were trying to build better lives for their families to come. What you're talking about is excitement, gambling, and escapade with so much risk attached.'

'What's life without some risk?' she could imagine herself finding the courage to say. Easy in thoughts, not in person, she reminded herself.

But her mother would be ready with a brisk rebuke. 'And find out that balloon soaring to the sky is just hot air and no substance.'

Mary Fairweather was not a shrew; Grace knew her mother to be generous and affectionate, but also fiercely protective of her husband and her only child. If she came across as a purse-lipped naysayer, it was because either Grace or Hugh – or their business – might, in her mother's mind, be threatened. She would not enjoy listening to Grace's plans, and to have Alfie at the centre of them would surely make her lips become so thin they'd disappear.

On one hand Grace would find her mother's reaction amusing, but she didn't relish the fractiousness that was about to come into her life. She'd have to fight for Alfie's acceptance and, curiously, she felt ready to be his champion. It would be hard to explain, but she suspected her father would understand. If she could just take her mother back to the early days of falling in love with Hugh, she might be able to make Mary Fairweather understand what this exciting moment felt like.

For she had fallen in love with Alfie; she could finally admit that to herself. Right now, with his love and his praise and his bright energy for her dream . . . well, it felt possible, so near she could almost touch it. He made her feel indestructible and together, she could imagine they might be formidable.

'Grace?' Alfie was looking at her expectantly, his breathing still a little fast from his high jumps.

She smiled at his antics. 'What was that for?'

'That's how you make me feel. And that's how our new partnership feels.' He offered an arm. 'Shall we walk?'

'Oh yes, I must settle down all that I've devoured. Thank you, Alfie. It was wonderful.'

'Just the beginning of how I'm going to spoil you, Grace.'

Could she trust it? A vision of George Dooley came to mind.

'I believe you,' she said, trying to keep her voice neutral. 'But how are we to raise this money we need? I have some, certainly enough to get us started, but achieving that "experience" in the shop – which I now can't stop thinking about – is going to cost a lot more than what we can earn from a barrow in Martin Place.'

'Let's agree that you concern yourself with the range of product and leasing the shop itself. I'll worry about all that other stuff.'

'On a delivery boy's wage?'

'No.'

'Then—'

'Grace, just let me do what I do.'

Grace frowned. 'So George Dooley can come wandering in and make demands at my parents' shop? If he can't get it from you, Alfie, he'll demand it from us.'

'Why would he do that?' Alfie actually laughed.

And now she was trapped. She didn't want to say 'because if we're married, then he can come after your wife'. She wasn't ready to admit that she wanted to marry him – not yet. But she found the answer within enough time so that she didn't look lost for words. 'Because if we're business partners, I will be liable for your debts.'

He smiled and she wondered if he could read her mind. Alfie might be uneducated, but he had worldly smarts about him. She sensed that along with his incredible mathematical skills, he could read a person as easily as she might read a book.

'I promise I shall bring no debt to your door, only profit. But you must trust me and not question me or try to corner me. Alfie Sweeting must fly as free as a bird,' he said, flapping his arms as though they were wings and managing to annoy a passer-by.

'Watch out!' the man said.

'Sorry, sir,' Alfie apologised and the man's horrified face was funnier than Alfie flapping his make-believe wings. Even so, her mother's voice in her mind, talking about soaring in the sky – *all hot air and no substance* – haunted her now.

'You have to promise me: no stealing.'

'Stealing?' Alfie looked deeply offended. 'There you go again, Gracie. Those childhood pickpocket days are behind me, darlin'. I came to Australia a free man and I intend to stay that way. But I'm not going to get rich quick delivering groceries, so I need you to get on with your part of our plan and let me tackle mine without any . . .' Now he was searching for the right word.

'Hindrance?' she offered.

'I was thinking about how a horse is shackled to the wagon.' He mimicked holding reins.

She understood what he was getting at. 'All right, Alfie. You come up with the funds to set up and decorate the store, and hire the staff we need, and I will not ask questions unless a policeman comes to my door.'

He put his hands up in mock surrender. 'No police, that's a promise.'

If she was being honest, she didn't know what she'd just agreed to. Alfie's reply didn't for a moment convince her that he was being transparent, and she knew whatever he had in mind may not be entirely legal.

But then again it could be. She shouldn't think the worst of him; she imagined people had probably been doing that for all of Alfie's life because of where he came from, how he sounded, how he looked. If he always dressed as he had today, he could pass as a man of means, a man of business. Maybe that was the answer, and it was as simple as giving him a fresh wardrobe and a regular haircut and shave.

Clothes make the man. She remembered that phrase from her schooldays. It was true. A man's attire communicated so much about his character and status, even if it were simply a shroud to cover his true nature.

'I have to ask, Alfie. Do you mean to earn the money gambling?'

Alfie held up his palms. 'Only with the legal kind, Grace. At the racecourse.'

She knew her body language was giving away her soft despair because Alfie stopped walking and pulled her into Martin Place, away from the stream of pedestrian traffic. He led her beneath the cool of the grand arcade of the Italianate-style general post office of New South Wales, where few people were on a weekend.

'Listen,' he implored her. 'I know you don't approve of gambling, but I'm good at it, Grace. You must trust me on this. I can win the money we need faster at the racecourse than with a year of hard work.'

'But I've been raised to know that the only way to get on is through hard work. There is no easy way to get rich, other than criminal means.'

Alfie shook his head. 'I'm just going to place some bets, that's all. I'll keep it small and I'll bring my winnings to you.'

'I don't want—'

'For you to keep them safe. I won't reinvest my winnings and risk them. I'll put them straight into our savings for the new shop. And when I've won enough, I'll stop.'

Grace held his gaze. 'Is that a promise too?'

He crossed his heart, puddle-grey eyes staring into hers, and then without warning he leaned in and kissed her gently. She didn't resist him. It was becoming increasingly harder to resist Alfie and his charms.

9

Alfie stood near the top of William Street in Woolloomooloo; a stranger word he'd never heard uttered, and no one could tell him how the name had come about. When he'd first arrived and gone hunting for gambling opportunities, a gentleman bookmaker had commented to him that it had a connection with an Aboriginal burial ground. But no one was sure. All Alfie knew was that poverty lived here as happily as it did around The Rocks, and just like The Rocks there were good, hardworking people here making the best of things, right on the edge of where the better heeled lived.

It was merely a ten-minute walk to the dangerous territory of Darlinghurst, which sounded innocent enough, but Alfie didn't need to read the newspapers to know that the nicknames of Razorhurst, Gunhurst and even Dopehurst were well and truly earned by the suburb on the fringe of the city. It was in this neighbourhood that crime of every possible kind was flourishing. He knew the atmosphere well, because he had lived it in the East End of London back in his youth.

Alfie turned west to look back at the city, where he knew Grace was having a day off, a picnic with her parents. It was Sunday.

He'd told her he had picked up an odd job in the east; the lie had come easily, even though he hated to betray her. The financial mountain he was aiming to scale, however, was daunting and he'd come here to see how he might go about raising his half of the money required to open the Sugar Palace.

It had been two weeks since they'd convinced each other that they were going to set up the most exciting store Sydney could offer for an affordable treat and, more importantly, at least in Alfie's eyes, that if they pulled it off, then their wedding would follow. He had begun to daydream about finally having a family: a loving wife in Grace and his own children to hold in his arms. He would give them all the love in the world . . . all the love that he hadn't experienced in his childhood. And if he could help to make Grace's dream come true, then they would be able to make their children's lives far better than he could have imagined when he was running jobs for Sabini back in London.

The missing finger seemed to tingle in memory of his punishment. George Dooley was capable of that kind of violence, Alfie knew, but he wouldn't be nearly so polite about it. He remembered Sabini gently explaining why Alfie must lose that finger and how he'd respected him even as he'd hated him.

Alfie shuddered. Never again.

But even as he thought that, turning away from Grace to do something she would not approve of, he had to take the risk if he was ever going to raise the money. He had a choice to make. There were two women he might approach, bitter rivals. One was Tilly Devine, notorious madam and criminal entrepreneur, whose headquarters were in the very neighbourhood he was standing in. Or he could head east into dangerous Darlinghurst, where the frightening Kate Leigh lived and dealt in the underworld. Her reputation for violence was well known and she undertook it with the kind of casual ruthlessness that could make any man's knees buckle.

Both were extraordinarily wealthy but equally dangerous in their own way, and it was hard to choose between them. In the end, it was like a toss of the coin with the weight ever so slightly in favour of Tilly, and only because she was originally from England.

The decision was made.

Alfie walked deeper into Woolloomooloo, knowing that every step he took brought him closer to the kind of treachery, violence and cruel attitude that had ruled his past. Money in the city's east changed hands as fast as water might flow from a spout, in constant motion whether it was paying for girls, gambling, drugs or having someone assaulted or killed.

He imagined what Grace would think of him and he shuddered again at the idea that she might ever find out. He would never tell her; the barrow to start selling her goods in Martin Place was being readied now and while he might have to exaggerate the takings to keep Grace in the dark, he was confident his idea would work. Betting at the racecourse was simply a notion for Grace's benefit. He didn't feel the horses could achieve what Tilly Devine's trade could. But he wouldn't do it for long. That he promised himself as he drew closer to the address he'd hunted down.

Just long enough to get the money to open, he swore under his breath as he arrived at a squalid-looking terrace. A girl stood outside, regarding him with eyes like dark saucers.

'Is this Mrs Devine's place?' Alfie kept his voice casual.

'Who's asking?' the girl said.

Well trained, he thought. 'My name is Alfie Sweeting and I was told she may have some work for me.' He gave his trademark grin; it usually worked on women and girls of all ages.

The girl practically scoffed at him. 'She works with *girls*.'

'What's your name?'

'What's it to you?'

'Just being polite.' He grinned again, trying to get her to smile back.

She didn't. 'What sort of work?'

He had to hand it to the girl; she was blunt and unafraid. 'Er, it might be better if I have this conversation with her.'

The nameless child, who was perhaps thirteen years old by Alfie's reckoning, stared at him for a moment longer, then turned on her heel, disappearing behind a wonky timber gate that joined an equally ramshackle raw timber fence. She was as unkempt as the house she seemed to belong to. He wondered if he'd looked like that as a child and decided that he probably did; he too had worn raggedy clothes and had unwashed hair that needed a cut.

He didn't know what he was supposed to do, so he waited.

After several minutes, a woman clad in a shiny floral dressing gown sauntered out the back door behind the youngster who had opened the gate. The woman had made little attempt to cover the tops of her large breasts, not bothering to tie the garment she'd presumably hurriedly pulled on, but simply holding it in place with a casual grip of one hand.

Alfie pulled his flat cap off as she stopped in front of him. 'Mrs Devine.'

The girl laughed first and the woman followed with a lazy chuckle, then a chimney of smoke blown upwards from the cigarette she held loosely in the corner of her mouth. 'No. I'm Maddy. What do you want?'

He repeated his request.

'Mrs Devine doesn't see just anyone, you know.'

He needed to think fast. What could possibly persuade her to meet a stranger, other than money or perhaps a threat? It was out before he could censure himself. 'Tell her I'm one of George Sabini's boys.'

'What's that supposed to mean?' Maddy asked, unimpressed. 'Is that supposed to send me running back full of fear?'

'You know my name. You know who sent me. Tell her.'

'All right, handsome,' she said, amusing the girl. It must be how all the women in the brothel behind that door talked. 'But I'll warn you now, Tilly kills for being looked at the wrong way,' she said and then burst into laughter.

His face must have betrayed his worry. Devine certainly had a reputation for violence, he knew that much. He gave a shrug, trying to relax his shoulders. He couldn't show any fear.

She continued. 'If we're not back in five minutes, walk on and away from here.'

He nodded, then put his cap back on as if to say it was her funeral if she chose to treat him that way. She didn't need to know that the sun was high enough in the sky to create a glare.

'Watch him, Hols.' The woman swung around, gown flaring and almost giving Alfie an eyeful as she went back inside.

The girl squinted up at him from where she now sat outside the gate playing jacks. 'I'm watching you,' she threatened in an amiable tone.

'I won't be moving for five minutes,' he assured. After a while, watching her play, he spoke again. 'Did you know that game used to be called knucklebones?'

She laughed at the name. 'I don't think so.'

'Yes, it did. And that main pebble you're using – we called it the jack. That's how the new name came about.'

'Did you use the knuckles of the people you killed?' She seemed more interested in what he had to say now. 'You wanted Maddy to think you're a gangster, didn't you?'

He gave a soft burst of a laugh. 'No!'

She smiled. 'So you were someone's errand boy?'

'No to that too,' he said, feeling scrutinised and failing to hide the truth.

'All right, I'll bite, handsome,' she leaned on the word, letting him know it wasn't necessarily what she thought of him. 'Whose knuckles were used?'

'We used mutton bones.'

'Oh.' She seemed disappointed. 'You would be so much more interesting if you had lied and said you used the knuckles of all the men you killed.'

'Hols . . . Is that really your name? I've never killed anyone and don't intend to.'

She sighed. 'My name is Holly. And killing someone is sometimes the only way to get things done.'

It was his turn to laugh. 'How old are you?'

'Fourteen. And don't tell me I look small for my age. I know I am. I'll start work soon as I turn fifteen.'

'When's that?'

'Dunno.'

'You don't know your own birthday?'

'I was an orphan. Tilly bought me.'

'Bought you?'

'Five pounds. That's a lot of money, mister.' She gave a scowl. He put his hands up. 'It is.'

Holly shrugged. 'She said I'll make it back for her in no time when I start proper work.'

Alfie frowned. 'What sort of work?'

'You're here to see Tilly and you're asking me that question? Use your imagination.'

Ahh. He was helplessly entranced by her manner; he didn't even know her, but he hated the idea of what lay in store for her. She seemed so worldly and there was a bright intelligence in her eyes. 'So are you now considered Tilly's daughter?' She sounded like she should be with that blunt manner.

That amused her. 'I wish I was. I belong to Maddy.'

'So *she* has become your mother?' he asked.

'No, I didn't say that. I *belong* to her. My real mother died. Tilly paid my father for me. He couldn't get rid of me quick enough. Probably kept him in grog for half a year on the proceeds.'

'Oh,' Alfie said, roundly corrected and desperately saddened at once. 'My mother died on me too.'

'So what?'

Blimey, she was tough. 'Well, it might help if—'

'How would your mother dying help me?' She put her hand up to shade her eyes, now fully regarding him.

'It wouldn't,' he admitted.

'Then why say it?'

Why indeed. 'I thought if you knew . . .' He trailed off. She was right. They weren't friends. And he was making a fool of himself. She was far too smart and probably spoke to dozens of men a day, arriving at this place to enjoy the attention of a woman for a brief time. And it seemed she was already resigned to taking on the role alongside the women who worked here.

'Holly . . . Is that your real name?' He wondered how much of what she said was true.

'No, my name is Matilda, same as Tilly, but we couldn't have two of those, so she called me Holly.'

'Matilda is pretty.'

'Are you trying to get off with me, mister?'

'No.' He put both palms up in a placating gesture. 'Not at all. I'm getting married.'

'So what? Most of the men who come here are already married.'

'Not me. I'm marrying the brightest, most gorgeous woman in Australia.' He smiled.

'What's her name?'

'Grace.'

She gave a nod. 'Pretty enough.'

An idea struck him. 'Listen, Holly. Grace and I are opening a shop in the city. If you ever want to do an honest day's work for an honest wage, and in lovely surrounds where you will wear a smart uniform and be respected by our customers, you come and find me. Do you remember my name?'

'Alfie Sweeting,' she said. At his look of surprise, she rolled her eyes. 'What sort of shop?'

'I can't say much more right now, but I can assure you it will be the talk of the town.'

'What would I do?'

'Simply serve behind a counter – nothing hard about it, but I think your fast mind is exactly what we need. I presume you can count and add up?'

'Of course. Maddy insists upon it or men take advantage.'

'Ask for me at Fairweather's grocery store at The Rocks. Or better still, I'll have a barrow in Martin Place soon – you won't miss me.'

'I thought you said a shop?'

'I did. But while we get it ready, we're going to be testing our products on the public.'

She said nothing more because the gate opened. Maddy was back. 'Well, it seems your friend Sabini held some weight with the boss. Tilly will see you. Follow me, handsome.'

10

Grace sat on the grass, a rug beneath her, chewing morosely on a sandwich. Hugh Fairweather shared the rug, while her mother sat primly on a small bench with the picnic basket next to her.

Her father sighed into the tense pause. 'Mary. We wanted this to be a nice family day. We get so little time to ourselves.'

'Blame your daughter, Hugh. She's the one who has smothered the mood.'

Smothered the mood, Grace repeated silently. 'A wedding should bring joy, Mum.' She set her half-eaten egg sandwich on the plate beside her.

'Not this one,' her mother replied, chewing deliberately but looking as though she tasted nothing.

'Why not? I'm happy. Isn't that worth all your joy?'

'Grace,' her mother began in a tone of exasperation. She often used it on both Grace and her father, conveying the attitude that she was always right and was now going to prove it to the witless pair she shared her life with. 'I like Alfie well enough. I realise he has a worldliness and bright mind that no formal education provides.

I can tell he amuses you, and I know he's different to the other young men you have stepped out with.'

Grace shrugged as if to say, *well then*? 'He sounds perfect.'

'Quite the opposite,' her mother countered. 'Because for all of those pleasant-enough aspects, Alfie strikes me as being unreliable – and you know I'm understating that.'

'No, I don't. Why don't you say exactly what you mean?' Grace kept her tone neutral, not wishing to inflame the discussion but needing to be clear about her position within it.

'I mean that he will let you down, my girl. It's as simple as that. Your father knows it too – he just lacks the courage to risk hurting your feelings.'

'Mum, how can you possibly know that? You're not a fortune teller.'

'I don't need to be. You're clearly blinded by your affection for him. But I am not. That means I do not view him through the rosy lens that you do, and I can see the real Alfie and his faults . . . not just the fascinating bits.'

'But surely you could say that for every man or woman who wishes to marry,' Grace protested. 'We can't know everything about each other. We have to love those good bits and let that make the marriage strong.'

Her father had been watching them silently, a tense expression on his face. 'Your mother is just trying to save you pain, Grace.'

'Not you too, Dad,' Grace murmured, sounding injured.

Her mother interjected before he could qualify what he meant. 'You're our only child. Everything we do, we do for you. So I'm not going to let some smart-talking Londoner, who has the capacity to think like a criminal, just walk in and take what's ours.'

'My dear, that's a little harsh. She's not a commodity,' her father commented, looking unhappily at his sandwich.

Mary ignored him. 'Grace, look at me.'

Grace raised her gaze defiantly.

Mary placed a hand over her heart. 'Can you honestly say to me that Alfie is an honest, law-abiding citizen, who will look after your interests before his own and who is capable of being as good a father to your children as your father has been to you?'

Grace knew she shouldn't jump in and say yes immediately. Instead, she deliberately paused to look out towards Farm Cove; it was a pretty view from where they sat on the rise in the Botanic Gardens. She blew out a breath slowly and turned to face her mother's serious, intent gaze. 'Mum, I don't know what you think you know about Alfie, but I know him better than you. And whatever his past points towards, he has set himself a new direction: me. Me and our marriage, a whole new enterprise.' She might as well say it all and get it done with, she realised. 'We're going into business together and—'

She wasn't surprised at the gasp from both parents that stopped her mid-sentence.

'What do you mean?' Her father looked astonished, while her mother's lips drew themselves into that anticipated tight line of disapproval. 'We want to hand the business over to you in time.'

Grace knew she needed to be gentle now, and began her explanation in a soft tone. 'Dad, I don't want to be a grocer.'

'Well, neither do I!' her mother snapped.

Shocked, Grace looked at her, then at her father, who looked equally taken aback.

Now that she'd made the admission, her mother dug in. 'It was never my dream, but I've been getting on with it for years. Now we have a solid family business that you have been trained to take on.'

Grace didn't respond immediately, wanting to organise her thoughts, but her father filled the taut silence.

'What do mean by that, Mary? I thought we both agreed that a grocery was—'

'You did, Hugh,' her mother said, frustration spilling as she cut across his words. 'I did it for you because I loved you and because I wanted to support you in your endeavours.'

'But . . .?' he asked.

'But nothing.' She shrugged, suddenly embarrassed by her husband's and daughter's accusing looks.

'No,' Hugh said. 'This seems to be a day of truths. Why don't you tell me what I don't seem to know?'

'Oh, Hugh, come on.' Her mother flung her sandwich at the nearby pigeons who had been waiting watchfully and now, in a flap of wings, began to fight over the bread, bits of egg spilling onto the grass. 'I had my daydreams but then I met you. What more is there to say?'

'That you don't enjoy being a grocer's wife and that after twenty years, you're struggling to hide it?' Grace offered.

Now both her parents turned their attention on her.

Grace shrugged. 'Why can't we be honest? Dad, you like being a grocer, but Mum doesn't. It's probably because her family looks down upon her, even though it's her hardworking, independent spirit that has helped you to turn a small shop into arguably the best grocer in Sydney city.' It was the right string of words to put together in that moment. She watched her father straighten his bearing, while her mother looked instantly prouder. 'You're an amazing couple. You complement each other's strengths, and you fill in for each other's weaknesses. Mum, your family should take pride in the fact that you help run a busy, profitable business. Dad, if not for you, we wouldn't have this flourishing shop that has grown and keeps growing. Everyone knows Fairweathers. Everyone likes you and wants to give you their business – I know this because those offices at the top of George Street could just as easily give their money to that other grocer that's closer, but they're happy to pay your delivery expenses. Ask yourself why. It's because of you and Mum and how you treat your clients – you both respect and welcome all customers.'

Grace paused, watching her parents share a glance of pride between them. 'The point is, Dad, you chose this business. And Mum, you chose Dad. You could have waited, married someone else, maybe been a lady of leisure from the North Shore, but knowing you as I do, I can't imagine that would have been enough for you. Even if running a grocery store wasn't your dream, you would have wanted to do something with your skills. Look at how you keep our business on the straight and narrow with your excellent accounting and ordering skills. Left to Dad, we'd have too much of this or not enough of the other. But Mum, you made your own decision to marry Dad and go into this life.'

'So what if I did? I don't regret it.'

'Good,' her father said, 'because I couldn't have done it without you.' He smiled at his wife and winked.

Satisfied that the potential rift had not been realised, Grace knew she needed to strike and make her point. 'But *I* didn't choose this life,' she risked, forcing both her parents to return their attention to her. 'I was born into it.' She shrugged again. 'You've always known I've had ambition to do something with my confectionery.' She watched her mother begin to lean forward, about to jump in, and put a hand up. 'No, this needs to be said. I intend to see how far I can take it. Alfie and I are going to open a confectionery store, and we've made a promise that if we do, we're going to marry.'

'And if you don't open one?'

'It means we've failed each other, and I doubt marriage would be on our minds, but I don't intend to fail, Mum. I know I can make a sweet shop work in Sydney.'

'You'd turn your back on our store, my love?' her father asked, sounding plaintive.

It broke her heart a little to hear that note in his voice, but honesty was needed now. 'I have to do this, Dad, or I'll never be happy. I must try, anyway, and you're not near retirement yet.' She opened her palms. 'Can we talk about your shop when the time comes and we need to make these important decisions? Right now we're worrying about events that haven't happened.'

'You're right,' her mother said, closing the lid of the picnic basket she'd been steadily repacking. 'Let me just say this, my girl . . . and it is said with only love and care for you. When Alfie lets you down, we will be here for you.'

Grace fixed her mother with a stare. 'Thank you,' she said, trying to sound as sincere as she could. 'But he won't let me down.'

'Then I suppose I had better return to planning a spring wedding – just with a different groom,' her mother replied.

———————

Alfie's patience was rewarded. Now inside the house in Woolloomooloo, he was confronted by a plain woman with thin lips that flicked down at either side. Tilly Devine, the woman who'd made a name for herself in Sydney since she'd arrived five years earlier, sat in front of him on a ratty armchair covered in green fabric.

He was struck by how different she was to his Grace, whose pretty face he could stare at for hours, and whose lips were full, round and eminently kissable. Tilly would have to pout generously to even find her lips, and that probably explained the thick streak of dark-plum lipstick she'd used to enhance their shape. She wore a scarf around her head like a turban but had allowed stringy dark curls to peep out. Her eyes looked to Alfie like two lost buttons, searching for something that wasn't there. He wasn't fooled, though; Alfie had learned from a young age to read the body's language, and while Tilly's eyes gave off what struck him as practised disinterest, he could sense she was highly focused on him.

Why else would she have permitted him an audience? The name Sabini would have triggered just the right amount of intrigue; Alfie knew there was little chance she didn't know of the man.

While Alfie had eyes only for Grace, he suspected to many Tilly would be considered attractive. Her legend reached all the way to the harbour. This was a woman who had known a hard upbringing and the beat of a fist against her. It had moulded her into a woman who gave off a sense of power and he felt that now, emanating underneath her scrutiny. It was confidence, he realised. The name Tilly Devine was supposed to breathe fear into many. He was well-versed in the story of the London war bride who had followed her abusive husband to Australia, leaving their son behind to live with family.

In Sydney, Tilly had returned to the streetwalking ways of her early days, and when her looks had begun to fade she'd set up a profitable group of brothels in the city. Tilly was into everything, Alfie had learned, from running her notorious razor gang to supplying sly grog, and plenty in between.

'She'd think nothing of slicing you up with her blade,' one fellow told him when he began his gentle enquiries. 'Just as happy to do it herself as order your slashing from one of her girls or louts.'

Alfie knew not to show his trepidation in front of her. He'd made that mistake only once and he'd lost a finger; he intended to emerge from this house as whole as he'd arrived . . . perhaps with the potential to be richer.

'So you know the Italian,' she began.

'I would never call him that,' Alfie replied. 'But I used to run jobs for Mr Sabini, until I left London.'

Tilly smirked as she nodded towards his hand. He hadn't hidden it, but he also hadn't waved it about. 'He loved to cut a little finger off to "educate" his lads,' she said. 'I won't ask why, because I'm not particularly interested in you or that Italian gangster.'

This seemed to amuse her, drawing her mouth into a gummy smile of unevenly arranged teeth. Lines crinkled deeply at either side of her eyes; Tilly's best days were past her for looks, but not for her wily ways. Apart from her bitter rival Kate Leigh, the other fearsome woman in Sydney, few gangsters could hold a candle to Tilly's intelligence. 'Why don't you explain quickly why you're wasting my time, little man?'

'Fair enough,' Alfie said, meeting her gaze. 'I'd like to offer my services.'

'Oh, yeah?' She gave a nod, her expression filled with disdain. 'And why would I need the likes of you?'

He liked her accent. It felt like home. 'Because we're both Londoners and we understand each other.' He was making sure his own East-End manner shone through. She was from Camberwell in the south, but he didn't think that would matter. When one was on the other side of the world, London was London. 'But perhaps you don't need me at all. I think I need you more than you need me.'

This brought another smile, full of cunning, but he sensed there was a mote of fascination in her unremarkable, mid-blue eyes.

'I like your honesty. Most men I meet think they're smarter than me.'

'I don't think like that, Mrs Devine. I am about to marry a woman who is far cleverer than I am.'

'Good. Perhaps your marriage will last if you keep thinking like that. Is she pretty?'

'I'm yet to see a prettier girl on either side of the world.'

'Does she want a job?' Tilly cackled another big laugh, cruel this time.

'No,' he said, keeping his face and voice neutral. 'She's a businesswoman . . . a bit like you.'

'Is that right?' Tilly said, her humour disappearing. 'What sort of business is that?'

'Simple groceries for simple folk,' Alfie said, realising he mustn't challenge her. 'But she's branching out into sweets.'

'What, toffees, you mean?'

Alfie nodded.

'You'll have to bring me some for my girls. We all like lollies around here. That's what they call them in Australia, Alfie darlin', not sweets.'

Again he nodded, giving the impression that he was happy to be corrected.

'So what's your bride's sweet shop got to do with me?'

'Nothing,' Alfie replied carefully, not wishing to point out that she was the one who'd asked about Grace. 'No, I'm here offering to transfer some of your . . . shall we say, clandestine goods.'

Tilly twisted her thin lips into a smile. 'That's one of the Italian's favourite words, I seem to recall.'

Alfie risked a chuckle. 'You'd be right. Mr Sabini liked to conduct his business in a gentlemanly manner.'

'Even cutting off fingers for punishment?'

'Especially then.'

She fixed him with a hard gaze. 'Why do I need your help, Alfie boy?'

'I don't know that you do. I need to earn some money quickly. I'm setting up a barrow in Martin Place to sell sweets, and I can walk that barrow from the quay to any place you say within the city, and I will look as innocent as an angel doing so. Beneath my sweet offerings I can carry anything you like, but I was thinking about opium from the docks. I don't think grog's a good idea, because the bottles will make a noise and I'll be found out.'

'A barrow boy?'

Alfie didn't take the bait. 'It's just a start. I'm using it as a way of getting customers used to Grace's range of products.'

'Smart.'

'Thank you.'

'A barrow boy is no good to me though, darlin'. Anything else you care to offer? Maybe I buy into your little venture.' She raised her brows.

Alfie smiled to show that he appreciated her suggestion, but also to cover the trill of alarm he felt at that idea. He could just imagine Grace's expression at finding out the likes of Tilly Devine wanted to be an investor. 'What about the gee-gees?'

'I'm not into that sort of racketeering.'

'But not above it, surely?' he chanced.

'I don't have any set up for it, love.'

'But you've got it all, Mrs Devine. You've already got men coming here with money to spend. It can all happen at once. I can run it for you from the back garden.'

'They call it a yard over here,' she corrected him. 'You need to fit in, Alfie boy.'

'Look, it's simple off-course betting. I know how to do that.'

'Yeah, but I don't, and I'll never move into any sort of situation I don't understand. It's how I've dodged a lot of trouble. And the fact that you know how to run that sort of scam only gives me more reason to say no.'

His face must have betrayed the question in his mind because she answered the unasked query.

'Because it gives you the power.'

She had a point. 'What about peddling off the barrow?'

She blinked. 'Go on.'

'I know you mostly distribute your "snow" in the east, but through me you could access the Sydney cove and the bottom end of George and Pitt streets.'

'There's a reason I don't distribute there. Why would I open myself up to rivals telling me I'm trespassing?'

'Because you wouldn't be. I'll act as an independent. You

supply the cocaine, I'll sell it off my barrow, never coming east and stepping into your regular neighbourhood. I give you fifty per cent of the profits after I've paid for the drug at a wholesale rate.'

Tilly's cold gaze narrowed and focused, like a camera lens turning, bringing him closer, clearer. 'Seventy.'

'Fifty-five,' he said, shaking his head once.

'Sixty and don't bother throwing another number at me. See yourself out instead.'

Alfie nodded. He'd done better than he'd imagined; he'd had twenty-five per cent in his mind for himself, and forty was already far more profitable than he'd hoped. 'Sixty to you, forty to me,' he agreed.

She spat on a hand and offered it to him. He did the same and they shook on their deal.

'If you get caught by the police and feel like squealing, Alfie, I would warn you to get yourself on the next boat out of Sydney and sail far from Australian shores . . . I'll let that creative mind of yours ponder exactly what I'll have done to you before you draw your last breath.'

'Mrs Devine, if I'm caught by the police, I am an independent peddler of the Chinese snow, I swear. I have nothing to gain by involving you.'

'Glad we understand one another, although I have to ask: why won't your sailors simply walk into the nearest apothecary and buy it over the counter? It's available.'

Alfie nodded thoughtfully. 'You're right. I wanted to test that very theory, so I organised for someone I know to buy three grams only this morning.'

'Three grams!' Tilly looked uncharacteristically shocked.

'You can buy up to five grams and stay permanently lost to the euphoria – I think that's the word the chemist used – for a couple of weeks.'

'And?'

'And my acquaintance was immediately approached by some-one who claimed to be a plain-clothed detective.'

'Lucky you didn't do the purchasing,' Tilly noted.

Alfie risked tapping the side of his nose, as if to say, *I'm not stupid.* 'He was questioned on the spot, but we'd already agreed to a story, which he shared with the chemist, so both of their accounts matched. He told them he is a returned war veteran – which he is – and left a leg behind in France – which he did – and now he feels its ghostly presence constantly. It's not there but the severely wounded leg that was amputated, without morphine and little more than a few swigs of brandy, now gives him nightmarish pain. And only the cocaine allows him some relief.'

'And they bought that?'

'They did, Mrs Devine, because old Charlie boy looks the part, with his trouser leg pinned up against the stump at mid-thigh level. He's convincing, you could say.'

'What did they do?'

'Gave him back a gram and a warning. The chemist got a dressing down and a more severe warning of arrest next time.'

'So they're watching,' she said.

He nodded. 'I'd guess they've been looking at several chemists, and they'll lock that side of the business down . . . and it won't be gradual. There's a lot of do-gooders out there, Mrs Devine, and they want the cocaine use stamped down hard.'

'But they won't be watching you with your sweetie barrel full of licorice and humbugs, is that what you're saying?'

He shrugged as if to indicate she was welcome to draw her conclusions. 'Sixty–forty, as agreed . . . on profit.'

'When?'

'Next week?'

'How much?'

'Shall we start with an ounce?'

Tilly's laugh showed her entire top gum this time, and she uncrossed her legs and rose from her seat to shake his hand for the second occasion. 'That's nearly thirty grams,' she warned.

'Fine with me.'

'What will you cut it with?'

'Boracic acid, but I'll keep it light so the word spreads fast that it's good stuff. Then I'll thin it.'

'How many packets?'

He made a face as he calculated, drawing in a breath as he did so. 'Two hundred?'

'I could make an extra fifty packets.'

'I know, but you wouldn't get the return trade I will down at the quay.'

'Okay, Alfie Sweeting. Let's see if you perform as well as your mouth does.' She took a breath and yelled out, 'Maddy!'

They heard footsteps ascending the stairs and Maddy appeared from around the door, enquiry in her expression.

'Send that kid of yours to our friend here. One ounce.'

Maddy nodded, glanced at Alfie and departed.

'You be back here one week from today, with the price of the Tokyo.'

He blinked; that was a new name for it.

''S'wat they call it in London apparently, and it's catching on here,' she said.

'Good word.' He had no idea what Tokyo was.

'It's Japanese,' she said, again managing to answer his unsaid query.

Alfie frowned. 'Isn't it coming from China?'

'Never you mind where I source my snow from, Sweeting. Thirty shillings for the ounce. You sell it alongside your toffees,

126

and you'd better be honest about the profit, because you will be watched, my lad. I'll have eyes on you.'

He nodded. 'I'm an honest dealer, Mrs Devine.'

'Go on with you then. The kid will meet you outside with the stuff.'

He nodded his thanks and made to leave.

'Alfie?'

He halted at the door, knowing what was coming.

Tilly drew a line across her throat. 'I won't hesitate to throw you in the harbour, lad, if you cross me.'

'I know,' he said. He knew she meant it.

11

April 1925

Alfie had left his job as the Fairweather's regular delivery boy, and Grace had been allowed time by her parents to cook up a storm with her sweets for the barrow. She figured it was their way of giving a cautious blessing to her new venture, doing their utmost to be supportive.

'Can we come and see this new "instant shop" in Martin Lane?' her mother enquired, watching Grace dance around the small kitchen with various pots boiling and simmering with liquid sugar. 'Oh, it's called Martin Place now, isn't it?'

'I would be honoured if you would. I won't be staying, though. Selling the product is Alfie's concern. Mine is getting the recipes and the look of the shop right.'

'And when can we see the grand unveiling of your shop?'

'Very soon,' Grace replied, eager in tone, keen to make her mother feel welcome. 'It's going to be so colourful, Mum. People won't be able to resist coming in to have a look. And once they set foot over my threshold, I've got them and I won't be letting them out until they buy something.'

Mary Fairweather laughed. 'I don't know where you get

that sort of talk from, Grace. Imagine if we treated our customers like that.'

'I do imagine it, and I know I'm right to think like this. You keep staples in the grocery store, Mum. People need what they come in for. The only frivolous goods on offer are these sorts of things,' Grace said, pointing to her pots and pans. 'Just a moment.' She frowned and tested her ball of sugar on a cool plate. 'Nearly there.' She wiped her hands and returned to her mother's interested gaze. 'But I'll be selling goods that people do not need – that are a luxury, in fact.'

'Then, Grace . . .?'

'No, wait, Mum. That's the point. Poorer people cannot afford most luxuries – they can't permit themselves to dream too much, because there are hungry mouths to feed and so much strain on what might be a single wage. What I'm offering is a tiny escape. It lasts for only a brief time, but it's affordable, even though it's a luxury. I believe all the people who live around here – and all the workers in the city – will be able to justify a minuscule outlay to enjoy a treat in their busy, demanding lives. I'm not making these for people like Mrs Chalmers and her children – although I have no doubt they'll enjoy them just as much as the next person. These are for the working-class families, like Mr and Mrs Hobie in Cumberland Street, who might share a bag of toffees on pay day. Simple, easy, affordable even on their wages . . . and, above all, it's *not* just a necessity.'

Grace clapped her hands suddenly in glee, startling her mother with her enthusiasm. 'This is the point, Alfie tells me. Everything about a working-class family is about necessity. But what we're selling them is a moment of pure indulgence. They can treat themselves and they don't have to go into debt to enjoy that small pleasure. It's like going to the cinema, or to a dance, but the whole family can enjoy my goods.'

'And you don't think Hillier's might try and crush you?'

Grace laughed. 'No, Mum. Hilliers won't even notice us. We'll be like a flea on the bottom of an elephant's foot, although I don't intend to remain that way. However, for now, we shall be so far down in their estimations that they won't even notice when we creep up on them and overtake them in popularity. We'll be like little moles, tunnelling underground and then suddenly popping up!'

Mary wrinkled her nose. 'Fleas and moles. Another of Alfie's comparisons, I suppose?'

Grace gave a helpless shrug. 'He was a tunneller, what can I say. The bravest of the brave.'

'He's certainly very brave with *your* savings, I must say,' her mother snipped.

Grace didn't overreact. 'Alfie is making his own contribution, matching me dollar for dollar as it happens,' she said, deliberately keeping her gaze on the sugar she was assessing, waiting for it to turn to toffee. The boil had slowed, the bubbles had become larger, bursting with deliberate tension and darkening by the moment. Its progress prevented her from turning back to her mother, who was clearly spoiling for some sort of confrontation over Alfie.

She knew her mother was still smarting from their picnic conversation and her determination to flee the family nest into a marriage with Alfie. Mary couldn't help showing her disapproval and, curiously, that Alfie's resignation from the role of delivery boy seemed to have cut the deepest. It was as though she took it wholly personally that Alfie had the gall to look their job in the eye and turn away from it.

'Look, Mum,' Grace began reasonably. 'I know him leaving Fairweather's has all sorts of implications, not the least of which is you and Dad feeling let down, but he's found a good replacement – I think Billy will work out well – and it allows Alfie to help me.'

'So long as it doesn't leave egg on your face . . . or ours.'

'It won't. He's got a new job now at the barrow and he's doing some work on the east side of the city that pays him very well, twice as much as we could.'

'Grace, my darling girl, you know very well what the east side of the city offers. Whatever work he's doing, it's not honest.'

Grace couldn't hold back now. 'Why do you have to do this? It's as though you don't want me to be happy, Mum. Everything that makes me feel independent or empowered—'

'Empowered?' her mother repeated, filled with astonishment. 'What does that even mean?'

'Times are changing. Look around you. Women are becoming more vocal and more determined about what they want, and it's not always doing the bidding of men. I was born just as women were getting the vote in this country. You educated me properly so I became a strong, independent woman.'

'Exactly!' her mother agreed. 'I didn't want you marrying the first fellow who came along after Norm. This one has few prospects, but probably spoke sweetly to you.'

Grace ignored the insult. 'Why do you imagine Alfie has no prospects? He got himself here all the way from London alone, with no money, no knowledge of life here. It was brave and it was because he could imagine a better life. Now he's trying to live it, improve his chances.'

'He was probably running away from something.'

Grace sighed. 'Well, that's just like you, Mum. You always move into that negative thought. You won't allow room for others to be optimistic.'

'I've lived longer than you, Grace. I know how people's minds work, especially loners and desperates like Alfie.'

Grace shook her head. 'He's neither of those things.'

Mary scoffed. 'And what has he told you he's doing in the east

131

side of the city? You know as well as I that the east is where all the gangsters live and breathe.'

'So Alfie's a gangster now?'

'Well, unless he's delivering drugs or illegal grog, I can't imagine how he's making money. Maybe he's gambling.'

Grace found a reserve of patience she didn't know she possessed. 'Mum, I have to work this toffee. We can talk about this later. Will you excuse me, please?'

'Can I help?'

'No. I think I'd rather do this alone.'

Grace watched her mother's eyelids narrow defensively. Obviously with a lot more to say but no heat into which to fling her words and get their best effect, she backed off, leaving Grace to her toffee and a tray of recently cooked peanuts.

She'd given them time in the oven to brown and develop a prominent nutty flavour, and now, with the sugar syrup at the correct temperature, what she knew as the soft ball point, she lifted the heavy cast iron pot from the stove and with great effort poured the now amber, slightly smoking liquid over the peanuts. This was dangerous work and as she toiled she realised she'd need to work out methods for safety if others were going to help her. Eyes needed shielding from splashes, hands and arms needed guarding against splatters of hot toffee and, frankly, as much as she thought herself strong and independent, this pouring probably needed to be done by a man with more strength than her. She was going to waste too much of the toffee because she couldn't tilt the pot with one hand and scrape out the fast-hardening sugar with the other. She made a mental note that this product would take two people in the kitchen.

There was nothing new about peanut brittle; it was already a popular favourite with the people of Sydney and sold all over. However, Grace had decided she would take it to a new level. Once she had shattered her brittle into manageable small chunks, she planned to coat them with rich chocolate. She would dip each nugget twice to ensure a thick blanket of dark sweetness that gave easily on biting, before the crunchy middle of nuts and toffee. It was innovative, she knew it, although would perish faster.

Even so, in her imagination, these would sell briskly from the barrow and she hoped to have at least fifty bags made up by this evening. She looked towards the shelves on the kitchen wall, which her father had put up just for this purpose. She loved that he was showing genuine support for her new venture and making accommodations to help her. She tried not to compare his interest to her mother's disdain.

A cat that didn't belong to them – though she seemed to call by daily as if she did – curled around the edge of the kitchen door, tail high and drawing an imaginary eight with its movement.

'Oh, hello, Sooty.' Grace had decided to name their visitor long ago because the feline breezed in so regularly. She was calling into several homes, it seemed, to see what might be on the menu, but she was a good mouser so no one seemed to mind. Grace had seen her through two litters of kittens and feared she might be pregnant again. 'You see, both of my parents' attitudes come from their love, except they show that love differently, Soots. My father expresses his love with generosity and a how-can-I-help approach. My mother, however, expresses her love with worry and caution, feeling the need to warn me constantly against all that can go wrong.'

Sooty gave a mewl.

Grace regarded the cat. 'Neither's right, neither's wrong. They're just good parents, looking out for me.'

The cat kept twisting about her legs, hoping for a morsel, and Grace obliged, moving to the cupboard where she cut off a piece of silverside, which she knew her father was planning to eat that evening. She didn't think he'd miss it, and wouldn't mind if he knew it had filled an empty belly. 'There you go, Sooty. Now don't hang about or my mother will catch you begging.'

The cat pounced on the piece of meat and devoured it in a heartbeat. When she was sure there was no more forthcoming, she drifted away as silently as she'd arrived. Grace would see her again tomorrow, she was sure. She rinsed her hands and studied her shelves of goods while the toffee brittle cooled and cracked behind her. There was plenty for the barrow and she was feeling confident about sales. If this worked, they were likely going to need a factory; it couldn't all be cooked up behind the grocery shop. Even this amount of product had taken all the available space and there were never enough pans or heat sources. She'd had to cook each item separately over so many days, but it had been worth it. She ran her eyes over the parcels of old time rock, the bright pink and creamy white of coconut ice and toasted marshmallows coated with desiccated coconut, which vied with boiled sweets and barley sugar.

Her father gave a sigh as he entered the room, disturbing her thoughts. 'Well, Grace, doesn't that all look bright and appealing. I'm so impressed.'

'Thanks, Dad.' She gestured to the tray of brittle. 'I'm going to smash that and coat it in chocolate and then I think I'm ready.'

'Go on then,' he urged. 'I love peanut brittle, as you know.'

She grinned and took a small hammer she'd found in the store and used it to break up the nutty toffee into jagged shards. 'Help yourself.'

He did, making a sound of deep delight as he crunched into the chunk he'd chosen. 'You take that toffee almost to bitter . . . but you just stop in time.'

'I've learned that you have to be brave with toffee in order to achieve that deep flavour. I need it to hold its own against the richness of the chocolate.'

'I like the salty taste too – have you added some?'

She grinned. 'I took a risk. It's my secret ingredient. The butter just wasn't giving enough.'

'It's scrumptious, Grace.'

'Good, it needs to be.'

'How much are you selling these for?'

'Well, I've worked out through all my testing here that buying a box of chocolates feels more special than the bag of lollies that you scoop up from a drum. So I'm pre-bagging the product, but in these specially made paper bags, see?' She bent down to rummage in a box on the floor and pulled out a red, diagonally striped paper bag that opened to stand tall on the counter with a flat bottom. *The Sugar Palace* was emblazoned on the front in a clear, bold font that was both playful and easy to recognise. She explained this to her father.

He looked bemused. 'You're using psychology?'

'I've been reading about colour, and people respond to it in different ways. Now, imagine if this bag was blue – a colour we all love because it speaks of the sky and the ocean, but it also brings to mind something more solitary and potentially sorrowful. I don't want that message conveyed, no matter how subliminal.' She shrugged. 'And I won't do yellow, no matter how sunny and uplifting it is, because it won't show against white, and the colour can go curious if the printing doesn't come up well and then it speaks of nausea and not feeling well.'

Her father laughed.

'You may find this amusing, Dad, but I know that exists deep in our minds. And before you say to have the yellow against a dark background, I would risk the bag reminding everyone of a wasp and then there's that subliminal message again about being stung when you come to the Sugar Palace.' She grinned. 'I'm leaning towards richer pinks and bright red. They have oodles of positive elements, plus it's said that red contains pigments of all the colours, which I rather like.'

'And it will look bright against the white.' He winked.

'Exactly. Now, green is lovely. I toyed with green, but it didn't compete strongly against the red, which stood out from across the street. The green blended into the colours of the buildings and what people were wearing, while the red demanded attention. It's easy to read against the white background and look, Dad, when I add this . . .' She folded the top of the narrow packet and then stuck the flap down with a tiny gold-foiled sticker with black writing.

He stepped closer to read it. 'Enjoy!' he murmured. 'Oh, that's clever.'

'It's wishing them pleasure with their purchase, but somehow conveys a thankyou – do you agree?'

'Definitely. My, my, Grace. Where have you learned all of this?'

She smiled. 'I've been learning all my life, Dad, standing at your side and watching how you package goods and which brands seem to win more attention. You've taught me that it's not necessarily because they're pricier or even better quality, but more because of how they're presented.'

He gave a nod, clearly pleased. 'They'll look good on the barrow.'

'Alfie's picking them up soon, so I'd better get a wriggle on.'

12

Alfie watched Grace stand back and admire their barrow, piled high with brightly coloured packs of sweets. He had to hand it to her, her eye for presentation was brilliant and the products themselves looked enticing, each sweet shiny in its well-boiled sugar or thick coat of chocolate.

She gave him the thumbs-up from the steps just outside the main doors of the GPO, and returning to his side, she kissed his cheek. 'It looks so amazing it makes me want to weep.'

'Why?' He looked concerned.

'Happy tears, Alfie. I can't believe those are my lollies. They look so appealing. And I love the way you've painted the barrow red, and the signage is perfect. And that brightly striped fabric skirting . . . It's inspired. Women won't be able to resist.'

'That cost me a favour or two but it's worth it. I'm glad you approve, Gracie.' He needed her attention away from that skirting; he couldn't even imagine telling her what sat beneath it.

'Approve? I adore it. I want to stay and watch people coming to buy, but I'd better get back to the shop. I promised I wouldn't be long.'

'You get going,' he said. 'It's up to me now, darlin'.'

'Do you really think you'll sell it all?' She sounded excited.

'That's my goal. Watch this.' He reached for a bag of the boiled sweets she called acid drops and tipped them into a small basket.

'Wait, what—?'

'Trust me now,' he said, shooshing her. He took a bag of peanut brittle and gave it the same treatment, and then the honeycomb too. 'Just watch.'

In a singsong voice he began to call out, like the barrow people he remembered from London. 'Oi, oi,' he began and a stream of invitation came out in a loud, welcoming voice that was laced with humour. '. . . And I can assure you this brittle has some snap to it, my word. Watch out, sir – can't have your dentures in jeopardy. Maybe it's the marshmallow for you, just tuppence a bag.'

Alfie winked at Grace as the people using Martin Place to cut through between George and Pitt streets were tempted, one by one. 'No obligation, madam, but I swear, once you taste my boiled sweeties, you're going to want another, and another. What about you, sir? How about some peppermint cake?'

He was aware of Grace watching as he pushed two small baskets of sweets into the hands of a girl and boy who flanked the main GPO doors. She didn't know about them and he knew she would be intrigued, especially as the children began to call out her wares as Alfie had taught them. Grace approached as Alfie moved back towards the barrow, but he eavesdropped while speaking with his customers.

'What's your name?' Grace asked the girl.

'I'm Holly.' Alfie saw Holly grin from an innocent face; freckled and wide-eyed. 'And this is my friend Petey.'

'I don't know you. You're not from The Rocks?'

'No, we live in Darlinghurst.'

'Oh,' Grace replied, surprised. 'How do you know Alfie?'

Holly smiled innocently again. 'He's doing some work with my family, helping them to expand their business,' she said. *Good girl, Hols*, he thought.

'Right, and—'

'And Petey's our neighbour,' Holly said. 'Um, would you like to buy any?' she said, holding up a small plate with a selection of sweets on it. 'You can try first.'

Alfie wanted to cheer as he heard Grace chuckle. 'I made those lollies.'

'You did? Well, I never. I want to eat them all, but Alfie said he'd hold back our wages if we did.'

'Did he? And how much is Mr Sweeting paying you?'

'Penny a day. Just two hours,' Petey joined in. 'Come on, Hols. He said we get more if we send customers to the barrow. Sorry, miss, but we have work to do.'

Alfie was grateful for his keen hearing. He knew Holly had the street smarts and all-too-grown-up wisdom to say plenty but give away little. She was going to be a formidable woman in years to come. Maddy, he presumed, had done a very good job in giving both children a scrubbing, brushing Holly's hair until it shone and tying it in a ribbon, and she had pulled together clothes that were clean and ironed, making the pair of urchins look so presentable that even Grace's mother would likely be impressed. They were good kids. Very much in his mould, he realised. They'd learned the way of the streets and of rogues and could match them. If anyone could sell those lollies alongside him – and his other more secret wares – it was that pair.

'Oh my gosh, yes. I have to get some of these,' a woman shopper exclaimed, making him focus again fully on his task.

'Why not take two bags, madam?' he said and Grace laughed.

'You know I think I will. One of the brittle, please, and one of the marshmallow.'

'That's fivepence, madam. And here, why don't you take a small sample of the peppermint cake with you?' He tapped his nose. 'You'll be back for some next time, I promise.'

'Ooh, you're wicked, you are,' she said, dropping pennies into his hand, which he whisked away into a small satchel he wore around his waist. He'd brought it from London, a relic of a different era, from his time running around the streets of the East End. He'd never imagined he might find a practical use for it but now it was serving its purpose splendidly.

Another customer pointed, still chewing his sample of peppermint cake. 'I'll take some of this and the chocolate fudge, please.'

'Ooh, very good choices there, sir,' Alfie said. 'That'll be fourpence, and please try the marshmallow for your trouble.'

'I will, thank you,' the man said, handing over four coppers that Alfie threw in his bag.

'Tell your friends about us, now. This is a new business, and we appreciate your custom.'

The man tipped a finger in a salute and moved on. Alfie had to serve another half-dozen customers before Grace could wish him farewell.

'I can't believe it. At this rate you'll be done by midday.'

He winked. 'Stick with me, darlin', and you'll be the belle of Sydney soon enough.'

She laughed. 'I'm impressed by your staff too,' she said, glancing back at the children, who were not letting any person leave the GPO without being pointed towards the barrow. Together Grace and Alfie watched Holly smiling at a potential customer.

Alfie nodded. 'They're so good at it.'

'I can tell . . . and cheap.'

'Their mothers were happy to have them off the street and doing something that contributed to the family coffers.'

Grace smiled. 'You're a good man, Alfie.'

He wasn't so sure about that but he enjoyed knowing she thought so highly of him. Even so, he needed Grace to be gone so he could get on with tipping the wink Holly's and Petey's way to have them looking out for a new sort of customer.

'Right, shall we meet up a little later?' Grace offered.

'Of course.' The clock of the GPO chimed that it was eleven. 'Why don't we see each other here at four?'

'I'll see you beneath India then.' She grinned and gave him a peck on the cheek.

'India?' Alfie frowned, baffled.

Grace pointed to one of the great sculptures on the side of the post office building that fronted Martin Place. He blinked, still confused.

'India,' she repeated, pointing more directly at the carved face of an Asian woman wearing a grand headdress and jewellery with a large ring through her nose. 'It's a saying in Sydney. Lots of young lovers meet here.'

He blew a soft whistle. 'Well, you learn something new each day,' he said, sounding impressed.

'I'll tell you all about them later.'

Grace blew him a kiss and he pretended to catch it and place it over his heart. Blimey, but he adored this girl, he thought as he watched her hurry away. She was so pretty, with a flush at her cheeks and a skip in her step. He thought of the shelf beneath the cart's bright skirt and worried that he was running the biggest risk of his life.

Holly hurried up towards him. 'Ready?'

Alfie nodded. 'Be careful. Take it slow and steady.'

'We know how to do this, you watch.'

She wasn't lying. The two youngsters astounded him in how keenly they were able to sniff out the right mark. It was always a man. With the women they went through their 'sweets' routine, as he'd begun to think of it, and he wondered how Holly knew to adroitly let up to ten men pass her by with just call-outs about the sweets, often winning their attention enough to send them towards the barrow for a sale . . . but then that one fellow she spoke to swiftly would sidle up and look at him expectantly.

One stood before him now. '*She* sent me here,' he said, nodding towards Holly.

'A pinch?' Alfie murmured, reaching for a packet of fudge mixed up from condensed milk. It wasn't their bestseller of the day, so he could afford to give it away.

'How much is that?'

Alfie pursed his lips as he blew out a calming breath noiselessly through his nose. 'A pinch of salt on this very sweet fudge will make it sing in your mouth, mate,' he tried. He had to be sure this was no plain-clothed policeman; he'd heard they were on the rise.

The man looked confused and also a little dazed. Alfie glanced over at Holly. She gave him a firm nod to say the man was no copper.

How could she possibly know that? He needed to trust her though, or this was all a waste. 'A pinch is sixteenth of an ounce,' he whispered and reached under the skirt of the barrow for a bag, pretending he was looking for some particular sweets. 'Here you go, sir.' He toppled a tiny twist of paper holding white powder neatly into the bag of fudge.

'She said five shillings *uncut*.'

He hoped the bloke would understand the code. 'No acid in this fudge, my friend. You can do with it what you like.'

Five coins were placed in his palm and swapped for the bag of fudge. Alfie blinked with relief as the man moved on. He imagined that fellow would now mix – known as cutting – the pure cocaine with boracic acid and sell it on to new customers. Alfie didn't care. Five shillings was profit enough to make his heart race, and he needed no cocaine to achieve that rush of pleasure.

He served a few more legitimate customers and was further pleased to be able to say that they had run out of brittle and marshmallow. He made a mental note to let Grace know the order of popularity of her products.

'But, madam, you can't leave without anything,' he said to one disappointed-looking customer. 'I'll tell you what, this bag of vanilla fudge is with the compliments of the Sugar Palace if you buy some of our licorice or peppermint cake.'

Her eyes lit. 'For free?'

'The fudge, yes, indeed. Two bags if you buy one of each.'

'Well, well,' she said, brightening. 'My husband likes fudge, and I am partial to licorice.'

'Keeps you regular, madam,' Alfie chanced with a wink.

She didn't seem to mind his cheekiness and nodded. 'I also like how it tastes, young man.'

'Here you go. You enjoy those and come back next time, and I'll set aside some peanut brittle for you. We're going to try some almond rock as well – you may enjoy that too.'

Another two customers sidled up separately, one watchful, one overly casual. Alfie glanced Holly's way and she gave a near imperceptible nod. *Blimey she was good.*

Those customers soon went off happily with bags of sweets they would likely not eat as well as the tiny twists of cocaine they were more than eager to consume.

The clock's bell chimed sonorously from its tower at midday, reminding Sydney that it was time for everyone to take a break and have something to eat and stretch their legs. It didn't take long for people to spill from offices all around him and for the Sugar Palace barrow to be swarmed by a queue of customers. Even Holly and Petey had to leave their posts to join in serving.

Suddenly it was a chorus of their three voices:

'Who's next, please?'

143

'Yes, sir?'

'How can I help you, madam?'

'Sweet tooth, sir? Oh, it's for your wife? Then may I suggest the fudge?'

'Might as well take two bags, sir,' Alfie heard Holly say and had to resist grinning. 'Because you'll want more as soon as you've chewed the last toffee.'

'We've got rich licorice toffee! Soft, sweet fudge in chocolate or plain! Try our range of sour drops!'

'Yes, madam, those sour drops will get your eye twitching, but you'll love it,' Alfie quipped to one customer.

'All out of peanut brittle, sir,' he heard Petey confirm, 'but I can recommend these rich, chewy toffees, sir. You won't regret buying a bag or two and, look, if you do buy two, we might chuck in the last of the sour drops.'

'And what about our special?' Alfie whispered to the two children in a brief reprise from the crowds. His fast gaze had picked up their equally swift hands exchanging coins for bags of sweets that had a little something extra within. He marvelled at the light-fingered way they moved. In fact, he decided, they had probably cut their teeth for Tilly as pickpockets in their neighbourhood.

To their credit, he felt his change bag getting heavier. If they were slipping away any of the illegal takings, then he certainly wasn't aware of it and he believed it to be near impossible to use sleight of hand against him. *I'm the maestro of the misdirection*, he thought to himself. The children had likely been told to remain honest with him because everyone in the know would benefit.

'I've sold ten bags of sour drops,' Holly said. 'Er, yes, madam, how can I help you? We seem to be running out fast of everything,' she said, leaning on the last word pointedly.

'All gone,' Petey confirmed taking a moment to check beneath the skirt. 'We're right out of the special.'

'Er, folks,' Alfie said loudly to catch everyone's attention that he could, but privately feeling the excitement and power of pulling off a heist. He'd never been involved in selling drugs before now. He'd carted them all over London for others, barely aware of what he was moving. One time it was coffee, another it was sugar, but each time there were hard-packed bricks of 'snow' as they called it and even the 'golden dragon' – opium – a few times. But he never had to touch the bricks, simply deliver the sacks of innocent-sounding goods. Today he was the handler. He was the buyer and agent. He was the distributor of illegal cocaine. And while he didn't relish the title, he couldn't help but enjoy that old buzz of underground trading.

'Folks!' he called again. 'We only have left what you see on the barrow. Because your choice is now limited to toffees, fudge and some very pleasant aniseed drops that would be soothing to that cough, madam, I am going to lower the price across the range.'

The queue was still long enough that it eagerly pressed forward, each of its members with a slight frown of concern that they may miss out. Alfie wished he could capture this moment for Grace. She would be so proud, and rightly so.

Later, in the laundry backroom where he slept, Alfie counted out the proceeds of the cocaine.

Holly nodded. He had gathered that she might not be a reader, but he could see by the silent movement of her lips that she could add up. 'That's a good haul,' she said, confirming his suspicion and telling him that, despite her youth, he was talking to an equal . . . in Tilly's estimation, anyway. He also reminded himself that having Holly and Petey work alongside him had been Tilly's idea, so they were probably there as eyes and ears on her behalf.

'It is. We can do better next time, now that they know how to find me. Come on. I'll get you back, and I can pay my dues to the boss.'

Petey grinned, chewing one of several licorice toffees he'd enjoyed that had turned his tongue black. 'We did all right with the lollies too.'

'You were both great, actually, which is why this is for you.' Alfie gave each child a shilling. He knew it was a lot, but he remembered the moment that Sabini had tossed him a shiny sixpence when he was about ten. It had felt like a fortune. Even his father had made a remark, but Sabini had shaken his head.

'Your son did well today. Hey, boy,' he had said, addressing Alfie directly. 'You impressed me. You know what that means?'

'Means you like me?'

'I don't have to like you, kid. I have to like how you conduct yourself. And you did well today. You can be my lookout anytime, lad. You've got sharp eyes and an alert attitude.' He nodded at the coin in Alfie's small palm. 'Don't give that to your old man – that's for you. Go treat yourself.'

Treat himself! Six whole pennies, wrapped up in the shiniest sixpence he'd ever seen. Before his father could stop him, he'd dashed to the shops to spend it all on food.

He'd returned to his mother's expression of dismay. 'Did you steal all that?'

'No! I earned it. Mr Sabini gave me money.'

'He gave *you* money?' She eyed him through a disapproving gaze. 'And what did you do in return?'

'I was just on lookout, nothing bad, Ma. Look, we can eat well for a few days, and I bought some sweets for the kids.'

He saw tears water in his mother's eyes and knew she was torn. She didn't like Sabini. He'd heard her say as much to his father, and it had ended in another blazing row with her lip bleeding, again, and her head sore from being banged against the wall. But they needed the food; they both knew that.

She'd nodded tiredly. 'Change her, son, will you?' She tipped her head towards the toddler with a wet nappy dragging on the floor. 'She'll get a rash.'

Now, squatting in the dingy underground room of the laundry, which smelled of damp, moss and decay, Alfie realised that he was feeling like his mother had all those years ago. In a sharp moment of clarity, despite the sense of glee he'd felt at pulling off his plan, he knew he didn't want to be counting money from selling cocaine. He wanted to be rid of his criminal past and to cast off the shadow of people like George Dooley, who would just as soon kick him unconscious and leave him for dead in the gutter as lend money to him so they could keep him on a string of debt.

All he wanted to do was open the Sugar Palace with Grace and pursue a new life of enterprise and honest business as her husband and working partner.

'*And so you take the fast, criminal way, Alfie,*' he heard his mother say. '*When good business is all about hard work and years of patience.*'

Well, he didn't have years. And he had no patience . . . not with a policeman with prospects, who could offer Grace a better life, waiting in the wings. He smiled grimly into the dim light . . . not a better life, just easier. A better life, if Alfie could organise himself, was always going to be with her as Mrs Sweeting.

'Alfie, are you coming?' Holly asked, bemused, from the ladder that led from underground to the basement of the laundry and up to the street. 'You looked like you were lost there.'

'Not lost, Holly. Just thinking,' he said and tapped his temple. 'Always thinking.'

13

Grace met Alfie later that afternoon as arranged. She ran up to him laughing, feeling like a teen again with the new carefree sensation of being in love with life and all that it was delivering to her at present.

'Under India, as promised,' he said, grinning and daring to sweep her into his arms to kiss her quickly.

'How did we go?'

'Brilliant, darlin'. We sold out.'

'You didn't!'

'Well, I admit I cut prices towards the end of the midday break, because we'd sold out of what most people wanted. That way I was able to move on all the bags of toffee and the barley sugars and aniseed twists.'

'Not popular?' That was disappointing.

'It's not that,' Alfie reassured her. 'I think our customers will enjoy them, but the peanut brittle, honeycomb, peppermint cake, marshmallow and chocolate fudge just went.'

She breathed out a sigh of relief. So they had liked her products. 'Tell me all about it. I have to know this.'

He grinned. 'First, tell me about these,' he said pointing towards the sculpture of India. 'You promised. And then I'll take you for a hot chocolate or something and we can talk business.'

She smiled back at him. 'All right, well, all the carvings around the corner that front Pitt Street caused a big stir because of their . . . well, their daring, shall we say? But these ones facing Martin Place are much admired and you can see why – they're very beautiful and represent all the countries that Australia has a strong relationship with, whether it's Britain through our King, trading partners or even an important country or continent.'

She watched Alfie frown, and continued. 'This is the General Post Office, Alfie, so these marvellous sculptures sort of boast to all the people of New South Wales that our major city can reach all these countries, states and continents from within these walls.'

'Oh, I see. You mean we can write letters or send telegrams.'

'Exactly! We send and receive parcels and do all sorts of international transactions out of this one building. It's like the main focus for our city, isn't it? Everyone has to come here at some point, and look'—she pointed—'these sculptures say that you can reach from Belgium to Polynesia, from Germany to Italy and from Scotland to South America . . . all you have to do is step inside these doors.'

He gave a low whistle. 'That's clever promotion.'

'It's smart, I agree. And we need to be that smart for the Sugar Palace. Now, come on, I'm dying to know more about the barrow sales!'

'Do you want a hot chocolate?'

'No, a cup of tea will be perfect. Come on, I know a place.'

They talked as they walked, heading towards Pitt Street.

'Let's start with fudge,' Alfie began. 'Chocolate is more popular than vanilla.'

'Why?'

He frowned and considered the question as she led him across Pitt Street towards a narrow doorway that opened into a tiny café. They stood in front of the counter waiting for the waitress to finish serving another customer.

'Hmm, well, my guess is that a lot of the women could probably imagine themselves making plain fudge at home, but the chocolate is a notch up and more interesting. It's certainly delicious, and the samples went down a treat.'

'Okay, maybe I improve the vanilla then, by complicating it with some cherries and nuts sprinkled on top. That would make it look more interesting.'

'Do it,' he encouraged her. 'Barley sugar is too boring among the range. You can buy that anywhere, and it's very old-fashioned. Aniseed twist looks appealing, but I suspect they feel medicinal to customers rather than it being a treat. They'd sooner buy some sort of cough sweet in a chemist.'

She smiled. 'You're right. Let's get rid of both of those.'

'Now, the sour drops were a hit. But I'm wondering . . . because they're glassy, see-through, maybe you could make them more colourful.'

She nodded. 'That's easy. Good idea.'

'And I would definitely introduce peppermints.'

'We have the peppermint cake . . .' Grace frowned. 'Oh, er, just a pot of tea, please,' when the lady caught their attention at the counter.

'For two, love?'

'Please,' Alfie answered for them. He gestured for Grace to choose a table. There was one beside the wall and looked private, so Grace moved towards it and they sat. 'Well, peppermint cake is delicious and it went so fast, but I think some peppermint boiled sweets in that glassy look would be great.'

She nodded, frowning in thought. 'I could make them a lovely pale blue, so they look fresh. Peppermints are good for breath freshening.'

'And for brightening you up. If you're sleeping, poring over boring office stuff, you could suck a peppermint and wake up a bit.'

Grace laughed. 'What do you know about boring office work?'

'It *sounds* boring. I'm sure I'd fall asleep.' He grinned. 'So let's add those to the list – I can move those easily.'

'Marshmallow?'

'Flew!' He flapped his arms like wings to make her chuckle. 'More of those . . . maybe some in colour?' he asked.

She twisted her mouth in a look of uncertainty. 'No, I think adding colour into that egg white can go too bright. I hear what you're saying, though. How about I do some plain and then some covered with toasted coconut or chocolate?'

'Oh, you know what would work, Gracie, darlin'? What if you did chocolate, nuts, cherries and coconut with the marshmallow somehow? It could be like a . . . like a . . . what do they call it? Flourish?' He gave a mug of despair, knowing that wasn't the right word, especially when she burst into laughter.

'I know what you mean. Combining everyone's favourites into one treat . . . How about our signature treat?'

'Now you're talking. That could become a product that is unique to us, and that everyone wants.'

She nodded thoughtfully. 'I'll have a play. I really like the idea of having at least one product that people know is only available at the Sugar Palace so they're prepared to make a special trip to our store.'

'We can trial them through the barrow for free – hand out small sweets or pieces.'

'Good. I'll put my thinking cap on. In the meantime, I'm thinking of making both plain and chocolate-coated brittle and same for the peppermint cake. What do you think?'

Alfie tapped his chin in thought. 'Perfect for now. Not so good in summer.'

'By summer, if all goes to plan, we won't have a barrow to bother with. We'll be in a shop and I can control temperature a bit better, but maybe you're right that plain is easier in summer to pack and sell. I think we need more boiled sweets if we're doing away with the aniseed twists and barley sugar.'

'How about some lollipops in a load of colours that we can hang off a string or pile into some sort of container – they'll look bright and attract people, especially children. Ha'penny each or something?'

'I don't know why I haven't thought of that before. They would be so easy to make in bright colours.'

As the tea arrived with a clatter onto their small table, Grace looked around and caught sight of a newspaper that someone was reading. The headline featured the use of an automated traffic system using coloured lights to control the flow of vehicles at busy intersections.

Alfie glanced over his shoulder to where she was staring, deep in thought. 'What's wrong?'

'Nothing,' she replied, returning her attention to him. 'I heard on the radio that the Sydney council has opened talks as to whether the city needs one of these new-fangled traffic light systems. You know, like the ones in America.'

He shrugged, looking bemused. 'Well, I'm very glad we're staying focused,' he said with a grin.

'But I am.' She laughed. 'I'm thinking about a sweet that repre-sents the traffic lights – red, green and yellow.'

His mouth opened in surprise. 'Wow. You really are clever, Grace. I can see them already. Little balls in those three bright colours. We could simply call them Traffic Lights.'

She nodded, forming a small space between her thumb and forefinger as she imagined the design. 'Or even a bit like the aniseed twist.' She gave a small shrug. 'I've made the mould, and it would be a shame to throw it away. I could turn those small oblongs into a three-coloured fruity version, perhaps.'

Alfie mimicked licking a lollipop. 'How about a traffic lights lollipop?'

'Yes, we could probably do that easily enough too. And as we're building that into a new product, why don't we add a gobstopper to the suite? It could have green at the centre, yellow around it and the outer layer would be bright red.'

'Changing colours?' he said, helplessly forming an expression of awe.

'Exactly!'

He shook his head. 'Absolutely brilliant. And that's plenty for the barrow, Gracie, but in terms of the shop, have you been thinking about a much larger range?'

'It's all I think about,' she admitted with a sigh, pouring her tea and one for him.

'Oh, now, I'm hurt.' He pouted, then grinned.

She laughed at his playfulness. 'You know what I mean. Milk?'

'Always,' he replied and added a sugar lump to his tea, which fizzed slightly as it dissolved.

'I do have some ideas for the shop in particular. I want to make some individual chocolates.'

'That's Hillier territory, isn't it?' he asked with raised eyebrows.

She sipped her tea. 'Hillier's does not own the chocolate industry in Sydney, Alfie.'

'No, I know, but—'

'But what? I'm not scared of them. Our customer will be different, but that doesn't mean that ours don't enjoy boxed chocolates . . . with a difference.'

'What kind of difference?'

She lifted a shoulder, slightly defensively. 'We have to dare to be different so we're not going in direct competition with Hillier's or any of the other high-priced chocolatiers. So I was thinking that instead of exquisite chocolates, and ribbons, bows, fancy tins or boxes, and clever centres . . .'

'Yes . . .?' He waited.

Grace warmed to the subject that had preoccupied her mind since feeling the weight lift of an impending marriage to someone who did not hold her on any sort of pedestal. 'I was thinking, how about we do simple enrobed chocolates, like nougat, a brazil nut, a piece of fruit, a toffee?' She shook her head as if the choice was limitless. 'Chocolate-covered ginger from Queensland, um . . . oh, I don't know, chocolate-covered cherries in syrup from Tasmania, chocolate-covered apricots from South Australia.' Her voice got more excited. 'Chocolate-covered licorice toffee!'

'Blimey, darlin', now you're talkin',' he said, laughing. 'Sounds brilliant, Grace. You're going to conquer the world!' he said, punching a fist sharply in front of them.

She smiled, taking a sip of tea. There was the difference with Alfie right there; Alfie had professed his love for her and she believed him, but he respected her, admired her. His love offered so much more than Norm's – if Norm had even loved her at all. Alfie completely believed that she could achieve her goals. Even better, he wanted to help her reach them. He didn't look for praise or for the limelight to shine on him. He seemed happy to be in the background, enjoying the notion of potential success at her side. She loved him more for being the antithesis of Norm, who had made it fairly obvious that her role in life would be to make his star shine a little brighter.

She shook her mind free of Norm and focused on the affectionate grin emanating now from Alfie. 'I'm glad you like the idea,' she continued. 'But here's the real difference. We do plain little boxes of each. No one has to come in and choose them from a cabinet, where an assistant with gloved hands daintily picks them up and puts them into a beautiful box lined with tissue.' She shook her head. 'All of that costs money, and it makes people feel intimidated. Instead, I was thinking we could do pre-packed boxes, that fold over like this.' She folded a paper napkin to show Alfie what she meant. 'Our customer buys a box of chocolate-covered ginger, let's say. No frills or fuss, but delicious nonetheless and far cheaper.'

He nodded, enthused. 'Have you costed it up?'

'No. I will, but my years in the grocery store already tell me that it will be achievable.'

'Always colourful, though, Grace. Don't do dark brown boxes for dark chocolate and lighter brown for milk.'

'It's more obvious to the shopper,' she said, sipping but paying close attention to him.

'Maybe that's true, but those colours fade into the background. You want your Sugar Palace to be a riot of colour. It should feel like an event when the customer walks in, remember – a fun experience for the time they're in the store. So we need colour in every corner.'

'So perhaps something like red for the dark and green for milk varieties?' she offered.

'That's more like it, but that feels too much like Christmas.' At her frown he shrugged. 'You don't want to confuse people. Maybe . . . um, purple and yellow, or blue and orange.'

She blinked. It was a wild suggestion but there was no doubting that they would stand out. 'I suppose,' she muttered, sipping her tea. 'Not too garish?'

'I don't know what that means.'

'Loud, gaudy . . . erm, too much at once,' she suggested, with lightly flapping hands.

Alfie grinned. 'You know, Grace, I once did some jobs for an artist. I was just a messenger, running errands for a few pennies.

I was a kid, happy to earn a ha'penny wherever I could and help Mum out with money for food.'

She took another sip and set her cup down. Alfie didn't say much about his days in London, so she was always intrigued when he let her in to the stories of his childhood. They seemed fraught with poverty and yet far more interesting than her own. 'In the East End?' she asked, to show she was paying attention.

'No,' he replied. 'A bit more south.' It came out as 'souf" and once again she was delighted by his London accent slipping through. 'Anyway, one day he had me pick up some new paints for him and I took them up to his studio. "Set them down there, Alfie, my boy," he said, and he was busy, you know, preparing for a new piece of work. I'd never been up the stairs into his attic studio, and I loved how it smelled of the oil paints, the turpentine he used to clean his dozens of brushes and the slightly, um'— he rubbed his fingers together as he reached for the memory—'er, nutty, bitter smell of linseed oil, which he had in a huge bottle. He said he used it to make his paints move more easily. And the way the sunlight angled in,' he continued, filled with enthusiasm. 'It would create a shaft of light that picked up the dust in the air that danced about. He always looked like he was standing in an old painting himself.' He grinned. 'Anyway, he was busy and I was waiting to be paid and found myself staring at this big piece of paper hanging on the wall.'

She watched Alfie mimic a big square in the air. 'Go on,' she said, with no idea where his thoughts were leading them.

'On the paper was this circle,' he said, helplessly drawing that shape in the air as he remembered. 'And it was split into loads of smaller circles, like a dartboard.'

She laughed, nodding. 'Concentric circles, those are called.'

'Ah, well, there's that education of yours shining through, Gracie.'

'Keep going with your story. I feel like I'm standing in that attic studio with you.' She smiled.

'Well, this had all these circles separated by colour. And the artist, an Italian man called Mr Giaccio – I never knew his first name – saw I was frowning at the colours. He explained that it was the colour wheel. It was invented hundreds of years ago – it sounded to me like back in the days when men wore velvet tunics and tights.' Alfie grinned. 'Mr Giaccio said that the scientist who proved gravity – whatever that means – also worked out a theory for colour. Are you still with me?'

She nodded, not offended. 'Isaac Newton?'

'That's the name!' He sounded impressed. 'Anyway, this chappie, Newton, worked out that for every colour there is an opposite – well, he called it complementary or something, which I didn't understand until he said "opposite" – and if you mixed those opposites you always ended up with the neutral, he called it, of grey.'

'What?' Grace tried to think it through.

Alfie nodded, laughing. 'It's true, and Mr Giaccio proved it. He mixed purple and yellow, then orange and blue to show me what happened and, yes, they became grey. He taught me that the smaller circles were the same colours but of less . . . intensity, I think was the word he used.'

'I think I'm catching on. Are you suggesting we use "complementary" colours,' she said, emphasising the special word, 'to show our opposites of dark and milk chocolate selections?'

'Exactly,' Alfie said, touching a forefinger to the side of his nose. 'So the customer knows whether it's available in milk, in dark, or perhaps even in both.'

'I love it!' she said, fully supportive of the idea. 'I hadn't thought of doing a mix either. That's clever. I think purple and yellow are very bright and unmissable.'

'So maybe, then, think about how you'd apply those two colours into the rest of the shop – your uniforms, shop styling and frontage, even the bags. If purple and yellow are your choices, they should be reflected in everything that the Sugar Palace says about itself.'

'Alternatively, I could go with the colours of the rainbow and just use the purple and yellow to separate the boxes of dark or milk chocolate.'

'Yes, you could. Whatever you decide on, Gracie, it needs to be strong, bold and instantly recognisable as your brand. That way, someone who may be on the ferry and travelling to the north side of Sydney can be your advertising, walking around with your beautiful, brightly coloured bag. Everyone will either want to know what they bought, or it will remind them to call into the Sugar Palace when they're in the city next.'

'Oh, now you've got me thinking,' she said, swallowing the dregs of her tea and all but clapping when she set the cup down. 'Come on, I know just the person who can help us.'

They left the café and Alfie, putting his arm around Grace, nearly bumped into someone. 'Whoops, my fault . . .' he began in a jolly tone but the rest of his apology got stuck in his throat when he looked into the sneering face of George Dooley.

'Hello, cockroach,' Dooley said, cutting his gaze to Grace. 'What do you see in this little toad, missy? You could do so much better, looking the way you do, and a shopkeeper's girl at that. I heard Norm Jenkins had a ring on your finger.'

'Then you heard wrong, Mr Dooley,' Grace leapt in before Alfie could defend either of them. She held up her left hand. 'And I'll thank you to address me courteously. Perhaps I'll soon be Mrs Sweeting,' she said, enjoying watching Dooley's expression drop. 'But for now, you can call me Miss Fairweather, or please don't speak to me at all.'

'Don't you take that tone—'

'Or what, Mr Dooley? Senior Sergeant Jenkins may have to come calling on you if I tell him that I am feeling harassed.'

'Harassed?'

'You came into the store—'

He laughed at her. 'To buy cigarettes and—'

'To make threats, actually, and that's certainly what I will be saying to the police if you cross me again. Now, please leave us alone.'

Dooley scowled. 'I can see you two are very cosy.'

'I can't see how that's any of your business, Mr Dooley,' Grace responded, not bothering to disguise her dislike for the man.

'Well, I'd like a little word with Alfie here.'

Grace looked at Alfie and he nodded. 'You go on, Grace. I'll meet you back at your place.'

'But Alfie . . .'

'No, it's all right. Mr Dooley and I need to settle our differences and part company once and for all.' He sounded determined.

'All right. Don't be long.' Worried, she gave a tight smile and walked off, hoping he meant what he said.

———————

After Grace had walked away, looked back over her shoulder at him and he'd raised a hand in farewell, Alfie focused his attention back to Dooley.

'Looks like you caught your old chap in the till there, Alfie boy. Do they know how light-fingered you can be?'

'You leave the Fairweathers alone, Dooley.'

'Or what?'

'You'll find out. I mix with a different sort now.'

Dooley didn't look surprised. If anything, his expression turned even more smug. 'A little birdie says you might be mixing with one of the razor gangs now.'

'Is that right?' Alfie asked, sounding innocently intrigued. 'Well, I wouldn't know what you're talking about.'

'What's this barrow I also hear about?'

Alfie smiled to cover the chill that suddenly traced his body, as though his blood had iced through. 'I thought you knew everything, Mr Dooley. Surely you've discovered that Grace and I are now selling sweet treats in Martin Place?'

'I did hear something along those lines,' he admitted. 'But it sounds fishy to me.'

'Fishy?' Alfie laughed. 'Couldn't be more innocent, Mr Dooley. Grace is as straight as a die.'

'Yes, but you're as bent as my old granny's spine, may she rest in peace.'

'No, Mr Dooley. I'm honest these days. All above board. Very soon you'll see what our work at the barrow is leading towards.'

Dooley poked Alfie in the chest. 'Nothing that Tilly Devine does is straight, my friend, and when I find out what your relationship is with her, I shall have no second thoughts about turning you in.' He shrugged, smiling. 'Unless we can scratch each other's back, perhaps.'

Alfie wanted to turn and run but knew he couldn't. 'How so?'

'You cut me in on the action.'

'I don't know what you mean, Mr Dooley, sir.'

Dooley held up two fingers and pointed them at his eyes, then turned his chubby hand towards Alfie and pointed them his way. 'I am watching you, boy. And when I know what you're doing, with whom and how, I shall have you.'

'Can I go now, Mr Dooley? My girl's waiting for me.'

'She's too good for you, Alfie. It will end in tears for her.' He gave a firm nod, looking Alfie straight in the eye, then turned on his heel and left.

14

Grace was walking with Holly towards the GPO from The Rocks, hauling a small cart of Grace's confectionery between them. They were now into their fourth week selling from the barrow in Martin Place, and Grace couldn't have been more thrilled with how customers were responding to her products. Their start-up capital was growing by the day and together with her savings, she felt they'd be ready. Alfie had told her he'd pulled together some funds from odd jobs and some wins on his betting. She wished he wouldn't, but he had assured her repeatedly that he would only be a gambling man until the shop opened and he could support his side of the budget. 'You don't have to worry about me, darlin'. I'm not hooked, I'm just good at it,' he said with a wink.

Grace only visited every few days even though she could hardly stay away, wanting Alfie and his young helpers to feel like she trusted them completely – which she did. Still, she couldn't help but feel excited every time she saw people buying her sweets.

'Alfie was in a hurry this morning. He could have waited and saved us the bother.'

'Taken it all at once, you mean?' Holly queried.

'Yes. Now we need to make this extra trip.'

'I think he wants to surprise you with the barrow looking all splendid, Miss Fairweather. It's nearly the last week selling from the barrow, and he wants it to be perfect.'

Grace sensed caution in her words. She liked Holly. Here was a child with no education and yet she seemed more worldly than Grace at times . . . like now. Was Holly protecting Alfie somehow?

'Please call me Grace. Otherwise I just sound like my mother.'

Her companion grinned.

'What do you think you'd like to do when you grow up, Holly?'

'Grow up? I'm nearly fourteen, miss, and anyway—' She stopped.

Grace frowned. 'And anyway? What happens next?'

Holly looked to be choosing her words carefully. 'The folk I live with will expect me to . . . er . . . to work.'

Yes, serious caution. 'I see. What sort of work?'

'Not the sort you're used to, miss.' Holly chuckled and sounded like she hoped that might be the end of the questions.

'Oops, let me just straighten up these sherbet lollies or they'll roll right back down to Circular Quay and the ferry commuters will get a surprise,' Grace said, and Holly paused to help her fix their load. 'Where do you live, Holly?'

'Woolloomooloo.'

'And do you like living there?'

'It's all right. I don't know anywhere else.'

'I heard you coughing badly when you first started working at the barrow, but now you don't. I wonder if the air around here and the fresh breezes off the harbour might be better for you.'

'Might be, miss. But I have nowhere to live down here.'

Grace took a deep breath. 'What if I said you could live with us?'

Holly halted her steps and stared at her. 'But why?'

'To improve your breathing and—'

'No, why are you asking me this? Why would you want me living so close?'

Grace sighed softly. She'd brought this on herself by speaking before she had lined up her thoughts and, indeed, she could have chosen a more appropriate time than halfway to Martin Place with a cartload of confectionery. 'I have to presume that Alfie has mentioned to you that we plan to open a shop soon?'

Holly nodded, her gaze narrowing in anticipation of what was coming next.

Grace continued. 'Well, I think you'd be brilliant working with us in the shop.'

Holly blinked rapidly a couple of times.

No, Grace, thought, *she was not expecting that*.

'Proper work?' Holly qualified.

Grace grinned. 'Yes,' she said, keeping her voice light. 'Proper work, proper wages, proper hours, a proper uniform and proper respect for you as a valued staff member.'

She was shocked to see Holly's eyes turn misty with tears. None fell but the emotion couldn't be missed.

'Do you really mean that?' the girl asked softly.

Grace put down her side of the cart's handle and moved around to hug Holly; she could feel the child's ribcage through her baggy clothes. Pleased the youngster didn't pull back, she let go and looked into Holly's eyes. 'I mean it with all my heart. I think you're savagely smart – possibly one step ahead of all of us,' she said, stroking down a wayward lock of the girl's hair. 'I think we need people like you around us, and personally, I could do a whole lot worse than have you behind my counter with me. I've seen how quickly you add up and subtract.'

'I'm not as good as Alfie – he's amazing.'

'Yes, he is. He's one out of the box, but he's had a lot more practice than you, Holly. You'll be as good in a few years, mark my words. But it's not just that. I see how you observe people and weigh them up. That's a life skill that many take most of their life to develop – if they ever do. You're just thirteen!'

Holly grinned. 'No one's ever said I'm much good at anything before.'

'Well, they should have. I'd like to offer you a full-time job with the Sugar Palace, and you could live with me too, if you'd like to. Would your family agree?'

Holly looked down. 'I don't have real family, but I have people who have allowed me to live with them.'

'I see. So would you consider my offer, then?' They eyed each other. 'I promise there's no trick to this,' Grace added. 'Honest work, honest wages, breakfast and a hot meal each evening, and if you're hungry, you can have something at midday too.' She could see how tempted the girl on the brink of womanhood was. 'Who cares for you, Holly?'

'Cares for me? No one. I look after myself.'

'But who is the adult around you?'

'Maddy.'

'But Maddy's not your mother?'

'No.' Holly shrugged. 'I told you, I'm an orphan. I have no real family, but Maddy has been around me. We share a bed.'

Grace swallowed. 'And would Maddy be very upset if you were not around?'

'I don't know,' Holly replied.

Grace suspected she did know but didn't wish to say. It was only just occurring to her now that Holly probably moved among one of the female gangs who haunted the eastern end of Sydney, run by fierce women like Tilly Devine and her ilk.

'All right, well, you have a think about it. And talk to whoever you wish. If you feel it's a good idea, Holly, then I would love to have you work with us and—'

'I'd like to,' Holly cut in, surprising her.

'You'd like to . . .?'

'Work at the Sugar Palace, wear that uniform, earn those wages and have that hot evening meal. Yes!' she said, giving a beaming smile that Grace had not witnessed previously.

'And would you live with me?'

'When you marry Alfie, I will.'

Grace laughed. 'Are you so sure I will?'

'Yes,' Holly said, suddenly serious. 'You'd be mad not to. Alfie really loves you.'

'Advice from a thirteen-year-old?' Grace asked in a bemused tone. She began hauling the cart once more.

Holly followed suit, joining her at the front and pulling alongside Grace. 'Do my thoughts not count?'

'It's not that,' Grace said, sliding a look towards her. 'It's just you haven't seen a lot of life or men to know much about this at your age. How do you know he's right for me?'

Holly stopped, forcing Grace to stop walking too. They were just a hundred steps from Martin Place so it was frustrating, but Grace tried not to show it.

'I know you believe that. And I know you want to think that every little girl has had your life, miss, but not all of us have. Not all of us can choose what we want to do, as you can.' She pulled at the cart, looking away.

'Holly, wait . . . I'm sorry, I didn't mean to—'

'Yes, you did. Just because I'm a lot younger than you doesn't mean I haven't seen life – and perhaps I've seen lots that you haven't had to or have been protected from by your family. As to men, I probably know a lot more about them than you can imagine. And most of them are nothing like Alfie. He's kind and sweet. He worships you. All he thinks about, all he talks about is you – and helping you to be a success with your dream. I've met enough men around my way and I know you could do a whole lot worse.'

'Holly,' Grace tried again, feeling every inch of that dressing-down. What had that child seen? She didn't want to imagine.

'Come on, miss, he's waiting. I will work for you because like Alfie, I've got stars in my eyes too for what you're doing. And I want to better myself. I don't want to live how I'm living or be at other people's beck and call. I want to wear nice clothes and earn my own money, make my own decisions. I don't want any man in charge of me.'

Grace nodded, determined to make amends for what she now realised had been patronising. She had so much admiration for this youngster, who sounded a decade older than she was. The truth was, Grace realised, that she was in awe of the composed child in front of her. 'You start in a week, Holly. We'll measure you up for a uniform and new shoes in a day or so.'

There was that smile again. It came out of nowhere. Holly's expression hadn't been stormy so much as overcast, but now it was as though the sun had been sitting above the grey and had broken through. Grace knew in that moment that Holly was going to be intrinsic to the success of her new shop.

———————

Holly was right; Alfie had got the barrow looking perfect and it was now freshly stocked with the last load that they had delivered. There was already a queue of people waiting and Grace was again impressed by Alfie's brilliant sales technique.

'That's how they do it in London, he told me,' Holly said, nudging Grace.

'No Petey today?'

'He's coming soon, but Alfie and I can manage,' she said, full of confidence and swagger as she returned to her favourite, high-traffic spot outside the main post office doors.

Grace was sure they could. They certainly didn't need her, only her product. She didn't mind, though. It gave her more time to help out at her parents' shop; there was now only a few more days that she could. From Friday, her whole focus would be on the new store opening in George Street. This afternoon she would approve the shop fit. It felt like a milestone moment but frightening, given all her savings were going towards it.

At that moment, as though he could read her thoughts, Alfie looked over and winked, making her heart leap. Maybe Holly was better attuned to the world of men than she was. Alfie adored her, that much was true. They seemed like a good match. She knew too many women who stayed in their marriages for convenience, security . . . children. But she couldn't see herself ever tiring of her affection for Alfie. Almost everyone she saw him with – the customers, even these kids – responded to him so well. She noted Holly gleefully laughing at something he'd yelled to one of the customers further down the queue. Alfie would make a great father, there was no doubt in Grace's mind.

She waved her farewell to him and turned towards George Street and home, missing the moment when she might have caught sight of George Dooley entering Martin Place from the opposing Pitt Street end.

Holly had not missed Dooley's arrival. She might have been focused on accosting any potential customers coming and going, but she had been trained by Tilly Devine herself to keep a roving gaze, constantly on the lookout for danger. Holly had proved so adept at the task that Tilly had appointed her the role of innocent-looking backstreet spy at just eight years old. She'd taught Holly how to whistle and, in that innocent sound, to communicate a message, or how to skip outside the back gate to communicate a different one. If she burst into song, belting out the chorus for 'Waltzing Matilda', that sounded danger to Tilly, who could then bellow a warning to anyone in the house at the time. This was mainly used against police raids or rival gang threats.

As cunning and street smart as Holly had become, though, she'd grown up wanting more from life. She'd had the conversation with Alfie.

'I feel jealous of all those posh kids who go to school.'

'Believe me, Hols, you know more than them about life – and it will serve you well. And you can already add up.'

She'd frowned. 'Alfie, do you understand what my future is?'

She remembered how he'd looked down and shrugged, his embarrassment obvious. 'You don't have to—'

'I do, though. That's what Tilly expects. Maddy's already beginning to talk to me about it.'

'When, Holly?'

'She reminded me only last week that I'll scrub up nicely for the gentleman callers.'

He had looked away. 'I mean, when do they intend to, er, change your role?'

'After a few bleeds.' She'd watched the shock crash across his face, his expression turning haunted. 'I've already started,' she added.

Grace's offer, which had come out of the blue, suddenly made sense: Alfie had likely spoken to her about Holly's predicament. Holly liked that he cared about her. She hadn't expected him to, nor Grace, and yet her offer had made Holly's hopes soar. She couldn't remember a brighter moment in her life than when Grace had presented her with the chance of a proper job and somewhere to live. All her insides had fluttered like a flock of birds being startled.

If Alfie had decided she needed protection, she would protect him too. Holly cut through the pedestrians in Martin Place, zigzagging towards the barrow where Alfie was performing, all faces in the queue turned towards him as he told a funny story about nearly choking on a gobstopper as a child. She cast her gaze around to find Dooley, now just twenty steps away, a mocking smile angled towards Alfie and his audience.

She made the decision and then it was too late to hesitate.

―――――――

Grace walked around her new store, resisting the temptation to hug herself. The feeling of anticipation had begun to shift from what had been a low hum at the back of her mind these last few months into what now felt like a buzz near her ears. The thrum of excitement vibrated through her and she could have sworn her blood was moving faster around her body whenever she stood in this space. Her dream – hers and Alfie's – was becoming reality and very soon the current smell of fresh paint and freshly installed timber cabinetry would be overwhelmed by the unmistakable scent of sugar.

The man pulled a pencil from behind his ear and ran it quickly down his calculations in a book. She watched him nod and then lick his pencil tip and sign his name on the bottom.

'There you go, Miss Fairweather,' he said brightly. 'That's the bill for the cabinetry work, its installation and all the painting.' He tore the sheet from the invoice book and handed it to her with a friendly nod. 'Thank you for your business.'

Her smile covered a momentary panic and if he sensed her hesitation to take the list of costs, then he didn't show it.

'Wishing you every success with your new shop, Miss Fairweather. I shall enjoy visiting with my family once you're up and running.'

'Thank you, Mr Benson. Tell all your friends too.'

'I sure will. Have you found all your staff yet, if you don't mind me asking?'

'Er, to be honest, I'm not sure how many we shall need.'

'It's just that my Lizzie would love to work in a store like this. She's just turned sixteen.'

'How is her arithmetic?'

'She didn't enjoy it, but she certainly knows how to account for her pocket money.' He gave an embarrassed grin.

Grace smiled. 'And her reading?'

'Oh yes, she reads just fine. I doubt she'd be much good at writing letters, though, Miss, to be fair.'

'I'm looking for bright, energetic, smiley girls who enjoy serving customers. If you think Lizzie might fit that mould, Mr Benson, then maybe have her drop off her credentials.'

'Credentials?'

'Oh, you know, her schooling, but particularly any relevant experience with serving the public – even jumble sales at the local church. I'd also like to hear why she thinks she'd be a good member of staff at the Sugar Palace.'

Mr Benson blinked, slightly bewildered, as she'd expected. If he explained it to his daughter well enough and she grasped what was expected of her, then Grace was confident she'd see Lizzie soon enough. If she came alone to deliver her credentials, it would also mean she was enthusiastic and not simply being bullied along by parents who needed their child working. 'I'll do that,' he said and collected his things to leave.

'Tell her I look forward to meeting her, and Mr Benson?'

'Yes?' he said, turning from the door.

'Would it be all right if I paid this in two parts, with the first next Monday?' She held up the bill.

'That would be acceptable. Thank you, Miss Fairweather.'

When he left, she was finally alone in the Sugar Palace. Now she did hug herself, but there was no time to dwell. Her job from here on was to make enough product to stock the shop daily, which was going to take more than just her. Incredibly, her mother had put up her hand to help. Mary Fairweather had watched Grace for weeks as she cooked up sugar, made her toffees and whipped egg whites for marshmallow. She'd done endless tastings in the grocery store and at the barrow to get the balance in flavours, colours, shapes and sizes just right.

And remarkably – to Grace anyway – her mother had become caught up in the excitement as well. Her father had shaken his head, sharing his thoughts on several occasions that he hadn't seen his wife this galvanised since she was planning their nuptials or preparing for Grace's birth. Grace had also taken them both to watch Alfie in action at the barrow earlier that afternoon, when the shop always got quiet, and she knew them too well to not recognise how impressed they were, despite their initial silence.

Walking back down to The Rocks, her father had finally given the praise she'd hoped might come. 'He's very good, I'll give him that.'

She'd smiled. 'Somehow he moves every bit of product. I know he all but gives some of it away towards the end of the day, but he says that's how it used to work on the barrows in London. Nothing is free other than samples. He has great ideas like "if you buy the rest of the vanilla fudge, I'll throw in a bag of chocolate fudge." Or with the perishables, like the toffee apples, he sells those hard as early as he can, but if he's got some left he starts to discount them, "buy two and get a third free". It's smart. He doesn't give it away, but he also doesn't have wastage.'

'Well, I think your range of product is superb, Grace,' her mother admitted. 'When I watch you cooking madly and shaping so furiously, it just all looks like a lot of hard, unheralded work but to see it displayed so well on the barrow, all those lovely colours and clever towers of lollies, I am really impressed.'

'We both are,' her father followed up, putting an arm around her. 'Aren't I lucky to have two wonderful women in my life?'

'Oh, go on with you, Hugh, you old charmer,' her mother replied and Grace had felt nothing but pleasure at the return to the warmth she had grown up with. She loved it when her parents spoke romantically to each other. Now she just had to get them over the line with Alfie, accepting that he was the one for her.

'Alfie has made enough money from the barrow for us to open the shop within a week.'

'It's some achievement,' her father said with a proud nod. 'I take my hat off to the boy. He's delivered on his promise to you.'

They'd arrived back at the shop and her father had just turned the key in the lock to let them in. Suddenly Grace had felt she should no longer hold Alfie at arm's length. With Holly's warning about Alfie being too good to let go echoing in her mind, and his obvious determination to make her dream a reality on show, she felt it was right to cement their relationship. 'As you know we're planning to marry. He'd like to talk to you, Dad, if that's all right?' Another fib. Alfie wouldn't see the need, but she would insist upon it. Her parents were conservative and her mother a stickler for the right behaviour.

She ignored her mother's small gasp as the shop door was closed behind them. 'And you're absolutely convinced this is not too soon after ending your engagement to Norm?'

Grace shook her head. 'Norm is going to make a good husband for someone.' That was her third lie in as many minutes. 'Just not for me. Alfie and I are so well suited. You just have to trust me.'

Her mother blew out a sighing breath, obviously fighting hard against offering her opinion again.

Hugh watched her carefully. 'It's *her* heart, Mary.'

'Which I'm frightened he's going to break.'

Grace forced herself to not bite back. 'You can't know that. Don't judge him yet. Give him a chance. I'd appreciate your blessings for our love, our endeavour and our determination to make this venture of ours successful. If you don't want to help me celebrate a wedding, that's fine. I'll go to a registry office and—'

'Now, hold on. Stop,' her father said, trying to calm the conversation. 'What's happening to us, Mary? The three of us have been inseparable and now we've got all this fractiousness. It's plain you don't approve of Sweeting, but I have to agree with Grace; this is her heart, her life, her feelings. If she trusts Alfie – and even if you or I don't – then we must trust her.'

Her mother blinked. 'I agree. Grace, we trust you completely. Whatever you do, we know you'll work hard at it and make it successful through your determination and that goes for marriage. So . . . you have our blessing.' Before Grace could respond, her mother added, 'But my darling girl, you should never feel you cannot walk back into our arms at any time. Any time, do you hear me?'

Grace nodded. Her father shook his head with relief and her mother lifted and dropped her shoulders as if girding herself for a challenge.

'You get on with opening your new store. I know you'll make us proud. I'll get busy with picking up the threads of a wedding. New date, new groom, new life,' she said, nodding at Grace with a smile that landed on her with only tenderness.

15

Alfie had clocked George Dooley smirking on the outskirts of the queue a few minutes after Holly, and he felt shaken at the sight of the big man. He could hardly make a run for it and leave the barrow unattended; if he did and word got back to Grace, there would be no explanation that might satisfy her.

Dooley, meanwhile, looked to have all the time in the world, standing back and watching the proceedings with his arms crossed. He was patient, waiting for the busy lunchtime crowds to disperse before he made his move. In fact, he waited until Alfie could no longer pretend to be otherwise engaged.

Darting looks towards Holly told Alfie she had mercifully sent every potential cocaine buyer away for today. He was angry at the trade and useful dollars he'd missed out on. Not only had Grace innocently got used to the extra cash he was piling in towards their new venture, but he'd have to make up any losses to Tilly. Thank goodness for Holly, who had shown the insight of an adult – a very wise and cunning adult, in fact – to head off the other type of customer.

'Mr Dooley,' Alfie said politely, raising his cap. 'Can I interest you in some sherbet sweets, or perhaps some peppermint cake for Mrs Dooley?'

'Only if it's free, lad,' the horrible man said, chuckling.

'I'm sorry, I can't do that.' Alfie smiled, amazed that he could sound as relaxed and confident as he did. He noticed Holly hurrying away another man who'd been approaching with a sly look. 'You can come back at the end of the day, when I do often reduce the rates by half or two thirds depending on what I have to move. But I don't give it away for free.' He tapped his nose. 'That's not good business.'

Dooley gave another chuckle and raised his eyebrows. 'I'd like to know what other sort of business you're doing here, lad.'

'I can't imagine what you mean, Mr Dooley,' Alfie said, smiling with feigned innocence, his insides feeling suddenly watery.

'I hear on the jungle drums that you're doing a roaring trade.'

'As you can see,' Alfie said, waving a hand at his barrow. 'This was loaded up this morning and topped up just before midday. There'll be another push when all the office workers leave for the day. I'll be here until five-thirty selling madly until the last lolly has gone.' He kept his tone conversational, drawing away from where Dooley wanted to take the discussion.

Dooley gave a sly grin. 'So why is it, Sweeting, that I keep hearing whispers that you're working with one of the gangs over east?'

'Not me, Mr Dooley,' Alfie said, risking the lie. He was sure the man was fishing. 'Whatever makes you say that?'

Dooley shrugged expansively. 'So you won't mind me taking a look around your barrow?'

'Everyone looks. It's a free country,' Alfie said, feeling worms stirring in his belly, like a sod of earth had been suddenly turned over to reveal the secret lives beneath, twisting and turning in shock.

Dooley walked around the barrow at close quarters.

'Fancy anything?' Alfie tried. 'The toffee apples are seasonal. Best to get yours now before Grace stops making them once the warm weather hits.'

'So you're using the barrow for what purpose?' Dooley asked. 'I thought your little squeeze wanted a real shop.'

Alfie suspected his nemesis was playing dumb. He explained the plan. 'And if all goes well, we open up in a week's time,' he finished, sounding chuffed, but Dooley's expression remained unimpressed.

'Well, you certainly are punching above your weight, Alfie boy, with that Fairweather girl.'

Alfie kept his tone neutral. 'We're getting married soon, Mr Dooley. I'll ask you to respect my sweetheart.'

'Oh, I do, I do, lad. I think she's beautiful and smart, but I doubt she's got a single clue about who she's contemplating marrying.'

Alfie gave a shrug. 'I don't know what you mean by that. I've gone straight, I told you. Grace knows about our past dealings, but we don't have any these days, Mr Dooley, so I'll politely ask you to stop calling by – unless I can interest you in some toffees?'

'Strike me, but you play the innocent so well, Sweeting. Tell me then, if you're all straight up, how come I spot one of Tilly Devine's cockatoos keeping a lookout for you?' Dooley thumbed a fat digit Holly's way.

'Holly? Oh no, you've got that wrong. She works with me now.' Alfie looked past Dooley's beefy shoulder and called out. 'Er, Holly, could you come here, please?'

Holly strolled up, looking suspiciously at both of them. 'Yes?'

Alfie gave another innocent shrug. 'Mr Dooley doesn't believe that you work with me.'

'But I do. I find customers and point them your way,' she said, sounding offended. 'I get threepence a day for my trouble now. We've had a raise.'

Dooley bent down and pointed a finger at her chest, a little too intimately for Alfie's liking. He bristled as Dooley poked her. 'I've seen you up at the Woolloomooloo house of no good.'

'Oh, are you one of the customers, sir?' she asked and Alfie, despite his concern, had to stop himself from grinning.

'No, you little wastrel!' Dooley said, raising his hand to her.

Before he could think about the consequences, Alfie leapt in front of Holly. 'Don't you dare do that, Mr Dooley. Don't you touch her.'

'Aren't you lucky to have a knight in shining armour, Miss Smartypants?' Dooley sneered at Holly, who peeked around from Alfie with a defiant gaze. 'I was only teasing anyway. You're very jumpy, Sweeting. Have you got something to hide?'

Without warning, Dooley ripped back the barrow's skirting to reveal the special shelf Alfie had built. 'What have we got under here, then?'

Alfie blanched. 'Listen, Mr Dooley,' he said, beginning to fashion an excuse, but he pulled up sharply, momentarily horrified to see the small sack that normally held their pouches of cocaine no longer there. He watched in taut silence as Dooley rifled through the remains of their confectionery stores and then began running his fingers around the underneath of the barrow. Alfie thought he was going to be sick all over Dooley's shoes.

But he felt a squeeze of reassurance from Holly, her small hand in his. She said nothing but her gaze told him everything he needed to know as she subtly looked down towards her dress. Holly had removed the cocaine while Dooley was still far away, and the small sack was now tied around her waist and hidden by her long frock.

Emboldened by her audacity, he schooled his features to a puzzled frown. 'I just don't know what you're looking for, Mr Dooley. Maybe I can help?'

Dooley swung on him, red-faced now, enraged. He waggled a finger in front of Alfie's face and Alfie could smell the liver and onions that the man had eaten for his midday meal. There was no doubting that ghastly smell coming off his breath.

'You little turd. I just know you're selling more than confectionery from this barrow. It doesn't make sense that you're not, not with that whore's urchin as your lookout.'

'Enough!' Alfie said, having spotted customers on their way. A new courage was building. 'Go away, Mr Dooley. I'm not taking any more of your bullying or your insults, and if I ever see you raise a hand to a child or speak to Holly in this way again—'

'You'll what?' Dooley sneered.

'I'll report you to the police.'

'So will I!' Holly chimed in. 'I've seen you oiling your way around the east,' she accused. 'Not only are you not liked, no one trusts you.'

Dooley looked taken aback by the sudden offensive taken by Alfie and Holly.

'One more thing, Mr Dooley,' Holly said. 'I don't work for Tilly any longer.'

'Yeah?' He chuckled. 'Apparently you work for this joker.'

'I work for Grace Fairweather, actually. She hired me today.'

'What?' Dooley said. Alfie had to privately admit he was surprised too.

'You heard me. I have a full-time job, proper wages coming my way and all that. I get to wear a uniform. I belong to the Sugar Palace now.'

'I don't believe it,' Dooley said, loading his voice with derision.

'You can ask Miss Fairweather if you don't believe me. I start in one week. I'm being measured up for shoes too.' She advanced on Dooley. 'So you can just leave us alone, or I will report to the police that you've been pestering me – and we all know why fat old men pester young girls.'

His scar elongated with his snarl. 'You dirty—'

Holly kept her cool, now waggling her finger at him as he had done to Alfie. 'Be careful, Mr Dooley. I'll tell them all the terrible things you've promised to do to me.'

Alfie found the courage to express the helpless chuckle that bubbled to the surface now; few could get one past Holly. 'Go away, George,' he said, amazed at how disdainful he managed to sound. 'You have no more business here, and I don't want to see you around this barrow unless you're paying the King's coin in fair exchange for my product.'

Dooley backed away, perhaps knowing he was beaten. 'I'll catch you yet, Sweeting, and when I do, it will be more than your finger going. As for you,' he said to Holly, 'I'll be watching.'

He left, striding away to George Street and turning right at the corner.

'You've got customers,' Holly said to Alfie, nodding in their direction. 'Don't worry, we made more than enough with the morning and lunchtime trade. You'll be able to cover Tilly's costs.'

'I want to be free of her, Holly. I'm done with selling for her.'

Holly nodded. 'We'll have to sell off what's left in your load and then you can talk to her.'

'Let's get busy then. I doubt we'll see Dooley again.'

'I wouldn't be sure about that. He's a horrible man, but he's not stupid. Once he gets a whiff of something, he won't let it go.'

Alfie sighed. 'You're probably right. You were brilliant, though. Did Grace really employ you?'

Holly nodded, smiling helplessly. 'And I accepted. I'm going to live with you too.'

Alfie nodded, his mouth open in surprise. 'When?'

'When you get married. So hurry up and make it happen!'

Mary and Hugh Fairweather were on a rare night out. It was their wedding anniversary, and Grace had shooed them out of the grocery store, working alone for its final hour. Now she'd turned the sign around to *Closed*, swept and dusted down for tomorrow before dutifully emptying the till, separating notes and coin before counting the 'float' for the next day's trading, which she put in its bag; the day's takings she put into another dedicated pouch with the note stating the amount, bound with a rubber band. She had already tallied the difference, written it on a separate note and slipped that in too.

Both amounts were put into the safe they kept out the back. Grace heard the doorbell and smiled. That would be Alfie. 'Just coming,' she called. She heard no reply but she closed the safe and hurried out into the shop, only to be confronted by George Dooley. She swallowed her immediate fear. 'We're closed, Mr Dooley.'

'Door was open,' he remarked, smiling, but not kindly.

'The sign says closed.'

He gave a tsking sound. 'You should lock that door after hours. A young lass like you should be wary. Are you alone? Actually, I know you are – I saw your parents leave.'

'It seems I have no one to be wary of but you, Mr Dooley. No one else is letting themselves in, uninvited.'

He grinned, broadly now. 'My, but you're a confident creature. Far too much for that Alfie Sweeting, I'd wager.'

'Mr Dooley. I am not a young lass. I am not a creature. My name is Grace Fairweather and I'll thank you to address me that way, or as Miss Fairweather, I don't mind which. I don't call you Georgie, or Dooley, or fat man or Scarface, do I?'

His amusement blinked away. 'What did you say to me?'

'I'm sure you heard me, Mr Dooley. Address me with respect, or I shall not respect you. We have no business together and unless you're a paying customer, you have no reason to be here.'

'That's what your toad of a boyfriend just said.'

'He's not a boyfriend. We're to be married.'

'Oh ho. I'll bet he wants that ring on your finger as soon as he can push it on.'

Grace sighed. 'Mr Dooley, I am losing my patience.' She watched him as he tried to regain control by forcing a fresh smile. It seemed he preferred to be in charge of any situation.

'Yes, indeed, his hands are full with you, Miss *Fairweather*,' he said, emphasising her name.

'Right, well, I cannot serve you once the shop is officially closed. So I'd like you to leave.'

'Or what?'

She frowned, forcing herself to appear unfazed by his presence, although inwardly she was frantically searching for ways to be rid of him. 'Is that a threat? Do I need to call the police?' Her voice was hard but not impolite.

'You mean your man Norman?' Dooley scoffed. 'I doubt he'd be in a hurry to help you.'

'Really, is that what you think? Whatever's happened between Norman and me does not make him any less of a policeman. Plus, he's conscientious. I suspect he'd be here in a flash if he was asked.'

'And you think you can get past me to raise the alert?'

'I would certainly do my best,' she said, fear beginning to claw in her gut. She stared at him coldly. 'Get out!'

He tsked again. 'That's no way to speak to someone.'

'I think it's the only sort of language someone like you understands.'

'Very high and mighty, Miss Fairweather. You know that high-mindedness may come before a fall.' He made a solemn face.

'I'm fair to all but the fact is, I don't like you, Mr Dooley. You serve no purpose in my life except to poison it, and I owe you nothing. Now, I've been polite and I've also firmly asked you to leave and I can't imagine why you're even here, other than to—'

'Other than to caution you,' he cut in.

'Caution me?' She gave a gasp. 'Over what?'

'Selling illegal goods from your barrow.' He spoke slowly, pointing his finger towards her face with each word.

She laughed. 'We have a licence, and when did selling confectionery become illegal, anyway?'

'I'd suggest you discover whatever else is being sold from your barrow under your name, Miss Fairweather. Ta-ta,' he said, giving her a little wave. 'I wouldn't trust Sweeting,' he added, 'or that little tart he hangs around with. She's one of Tilly's, I swear. She's probably bringing the drugs – snow, I'd say – and that sweet little girl is knee-deep in a different sort of trade from your innocent-looking barrow.'

Grace couldn't hide her shock. Her voice was small and strained when she spoke. 'Where's the proof?'

'I don't have any, but I've been around Alfie's sort long enough to know they don't change their ways.' Dooley wagged his finger in a way that was fast becoming annoying. 'Mark my words, he'll be your downfall, and imagine all the sourness *that* will bring to the good name of your parents. Don't ever say I didn't tell you that Alfie Sweeting is a fraud, and he's romancing you to advance himself.' Dooley rubbed his fingers together in the universal sign for cash.

'Get out!' Grace snarled again. 'If you ever set foot in here again, I will call the police and claim harassment.'

Dooley laughed, then he blew her a kiss and left her with the sound of the tinkling doorbell. She hesitated for a heartbeat before rushing up and locking the door, breathing heavily and with relief.

She didn't want to allow Dooley's mocking words any space in her mind, but they echoed all the same. He'd driven a wedge of concern into her thoughts. It was about ten minutes later that Alfie arrived, by which time Grace had corralled her emotions and cooled down, telling herself that if Alfie was playing with fire, then she'd let him burn himself before she went looking for the scorch marks. She knew Dooley was a troublemaker and she would not allow his stirring to create unnecessary ripples in her life if they were just his agitations, based on no fact.

She allowed herself to believe in the possibility that it was true; Alfie's background was shady, and he was certainly no angel. But she also knew that whatever his past suggested, he was setting out to break from his old ways and she was not going to help Dooley with his mission.

She recalled Holly's words about Alfie and, frankly, she trusted the thirteen-year-old more than she did George Dooley.

'Sorry, I'm late, darlin'.' Alfie pecked her cheek as she opened the door for him. It was dark outside and he brought a chill in with him; Grace did not allow herself to regard that as symbolic. 'I made sure I saw Holly most of the way home.'

'Good.' She nodded, determined to shake off Dooley's presence, and hugged him. 'I don't like her being out alone.'

He grinned. 'Well, that's one girl who can take care of herself, I promise you. Is it true you've offered her a job at the Sugar Palace?'

'It is,' she said brightly, leading him away from the door. 'Come on, I've cooked – I'll tell you more upstairs. Let me just switch off down here.'

She joined him upstairs and told him about her conversation with Holly. 'I have no doubt in my mind that Holly will be an asset in many ways,' she said. 'She's whip smart and thinks fast. We'll need that sort of presence in the store.'

Alfie nodded. 'You're right. I've met some operators in my time, but few like Holly. She's as sharp as a razor blade—'

Grace seized her moment. 'Is that because she's familiar with one of those eastern neighbourhood razor gangs, Alfie?'

'What?' He looked momentarily trapped and his face slackened in the way she'd seen mice deliberately flop and feign death so the cat would drop them – and then they'd be off in a flash. 'She lives at Woolloomooloo but—'

Grace refused to let him out of the jaws of her question. 'Now, listen. We are business partners, Alfie, and we are talking of marriage. We have to be honest with each other, or we'll fail before we begin.'

He looked chastened. 'Holly hasn't had a happy upbringing,' he began. 'Whatever her start in life, we've already changed it and now your offer of work and a place to live . . . It's an enormous shift for a girl who was looking at a very different life ahead.'

Grace nodded. He was treading around the question, but in his way he was answering it. 'I dread to think what they had in store for her.'

His expression fell further and he nodded gravely, because he'd not discussed Holly's likely fate in the east. 'You've done something wonderful for her.'

'You began the process. I'd never have met or even known about Holly if not for your barrow. The thing is, I suspect that she feels an enormous loyalty to you. So she's going to follow your footsteps.'

'What do you mean?' He frowned.

Grace paused a heartbeat. She needed to be clear without calling his trustworthiness into question. 'She's looking for leadership, Alfie.'

'From you. Not me.'

She shook her head. 'George Dooley called in on me tonight.' His look of horror told her plenty. 'So, presumably he'd already paid you a visit?' She looked hard at him.

'What did he say?'

'He really doesn't like you, does he?'

'Whatever he might say, he doesn't like anyone who pays their debts because it gets them off his hook.'

'And you're off his hook?' She still hadn't looked away, trying to read him.

'Completely, Grace. I told you, I'm going straight.'

'He doesn't think so.'

'Dooley's a bully and stirs up trouble wherever he goes.'

She nodded. 'I think you're right. I think he's deliberately creating doubt between us.'

'Don't doubt me,' Alfie said, pulling out a huge wad of money and placing it on the table. Then he dragged a small sack of coins and put those alongside it. 'Today's takings and the last of my winnings. I'm done with gambling.'

Grace stared at the money. Was it really all from gambling? 'Is that a promise?'

He fixed her with his handsome gaze. 'I cross my heart.' He nodded at the cash. 'That should give us all we need to begin. We don't even need the barrow now. We stop.'

'Won't you be missed in Martin Place?'

He smiled. 'I've paid for the barrow for another week, but I've had a sign made up that points people to our new shop, so when people come to buy your treats, they'll know where to find us. Come on, no more frowning. Let's eat. And tomorrow night I'm going to take you out dancing.' He stood in a rush and grabbed her hands to pull her up too.

'Dancing!' Grace spluttered, caught up in his infectious smile and the way he began to twirl her around the kitchen.

'Yes. Tomorrow it's music, dancing and champagne. And next week our grand opening.'

'Alfie—'

'No buts. Go find your best evening frock and dancing shoes . . . We are celebrating.'

The shadow of George Dooley retreated and was replaced with food, laughter and Alfie's tall stories about their customers. They began to plan more product, and Alfie's latest idea was that they already begin to look for factory premises. It all felt to Grace as though it was moving extraordinarily fast as they ranged across confectionery ideas and plant equipment.

The more they talked excitedly about the future, the more the threat of Dooley's warning dissipated in Grace's mind, but a new thought was forming. She'd act on it tomorrow.

16

Holly looked thunderstruck to see Grace approaching the house in Woolloomooloo. She pushed herself off the wall at the back gate where she'd been leaning and hurried towards her.

'Miss Fairweather,' she said, her voice high and worried. 'What are you doing here? And so early – it's barely eleven.'

'It's Grace, remember? I could ask you the same thing.'

They regarded one another with unblinking gazes. They couldn't be more different in looks, Grace thought; her own blonde hair was neatly swept up behind her neck and lay beneath a velvet navy cloche hat, and she was dressed in a drop-waisted navy crepe de Chine dress that hung exquisitely from her shoulders to a knife-pleated skirt. At her hips she'd buckled a wide belt. She had chosen her outfit with care. She needed to look serious, professional even – like a woman used to negotiating . . . and getting her way. And she was. She'd honed her skills with the various suppliers for her father's store and then added a fresher, keener edge doing all the bartering required for the design and set up of the Sugar Palace, from landlord to tradesmen. But she'd never faced any negotiation like the one that she knew she was walking towards.

Holly, by contrast, looked as though she hadn't slept well. She had dark shadows beneath her eyes and her hair was unkempt, unwashed. Her tunic was stained and her shoes scuffed. 'Don't, Miss.'

'Don't what, Holly?'

Holly tilted her chin towards the house. 'She's scary.'

'Do I look scared?' Grace asked, sounding assured but feeling all her senses on high alert.

'You look . . .' Holly shook her head.

'How do I look?' Grace frowned. Had she got it wrong?

'Amazing, miss. People who look like you don't come here.'

'And yet here I am. Take me to Tilly Devine, please. I was told I would find her at this house after spending the morning being turned away from grungy looking establishments in Darlinghurst where I thought I'd find her.'

Holly blinked but said nothing.

'This is her newest brothel, isn't it?'

Holly nodded unhappily.

'Why do you stay here, Holly? I mean with these women?'

'I like my freedom, miss. I don't want to be caned by nuns or imprisoned in some sort of orphanage.'

'So you'd rather . . .' Grace couldn't finish her question but luckily didn't have to as a woman hailed her.

She was glaring at Grace. 'Hey, you. What do you want?'

'I want to talk to Mrs Devine, please,' Grace said, cutting her frustrated attention from Holly to the newcomer.

'Oh, yes? And what do you need to talk to her about then? You don't look like you need our services,' the woman drawled, smiling with a cunning look. 'What's she after, Hols?'

'Grace, this is Eve. She works with Mrs Devine.'

Grace spoke confidently, meeting the woman's eye. 'I'm Grace Fairweather and I have a proposition for your boss.'

'You're lucky her husband isn't around. He'd pick you up and fling you into the next suburb from here.'

'Lucky he isn't then. It's not him I have business with anyway.'

'He'll be back soon. Don't say I haven't warned you. Wait here.' She turned and went inside.

'Now you've done it,' Holly said, looking distressed. 'What are you doing here?'

Grace's gaze softened. 'Holly, do you want to work for me?'

'You know I do.'

'Then you have to trust me.' Grace noticed a curtain upstairs moving and a woman's face appear in the window. 'Looks like I'm being checked out.'

'Be very careful, Grace,' Holly said, her tone grave. 'She's slippery. Don't trust her smile. She hates women who are prettier than her. And you're much prettier.'

'I'll be careful. Here's Eve.'

The older woman was back at the gate, curling a forefinger Grace's way. 'She says she's amused to hear what a woman like you might have to say. You stay here, Holly.'

Tilly Devine was younger than Grace had imagined, perhaps only half-a-dozen years older than her, but she looked like she'd been around the world several times. Grace sensed an enormous amount of cunning in the woman's greeting smile. She was attractive in a tough sort of way, with chin-length blonde hair – though perhaps the colour wasn't natural, as it leaned towards white – that had been savagely crimped with irons. She wore a satin housecoat in a busy oriental design, as though she was only recently out of her bed, but her make-up was thick, her lipstick a rich red like she had dipped her mouth in a saucer of blood.

'Grace Fairweather,' Tilly said in a mocking tone. 'What a pretty name.'

'Mrs Devine,' Grace replied, keeping her gaze firm and unblinking. 'Thank you for seeing me.'

The woman laughed. 'Call me Tilly. Otherwise I feel like my husband's mother,' she said and winked. 'And I shall call you Grace – is that all right?'

'It is.'

'Can we offer you something?' Tilly said, gesturing for Grace to take a seat in the boudoir of sorts. 'I was about to have a brandy.'

There was so much heavy draping, Grace was certain it hadn't seen a dusting in an age and felt she needed to clear her throat. The room smelt of perfume and old liquor. Various silk, satin and thick crepe outfits crowded against each other, hanging from coat hangers in an open wardrobe down one side of the room. 'A brandy?' Grace managed not to sound judgemental but she couldn't quite rid her tone of surprise. 'Er, no. I don't need anything, thank you.'

'I have a scratchy throat, you see.' Tilly moved to a dressing table where a decanter and several glasses sat on a tray; some had been used. She poured herself a slug into a fresh glass while Grace waited, perched on the end of a chair covered in striped satin.

Everything was garish in this room, either in colour or pattern. How did Tilly ever sleep, Grace wondered, although she doubted sleep was high on the list of activities for this space.

'Now, Grace, to what do I owe this surprise visit? We don't know each other, do we?'

'No.'

'I didn't think so. I never forget a pert pair of breasts.' Tilly laughed and Grace heard that cunning again. 'You look very prim, Grace, but don't get me wrong. I don't mean prudish. I think your outfit is deliciously elegant, and I could wish it were mine. I don't have anything that sombre. It would work well for me when I attend a funeral.' She laughed at the couched insult.

Grace shrugged. 'I can sell it to you or I'll throw it in as part of a deal,' she offered with care.

Tilly laughed. 'Aha, straight to it. No small talk for you, Grace. I'm impressed. Now what could we two girls from such different worlds possibly have to make a deal about? We hardly have much in common.'

'Enough,' Grace replied evenly. She removed her gloves, forcing herself to look unhurried, almost careless. 'We're both women, both in business, both trying to make our way in a man's world, are we not?' She sat back and looked up at Tilly with enquiry.

Tilly smiled. 'Oh, well, I must admit that I do very nicely from that man's world. In case you hadn't noticed, I offer them exactly what they want.'

Grace lifted a shoulder in a simple agreement. 'And I offer them something they can take home to their wives after they've got what they need from you.'

This seemed to amuse Tilly hugely. She threw back her head and chortled a laugh to the ceiling. 'Bravo! Yes. I hear you're opening a confectionery store. I gather you're the daughter of a grocery shop owner at The Rocks.'

'Then we aren't the strangers you think we are, for you seem to know plenty about me.'

'Oh, I keep my ear to the ground,' Tilly said, raising her eyebrows in amusement over the rim of her glass as she sipped.

Grace noticed she'd left a waxy red mark on the glass like a kiss.

'So, now that we've established we have some common ground, what exactly do you want from me?'

Grace suspected Tilly already knew, and that meant she would drive a harder bargain in the negotiation. Grace had her around the table, but could she engage her into making the deal she was after? There was no use hedging. 'I'd like Holly to leave your establishment and come and live with me.'

Tilly frowned. 'Holly? What would you want with that slip of a girl?'

'Mrs Devine, I know—'

'Tilly. Remember, we're friends now.'

'Tilly.' Grace began again slowly. 'I know that you are aware that Holly has been working with my fiancé.'

'Alfie Sweeting. Good-looking bloke.' Tilly made a duck bill with her hands, opening and closing her fingers. 'Got the gift of the gab, that one.' She sipped again. 'I like Alfie. He's nicer than most men who cross my threshold.'

Grace nodded. 'I like him too. In fact, I love him.'

Tilly gave a faint frown. 'Ah, pet, keep an eye on that one, though. Easy on the eye and easy to love, but I imagine hard to contain.'

'I don't plan to contain him at all.'

'Then you might be headed for trouble. That fella thrives on the edge.'

It was Grace's turn to frown. 'The edge?'

'No man's land . . . between the good and the not-so-good. He isn't a gangster, but he's not what you would call squeaky clean.'

'He's changing, Tilly,' Grace said, realising she was saying this aloud as much for her own benefit as the older woman's. 'He's come from a poor background where petty crime was his only way. But he wants to make a good life, an honest income. He'll settle into life as a shop owner and he has big plans for our confectionery shop.'

Tilly nodded. 'Well, I hope for your sake it works out how you intend. So how does Holly fit into this scene of wedded bliss and sweet enterprise?'

No point in hesitating. 'I've offered Holly a full-time job in the shop.'

Tilly reached over to a nearby table and opened a box, withdrawing a cigarette and a holder. She took her time with a glass lighter shaped like a rose, before taking an exaggerated drag with the cigarette holder at the side of her mouth.

Grace heard it tap gently against Tilly's teeth and wondered if it symbolised her grinding her jaw in rage. She watched the brothel owner blow out a thin stream of smoke above her head.

'Now why would you do that, Grace?'

Grace gave a calm smile. 'Because she has the right skills to make a very good member of staff.'

'There are dozens of girls who would do that for you.' Tilly frowned.

Grace schooled her expression to remain open and gave a nod. 'Yes, you're right in some ways, but I don't have the time to find them. Holly brings a lot more than simple service skills and charm. I can teach staff those techniques. But some people are born with sharp, quick-witted minds and an inherent intelligence that cannot be taught. Holly is one of those people. For now I have appointed two other members of staff, plus there's Alfie and me, but I'd love for Holly to join us too. She could easily, in a brief time, even manage the store. I feel Holly is someone I could rely on.'

'Clearly more than I can,' Tilly remarked.

'You don't need her. She's not yet fourteen.'

'And she's had her first bleed. I can't tell you how valuable she is to me. There are men who would pay triple, quadruple . . . anything I ask, to bed a virgin.'

Grace had to swallow her contempt. 'I gathered as much, which is why I would like to negotiate. I can make it worth your while to allow me to take Holly home with me today.'

'Negotiate? It's illegal to sell people, Grace, you should know that.' Tilly gave a hard stare, taking another drag of her cigarette.

Grace met her gaze. 'It's my understanding that you bought her as a youngster. It's also illegal to keep a child slave.'

'She's here of her own free will, you can ask her.'

'In that case, Holly has already accepted my job offer and my reason for being here today is to politely let you know that I'll be taking her home with me and she no longer needs your . . . care.'

Tilly put down the cigarette. 'Ah, now hold up. I thought we were negotiating.'

Grace sighed. 'Let's stop playing games. Holly wants to leave this place. She doesn't want to belong to the brothel, and I certainly don't want that for her future.' She held up a hand. 'I mean no offence. What the women who work with you choose to do is their business. No judgement,' she said, not sure she meant that but it sounded appropriate and had stopped the angry narrowing of her listener's gaze. 'But Holly has aspirations.' At Tilly's frown, Grace explained. 'She is so ambitious – perhaps she got that from you. She speaks of you with awe as an amazing businesswoman,' she said, trying to dance the fine line between obsequiousness and lies. 'But she doesn't want to be in your line of work, Tilly, and surely she'll soon become a burden, another mouth to feed.'

Tilly gave a gentle scoff. 'She already is.'

'I gather she earns her keep in a way that ensures a measure of safety for you.'

'And she's very good at it, as your Alfie will attest,' Tilly said, now licking a drop of brandy from the edge of the glass in a lascivious manner.

It was a guarded jab but Grace felt its thrust and subsequent pain all the same. 'I don't know what you mean.'

'No, I suppose you wouldn't. Ask your fiancé. He claims it's all for you anyway.'

Grace deliberately paused, watching Tilly, who didn't seem to mind the sudden tense silence as she sipped her drink and smiled, waiting. 'You said it,' Grace finally responded. 'Perhaps you should explain it to me.'

'I don't like sticking my nose into other people's business.'

'But I'm giving you my permission.'

Tilly sipped again and laughed. There was scorn in it, but this time Grace didn't feel it was levelled at her. When Tilly spoke, Grace realised she'd judged correctly.

'Men.' Tilly sighed. 'They do test us. How do you imagine Alfie got to know my Holly?'

There was no point in trying to play dumb. Grace could sense where this was leading. 'I presume here.'

'Correct. And what do you think your fiancé was doing here?'

Grace swallowed, nervous to answer that question. She shrugged. 'You tell me.'

'Perhaps not what you think.'

'What am I thinking?'

It was Tilly's turn to shrug. She lifted herself off the tattered chaise longue and wrapped the silken robe around herself tighter but didn't fasten the belt, showing off a neat figure enrobed in a lace slip beneath. She stubbed out her cigarette and took time lighting another. Tilly approached the grimy window and blew out the smoke before finally answering. 'You're wondering if he came here to sow some wild oats.'

'What a polite expression,' Grace replied softly.

'I'm mindful of your genteel ways.'

'I am not as fragile as you imagine. So he came here to lie with a woman and met Holly – is that what I'm supposed to know?'

'No, love. Alfie has never partaken of one of my lovely girls, more's the pity. They'd think they'd won the lottery sweepstake with that good-looker if they had,' Tilly said, giving Grace a lazy smile. 'And I'd know if he had.'

Relief flooded through her. 'So why was he here, then?'

'Alfie came here looking for my help.'

Grace forced herself to remain patient as Tilly paused again, clearly enjoying herself.

'And I gave it.'

The clouds in Grace's mind parted. 'You lent him money,' she sighed, realising now how Alfie had been able to come up with his half so quickly. 'I thought he was gambling.'

'Wrong on both counts, Grace. I imagine he's far too scared to tell you what he's been up to.'

'Then you should.'

'I usually protect my own.'

'But Alfie isn't yours.' Grace raised her chin.

Tilly gave that cunning smile again. 'He is while he owes me money, love.'

'You said you didn't lend him any.'

'I didn't. We did business together.'

A siren of alarm screamed through Grace's body, the hairs at the back of her neck standing on edge and a loud whoosh sounding in a loud beat behind her ears. She couldn't imagine that Alfie was a 'pimp', as they called the men who ran the girls offering sexual favours in the streets. Surely Holly wasn't—

'I can see where your mind is roaming, Grace. I can read it on your face and you'd be wrong.'

'Then why don't you stop toying with me and tell me the truth?'

'All right. I think you have a right to know, being so squeaky clean yourself and I gather, promised originally to a policeman.'

Grace gasped. 'You seem to know everything about me.'

Tilly gave her a wry smile. 'When you're in my line of business, it pays to be informed.'

'So . . . Alfie?'

'You're not going to like it.'

'Tell me.' Grace closed her eyes.

'He's been selling cocaine for me.'

Fresh shock coursed through her like a pack of greyhounds moving with graceful speed around the track of her body. Their drumming paws were the escalating sound of her heartbeat, accompanied by Grace silently, inwardly screaming. 'No . . . no, I don't think so,' she faltered, already knowing she was wrong. 'I can't see how.'

Tilly seemed to take pity on her. 'Listen, love. Alfie approached me with a proposal,' she said and then giggled. 'Seems you're both at it. I gather he'd made a promise to you about going straight. I think that because he's not involved in using the snow or peddling it directly to users, he's convinced himself he's somehow still on the right side of it, earning a quid from a distance. His customers come to him, you see. He doesn't look for them – I imagine that eases his soul.' She grinned and there was no warmth in the gesture.

Grace swallowed the lump in her throat. 'But I can't see how he's doing this. Alfie works the barrow and . . .' She stopped talking, thinking it through and finding the answer without any further prompting. 'He's using the barrow?' she finally asked in a small voice.

Tilly nodded. 'Clever little sausage. He sells your confectionery up top to most and sells another sort of treat to a special few from beneath that sweet little skirt he had made up.'

Grace groaned as if she was in physical pain, doubling up slightly before standing and going to the window to breathe out her despair. 'So that's why he needed Holly.'

'No better lookout than my Holly. She can smell a cop a mile off, but she can also sniff out a snow customer with the greatest of ease. She marked and fed him his customers.'

Grace covered her face with her hands. 'I can't believe this.'

'Well, I must say you're behaving calmly. That's impressive. I thought we'd need smelling salts,' Tilly said, cackling a laugh.

'Where do histrionics get you?' Grace said, sliding her hands away, her tone already hardened. It was not really a question, more of a statement of resolve. She moved back to the sofa.

The women eyed one another and Tilly seemed to guess what Grace was thinking. 'I have no reason to lie to you.'

Grace shook her head dejectedly. 'I believe you. I just feel stupid for believing him.'

'I'm not in the habit of defending men, but he meant well, Grace. Look, I like Alfie. He's nicer than so many of the men that I have to deal with across any of my businesses. He's funny and he is sincere in his promises – he just can't keep them. Like the money he owes me. He promised it would be paid, but here I am, poorer for trusting him.'

It was shock upon shock. 'What money?'

'Snow doesn't grow on trees, Gracie girl. Even you surely know that. Well, I suppose it comes from coca, so it's a plant,' she said, laughing with great amusement at her jest. Now she got up, turning to the window to fling it up. 'Holly! Get your arse up here now!'

She called down to where Holly must still be watching at the gate, and Grace felt as though her breath caught with despair to imagine Holly leap as though stung. Soon enough, they heard her footfall on the stairs and a knock at the door before it opened.

'Yes, Mrs Devine?'

'Tell Grace everything.'

Holly blinked.

'Don't play innocent either. I've told her, but she needs to hear it from you. She'll trust it coming from you . . . although I don't know how much she'll trust you after this.'

17

Holly felt especially cautious, like she was a highwire walker she'd seen images of in one of Tilly's American magazines. If she said the wrong thing from Tilly's perspective, the madam would have a nasty punishment waiting; if she said the wrong thing from Grace's perspective, then Holly would be hurting someone she liked enormously, and potentially damaging the future she'd begun to dream about.

While she felt safe and even amused around Alfie – and it was rare to feel secure around a man in her life – she felt ambition and energy around Grace. She liked that she could be herself with Grace and that the grocer's daughter took a genuine interest in her for no other reason than she found her interesting and wanted to help her make something of herself. Other people noticed Holly for far less altruistic reasons; she knew Tilly was only interested in what she could earn from selling Holly's body over and over again.

Grace was offering her a way out from that future, but she didn't know how to navigate this situation. And so Holly balanced herself on the imaginary tightrope and moved gingerly, one careful step at a time, hoping her sharp mind would make the necessary adjustments to guide her safely to the tightrope's end and keep Grace safe too.

Grace sat in an unhappy silence, waiting to hear what Holly had to say. Except Holly had no good news to give, and so she gave Grace the best that she could: honesty. She embellished nothing, telling her everything about the sly operation and made no excuse until her final words, which were from the heart. She hoped Grace could discern this. 'I never meant to hurt you, Grace,' she finished. 'I didn't know you when . . . when all of this was set up.'

Grace looked pale. 'How long has this been going on?'

'Since the barrow began,' Holly answered truthfully.

'So you've both been lying to me since day one in Martin Place.' Grace's body seemed to deflate in disappointment.

Holly looked at her newly scuffed shoes; Grace's father had polished them for her a few days ago. The Fairweather family had been kind to her, and there was the exciting prospect of a new home, a new job, a new way of life in her new future. Holly felt as though her own body was crumpling in tandem with Grace's, and for the first time in years, she wept.

It was a shock to feel the dampness of tears on her cheeks. She had taught herself from early on that crying was wasted energy. It might win sympathy in some circles, but Holly had quickly worked out that she didn't move in the kind of circles where adults took pity on children. In her circle, adults did the reverse; they exploited children because of their age and the power they had over them. And her time for complete exploitation was fast approaching; she had no doubt that Tilly was already putting up Holly's virginity to the highest bidder.

It was hardly going to be some movie idol who put his hand up. No. It would be someone like George Dooley who would heave his fleshy body onto hers and take away the only thing she possessed that was truly hers. She wanted to decide who to give it to.

Unable to stop crying, she sniffed loudly. She was shocked to feel arms around her but wasn't surprised that they belonged to Grace.

'Oh, Holly, come on now. It's done. And I don't blame you. You are a child, and in no position to disobey the adults around you.'

Holly wanted to cry harder. Grace seemed to understand so keenly exactly what was in her mind. She'd managed to quickly cut through all the excuses, all the placations, all the things that adults said and did in order to get someone to do their bidding. Somehow Grace could see that Holly had never had a choice, or a say.

And then she did break down and sob at Grace's next words.

'I forgive you, Holly. None of this is your doing. I promise that nothing has changed between us.'

She felt Grace hold her closer, tighter. No one in her memory had ever hugged her like this. It was a new sensation, a whole new experience, and it was like a fresh well had been struck. Her body began to tremble with despair that she had never had a proper childhood, never had an education other than what the streets had taught her, never felt any affection from the women she lived with, just the leering smiles of drunken or lust-filled men imagining themselves with a young girl. The tears flowed from that new well.

'Oh, how touching this is,' Tilly remarked in a caustic tone. 'Doesn't change the fact I'm owed.'

Holly felt Grace's body stiffen slightly before she released her hold on her and she mourned the loss immediately.

Grace sighed and took some time pulling a small handkerchief from her sleeve before handing it to Holly. 'Here, tidy yourself,' she suggested before turning her attention back to the brothel owner. 'What exactly are you owed? By whom?'

'I'm owed plenty. By your fiancé and by Holly.'

'Alfie owes you for the cocaine – is that what you mean?'

'It is.'

'But he's bringing it,' Holly chimed in, sniffing. 'He's got the money, Mrs Devine. We made up your bundle. He's bringing it over today.'

'I see.' Tilly almost looked disappointed. 'Well, if he doesn't, then I hold you responsible, Holly. You were my . . . how shall we say it? You might have been *his* lookout, but you were *my* little spy in this operation. I needed you there to keep Alfie honest. How much?'

'All of it,' Holly answered crisply. 'It's all there.'

'I heard that ratbag Dooley has been sniffing around.'

'He didn't find anything, miss. I made sure of that.'

Tilly laughed. 'You see, Grace. I've taught her well. Your husband-to-be – if he still qualifies as that – could have been marched off to jail by now for possession, if not for her wits.' She pointed at Holly. 'The fuzz are cracking down hard.'

Holly was glad that Grace wasn't responding, because Tilly loved this sort of confrontation.

Unsatisfied, Tilly pressed her case. 'All right. I'll give him today to bring me my money, but there'll be interest because he's late. I'm not a charity! He should have been here this morning with the money, so I might add ten per cent once we tick past noon,' she said, her mouth forming a mean smirk. 'It's steep, but I'm not in the mood to be taken for a ride.'

They all looked to the clock ticking ominously on a timber mantlepiece over a fireplace. It was just minutes before twelve.

Holly shook her head. 'He doesn't have that extra money, Miss Tilly. You'll break him.'

'I'll find a way for him to earn back what he owes.'

Grace stood abruptly. 'No, this stops here!'

Tilly didn't look bothered in the least by Grace's outburst. 'It stops when I say it stops, and I don't know how Alfie will magic up the ten quid he'll owe me.'

'Ten!' Grace exclaimed.

'Explain it to her, Holly,' Tilly snapped, looking as though she was finding the conversation tedious.

Holly sighed. 'Four pounds for the cocaine, and then Alfie must return the same amount as Tilly's cut, plus an additional pound service fee, making it nine pounds in total to Tilly. Add to that the late fee to make it ten pounds.'

Grace glanced at the clock. It was two minutes to twelve.

'Don't hope he's going to arrive, love. He'll never make it up the road, through the gate and up the stairs in that time,' Tilly assured her.

Holly could sense what was about to occur before Grace even flipped open her clutch bag and withdrew a purse.

'Ten pounds owed. Here.'

It was a fortune in some circles and they all knew it. Tilly hadn't been expecting that, Holly could tell. She'd learned how to read the madam, and if there was one thing she couldn't tolerate, it was being outsmarted . . . especially by another woman. Her long-running feud with Kate Leigh, whose sly grog, cocaine and illegal-betting businesses often crossed swords with Tilly's empire, was legend in Sydney. Neither woman gave quarter. They despised each other. Holly sometimes thought that Kate, when she faced her final judgement, might fare better than Tilly because Kate had a side to her that felt an empathy for the poor. She kept it quiet, but Holly had heard from reliable voices that Kate helped families in need with her ever-increasing wealth.

Grace was from a very different world, but Holly felt proud that she seemed to be holding her own against Tilly.

'Let that be an end to it. If Alfie comes back here asking for drugs or money, you'll know he'd be doing so without my knowing. I will never again pay his debt, so don't hope he has a benefactor. This is the first and the last time I'll cover for him. If he lets me down and comes to you, you can do with him as you please . . . but he won't because he values me more than your vile cocaine and its income.'

Holly watched Tilly blink as Grace held her stare. She wanted to cheer.

'Come on, Holly,' Grace said, picking up her gloves and reaching out her hand.

'Ah, not so fast, Gracie-girl. There's the small matter of my Holly here. You didn't think you were just going to walk off with her, did you?'

'I explained—'

'You explained nothing!' Tilly spat. 'D'you have any idea what I can earn from a young thing like her? Well, do you? I'll tell you – thousands. She's got a whole life ahead of her, being flat on her back and earning for me.'

'Not if I have any say in it,' Grace warned. 'I won't allow it.'

'No? What are you going to do about it?' Tilly looked past Grace's shoulder and Holly's heart sank; she already knew whose cruel shadow would be falling across the doorway behind them. 'Hello, my love. Grace, meet my husband, Jim.'

Grace turned to see a tall, bulky man with a face like a block of cement standing in the doorway. His gaze swam slightly as though he'd been drinking. This had to be the famed Big Jim – a violent bully and underworld figure in this part of town.

Tilly turned to him with a smirk. 'Jim, this is Miss Fairweather. She's come to take Holly away from us.'

'Oh, yeah?' the man grunted. 'Why's that then?'

'Miss Fairweather doesn't think this is the right sort of place for girls to grow up. All the wrong influences,' Tilly said, and Grace could tell she was deliberately winding up her husband to feel aggressive.

Jim turned to stare at Grace and Holly. 'Is that right? You want to leave us, Hols, do you, just when you were becoming interesting?'

Grace felt Holly's hand clutch her own, and she pulled Holly behind her, feeling sure that no one had ever stuck up for her before. The idea gave her courage and she found her voice, forcing the man to look at her and not intimidate Holly. 'This is a child, Mr Devine. And no man is going near her. Maybe I should go straight to the police.'

'I'll break your fuckin' jaw for you, Miss Fairweather, how's that? Then you won't be able to speak.' He gave a cruel laugh.

Holly leapt out from behind Grace. 'You won't touch her, you brute!'

He chuckled again. 'Won't I? I'm not scared of Miss Posh, Holly, coming here like lady of the manor and ordering the peasants about. I had enough of the likes of her when I was a sapper in the war, while her kind did bugger all except give orders and stay well away from the troubles.'

Grace put a hand on Holly's arm to calm her. 'My father fought in the war, sir, and like you, survived. And before you ask, yes, he was on the frontline in northern France. Unlike you, though, he doesn't brag about it; in fact he never mentions it. I think the people who trade off it or hurl accusations probably didn't do quite as much as they claim.'

Somewhere in the deep recesses of her mind, Grace recalled hearing something about this fellow – that he had a history of being reprimanded for shirking his duties in the military. Big Jim entered the room with intent, one meat-like hand clenched into a fist.

'Jimmy, darling, we don't want any trouble,' Tilly cooed. 'Grace here has a sweetheart in the police force who may not take kindly to his girl being roughed up.'

Tilly was smart, Grace saw. Big Jim didn't need to know the claim about Norman was no longer true.

'But I do think we need compensation for earnings lost,' Tilly continued, nodding at Holly.

'Earnings lost?' Grace repeated, appalled.

'You heard her,' Big Jim said, catching on. 'You want that scruff, you pay for her.'

Grace took a breath. She had to save Holly from these people. She swallowed. Her budget was so tight; if she had to pay for Holly too, she didn't know how she'd pay the shop bills – but that was tomorrow's problem, she told herself. Holly was more important.

'She's already covered her fiancé's debt,' Tilly remarked to her husband.

He gave a low whistle. 'Miss Moneybags, eh? Walking around with that sort of money in these parts is dangerous.'

Grace ignored him. Tilly was the boss here, and she knew she needed to be strategic. She might have taken Tilly by surprise once by paying Alfie's debt, but the brothel owner wouldn't fall for that again. Now it would come down to negotiation. She took the lead before Tilly could set the price too high. 'I'll pay you a pound,' she said.

'A pound?' Tilly scoffed as Grace suspected she might. 'You've got cotton wool in your head, girl.'

Big Jim was upon Grace, snatching her clutch bag. He emptied out its contents on the table as Grace and Holly gasped, more in fright than offence. 'No money in here, Tils. She's playing you.'

There was a knock at the open door. It was Eve. 'Mr Devine?' She sounded hesitant but continued. 'A fight's broken out downstairs.'

'Who?'

'Old Ned and Thrasher are having fisticuffs, and the girls are scared.'

'You go on, Jim. Sort it out. Us women have business to discuss,' Tilly said.

Grace was relieved to see Big Jim leave. She was also relieved that she'd tucked the last of her savings safely underneath her clothes; she only had it with her because she had been going to pay for the elegant till that had been installed at the shop and the last payment on the cabinetry after her visit to Tilly. It had been a precaution while she was up in the east, where pickpockets and thieves were rife. She had a five-pound note tucked in one cup of her brassiere and three pound notes in the other. She was not going to give up more than she had to.

Tilly returned her attention to the bargaining. 'I'm not taking anything less than eight pounds for this girl. That's only a few quid more than I paid for her, and she's finally become useful. I need something for my trouble.'

'She's not yours to sell, Tilly. I will speak to the police if we don't settle this amicably. Now, I'm prepared to pay something to compensate you, as you say, for the loss of a member of staff. But eight pounds is a fortune and you know it.' Before Tilly could respond, she added, 'And I don't want to hear about your potential earnings again. She's underage, and she is protected by the authorities from the harm of adults . . . in theory anyway. You know you're breaking the law, and I would suggest you don't need that kind of attention here.' Grace took a deep breath, giving Holly a tiny nod to assure her that she was serious. 'I will give you four pounds and that's my final offer. It's not to buy Holly. It is simply to make it easy for you to let Holly go, so she can be a member of my staff . . . and my family. I plan to formally adopt her, if that's what Holly wants.'

Holly gasped as Tilly took in Grace's words. 'My, my, Holly. You've certainly made the right impression with this one. I could regret ever giving you to Alfie Sweeting.'

'Four pounds, Tilly.'

Tilly regarded her coolly.

Hold her gaze, Grace pleaded with herself. *If you so much as blink right now she'll have you.*

'Five and you can have her!' Tilly snapped as if she no longer cared.

Grace hadn't realised she was holding her breath and couldn't show how much she needed to release it. She let the air in her lungs out slowly. 'All right, five. And I never wish to see you, your husband or indeed any of the women associated with this brothel around Holly again.'

'You'll miss us, Holly,' Tilly sneered. 'She'll have you in a corset and kneeling at Sunday school before you know it.'

Grace turned slightly away and dragged the five pounds from within her clothing, winning mocking applause from Tilly.

'Actually, Grace, you should come and work for me.'

'I'd sooner die,' Grace remarked without heat. 'Here's your money.' She put it on the table between them, not wishing to even risk touching Tilly. 'Right, Holly, fetch your things.'

'I don't have anything,' Holly admitted.

Grace took her hand and made for the door. 'Then let's go.'

'Nice doing business with you, Grace. My regards to Alfie, eh?'

Grace swung back. 'I'll tell you what, Tilly. If you refuse to do any business with Alfie in future, no matter how much he pleads, I'll make it worth your while.'

'Oh, yes? You going to pull a hundred pounds from next to your tits, are you?'

Grace smiled and made sure it was condescending. 'No. But I will supply your girls with sweets every week. It will be a gift from you, though – might earn you some favour. I'll have a box delivered to you every Friday, regular as the GPO clock. You can share them out however you choose. But if you break faith with me, I'll find a way to bring pain to your brothel operation through my connections with the police.' It was an empty threat, but Tilly didn't know that.

However, it seemed Tilly wasn't pondering the threat at all, but was curiously charmed by the idea of free sweets for her girls. She smiled – the first genuine gesture that Grace had seen from her. 'You have a deal. Let's shake.'

'No need. I trust you to keep your promise, as I will keep mine. Your first delivery will be next Friday.'

She and Holly left to the sound of Tilly laughing, walking tall and ignoring the fact that Big Jim was belting some poor bloke to his knees on the front verandah of the terrace house. Grace held Holly's hand tight and vowed she would never come to this part of Sydney again.

18

Alfie had indeed been on his way to pay his dues to Tilly. He'd left his digs at the laundry far earlier than he knew he needed to, but he had been too excited to sleep. Later that week, just in time for the afternoon outpouring of office workers into the sunlight, the Sugar Palace would open its doors for the first time.

If someone had asked him how he felt, he was sure he would struggle to find the words to describe the electricity that was tracing through him. Thinking about it, he decided it was like the sudden explosion of crackling energy that sparked from the trams as they lumbered their way up and down Pitt Street. Blue lightning that suddenly erupted and glowed brightly; that's how it felt. He was glowing with an internal energy that they were fulfilling a dream. Even better – a dream that meant he would marry Grace soon after.

It was hard to believe, he thought, but also somehow delicious to keep pressing in on the idea that just six months ago he'd been feeling so down at heel and like there was no hope in his life, nothing positive that gave him a sense of purpose.

But then he'd met Grace. And everything changed.

Suddenly he was a businessman. He was in love, contemplating settling down into married life and the notion of having his own home and children to populate it – their laughter to become its music – and, yes, reaching even further towards potential high income and the lifestyle of a wealthy businessman and entrepreneur.

It was all crowding in his mind pleasantly, like a seductive drug, lulling him into a careless rhythm in which he was no longer paying attention to anything around him.

His step was sure, even jaunty. His mistake, perhaps, had been to enjoy the look of the fine day and to walk rather than hop onto the electric tram or perhaps be faced with delays on one of the private buses. They, together with the horse-drawn cabs and the escalating number of automobiles, meant traffic had become frustrating lately. But for an able person who knew which route to take, it was much easier to simply stride out, cutting through less-congested streets.

He was now fully lost in his thoughts, navigating by memory while he chewed over the success of the barrow as a promotional tool. It had been his idea and he felt he'd proved to Grace that he was worthy of her; they had not only made very good money from the sales, but the new shop's name was being talked about. His latest idea was to run an advertisement in the morning paper for opening week but, better still, it occurred to him as he strolled towards Woolloomooloo, he should simply contact the editor and ask him to send a reporter to see what Grace Fairweather was achieving with some grit and imagination. A young woman opening her own shop . . . She was such a positive story, and with the Sydney Harbour Bridge very much underway with each passing week of clamouring work, Sydneysiders were enjoying all the optimism for their city. Grace was part of that happy development, and a story would be read by many and drive sales even harder.

As he made the mental note to pay the *Sydney Morning Herald* a visit, he was vaguely aware of having left the Archibald Memorial Fountain behind. He was walking down one of the paths towards the Anzac Memorial with the bandstand in his sights. Time to turn off and rejoin Macquarie Street to skirt around the cathedral. It was a cool morning, so there were some passers-by, but the park would be jam-packed with weekend strollers by lunchtime. Right now everyone was either having a lie in or at church.

As he instinctively veered in the direction of Woolloomooloo, he was suddenly shifted off balance and shoved towards a park bench beneath a sprawling fig that cast shadows around him, providing a welcome dimness for the murky figures that had man-handled him.

While it was no surprise – despite the shock of being accosted – to see the pockmarked face of George Dooley sneering at him, it was fear that now gripped him. He felt like every muscle in his body was clenched. Was it a beating he was in for? Was it another set of nasty threats? Or . . . he thought with a sinking heart, was it theft? How could they know?

'Alfie,' Dooley said casually, as though greeting an old friend. 'How coincidental to find you here.'

'Is it a coincidence, Mr Dooley?' Alfie asked, standing and straightening himself. He'd decided he wouldn't quake in front of Dooley; he'd be like Grace or even Holly, who would, even in the face of failure, fight back. This felt like Sabini all over again. Dooley had none of the gangster's charm but the end result would be the same – Alfie was about to lose something. *Then fight back*, he heard Grace and Holly say in his mind, as though they were standing beside him.

'Ooh, so cocksure now, aren't you, Alfie?' Dooley taunted him. He had the swagger of a man with back-up, and Alfie felt immediately unnerved but knew he mustn't show it.

212

Alfie tipped his head in a 'go ahead' gesture and one of his goons shoved Alfie roughly back onto the bench.

From his newly seated position, he tried to sound calm, if not defiant, despite his reeling fear. 'No, Mr Dooley. I'd like to think that we were both simply out for a stroll, but somehow the presence of your sidekicks tells me you've been following me.'

'Not following you, lad,' Dooley said, still sounding relaxed.

'Waiting for me, then?' Alfie offered, sounding far cockier than he felt.

Dooley smiled and the scar on his cheek lifted ominously in amusement. 'Perhaps. Actually, you're right. The lads followed you. I'm the one doing the waiting.'

'Why are you waiting for me, Mr Dooley?'

'Because you've tested my patience, Alfie. And now I'm angry.'

Alfie held up his palms. 'How can I help you?'

'Ah, now, you see, I like this more cooperative attitude,' Dooley said.

Alfie tried not to let his gaze dart too obviously sideways, but Dooley missed nothing.

'There's no getaway from us, lad. I can hear the cogs of your mind turning. And there's hardly anyone around at this time . . . just in case you were hoping to yell for help.'

'I wasn't thinking either of those things, Mr Dooley,' Alfie lied. 'I just want to know how I can help and then be on my way.'

'Good. Me and the lads here haven't had any breakfast, so we're keen to be moving too.'

Alfie waited. He sensed they'd reached the crossroads of the conversation, and it would no longer remain affable or even vaguely friendly from here. It was pretty obvious what Dooley was after, but he simply couldn't work out, no matter how hard he racked his mind, how Dooley knew he was carrying the money for Tilly. Well, he wouldn't offer it. They'd have to mug him properly.

He kept his silence until Dooley sighed. 'Hand it over, Alfie.'

'What, Mr Dooley?'

'The cash.'

'What cash? I don't—'

It sounded like a clap of thunder at his ear and it took a moment to realise he was on the ground, on his knees. He'd been hit from the side – a box to the side of the head. Alfie immediately put his hand over his right ear in response to the sudden acute pain.

'I didn't want to have to rough you up, Alfie, but I'd rather hurry this bastard thing up and go get my breakfast.' Dooley was crouching over him like a huge dog about to pounce, his voice coming from far away.

To Alfie it sounded like his brother's voice when they were little and talking around corners using old tins and a length of string. Pulling his hand away from his ear, he saw it was stained a shiny scarlet.

'Oh, that's a shame,' he heard Dooley say distantly. 'Looks like you've burst your eardrum. Now, do you want to help me out or do you want this gentleman here to burst the other eardrum for you? You can go deaf with that, you know.'

'It's in my jacket pocket,' Alfie said, unable to hide his pain or sorrow.

'No, you have to give it to me, Alfie, or otherwise that could be considered stealing,' Dooley said cheerfully. 'Get him up, lads.'

As Alfie was hauled to his feet, he managed to bear his own weight but he felt disoriented and unsteady.

'Now you reach into your pocket, Alfie, and get the money out that you earned through illegal racketeering.' Dooley held up a pudgy finger to Alfie's face. 'And before you think of denying it, lad, I know you've been working with Tilly Devine, selling her cocaine. I know you used your barrow and that little brat of hers to find customers, but I just don't know how you concealed the snow from me.'

'Perhaps he hid it in the sherbet, Mr Dooley?' one of the thugs to his left remarked.

'Oh my, then your pretty fiancée's customers are going to get quite the surprise when they dip in their lollipops, eh, Alfie boy?' Dooley said, enjoying himself. 'Now, hurry up, lad. Get the money out or my friend here will belt you again.'

Alfie's ear was paining him so much, he couldn't risk losing the other ear. He reluctantly slipped his hand into his jacket pocket and pulled out an envelope.

'Ah, there we go, boys. Now he's cooperating. I need you to give it to me, Alfie, so these gents can witness that you've handed it over willingly.'

'I don't do so willingly, Mr Dooley, but here it is.' He made a show of offering it so that he didn't earn himself another clout for his objection.

'Thank you, Alfie.' Dooley opened the envelope and riffled through the contents. He gave a sigh. 'Not as much as I'd hoped, son. Where's the rest?' He looked up from the grubby notes.

Alfie managed a shrug. 'It's all I have – that's from the sale of Tilly's cocaine. Grace keeps rigid accounting for the confectionery barrow, and I've already delivered Friday's takings to her. She would have taken it straight to the bank.'

Dooley fixed him with a hard gaze. 'I see. But this is a pittance.'

'Not really, Mr Dooley. That's nearly four pounds.' Alfie gave a whistle. 'And some of that is supposed to be mine.'

Dooley laughed. 'Well, it's mine now.'

'What am I supposed to say to Tilly?'

'I don't care what you say. But she'll learn a lesson about working with little people like you.' Dooley took a deep breath, hesitating. 'Are you sure this is all of it, Alfie boy?'

Alfie did a rapid, silent calculation within a couple of heartbeats. It was a risk, but he took it. 'Yes, sir. We sold each twist for a shilling.'

'I thought the going rate was much higher for the pinch size you'd be selling.'

'It was cut with boracic acid,' Alfie lied.

Dooley raised his brows. 'I wasn't aware Tilly cut her cocaine.'

Alfie shrugged. 'I can't say for sure. A customer mentioned he thought it was cut and I didn't want to risk word getting around, so I dropped the price.' He decided to press his luck. 'We didn't have a very good last couple of days, Mr Dooley. You interrupted us and Holly got scared and turned away customers, in fact.' It sounded plausible but would Dooley buy it? 'Tilly's already not going to be happy about that. I doubt she'd take kindly to knowing you took her money.'

Alfie watched Dooley's fist grab his shirtfront and drag him forward until he could look up the man's nostrils. 'I *didn't* take your money. You gave it to me.'

'But I don't know what to tell her.'

'That you owed it and used it to pay your debt. If I find out you've told Tilly Devine anything, I'll hurt your sweetheart.'

Alfie gave another shrug. 'I was going to tell her that you got in our way of sales, but now she'll come after me. This isn't fair, Mr Dooley. I don't owe you.'

'Oh, tell someone who cares, Sweeting, you pathetic runt. If you don't like the danger, stop playing with the big boys, eh? If you're going to walk around with money bursting in your jacket, take some minders with you.'

Dooley shoved Alfie so that he stumbled backwards. No one bothered to break his fall. He fell into the bench, first skinning his shins and then bruising himself as he landed.

Alfie looked up at Dooley. 'And you're not troubled by taking from Tilly Devine?'

A flicker of fear crossed the man's face, just a flash and then it was gone, dissolving back into Dooley's usual lizard stare. 'I would deny such a thing. And besides, I haven't taken anything from Tilly. I have accepted payment from you.'

Alfie pulled himself painfully to his feet. The ache in his ear had settled in and instinctively he knew he needed to shield that side of his face from wind. In that moment he thought of his mother, who would have warmed some oil and poured it into his ear, then stuffed it with cotton wool or a clean piece of rag to keep the air out. He knew now that the home remedy was used to keep infection at bay, and he was already running that risk.

'I'd better go, Mr Dooley. I'm not feeling well.'

The three men laughed.

'Off you go then, lad,' Dooley replied. 'And remember, if you need a loan, you know who to come to.'

Their amusement intensified and Alfie limped away. Despite the pain, he felt a small surge of triumph that he'd tricked George Dooley yet again. The man might be tall and mean, using brawn to get his way, but it was no match for intelligence.

Once he was sure he was not being followed, Alfie reached into a special flap he'd had sewn into his trousers, just beneath the belt that hung in the small of his back. Inside that cunning pocket was the bulk of the drug money. He'd have to get that to Tilly as soon as he could and first hope she'd forgive the lateness – he'd offer to pay a surcharge for his tardiness – and second, work out how to make up the shortfall within a few hours.

———

It was Holly who found him, shivering with fever in the basement of the laundry. He woke to her worried expression and frantic ministrations as she tried to tip water into his mouth.

'Holly,' he croaked.

217

Her relief at his consciousness was palpable. 'Try and sit up, Alfie. You must drink.'

He managed to lift up onto his elbows, sipping obediently.

'What happened?' she asked, turning his face to see his ear. It had been bleeding.

He shook his head helplessly and kept drinking, like a man who had just crawled from the desert.

'Dooley?' she pressed. At his nod, Holly groaned. 'I'm going to get that bastard.'

Alfie gripped her wrist. 'You go nowhere near him, Hols, and watch your language. You're a shop assistant now.'

She smiled. 'Did he get it all? Did you do as I said?'

'He only got a portion.' Alfie closed his eyes for a moment in relief.

When he opened them, he saw Holly nodding with a satisfied expression, and it struck him once again that he was dealing with a far wiser being than he had been at her age. Back then he was simply cocky, fast and smart thinking. But Holly had imagination; she was creative with her smarts, able to adapt and make an informed and wise decision about whatever situation she was presented with. It was Holly who had sounded the warning about Dooley.

Alfie recalled how he'd smirked when she'd first broached the subject of taking special measures. 'He'd have to catch me.'

'Don't be mad. He'll simply have you followed.'

'But why?' Alfie had asked.

'Because he smells a rat. And being a rat himself, he wants in on the action.'

Alfie had pulled a face of disbelief but Holly hadn't let up.

'No, you've got to listen to me. It costs you nothing to take precautions.'

'What sort of precautions? Tiptoe around in the dead of night, looking over my shoulder?'

'No. Split the takings.' At his frown she'd explained. 'Have some in your jacket, the obvious spot, but hide the bulk down your trousers. If he gets you and you have to hand over the money, he'll believe that's all there is and won't look for more because he knows he's jumped you.'

Alfie had smiled. 'All right.'

'If he takes you by surprise, act scared, take the beating, protest, carry on, but hand over the small amount and have a story ready for why that's all you have. Make it convincing – then get away. At least you'll save the bulk of the money.'

Even though it cost him some pain, Alfie now leaned forward and kissed Holly's cheek. 'You saved me plenty.'

'Good. So how badly hurt are you?'

'I ache but I'll heal. But it's the ear. I don't feel right.'

'Let's call Grace.'

'No, she must never know.'

Holly gave him a sad smile. 'Too late. She's waiting upstairs.'

———————

Within an hour Alfie was lying in a comfortable cot in Grace's room. Even her mother, despite pinched lips, had not protested as Grace's father helped Alfie up the stairs.

'Who did this?' Hugh looked appalled.

'We don't know, Dad,' Grace lied; Holly had told her who had injured Alfie. 'He was mugged in Hyde Park.'

'What was he doing there?' her mother asked, sounding aghast.

Grace knew she'd walked herself into a trap by trying to stick to the truth. Holly rescued her.

'He'd gone to buy Grace some flowers, he told me,' Holly said. 'There's a flower seller who has a barrow by the bandstand – do you know him?'

Hugh straightened from helping lay Alfie down. 'I'm sure we've seen him . . . probably, yes.' He frowned and Grace understood that Holly had counted on this uncertainty.

Holly nodded enthusiastically. 'He has the best roses in Sydney. They seem to last the longest,' she added.

'And no one saw this happen?'

Grace shrugged. 'I have no idea. Holly found Alfie at the laundry in this state.'

'I think we need the doctor,' Hugh said, sounding worried. 'He's clearly feverish.'

'Right,' Mary said and Grace recognised the tone of her mother taking control. 'What's the time?' Mary checked her wristwatch. 'Grace, go and fetch Dr Weatherall. Holly, you go to the cabinet in our kitchen – the one with the drawers – and get me lint and dressings, antiseptic and witch hazel. Hugh, once the doctor has seen him, you can help me to remove Alfie's clothing and get him into a pair of your pyjamas. Oh and, Grace, you'd better take some money and get a boiling fowl. We need to make up a soup that will help with any infection and get his fever down. Take money from the till and let me know how much so I can replace it.'

There was a moment's pause while everyone regarded each other.

'Well, get on,' Mary said. 'This boy needs help.'

And no more was said about what had happened, only that they needed to get Alfie well for opening day.

———

Grace had plenty to say, of course, but she held her tongue until she could be alone with Alfie, waiting until her parents had to go to the bank together.

'You'll be all right?' Mary said, eyeing Grace and Alfie, who was now out of bed and limping around, his bruises bright but covered by a pair of Hugh's pyjamas. George Dooley had made sure the blows had been struck with cunning.

'Of course,' Grace said to her mother. 'The shop will be closed for most of the time you're away.'

'Right, well, I imagine you have plenty to talk about.' Her father winked. 'Back soon. Come on, my love.' He led Mary out of the room.

'Where's Holly?' Alfie asked. He sounded nervous and Grace could guess why.

'I sent her on an errand.'

'Deliberately?'

'Yes.' Grace kept her voice in check, even though she wanted to scream at him.

'I'd like to think it's so we can sneak a kiss,' he tried, with a hint of his usual cheeky grin.

Grace made sure her expression didn't change as she knew he might hope. 'You'd be wrong.'

He gave a silent nod of resignation.

'I've not pressed you, Alfie, because you were so hurt and I've shielded you from my parents' questions, but now I need to know what actually happened – and please don't tell me the story about the flower barrow. Holly has already confessed that that was a quick but effective lie to get my parents off your back. She and I have made a pact never to lie to each other, and I'd like to think that you and I share a similar, unspoken pact.'

'We do.'

'Then tell me what happened.'

Alfie hesitated, and Grace decided to take away any dilemma about truth-telling he might be experiencing. 'Not only being in business together, Alfie, but us getting married depends on your honesty now.'

He told her everything; it spilled out of him as though it was being carried by a channel of relief.

'Cocaine,' she spluttered, her mouth full of bitterness. 'What were you thinking, Alfie?'

He hung his head in despair. 'I want to marry you, Grace, and the only way I could do that was to make the business a success. And the only way that could happen was for me to pay my fair share.'

'Are you blaming me?' she began, a tone of high disbelief in her voice. 'The barrow was enough. I wanted no more from you.'

'No, no, I'm not blaming you. I just wanted to provide the money fast, and while the barrow was a good idea, it wasn't going to happen quick enough.'

'What's another month or two?' she asked, shaking her head.

He shrugged, his eyes full of pain. 'I just wanted to impress you. I've got so little to offer you except my street smarts. I wanted you to stop working here, and to start building your new empire of sweet shops.'

'So you took the shortcut – and not just any old shortcut, but one that reflects on me and my parents, our good name.' Grace wasn't going to let him off that easily. 'Did you even consider for one moment what a catastrophe this would be for my family should it go wrong? How dangerous it would be for us?'

Looking crestfallen, he muttered the most obvious words: 'I'm sorry.'

She gave a growl of despair. 'I'm sure you are. It's easy to be sorry after the fact. But Alfie, selling drugs has just let horrible Dooley back in. And if Dooley's around it means you owe money.'

'I don't owe money.' Alfie paused. 'Well, I do now because he's stolen it.' He shook his head. 'But I can make it right. I don't understand, to be honest, why someone hasn't come looking for it.'

'That someone being Tilly Devine or one of her sidekicks?'

Alfie looked ashamed now. 'Yes. I don't want her coming here.'

'Tilly doesn't leave her dens in the east, you know that. She sends in muscle wherever it's needed.' Grace's tone was scathing. 'She's got plenty of people to do her dirty work.'

'We've got to warn your parents. You probably need to—'

'Tilly will not be sending anyone,' Grace said, cutting cleanly across his warning.

He blinked in surprise. 'How can you know? Has Holly heard something?'

'I have dealt with the situation.'

'I don't understand,' he said, frowning deeply.

'I've paid your dues.' Grace spoke with a tone cold enough to chill the space around them.

He stared back at her dumbly. Finally he spoke. 'What do you mean?'

She gave a slightly mocking laugh. She didn't like its sound in her throat, hating to become cynical – especially about him. In that moment she promised herself she would never take that line. Her mother did regularly, claiming it was simply because she was real-istic. But Grace wanted her love for Alfie to remain untarnished by suspicion or always presuming the worst of him.

So she took a breath, turned her tone neutral and explained. 'I paid a visit to Tilly Devine and settled the full amount of what you owed her.'

'What?' He sounded shocked and she understood why. 'Wait . . . how did you know about it in the first place?'

'Dooley told me his suspicions, and while I hated having to admit he was probably right, I figured he was because of Holly. Her suddenly turning up with you and being such a canny sidekick all fell into place. I don't blame her, Alfie. She might act worldly but she's still a scared child, simply doing what older, bigger, brutish people force her to do.'

'I'm no brute.'

'But you've allowed her to become part of your game. How are you any different to Dooley?'

That shocked him. 'How can you compare me to him? He's a bully, using his fists to get what he wants.'

'And you use Holly's adoration to do for you what others have to coerce. I have no doubt that Tilly insisted Holly work alongside you like a spy, but what she didn't count on was Holly being so enamoured of you . . . or the chance for a different life.'

Alfie paled immediately, as the truth of Grace's accusation hit home.

'I have told Tilly that if you ever go sniffing around her again, she has my permission to do with you whatever she chooses.' She paused to meet his gaze, shocking herself with her coldness. 'Make no mistake now, Alfie, you're on notice. I can't deny my love for you and that's why I did what I did, but I won't make a fool of myself again and I will not compromise my life for your weaknesses. If you don't think you can lead a clean life in honest trade and keep your promise to me, then we should agree to part ways.' Had she really just said that? It had come out on the gallop of her anger before she could hold the words back.

He took a step forward to placate her but she held up her palms, forbidding him.

'No, this needs to be said and agreed upon. I will not tolerate you risking our shop – our lives. I saw Tilly's hideous husband beating up some poor man on the verandah as though it was the most normal thing in the world. And he grinned at me as he did so.'

Alfie nodded miserably. She could tell he knew exactly what she meant.

'These people exist in a different world to mine. And I think you straddle it somewhere, Alfie. But if you want a life with me, you have to choose. You can no longer live on the edge of the law, laughing off your pursuers because you're smarter or quicker than them. They'll catch up with you – lies and deceit always do. Right now, your slate is clean – you owe nothing. So you must choose: my way or . . .' Grace shrugged, not knowing how to word the alternative. She looked down, feeling the pain of her decision like a bruise. 'Or please just leave my life. It will hurt to lose you, but it will be best for both of us in the long run. We can both avoid inevitable pain.'

Alfie looked panicked. 'I am not losing you, Grace,' he said, emphatic. 'I won't let you down. I was going to stop anyway. All I wanted to do was make enough money to pay my part and then I was done. I was going fully straight.'

'Well, keep what you have. You can pay it back to me in other ways . . . with trust. I'm handing over my trust completely by keeping faith with you. It's only you who can shatter the trust I've given you.'

'I'll never let you down again, Grace.'

Her mother's voice whispered in her mind. *You're so gullible.* But she ignored it and stepped into his open arms.

19

May 1925

Opening day approached. There was no further mention of Alfie's mugging; the Fairweathers seemed to grasp that Grace wanted to remain focused on the big event that loomed ahead of her. Alfie had lost money, that much was sure, but they had accepted the explanation of him being mugged and had made all the right tsking noises and offered him sympathy as he recovered. His hearing, the doctor said, would take time to return, although Alfie had told them it was already a little better than he'd expected it might be.

Even Norman had heard about it; he called in to see Grace at a time when her father was busy with customers and her mother, Holly and Alfie were up at the new shop decorating it to Grace's specifications, while she continued cooking supplies to stock it. He'd either chosen his time fortuitously, or he'd deliberately waited until he was sure he could speak with her alone. Nevertheless, he asked the obvious polite query. 'Is Sweeting around?'

'Why?' Grace replied, guessing the question was hollow.

'I've heard what happened to him. I thought I might speak to him about it.'

She had never pegged Norman as a liar, so perhaps he was genuine in having missed Alfie. 'Word gets around fast.'

'No, your parents told me. They're concerned that this sort of thing could happen so close to home.'

She looked back at him, slightly quizzical. 'Hyde Park is not that close.'

Norman shrugged, looking tall and imposing in his uniform. 'Even so,' he said, as if that explained it.

'Well, I'm sorry, but Alfie is at the store in the Queen Victoria Building, helping to get it ready. We open this week.'

Norman nodded. 'Congratulations, Grace.' At the look she cut him, he opened his palms defensively. 'No, I mean it. I really do think you're amazing the way you've followed through on your dreams.'

She frowned. 'How can you mean that? You likely wouldn't have let me do half of it when we were only engaged.'

'I do mean it,' he said quickly, sounding sincere and suddenly melancholy. 'I've given it a lot of thought since we ended our engagement, and I've come to the conclusion that I am perhaps too old-fashioned in my views. I've paid a terrible price for not waking up sooner and noticing that women are doing lots on their own and for themselves these days.'

Grace was stunned, and felt obliged to jest to cover her reaction. 'Tilly Devine and Kate Leigh, for instance,' she interjected with a sneer.

'Oh, the law will catch up with them one day. They think they're very smart, but their kind can't last.'

Grace was intrigued. 'Do you mean that?'

'I do. We'll get more manpower; it's already happening. We'll get smarter about how we deal with those lawbreakers. I have no doubt that committed policemen like myself will begin to outwit them at their own game. The drug sellers, sly grog people, the thieves, muggers and brothel owners . . . they actually believe they're above the law. And so they get cocky – and sloppy.' He shrugged. 'People like me will be waiting when they do.'

'I hope so, Norman. That's reassuring. It's bad for our growing city to have all this crime controlling so many people's lives.' Grace reached for a jug and poured several hefty slugs of cream into the sugar she had cooked down to liquid toffee.

Norman watched her with interest. 'That smells delicious. What are you making?'

'Chewy caramels.' She grinned. 'I make them in extra-large individual squares so we can sell them separately. You only need one. I'll be wrapping these up in greased papers we've already cut.' She nodded towards the sideboard, where a pile of square papers sat beneath a large pair of scissors.

'You sell them individually?'

'Yes, well, they're good value and it encourages people to try them, love them, come back for more. Also it makes it affordable for anyone to treat themselves or their family. A working mother could buy half-a-dozen for a couple of pennies and treat her children, but not have to buy a whole box or bag, which might be too extravagant.'

'Hmm, clever. Did your fiancé get badly hurt?' It seemed to pain Norman to call Alfie that, and it was obvious he wasn't yet ready to let the topic go, even though she thought she'd steered him away from it.

'He was hurt, yes, but his pride hurt more probably,' she admitted.

'So long as you don't get hurt in the process, Grace.' Norman's gaze softened upon her.

It was an odd remark to make. She hadn't been involved, so her old flame was likely referring to life in general with Alfie. 'Don't, Norman.'

He held up his hands, opening his palms to her. 'What? Can't I be concerned for you?'

'As my former fiancé, a friend or as a policeman?'

He shrugged. 'All three.'

She gave a gentle twitch of her lips – not quite a smile, but a gesture that said she felt flattered. She continued stirring the caramel bubbling on the stove, incorporating the cream she'd tipped in. She had it over a low flame, as she couldn't risk burning this caramel, but she wished she could speed up the process and get away from Norman's regard. 'I appreciate your consideration, and it's certainly handy to have a policeman as a friend. I hope that never changes . . . Our friendship, I mean. I'm glad we can both be adult about what happened between us. It was never—'

He took a step forward and she was pleased she didn't flinch. He looked like he wanted to touch her, to take her hand, perhaps, but she felt grateful she had a linen towel in one, wrapped around her iron pan, and a ladle in another, with which she was relentlessly stirring the caramel.

'I regret losing you, Grace. I miss you and I realise I made the biggest mistake of my life in letting you leave me.'

She did smile now, desperate to show that she did not hold any grudges and kept stirring as she spoke – the caramel was getting close. 'But Norm, you didn't let me leave. Let's be honest. You were always enthusiastic about our union,' she said kindly. 'It was me who broke our engagement. I let *you* down. You are not to blame yourself. I was the dissatisfied one and it wasn't about you, I promise. It's me! It was always about my need to have some independence and not be rushed into motherhood or being the good wife. Most women would be glad to have a good man, a good home, a nice life ahead of being a wife and mother.' Time had softened her feelings towards Norm.

Norm looked faintly pleased by this admission, but slightly puzzled too. 'So Sweeting doesn't expect this?'

'Expect? No. He wants it, of course he does. He adores the idea of us having a family together, but just as importantly, he wants my happiness. He could see when we first met how determined I was – how determined I am – to build something of my own first. I want to leave my mark, Norman. I don't want to leave my parents' house and their supervision just to step into another house of duty and supervision.'

'Is that how marrying me felt?'

She nodded. There was no point holding back any more.

'I'm sorry, Grace.'

She quickly reached for a small brick of butter she had already weighed and slipped it carefully into the bubbling brew, stirring vigorously. 'No more apologies, Norman. As you say, you're traditional. There are so many women who would love that about you. It makes them feel secure.'

He gave a shrug. 'There is no one else for me.'

She deflated before him, wishing he wouldn't do this to her. 'Oh, Norman, please don't make me feel guilty for being honest. I was looking out for both of us, saving us potential unhappiness.'

'Did you ever love me, Grace?'

The question was unexpected and so she had no ready answer. As she hesitated, she watched the sorrow seep into his eyes. 'I thought I did,' she said, trying to lessen the blow. 'I'd stepped out for dates, but you were special, Norman. You always made me feel safe, but then that protective manner tipped into something else . . . something that was controlling and . . .' She didn't want to say it.

'And what?' He frowned. When she didn't reply, he reached out to touch her arm. 'And what, Grace?'

She moved away and took the caramel off the stove. 'I've got to work with this now. Caramel doesn't wait.'

'Tell me . . . please.'

Grace sighed. She was hoping to avoid this, but she really was at a critical point in her confection. She stirred the caramel that was cooling slightly and told the truth. 'I was feeling suffocated and frightened that my life might become a prison. Hand me that square tin, please.'

He did so, grabbing the tin she had already prepared with a lining, but as he turned to her, his gaze looked mortified. 'That was never my intention. I simply wanted to love and provide for you.'

She carefully tipped in the liquid caramel, loving the smell of toffee that now scented the kitchen. She would never tire of it, she thought, and it reminded her of her idea to set up a pot of caramel in the store daily, so her customers would get to experience it too. She'd had the foresight to build a portable gas ring into the back storage area and she was sure that if she simmered caramel on it each day, it would perfume the store with exactly the right smell to encourage people to buy.

Finished pouring, she looked back at Norman. 'I know, but we've come full circle when I say this. Your need to protect and provide would have come at a price for me . . . in you feeling that I shouldn't work, that I should be content with being a housewife and a mother, and that I shouldn't go anywhere alone, or think for myself, or aspire to be anything more. I would have made you miserable.'

'What if I could change?'

He looked earnest as he said this, but she chuckled softly, not unkindly and, using a linen to prevent her hands from being burnt, tapped the tin of caramel on the bench, knocking out any potential bubbles. The batch could now cool and set.

He didn't like her laughing; he frowned now, the soft gaze gone from his handsome face. 'Don't you think you've rushed this engagement with Sweeting?'

She couldn't hide her exasperation. 'Is this a question my mother primed you to ask me?'

'They're worried, Grace.' At least he was honest. 'Their only child . . . I think it's only human of them to want what's best for you.'

'And you know they don't think Alfie is best for me – is that what you're saying?'

'No. Your parents are very supportive of your decisions. First to break our engagement and then to . . . well, to take up with this Sweeting so soon after. Your father made it very clear to me that he wants you to be happy.'

'I *am* happy, Norman. I can understand why you and others may feel it's all happened very suddenly, but where is the rule book that tells us when and how fast we must fall in love?'

He looked back at her blankly as she began to clear away her sticky utensils.

Her voice became a little more strained; she was running out of patience. 'It is quick, I agree. But I knew the moment I met Alfie that he intrigued me. He would tell you that he fell in love with me on sight. I took a little longer to love him, but not much.' She shrugged. 'I can't account for it. I'm not going to make excuses or even try and explain it. Alfie suits me. He makes me laugh, he wants me to be anything I want to be, he wants me to achieve everything I want to try and he is working to make my dream come true. I adore him for that, and I will marry him because, believe it or not, for any of his faults and for all of mine, we are well suited.' She waited a beat and looked pointedly at him. 'I'm not sure that *we* ever were.'

Norman stared at her with glum resignation. 'All right, Grace. But I want you to know this. If he hurts you, I'm coming after him. If he crosses from what's legal into what's not, I'm coming after him. And if he ever lets you down, I'm coming after you. There will never be anyone else for me, no matter how I might kid myself. The point I want to make is that in my own block-headed and short-sighted way, I loved you so much, and now I see more what I allowed to get away. So I'll be here for you. Just remember that.'

She nodded, deeply embarrassed but touched all the same. 'I will.' She went to the sideboard and picked out some of the treats that were ready to go to the store, tipping them into a paper bag. 'Here, take some of our sweets. Come visit, come buy, tell your friends about the Sugar Palace.' She smiled.

He gave her sad smile back, taking the bag. 'I'll think of you as I enjoy them.'

———

That week, her parents, Alfie and Holly worked hard along-side Grace into the small hours cleaning the store, setting up the products and making sure everything looked as inviting as possible by the night before their grand opening. They were all too exhausted to spend long admiring it, however, and Alfie agreed to walk Holly home. Mary had made a makeshift bed in Grace's room that would serve as Holly's permanent sleeping arrangement for the time being, as there were only two bedrooms. Holly didn't seem to mind, though, and Grace acknowledged that it was likely far more comfortable and private than what Holly was used to.

Alfie set off with Holly back to The Rocks, while Grace remained with her parents to lock up. She felt only more love for them, who had welcomed Holly in so graciously, sensing how important she was to their daughter but also that she had no family and needed some.

Her mother put an arm around Grace, so fatigued she was giving long yawns every few minutes. 'Don't admire it yet. Look at it tomorrow when daylight is streaming through those windows,' she said, nodding towards the brown paper still covering the glazing that faced George Street. 'You'll be amazed at how good it is – I know I am.'

'You mean that, don't you?' Grace said with a tired smile.

'With all my heart, child. I want you to enjoy only success. You've dreamed big and made it come true.'

'Well, I suppose it can only come true when there's a busy shop of happy customers.'

Her father moved in between them and hugged both women. 'It's even better than I imagined it would be, Grace. I can't imagine the rent and won't ask, but I'm astonished at your enterprise. We're very proud of you.'

'Alfie's worked hard to make it happen too,' Grace said softly.

'Yes, we can see he has. If he can stay on the straight and narrow, you're both going to set Sydney alight,' her mother assured her, and to Grace those words felt so uplifting that she was sure she was floating as they headed back down George Street to collapse into their pillows just before three.

Grace believed she had slept deeply for a few hours because she awoke in the same position she'd curled up in. Although she knew she needed to rest, she couldn't keep her eyes closed the second she heard the first chortle of the magpies that lived nearby, such was her feeling of anticipation.

Holly stirred soon after. 'Is it time?' she mumbled.

'It is. Come on, let's shower and get you into your uniform.'

Her new staff member dutifully went into the bathroom first, emerging minutes later with damp hair and a helpless smile. 'I couldn't be more excited,' she admitted.

Alfie arrived soon after, looking smart and as excited as Grace. Her parents both came to the door to see them off.

'I hope you have a queue right down George Street,' Hugh said, a proud smile on his face.

'Thanks, Dad,' she said over the top of Alfie's thanks and kissed her father's cheeks.

'We'll be up later.' Her mother smiled. 'We can't wait to see it.'

Grace kissed her mother and stepped back as Mary regarded her fiancé.

'Alfie, we might have set off on the wrong foot, but I know Grace has chosen you, and so her father and I wish you only success. We expect you to look after our girl in every way soon, but for now we just want to know that you'll support her in this new venture.'

Hugh chimed in. 'Sweeting, you have our most important possession – if we dare call her that – so don't you let her down. I know you've worked hard too to bring the Sugar Palace about and you have my admiration as a result. Don't lose it.'

Grace had never heard her father take such a firm tone, but instead of upsetting her, it sent a shiver of pride through her that her parents were so determined in their desire for her to succeed.

Alfie looked humbled. 'I won't let you down, sir.'

'Don't let Grace down,' her mother clarified. 'And then we shall be proud of you both.'

Alfie nodded at Mary and then grinned at Grace. 'Come on. It's past six-thirty and we have loads to do before we open up.'

'By the way, I've paid for an advertisement in today's newspaper,' her father said as they left. He smiled as her mouth dropped open in shock and gave a wink.

'Dad! That must have cost a fortune.'

He shrugged. 'You only have a grand opening once.'

She gave a squeal of pleasure and hugged both of her parents. 'Thank you both.'

'Go on with you. Don't be late for your big day.'

20

It was not yet seven in the morning when Grace, Alfie and Holly stepped into the store.

Grace's mother was right. When they finally tore down the brown paper covering the windows, which had been cleaned the previous day, daylight flooded into the store.

Holly and Alfie fell silent. Grace could sense them holding their breath, watching her as she did a full revolution of the space and then stood in the middle and turned slowly, soaking up this moment. It felt nothing short of magical for her.

She'd done it. They'd done it.

The Sugar Palace was real.

The shop smelled of cooked sugar in all its forms. In one heartbeat she could pick out the fizzy sweetness of sherbet and in the next, she caught the bitter note of toffee apples, which she insisted on having for day one. She closed her eyes and drew in another breath, immediately picking up the cloying sweetness of fudge that stood in a mountain of vanilla and chocolate, some studded with nuts, others with raisins. Grace then opened her eyes to take in the sticks of rock that she called 'sugar canes'; she'd made them in a multitude of colours that she knew would attract children. They were displayed in tall cylinders, and when the light caught them, they threw out rainbow glints.

Fluffy but silken marshmallows wobbled on a tray, while the rose scent of Turkish delight dusted with cornflour scented the air, competing frantically with the tarry aroma of flexible licorice straps, which she had rolled into tight curls, studding each centre with a candy-coated chocolate 'bean'. Orbs of boiled sweets in various colours gleamed in jars, while bullseye lollies of red and white stood alongside a tall jar of pyramid-shaped humbugs, striped in black and white, and another of the traffic-lights gobstoppers she'd designed. All around in vase-like cylinders stood lollipops of every colour she could think of, and the back shelves were filled with boxes – some purple, others yellow – of chocolate-covered treats in dark and milk.

She sighed.

'Happy?' Alfie asked.

'Delirious,' she replied. 'Well done . . . both of you.'

Holly beamed back at her. 'Are you still planning to give away the lollipops?'

'Only to children. Any child who steps across this threshold is allowed to choose one lollipop for free. Adults must pay.'

'Even if they're buying for children?' Holly qualified, looking as though she needed to be certain.

'Yes. We're going to follow through on Alfie's approach when he was running the barrow. We give away to attract new custom. The children who receive our free lollipops will grow up to be our new generation of buyers.'

'Get 'em young, I say,' Alfie said, punching the air and making the girls laugh. 'Joking aside, it's a good idea, Grace. It shows faith in your clients and it's a lovely treat for the kiddies.'

'I agree,' Grace replied. 'Holly, can you please make sure the other girls weigh out all purchases? The customer needs to see it being done properly. And please ensure the girls wash their hands before they move behind the counter. We need good hygiene.'

Holly nodded. 'You can count on me.'

Grace turned to Alfie. 'Are you really going to walk around with that sandwich board?'

'I am. I'm not too proud. Every penny extra you take, darlin', is for us. So I'll do my bit to round up customers.'

'Maybe you could carry a small basket of samples?' Holly wondered and she looked at Grace, slightly anxious at speaking out.

'Great idea,' Grace agreed, and Alfie nodded.

'The more generous we are and the more we give away, the more it returns us business. The more we smile, the more we greet our customers and ask them how their day is going, the more brightness we bring into their lives, the more often they'll come back. It's one of the invisible laws of selling.'

Grace checked her watch and glanced up at the store's clock. They were giving her the same time. 'We open in forty-six minutes. Holly, let's give the counter a final clean down, and I'm making you responsible for the two staff who will be arriving in about thirty minutes, all right? You can brief them. They're your staff essentially.' Grace smiled, and Holly seemed to swell another few inches taller in her new shoes. 'I'll work the till. The new girls are to serve, not handle money.'

Sensing Grace was finished with her instruction, Alfie nudged her. 'When I've done an hour or so with the sandwich board, I want to go and look at some warehouse space.'

'Today? Why?' Grace frowned.

'Because, Grace, my love, this is just the beginning. The tiny kitchen you have down at The Rocks is not going to be big enough to produce what you're going to need here. Mark my words, we'll need to triple our output by the end of the month.'

'Oh, Alfie, I don't—'

He put his hands up to stop her. 'Grace, you need cooking space, you need storage space so we can get ahead with stock, and you need space for the staff you're going to have to train to make your recipes.'

She blinked, half in wonder, half in fear that everything was moving so fast. 'But we've only just begun ... In fact, we're only beginning in thirty-nine minutes,' she said, checking the clock again.

'We have to expand ahead of demand. We can't be caught napping – any sort of merchant is ready with stocks to go. I learned that as a tiny tacker in London. If there's a gap between your supply and the demand, your customers will just go somewhere else. Luring a customer is one job, holding onto that customer as a regular is another task in itself. I'm sure you learned that behind your dad's counter.'

'I suppose,' she said, knowing in her gut he was right, although her father's clients were all from his neighbourhood – they had no other grocer that was as convenient.

'I know what you're thinking – I can almost see your mind turning, darlin'. But believe me, if your father failed to reorder his pails, for instance, and a customer needed one, they aren't going to wait with their bucket and hole for your dad to get new stock. As troublesome as it might be, they're going to walk around and find another store that can sell them a pail immediately – and what's more, they may be prepared to pay more expensively just to have it.'

There was no doubting he was correct. 'Where's the warehouse?'

He grinned. 'It's not too big. It's down at Pyrmont.'

'Set-up costs?' She blew out her cheeks.

'Well, that's what I'm going down there to learn.'

'If we're going to cook down there, then we need to build a kitchen.'

'I understand. Leave it with me to find out. Information is power, Gracie, so they say. Best we know what we're up against, and then we can make decisions. Ah, here comes the first of our staff – nice and early.'

It was the daughter of the landlord.

'I'd better get focused,' Grace said, feeling nervous and excited.

'You do that,' Alfie said and kissed her hard and fast. 'I'm proud of you. You too, Holly.'

Grace watched him leave with his sandwich board, promoting the Sugar Palace.

'Don't forget these,' Holly called, running after him with a small basket she had been busy loading up with samples. Grace could see she had chosen sweets that would not suffer for being transported around.

Grace smiled at their new member of staff, a young woman of about seventeen. She was tall, dressed neatly with freshly washed hair tied back in a ribbon. Perfect. 'Hello again, Sarah.'

The girl nodded, wide-eyed. 'Thank you again for this opportunity, Miss Fairweather. I won't let you down.'

Grace grinned. 'I know you won't, Sarah,' she said, squeezing the nervous girl's wrist. 'Ah, and here comes your other half. Welcome, Lizzie. You remember Sarah?'

The girls smiled at each other as Holly drew alongside Grace.

'And you've all met Holly,' Grace said. 'Holly will be your manager and if you have any queries, check with her. But remember, this is all new, so we're not expecting everything to go fully to clockwork. The main thing is that you don't panic or get yourselves anxious. You've done your training; carefully weigh out the customers' goods so that they can see what they're getting. Always pause when you reach the right weight and glance the customer's way, as I taught. Sometimes they'll just nod, in which case you get on with the sale, or quite often they'll say, "Oh, go on, just a bit more," and that's a method to sell more. Don't overdo it, but you'll be surprised how many will happily let you go over rather than under.'

The girls nodded, glancing with excited tension at each other.

'Keep your uniforms clean, keep your nails tidy and wash your hands constantly. Hair tied back at all times like Sarah's – thank you both for looking so neat today. Don't touch your face and then the product. Be diligent. If you need to sneeze or cough, excuse yourself and come out to the back. There's nothing more off-putting than an assistant with a runny nose or a hacking cough. And remember, smile at everyone. This is a happy day. Customers are coming in here to treat themselves, so spoil them. Never be afraid to let them try something. If they're not sure about the licorice, cut off a generous piece and let them taste it, or cut a piece of fudge in quarters and let them sample both flavours so they can choose which one they prefer.'

The girls liked this idea and grinned wider.

'And even now, I've had a new idea. What do you think, Holly? Shall we give everyone a free toffee with every purchase? I've made loads and it won't keep.'

'We're already giving away free lollipops to children,' Holly pointed out, and went on to quickly explain to the two girls what that meant. Grace was impressed with how succinct and clear Holly was in her instructions. Holly looked back at Grace. 'It's up to you.'

'It's our grand opening – let's be generous.'

'You heard our boss.' Holly grinned. 'So now with each sale, you'll give a toffee as a special thankyou.'

'The most important thing to remember, girls, is that we are trying to make our shop an experience for the customer. What that means is that we must try and help them feel that they're part of the sale. It binds them to the store.'

The girls frowned as Grace moved behind the counter and began to fill a shallow basket with her carefully wrapped toffee oblongs.

'What I want you to do is when you've completed the sale, you should offer this small basket over the counter for the customer to take a toffee, smiling as you do so. Say "Thank you for your custom. I hope you'll tell your friends about us, and that you'll be back soon."'

'In your own words,' Holly added to reassure Lizzie and Sarah. 'That's a great idea. Customers will look forward to that each time they come in.'

'Exactly! And we can vary what they receive and use it to test our products, especially new sweets.'

'Toffees today, chopped up rock tomorrow, perhaps sherbets the next,' Holly said, understanding.

'Yes,' Grace said with a pleased nod. 'Good.' She checked the time once again. 'Nearly showtime.' She grinned. 'Go and change into your new uniforms, girls. Holly will show you. Our doors open in fifteen minutes.'

'There's a small queue already,' Holly said over her shoulder as she led the girls behind the front of the store to change.

'A queue?' Now that Holly had mentioned it, Grace could hear voices outside. 'For us?' she said, filled with disbelief.

'Must be your dad's advertisement,' Holly called. 'I got you a newspaper – on the counter for you.'

Grace ran to it, turning the pages with anticipation until she saw the ad. It wasn't enormous but it was hardly small; no one could miss it. *Grand Opening of the Sugar Palace today!* it exclaimed. And her father had paid for what she knew was called 'spot colour'. The fire-engine red stood out from all the plain black type across both pages; anyone reading the newspaper would have their attention helplessly snagged by the explosion of colour. Her father had used her new branding of a striped red tent in the shape of a fairy-tale castle. It was arresting, as she'd hoped when she had briefed the artist, and she was thrilled with the result. That branding was now on her white packets and on all the boxes they'd use. The girls would be in complementary white pinafores and striped red aprons, with striped ribbons to tie back their hair and an oversized stripey bow at their neck.

Lizzie and Sarah stepped out to a beaming Holly and Grace, who actually clapped, giving a gleeful sound.

'You look marvellous,' she admitted.

It was her turn to feel a few inches taller. Overnight, she'd become an entrepreneur with her own store in Sydney's busiest street, with her own staff and now potentially her own new warehouse and kitchen.

She was filling with pride, and she felt nothing could possibly burst her bubble of joy.

21

The day moved in a blur. When imagining the first day, Grace had pictured herself calmly standing at the back of the shop to watch the proceedings. She was wrong. By half an hour after opening time, the shop was crowded and it was a case of everyone pitching in. Even Alfie didn't have an opportunity to savour the moment as he returned to see the store in frantic motion with Grace, Holly, Sarah and Lizzie at full stretch to cope with demand.

He went out the back to wash his hands, and Grace laughed at the sight of him as he returned; he had taken off his tie and used one of the striped ribbons instead, which looked marvellous against his white shirt.

He quickly pitched in alongside the women and soon hit his stride, using his barrow techniques to draw more sales from the customers. Grace was able to hear him as she busily worked the cash register.

'Madam, don't break my heart,' he said, placing a hand on his chest. 'How can you not want some of these marshmallows that are as silken as a new baby's bottom, as smooth as your complexion and as sweet as you?'

'Oh, go on with you, you smooth talker,' the woman said with a giggle. 'All right, I'll take four of them.'

'You won't regret it.' Alfie winked.

He offered lollipops to another woman who was holding the hands of two children. 'With the thanks of all of us at the Sugar Palace for your custom.'

'Are you sure?' the woman asked. 'I just came in for some peanut brittle for my husband. I, er, I don't have—'

'They're free,' he interrupted, sensing she was worried about having enough money. 'For the kiddies who are standing here so well behaved. Now, how much brittle can I get you?'

To another woman, looking amazed by the green lollipop just handed to her son at no charge, he offered a taste of fudge. Wearing gloves, Alfie handed her a full cube of it before she could even order her sweets purchase.

Grace glanced at the girls with a look that said, *Don't worry, just watch*.

'Now, when you taste that you tell me that doesn't speak to your heart, Mrs . . .?'

'Evans,' she replied obediently.

'Well, Mrs Evans, I think you were looking at some of our chocolate-covered ginger, am I right?'

'Yes.' She blushed. 'My husband loves it.'

'Does he indeed?' Alfie said, his tone filled with innuendo. His risk paid off. The woman and those nearby exploded into laughter. Grace smiled as he pushed his luck. 'Don't tell me your problems, Mrs Evans.'

Now more people were joining in the laughter.

'A quarter, Mrs Evans, or a little more for that insatiable Mr Evans?'

The woman cast her eyes up to the ceiling affectionately. 'Better make it half a pound.'

'Yes, indeed, he needs to keep his strength up.'

Those closest were guffawing, clearly enjoying the naughty but harmless banter.

'I'll just get that ready while you taste your fudge. Go on, don't save it. Enjoying your lollipop, son?' Her boy nodded dutifully. 'I'll be right back.'

When Alfie returned, Mrs Evans was still chewing. Her smile told him she had loved her treat.

'Now, there's your chocolate-covered ginger, and how about some fudge for you, Mrs Evans? Can I wrap up a little for you to take home?'

She blushed, swallowing. 'Why not. I'll take three pieces.'

Knowing he had a captive audience, Alfie pushed a little more. 'If you take five, you'll have a couple of extras just for you as I know your lad here is going to want a piece, right, son?'

The boy nodded again, licking enthusiastically at his lollipop and turning his tongue green.

'Go on then,' she said, smiling again at Alfie's querying look.

Grace moved behind Holly and the girls who had been watching while serving. 'That's called selling up. Try it.'

'I could never do that,' Lizzie said.

'Sure you can,' Holly said, moving behind her to reach for one of the sweet jars. 'Start small . . . Topple a little extra in like I do and then apologise and say, "It's a wee bit over."' She grinned. 'They'll always say it's all right.'

'That's selling up too,' Grace agreed, mightily impressed by how quickly Holly had caught on.

They'd already decided that they'd remain open through the midday break that a lot of shops closed for. Around eleven thirty, during a brief lull, Grace congratulated the girls on their morning's work.

'Well done. Now I need that same energy for the rest of the day.

Why don't you both take a break now? Have you brought some food?'

'I've got a sandwich, miss,' Lizzie said.

'Good. Do call me Grace.' She smiled. 'And Sarah?'

She nodded. 'I've brought something too.'

'Right, well, get out into the fresh air and eat. You can sit at the back, but I'd prefer you to see some sunlight. We can hold the fort here. I'm expecting it to be busier from just after twelve, so you need to rest and be ready for the onslaught. Oh, and try some of the product. There's no point in you selling it without knowing what it tastes like. What do you feel like?'

'Marshmallow for me, er, Grace,' Lizzie said.

'I'd like to try the nut brittle,' Sarah replied.

'Good. Help yourselves and this evening, before you go, you'll take home a small range to sample. By the end of the week I want you to have both tasted everything so you can sell with confidence to your customers, all right?'

They nodded with surprised smiles and went off to get their lunches.

Alfie wandered over, having just finished with a customer and joined them as Grace was asking, 'What about you, Holly?'

'I'm too excited to rest. I started counting the number of customers I served but stopped bothering after fifty.'

'I must have served the same,' Grace admitted. 'And there I was thinking I'd be out the back doing administrative stuff.'

Alfie grinned. 'You're a hit, darlin'.'

'No, Alfie, you're the hit,' Grace replied. 'You're charming everyone.'

Holly laughed. 'You're so naughty, Alfie, but the customers love you.'

He gave a shrug. 'I grew up doing this sort of thing.'

'Second nature, eh?' Grace smiled.

'It all felt so easy,' he said. 'And like you, Holly, I could do it all over again and not feel tired.'

'Well, I think I should break it to you both that we will have to. I can't see it letting up.' Grace didn't want to sound overconfident, but she knew she was telling the truth.

Alfie kissed her cheek. 'It's not going to let up . . . ever. Holly will have to run the second store alone very soon.'

There was a moment's silence and then the three of them shared a comfortable burst of laughter.

'How did you get on with the warehouse?' Grace asked.

She watched Alfie's gaze become ever so slightly hooded. 'I'll tell you all about it later – but it's going to be great,' he said, his voice sounding bright but slightly forced. 'Here comes someone,' he said and before Grace could reply, he was already moving away to hail the customer.

'Good morning . . . or is it good afternoon, sir?' Alfie grinned. 'Come on in, I won't hurry you. I know it can feel a little over-whelming at first with so much to choose from.'

Holly nudged Grace. 'Alfie can handle it out here for a few minutes. I think we should do a stock check so we know what's likely to sell out before the end of the day.'

'Sell out?' Grace couldn't imagine it.

Holly shrugged. 'Your marshmallows won't make five o' clock, and the toffee apples will be lucky to see the big hand hit three.'

Grace grinned but couldn't fully hide her astonishment. 'Good, they're our two perishables.'

'You'll be making more brittle tonight, and those toffees we've been giving away are running low. I think we'll need to triple our quantities next time, to give you some breathing space.'

Grace followed Holly into the back area of the shop. 'Good grief, Holly, I had no idea. Thank you for keeping tabs on everything.'

Holly shrugged. 'One of my jobs at the brothel was to keep numbers in my head.'

'Of what?'

'Everything. Customers, who was with who. Which girl was overworking, who wasn't getting enough trade, that sort of thing.' She blew her cheeks out. 'A bit like Alfie and his banter, it starts to happen without thinking.'

'But you're across a wide range of stock, Holly, most of which you haven't handled personally. I don't know how you do it.'

The girl smiled. 'I don't either, Grace. I've always been like this.'

'Counting, you mean?'

Holly nodded. 'I count the steps I take when I'm walking, I count how many birds I see flying overhead, and in the city I count how many trams go past or how many men are wearing hats or women have brown coats. It's not something I plan, it just happens. And in here it seems to come naturally to just count the sales and the levels of stock.'

Grace's mouth opened in surprise. 'You counted sales?'

Holly shrugged. 'It won't be to the penny.'

Grace reached out to touch her shoulder. 'But still. How accurate exactly?'

'Accurate?'

'How close do you think you'll be?'

Holly gave a soft hiss between her teeth. 'Put it this way, I don't think you're going to have any troubles paying rent or wages for today.' She grinned.

Grace returned the smile. 'You're amazing, Holly. I don't know how to describe your gifts, but I'm glad they're here and we benefit from them.' She gave Holly a hug.

'No, it's me who needs to thank you. I could hug myself for no longer being under the nasty eye of Tilly.'

'There's so much to look forward to suddenly,' Grace said with a pleasurable sigh. 'Maybe I can think about getting our own place.'

'For you and Alfie, of course you should,' Holly said, busying herself folding up boxes. 'We're going to have to do this every few hours, I reckon, to stay ahead.'

Grace grinned. 'I meant for you and me . . . and Alfie as soon as we're married.'

Holly turned and her shining eyes said everything.

'I'd better help out there,' Grace said before there were tears. She stepped back into the shop and could see Alfie busy with two customers. A trio of adults entered the store, looking around with awe; Grace felt her spirits lift even further to watch their enchantment. The older two smiled at each other, while the third – a woman in her early twenties – left their side to wander. She had only wonder in her expression. Grace heard the gentleman say, 'What an exciting smell of sugar. We'll all pick one treat, shall we, dear?' They were probably married and the young woman might be their daughter, Grace guessed.

Grace watched the slender woman with neatly tied back hair the colour of her honeycomb nod, wide-eyed, her gaze turned upwards as she scanned the bright shelves. She turned to the man.

'Look at the mountain of marshmallow, Dad,' she said, pointing. Grace laughed delightedly to hear the woman murmur, 'I'd like to sleep on those.'

She joined the family, determined to be the one who served them. 'Hello, I'm Grace. Welcome to the Sugar Palace.'

'That such a place as this exists is a wonder,' the gentleman said, inhaling and smiling.

Grace went to the counter and picked up a glass bowl. 'For your comment about sleeping on marshmallow, would you care to try one?' she said to the woman.

'Really? I'd love to, thank you. I'm Fleur,' she answered. 'We're from South Australia and we don't have anything like this in Adelaide.'

'Do I get one of those too?' the woman asked, sounding slightly put out.

Grace smiled. 'Of course, madam. A marshmallow like your daughter, or a piece of fudge, perhaps?'

'She's my stepmother,' Fleur corrected. 'My mother died.' It was blunt but spoken in a neutral tone. 'This is Irma and my father, Henry Appleby.'

'Welcome to the store. You've travelled a long way.'

The older woman ignored her, eyes on the treats. 'I'll have fudge, I think.'

Grace obliged with a smile. 'Mr Appleby?' she said, holding out the tray towards him.

'We plan to buy; you don't have to—'

'I'm the owner, Grace Fairweather, and it's my pleasure.'

'How splendidly generous of you. We're in Sydney just briefly, but I know we'll come back here if we're ever in town again. I'm here for a conference of people in the same industry as myself, so I thought we should take the opportunity to travel up and see the Sydney Harbour Bridge being built. History in the making – we aren't going to see its like again, I suspect.'

'I live beneath it, actually,' Grace said. 'I'll be very glad when it's finished.' She grinned. 'It's so noisy and grimy. I think the clanging of metal and the dust is so much a part of our life down at The Rocks that we won't be able to sleep when the city finally turns silent again.'

'Come to South Australia and set up a Sugar Palace in Adelaide,' Fleur said. 'I'll help.'

They shared a smile and the purchases the Appleby family made were far from modest. She knew it was a combination of the quality products together with the experience of entering such an exciting space, but more than anything, Grace knew it was friendliness, smiles and generosity that was going to keep this level of custom going for the Sugar Palace.

22

'Alfie,' Grace said later, in a rare quiet moment in the store. 'I've made a decision today.'

'The answer is yes,' he said.

'To what?'

'To marrying you, darlin'.' He grinned.

She gave him a friendly shove. 'This is serious.'

'I am serious.' He touched her shoulder. 'Go on, tell me.'

'I've decided that I'm only going to employ women – young or older, I don't mind – at the Sugar Palace. And part of the deal of employment is that I'm going to pay for them to take training courses as soon as I can.'

He frowned. 'What do you mean?'

She shrugged. 'Well, Holly might want to take a course in chocolate making, Lizzie might enjoy improving her education with a course in business management, and Sarah might like to be trained in design of some sort – she seemed to have an artistic flair when I watched her doing displays. I want to encourage it.'

He nodded. 'Right. And where might Holly take a chocolate course in Sydney?'

Grace grinned. 'Not Sydney.'

'Oh?' Alfie looked puzzled.

'Not even Australia – Switzerland. She can learn a new skill and then adapt it to our sort of affordable product. Just because we cater to a lower income earner doesn't mean we have to skimp on quality or creativity.'

'Switzerland! You mean on the other side of the world?'

'It's where I last saw it on a map.' She laughed.

'Holly, alone in—'

'I didn't say alone. I shall go with her.'

He blinked. 'Blimey.'

'You could run everything until we return.'

'Grace, this is day one.'

'I know.' She smiled at his disbelief. 'Just planning. I always dream big – you know that. You do too.'

He shook his head. 'Let's close and then we can celebrate.'

'No, Alfie. Let's close and let the girls get home for a rest and a meal. They're exhausted. We can tally up the day's takings and then you and I can talk.'

He winked. 'That sounds scary.'

'Needn't be. We're business owners now, and you keep saying we need to plan ahead. We'll clean down the store – you do the till,' she said over her shoulder as she headed for the back to grab the cleaning supplies.

After closing, the girls sent home, Grace and Alfie stopped at a nearby Chinese restaurant in George Street.

'I'd never come into one of these places without you,' Alfie admitted, grinning a thankyou towards a petite smiling waitress who showed them to a table.

'Why?'

He shrugged. 'I wouldn't know what to order. We didn't eat this kind of food in England.'

'My mother is suspicious of it,' Grace said with a laugh, 'but Dad's all in. He says the Chinese folk set up all over the goldfields in Victoria. I think originally it was to feed the Chinese miners, but now everyone enjoys the food. You should walk through the fresh vegetable markets sometime and see—'

He shuddered, cutting in. 'Markets make me nervous,' he said.

Grace could tell he didn't mean to but he glanced at his missing finger as he spoke.

'Do you know, Alfie, it's out of politeness to your injury, but I've never asked you about that.'

He looked immediately self-conscious and let go of her hand to place his in his lap.

'Would you tell me about it?'

Alfie sipped from the glass of water that had been placed on their table. He shook his head, seeming lost for what to say.

'No secrets, Alfie,' she urged him. 'I'm presuming you lost it in France?'

He sighed. 'Before then.'

'Oh.' That was a surprise. 'An accident?' she probed.

'No.'

Frowning helplessly, Grace pressed him. She wanted to know. 'It was deliberate?'

He gave a mirthless smile. 'Not by choice.'

She grew restless; he was stalling, that was obvious. 'All right, now I insist on knowing. Who did this to you?'

Their food arrived. It was a dish of glossy noodles with a rich smell of garlic and ginger, and a plate of sweet and sour pork, dotted with lightly fried carrots, celery and corn.

Grace waited while the waitress laid down the food and repeated their order in a soft, breathy voice.

255

'Please enjoy,' the woman said, gesturing politely to their dishes. She laughed when Alfie picked up the chopsticks and dropped them again clumsily. Pointing to the fork, she smiled sweetly. 'Perhaps Mister might find the fork and knife much easier.'

'I think we both would,' Grace said to their waitress's gracious remark.

As the porcelain-faced woman gave a soft bow and stepped away, Grace impaled Alfie with her gaze. She had no intention of letting him off the hook.

'Blimey, but she's beautiful, isn't she, Grace? I'd eat anything she told me to eat.'

Grace grinned but held her gaze. 'Your finger, Alfie. How did you lose it?'

Another sigh of reluctance. 'The food's going cold,' he tried.

'So will my appetite if you don't tell me the truth. Is it so hard?'

'It is. The memory alone is painful.'

A current of guilt wired through her momentarily but Alfie, she had come to realise, could be like quicksilver. He could divert, he could jest, he could talk his way out of most corners and this made him feel slippery at times. She didn't want that untrustworthy tag against his name, especially if it was to become her name too and that of her children's. So, no: it must be truth and trust as she'd warned him not so long ago. She wanted his real story.

She suspected that he could glean this from her unyielding expression and her silence, for he blew out a breath of resignation and started talking slowly while he twirled his fork in his noodles. She said nothing, eating alongside him quietly, listening to every sad word of his tale. When it was finished, he barely glanced up from his noodles.

'So this Salini fello—'

'Sabini,' he murmured.

'He's a gangster,' she said flatly.

'Not just a gangster. He's the head of what they call a mob. He has his own "family" in London. They all work for him.'

'You were one of them?'

'No. I think it's fair to say that my father worked for Sabini in various roles but no, I was only on the edge of it all – I was just a kid, running messages, moving stuff, at the beck and call of some of his men to make a few quid here and there.'

She nodded. 'But you were embedded deeply enough in that world to pay a high price for disobedience.'

He looked down. 'I was naïve.'

'But you've matured now,' she qualified.

He looked up at her, wounded. 'Of course.'

She tried to explain. 'You can't blame me for being concerned that you're back in that world, with Dooley being so—'

He shook his head. 'No, Grace. Dooley's just a bully. He's not attached to a gang. He's a fist for hire.'

'I don't see the distinction, frankly.'

'Oh, but there is one. There's a hierarchy, even a code of how a mob family operates. The rules are strict. What Dooley did to me in the park wouldn't please someone like Tilly Devine. She's not exactly Sabini, but she understands the code and she wouldn't rob from her own. It's just not good business, for a start.'

Grace gave a mirthless, stuttering laugh. 'You talk about this code as though it's something to respect or be proud of, but really Tilly and others like her are out-and-out criminals, with thuggish ways and a careless attitude to everyone but themselves.'

Alfie put his fork down.

'Am I being unfair?' she pressed.

'Sort of.' He looked embarrassed.

'Explain it to me, Alfie, so I can understand what you seem to understand about the likes of Sabini and Tilly.'

'There's nothing to explain, really. I'm out of that world.'

'And still George Dooley haunts my life.'

He sighed. 'We're going in circles.'

Grace threw up her hands. 'Because I don't believe you're being entirely truthful.'

For the first time since she'd known him, she saw his eyes blaze with something she couldn't read. It wasn't hurt, it wasn't entirely anger, but it sat somewhere between the two.

'What more do you want from me, Grace? I would give my life for you.'

She swallowed her helpless need for truth; the conversation had turned dramatic. She breathed out. 'I would never ask such a thing of you,' she said, reaching for his hand but he gently moved it aside; it wasn't fast enough to feel like a rebuke, but it still denied her the affection she wanted.

He shook his head. 'I think you're just going to have to trust me. When you're like this I see your mother in you.'

That felt like a slap in the face; she'd never seen herself that way.

'I want to share my life with you,' he continued. 'I want to give you everything you ever want if it's within my power and I would give you my last breath.'

She waited for the 'but' and it came.

'But I'm not your father. I'm not going to be bossed around from morning to night.'

Grace bit her lip, forcing herself not to jump in and defend her parents.

'I'm in business, as you are, and there are negotiations that have to be done. Whenever there are two sides, then there has to be give and take until a common spot is agreed on. It's like marriage. We have to give and take if we're going to be successful in our marriage. I don't need you getting caught up in rental negotia- tions, or the day-to-day activities of warehousing or moving goods around. They have a word for the sort of thing I'm going to concentrate on for the Sugar Palace. It's called logistics.'

She repeated it in her mind, having never heard of it before.

'It's all about how to make a system work – moving around parts, people, equipment, goods . . . even information – from the military. So now that's my responsibility, and you have to let me shoulder that without interference.'

'Or?' She couldn't help herself.

'Or I just become your puppet and that's not going to happen, darlin'. We'll fail. I need freedom, independence. For my mind to roam free. That's the only way for it to be the cunning thing it can be when it comes to negotiations. We need you focused fully on our product . . . new ideas, fresh innovations in store, clever sales ideas and ensuring Holly gets the right brief and the right help within the store. When we open the next one, she's going to have to trust someone to be her in another shop.'

'The next one.' Grace laughed, incredulous, and sighed, breaking the tension that had formed a spikey fence between them.

Alfie grinned. The fence dissolved. Grace was aware of the relief shimmering through her like a shiny ghost whose presence only she could feel. She didn't want to argue with Alfie. And she certainly didn't want to unwittingly become her mother, dominating and demanding, and looking back over the conversation, she had indeed undermined him.

'I'm sorry,' he began.

'No, Alfie. I'm sorry,' she said and he reached for her hand. 'You're right. I have sounded like my mother.'

He made a grimace. 'I don't mean to single her out.'

'No, but she does emasculate Dad sometimes.'

'I don't even know what that means but it sounds painful.' He laughed. 'Don't do that to me, for 'eaven's sake.'

'I promise. And I won't put you on the spot again . . . ever. I give you my word. I hate Dooley, that's the problem. And I loathe Tilly for her insensitivity and cruelty.'

'Look, people like Tilly have their place. Uh-uh,' he cautioned as she opened her mouth to object. 'Lonely men need certain things,' he began and then realised he was backing himself into a corner. 'The brothel serves a purpose, but I'm glad we got Holly out when we did.'

'There'll be so many more girls like Holly, though.'

'Well, you can become a crusader and save all the underprivileged kids of the world . . . like me – that's why I ended up under the screws of the likes of Sabini – or you can do more by making the Sugar Palace a huge success and use your wealth to educate them, to employ them and to demand more schools, more government assistance. It has to start with people like you who can make a difference, who have the . . .' He couldn't find the right words. 'Have the clever tongues.'

'The eloquence?'

'Probably . . . all the right voices and the right contacts to be heard in the right places to make change happen. You're far more effective being heard by powerful people than waging war single-handed against the likes of Tilly Devine.'

'It's Dooley who gets in my craw, Alfie.'

'We don't have to worry about him any more. Now, come on, let's get you home. I've made a decision today too.'

'Oh, what have you decided?'

'I'm taking all of you girls on a picnic to the beach.'

Her face lit with pleasure. 'I hope you mean that. I think I've only been to the beach once in my life.'

'Blimey, darlin', we have to change that. Every other summer, my dad, for all his terrible ways, used to pile us into a coach and we'd go down to the seaside for the day. We couldn't afford it every year so us kids would look forward to it rolling around. We'd spend hours on Brighton Beach, screaming at the cold of the sea – even though it was a hot summer's day – skimming pebbles, licking ice creams and eating fairy floss. I used to love him on that day.' Alfie sounded so nostalgic and she wanted him to keep talking but her mind was tripped. 'Hated him most other days,' Alfie said.

'Wait, what's fairy floss?'

He smiled. 'I guess it hasn't made it here yet.' His eyes widened mischievously. 'And it's right up your alley, Gracie. It's sugar that is spun with air.'

'What?' All her manners had fled because of her intrigue. 'Sugar spun with air? I don't understand.'

'Ah, something I know that you don't, eh?' He gave a wink and stood up to leave. 'Come on, I'll tell you as I walk you back. It's pretty amazing stuff actually, and the only reason I came across it – because people like me didn't get to fairs – was that I had to run a message for Sabini to some of the carnival folk. While I was waiting, I watched a demonstration.' He paused to open the door for Grace. 'An American sales representative was showing off this machine that his boss – a dentist – had invented. According to him, they'd sold tens and tens of thousands of boxes of the spun sugar at some big world fair about twenty years earlier.'

'Alfie, what *is* it?' Grace demanded, almost breathless, pinching him to make him understand her eagerness.

His grin only frustrated her more as he guided her around a tram and then a hackney cab to cross over George Street. 'It's hard to explain,' he said, frowning. 'Oh, got it. I've heard you complain about your aprons always having threads of toffee on them.'

She nodded, baffled. 'So?'

'I don't really know the mechanics of the machine, but what I gathered is this contraption uses a small amount of sugar and blows air into it to make threads.'

Grace frowned. 'That can't be right. There must be heat for the sugar to melt and to become spun sugar . . . is that what you mean?'

'Yes!' he said, impressed she'd caught on. 'I remember now, he showed the carnie folk this cup – he called it a reserv . . .' He stumbled on the word.

'Reservoir?'

'That's it. You put your common sugar crystals in and a small amount of them are heated.'

'It turns liquid, right?' she said, following the explanation. 'Then what?'

He made a circular motion with his hand. 'It spins fast, and air is somehow blown into the main part of the machine, where the liquid sugar arrives, and it turns into these really, really fine threads of sugar. I mean it's finer than hair, Gracie. It's like . . . it's like . . .'

'A sugar cloud,' she said, instantly able to picture it.

'Exactly,' Alfie agreed. 'I couldn't have said it better myself. They called it fairy floss and they were selling machines to fairs and circuses for the carnival folk to sell. The only real outlay is for the machine, I imagine, because it's otherwise just sugar.' He laughed at her silence. 'And now you're going to tell me the Sugar Palace is going to buy one by hook or by crook and start selling Sugar Clouds.'

She looped her arm through his, her mind racing in a pleasurable zigzag between product and marketing. He knew her so well already. 'Yes, Alfie, that's exactly what we're going to do. Thank you. It will be a sensation.'

'They colour it pink.'

She gasped with excitement. 'Then we'll do ours a pale blue so it looks like the Australian sky on a summer morning.'

Back home they did an inventory of her stock, her parents watching on with interest.

'I'm going to need more of everything.' She sighed. 'We'll be out of just about all of my ingredients within the month, and I daren't wait until we do run out because we can't risk not being able to supply immediately as the product diminishes.'

Her father grinned. 'Now you know my problem, Grace.'

'I do,' she agreed, 'but, Dad, I don't have anything to judge this by. I really thought we had enough sugar to last a couple of months, maybe more, but we went through more stock in one day than I thought we'd sell in the working week.'

'Not a bad problem to have, of course,' her father reasoned with a grin.

'Give me a list and I'll organise it all for you,' Alfie said.

'I can help too,' her father chimed in. 'I have some good suppliers who owe favours.'

Grace nodded. 'I'm going to need a lot of extra sugar. I'm also going to order a machine from America, Dad.'

'What's all this?' he queried.

'Long story. Alfie can tell you – he likes to set the scene.'

'Where are you going to put it all?' her mother wondered more pragmatically. 'We don't have room here for that level of storage.'

'That's why we'll have a new warehouse from the end of this week, Mrs Fairweather,' Alfie said.

At Grace's look of shock he continued. 'You have so much on your plate, darlin', I decided to take charge of one area that I know will make a huge difference. I took the plunge and signed the deal today.'

He'd asked her not to behave like her mother and tick him off in public. She didn't want to be like that, so she was going to have to trust him, and not try to control every single aspect of the Sugar Palace if they were to be proper business partners. 'Good gracious. A warehouse? Where?'

'At Pyrmont, as I mentioned. Nothing fancy. It's going to need some work to reach the hygiene levels we must stick to because we're selling food to the public. I've got a gang of men coming in who'll build all the benches and storage that Grace needs.'

'Where's all this money coming from, Alfie?' her mother asked, sounding shocked.

Grace blinked, hoping with all her heart that he didn't tap his nose and grin, or say something like *Don't you worry, Mrs Fairweather, it's all in hand*. He didn't.

'We made a very handsome profit today, Mrs F. I had every faith that we would, and my gut tells me every day is just going to get better, certainly in this opening month. We can more than afford the outlay. Besides, if we're going to generate the sort of business income that Grace has set her sights on, we must spend money on logistics.'

'Lodge what?' her mother asked, sounding insulted.

'Logistics,' Grace repeated. 'It's a military term, Mum.'

'Yes, I read it in the newspaper during the war, I'm sure. Movement of personnel and equipment, isn't it?' her mother replied.

'In our case,' Alfie said, 'it's easy production facilities for Grace, somewhere to store her ingredients and her finished product, and how we transport that product to and from the store to keep it stocked. It's about stock levels, reordering, knowing which are the most popular and which we can drop off, it's also—'

'Yes, yes, young man, I know what that all is, having run a grocery store for the past quarter of a century,' her mother grumbled. 'I just didn't know they had a new word that summed up all of that.'

'All right, Mary, let's leave these youngsters to their business.' Hugh looked at his watch. 'We have The Rocks shopkeeper's meeting.'

'I hadn't forgotten,' Mary snipped. 'Right, is Holly still in the bathroom?'

'No,' Grace said. 'She's exhausted. I've sent her to our room with a tray.'

'Right, I'll be ready in a jiffy, Hugh. Goodnight, Alfie. Well done on today.'

He nodded thanks.

'Night, darling. Don't stay up too late – you're looking rather drawn.' Mary kissed her daughter.

'I won't. Alfie and I will just finish up this list and then I'll be joining Holly at the pillow.'

After her parents had gone, Grace and Alfie got lost for the next couple of hours making detailed plans of what to cook when, what to store and for how long, especially the product lines that would perish the quickest, or ones that needed the protection of a coolroom.

'You'll be quite impressed by the coolroom,' Alfie said.

'I wish we could store everything in there,' she admitted.

'You'll need to do this,' he said, squinting his eyes and pointing at them.

'Why?' Her tone was as playful as his.

'Because the whole space is still a mess. But I promise you, it will be ready in a week for you to be cooking in. So I just need you to use your imagination tomorrow, all right?'

'I'm good at that,' she assured. 'Ooh, before you go, can you help me with this big bag of icing sugar, please?'

Alfie hoisted the sack onto a shoulder and walked it upstairs to her kitchen. 'You can't keep doing this,' he said. 'The sooner we get you into that new space to cook—' He missed his footing and stumbled slightly.

'Don't drop—' she warned, lurching towards him but it was too late. Alfie had dropped the medium-sized sack onto the floor and, as Grace had feared, it burst open in an eruption of feather-light sugar from the thick, brown paper sack.

After the initial coughing had settled down, Grace regarded Alfie through a haze of white dust.

'This is what a blizzard looks like,' he said, laughing.

Initially she'd been shocked, but now Grace shared the humour and wonder he felt, especially knowing she must appear exactly how he did: snow-dusted.

'We look like we've aged,' she said, trying to brush the white powder from his shoulders.

'No, we look like sugar angels.' He grinned from a face that looked like it had been hit with a big powder puff of stage make-up. 'What a lovely taste,' he said and as she went to wipe her face, he put his hand up. 'No, don't darlin'.'

'Why?'

'I want to kiss it off,' he said and pulled her close. She tasted his sugary lips and then he kissed the sugar from her cheeks too.

Sweet Alfie Sweeting. He suited his name so perfectly. When they finally pulled apart, she loaded an arch tone into her voice. 'Now you have to help me clean this all up before my mother gets back.'

'Easy,' he assured her.

Later, saying goodnight outside the back entrance of the shop that led up to her parents' home, still flicking at the light dusting of sugar on their clothes, Grace sighed and kissed Alfie, long and leisurely. Suddenly she no longer cared if anyone saw them or tut-tutted. This was the man she loved and planned to spend her life with. He still tasted of sugar, which felt fitting.

'Mmm, that's nice,' Alfie remarked, 'but also rather unfair to leave a lad in . . . shall we say, a high state,' he said, glancing towards his crotch cheekily.

She giggled, unsure if she should be embarrassed or allow the excitement to fizz through her.

'It's not a laughing matter, Grace.'

That only heightened her amusement. 'I'm sorry.'

He reached into his pocket, withdrew a tiny box and opened it. The moonlight caught a glittering gem, dark and delicious. They both stared at it in silence for several heartbeats.

'I was going to do this tomorrow at the warehouse but tonight with sugar all around us, it feels right. Put it on for me.' It sounded like a plea.

She lifted the delicate ring from the box and allowed Alfie to slip it onto her finger.

'It's a sapphire. Does it fit?' he asked in wonder.

She nodded, smiling. 'Snugly. I doubt I'll be able to get it off without soap.'

'Then it was meant to be. I'm sorry the sapphire is so small and—'

'I love it, Alfie. Shut up,' she said, quietening him with another kiss that was all about loving him.

'I guess I'd better say it then,' he said, opening his eyes and surfacing from the kiss.

'Say what?'

He looked at her seriously. 'Will you marry me, Grace Fairweather?'

She gurgled a laugh of pure pleasure. 'Tonight, encrusted with sugar, if I could.'

He put both hands over his heart and sighed. 'I don't think in my whole life I will ever have a sweeter moment than this.'

'Well, we have a whole lifetime ahead to create hundreds of brilliant moments.'

'I don't want to wait until your mother arranges it.'

'Please let her have this, Alfie. She has one daughter, one chance to let the world know she gave that daughter a lovely wedding. It means everything to her.'

He sighed and nodded. 'Then let's bring the date forward. Let's not hold off until spring. A winter wedding is fine with me.'

'Me too.'

'Tomorrow then?'

She laughed, threw her arms around him and hugged him hard. 'Very soon, I promise.'

'And our own place, Grace. I'm not living with—'

'I know. We'll start looking now.'

'You don't have to. I've found somewhere.'

She looked instantly baffled and surprised at once. 'You have?'

He nodded. 'I'll show you tomorrow, after I show you the warehouse.'

Small, pecking kisses deepened and lengthened.

Alfie groaned beneath her lips to make her laugh. 'Let me go, darlin' or I'll have to limp home.'

Grace laughed with fresh pleasure. No one had ever spoken to her so directly. It was lewd and yet so much fun to flirt in this way. She thought of how straightlaced Norman was by comparison to Alfie's ease around her. 'I do wish we could share a bed.' There, she'd admitted her desire.

Even in the darkness she saw his eyes glitter with promise. 'Very soon,' he promised, waggling a finger. 'See you tomorrow, my love.'

'I'll be at the store – I can only imagine it will be as busy as yesterday. Shall we say two o'clock? The girls can handle it after the lunch rush.'

'How about I pick you up? We can walk down together.'

'Perfect.' She smiled.

He kissed her hand, his lips nearly touching the ring.

As he was walking away, she called his name and he turned.

'I love you, Alfie.' She blew a kiss.

He pretended to be knocked backwards by it, staggering

and clutching his heart with a wistful sigh to make her smile as he walked away.

Clouds passed over the moon and threw them into darkness. The shadows instantly swallowed Alfie and all she could hear was his soft whistle retreating with his footsteps away from her. She watched the dark until she could hear him no more, wishing with all of her heart that they were already married, already in bed for the night and in each other's arms.

23

By seven-thirty the next morning, Grace and Holly had rearranged the shop between them.

'I think we need the lollipops just a bit lower so the smallest children don't struggle to see them,' Grace said.

Holly agreed. 'It also makes it easier for us to reach them – we won't have to get on the step-stool.'

They'd blown up multicoloured balloons, which had them both thirsty and breathless. After a pot of tea, they began to hang them in bunches around the store to add a fresh riot of colour to the already circus-like atmosphere that Grace was aiming for.

'Lots of colour, lots of products, towers of sweets and boxes of chocolates. I want it to feel as though everyone's walking into a carnival atmosphere. I think it's vital to overwhelm people – in a good way – with both the sights and the smells of sugar in so many forms they can't resist any of it.'

'I've never been to a carnival,' Holly said.

'What about the Royal Easter Show?'

'The what?'

'Oh, Holly!' Grace gasped. 'I'm going to give you the

childhood you've missed. Every Sydney child must go to the Royal Easter Show at least once.'

'What is it?'

Grace frowned, trying to define it. 'It's a lot of different things. It probably began as a small fair. I know it started a century ago.'

'A hundred years?' Holly sounded astonished.

'I've been going since I could toddle,' Grace assured her, 'and probably before then, because I know my parents love it. I think it likely started as an agricultural show – you know, a chance for farmers to bring their best and show off all the great produce in New South Wales to the big city folk.'

'What do you mean?'

Grace climbed up onto a small ladder to pile some empty chocolate boxes around the top shelves she'd had built. 'Hand those up to me, will you, please?' she said. 'Farmers could showcase everything from their prize bulls to pumpkins, or maybe a new vegetable, a new breed of sheep or cow.'

Holly nodded, understanding dawning on her face. 'Oh, right.'

'And then it just kept growing. Flowers, foods, all sorts of new products from around Australia with a focus on New South Wales. And then it just kept developing, I suppose, and became an annual gathering for everyone to celebrate all that was good about our state but also to entertain . . . There are exhibits and a fairground, donkey rides and petting zoos.'

'What is a pettyzoo?'

'Holly, you have a lot to look forward to,' Grace said, leaning back and admiring her handiwork. 'Look all right?'

The girl smiled. 'It looks wonderful.'

'Alfie and I will take you next year,' Grace promised. 'Would you like that?'

'Yes, but, well, we're new, aren't we? Can we show off our stuff?'

Grace looked down at Holly from her vantage, blinking once as her remark created a storm of thought. 'I think you've hit on something! Of course we should. If not as an exhibitor, we should definitely have some sort of stall there to sell to the public.'

'Like Alfie's barrow,' Holly said.

'I'm going to make enquiries today. I hope we're not too late for the showbags.'

'Showbags?' Holly looked baffled.

'Lots of food companies give out either free or very low-priced samples. For example, I reckon for tuppence we could sell one of our branded paper bags with some boiled sweets, a lollipop and some licorice.'

'That's worth a lot more than tuppence . . . You're giving it away?'

'That's the point. It encourages people to try our goods and then maybe they'll buy some, or certainly recognise our store when they pass by, even weeks later.'

Holly nodded. 'So it's like us giving out samples in the shop.'

'Exactly! Oh, Alfie is going to love this idea.'

'Where is he?'

'Coming by at two to pick me up. You'll need to hold the fort – we're going to look at this warehousing and kitchen space he's very excited about.'

'That's not all he's excited about,' Holly said with a cheeky smile. 'Don't think I haven't noticed the ring.' She laughed. 'I saw you trying to hide it from your parents this morning . . . turning it around so they didn't see it.' She gave a tsking sound and raised her eyebrows. 'I'd be very chuffed to show that off, especially if someone loved me as much as Alfie loves you.'

Grace blushed. 'We made it official last night but I haven't told anyone yet. I'm quite excited too, to be honest.'

'You should be. I would be.'

Grace gave her young friend a smile. 'Oh, you've got a long time before you start worrying about all that. You have to live first.'

Holly sighed. 'It's only since I met you that I've begun to daydream about my life.'

'Well, I hope it involves travel?'

'Travel? You mean around Sydney?' Holly said, sounding excited.

'No, Holly. I mean getting on a grand ship and sailing far away from Australia.'

Holly's mouth dropped open. 'What? I can't even picture that, let alone dream it.'

'Well, you'd better learn how because you and I are going to Europe next year.'

At that moment, any passer-by would have heard a very loud scream of joy coming from behind the closed doors of the Sugar Palace.

The new girls had arrived that day with a less wide-eyed look of fear than on opening day and were now moving confidently around the store. They seemed to know their duties on arrival, but everyone pitched in to ensure not an inch of the counter had so much as a crystal of sugar on it. The glass cabinets were cleaned of sticky finger marks where small customers had leaned and peered at all the delicious treats, and a long feather duster was passed carefully over every shelf.

'Good,' Grace said, glancing at the clock that was showing four minutes to nine. Opening time. 'Just long enough to check your hair, wash your hands and smooth your uniforms. You can re-tie that bow, Lizzie. The bigger and floppier the better – it grabs attention.' She grinned. 'And Holly, those lollipops in your hair are hilarious, but make sure they go in the bin when you're done.'

Holly grinned. 'I thought why not *wear* the product?'

'I think you're inspired,' Grace agreed. 'Come Christmas time this shop will be heaving with people. We can use candy canes in our hair and tie licorice around the bows. Keep thinking like Holly does, girls. There are no bad ideas, only ones we can't make work, but I want to hear every promotional spark of thought that lights up in your mind. I'll listen to every one of them and we'll consider them together as a team. Okay?'

'Okay!' they chorused like brightly feathered birds.

The morning flew by. Grace only just managed to roster the girls on and off for a quick mid-morning break, because the lunch-time crowd was upon them before they knew it. That was the busiest time of the day. It seemed the excited customers had seen the advertisement, or passed Alfie and his sandwich board, or recognised the shop as being the new incarnation of the barrow in Martin Place. But more than anything, it appeared to be word of mouth. It had spread like a grassfire – fast and furious – keeping Grace and her team all but running. She made a mental note that they needed a bit more space behind the counter. Something to remember for the next shop fit; when they were this busy, it was frustrating to wait for someone to pass or to let another through. And the till rang every half minute or so. Perhaps another till – so there would be one at each end of the counter – would make things much faster. It would be costly but a worthwhile investment to get more people through and prevent anyone from feeling frustrated by a queue and perhaps change their mind.

The pace finally began to slow as two o'clock approached. Grace glanced at the clock with disbelief that the day had gone so fast and sighed, craning her neck to see if she could spot Alfie beckoning from outside. There was no sign of him yet.

Holly, obviously noticing her clock-watching, sidled up. 'Can't bear to spend a few hours apart now, can you?'

Grace smirked. 'Don't be barmy. We have an appointment.'

'Well, he can't bear a minute away from you so you can be sure he'll be here any moment.'

Except he wasn't.

By half-past two, Grace stepped out of the shop's front door to peer down George Street for his casual, jaunty walk, but there was no sign of him. She walked back inside and served a customer who pounced on her with a question.

'That cinder toffee – how long will it keep?'

'I made it yesterday, very late afternoon. I would recommend it's all eaten by tomorrow afternoon.'

'Will you be discounting then?'

Grace laughed. 'Perhaps. Not yet, though. Do you want to wait until tomorrow?'

'Only if I can be sure you'll have some.'

'Now that I can't tell you. Have you considered the chocolate-covered cinder toffee?'

'Is that what those boulder-like things are?' The customer nodded towards the display.

Grace gave a polite chuckle. 'That's right. Perhaps we should call them chocolate honeycomb boulders. I rather like that.'

The customer grinned. 'That keeps better, does it?'

'Well, yes, it does because it's enrobed in the chocolate but again, I wouldn't let that chocolate spoil. How can you resist it anyway?'

They shared a smile.

'I'll take some of the boulders then, and I'll call back in tomorrow to see if you discount the undressed cinder toffee.'

'Good plan.'

There was only one remaining customer for the time being and Lizzie was serving her. Grace told Holly about the boulders idea, laughing again at the image.

'Why is that amusing?' Holly asked.

Grace loved her directness. 'Oh, I don't know, because it's sort of . . .' She shrugged. 'Sort of overly large, like something prehistoric.'

At Holly's critical slow blink she explained what she meant.

'You know, thousands of years ago dinosaurs roamed the world.' Then she found herself explaining what a dinosaur was.

Ten minutes later, when they surfaced from that conversation, it had been decided between them with excited laughter to rename the chocolate-covered cinder toffee 'Dinosaur Rocks'.

The last of the lunchtime customers had left and everyone sighed with relief.

'Well done, girls. That was a huge effort. Go and put your feet up for a few minutes, and I'll clean down here while I wait for Alfie.'

Holly frowned after glancing at the clock. 'It's nearing three, Grace.'

'I know. He must have got caught up with something. Go on, have a sit down. I'll do the dreaded glass of the cabinets.'

Grace got busy making squeaky noises with a chamois, rubbing off the smudges that had accumulated during the day. Customers came and went and the girls dutifully served. At the next opportunity when the shop was briefly empty, Grace asked the girls to do a quick sweep of the shopfloor. Before she knew it, the clock was telling her it was two minutes to four.

An alarm began to sound distantly in her mind.

———

Alfie was standing, dishevelled, after being manhandled by George Dooley into a Surry Hills house in Terry Street. It didn't take much to guess that below him a brothel operated. He could hear the groans of men and the muted but teasing voices of women and their feigned amusement. In his opinion, and from the little he gathered as he was bundled up the stairs to the top level, it was more of a knock shop than a brothel; he couldn't imagine there was any entertainment here. Simply an exchange of sex for money.

A woman with a face that could have just as easily been a man's regarded him with an expression that looked as though it were set in granite. The boss, presumably, but he had no idea who she might be. Her forehead was grooved with deep tracks and her mouth was set meanly. Alfie stole another glance but looked immediately down as he met blue-green eyes that stared at him as if he was something that had been lifted out of the gutter.

'Stand up straight,' she commanded from her seat, and Alfie obeyed, lifting his eyes to hers once more.

She smoothed already slick, greasy hair back towards her crown; her hair was in a bob he knew to be fashionable with a part as crooked as her nose. He didn't want to look at the hairs sprouting from her chin, although they commanded attention. She wore a fur coat inside. She was terrifying.

'This is him?' she asked her companion, staring at Alfie like he was an animal for sale.

'It is, Miss Smith,' George Dooley said and cuffed Alfie around the head. 'Introduce yourself, stupid.'

Alfie breathed out; he didn't want to be introduced to her. 'I'm Alfie Sweeting.'

'Do you know who I am?'

'No. And you don't have to—'

Dooley gave him a smack. 'Mind your manners,' he reminded him.

Alfie put a hand on the side of his head where the slap still stung. 'I was just going to say, Miss, er, Smith, that you have no need to formally introduce yourself. I don't know why I'm here. How might I be of service?'

The woman laughed, tilting her chin up and drawing attention to

277

her thick neck. 'Polite bugger, eh?' she said, cutting a sneering glance Dooley's way. 'You don't know why you're here?' she asked Alfie.

Alfie didn't know whether to nod or shake his head, so he did neither, waiting, hating how cowardly he felt beneath their bullying. It was like being a child again, watching his father beat up his mother, or quavering beneath the intimidating gaze of Sabini and his thugs.

'Dooley here tells me you've signed on for warehouse space down beneath where they're building that bridge. I really don't know why we need to be connected to the northern shore myself, but who am I to question governments?' She cackled another laugh.

Ah, that's what she reminded him of: the witch in that fairytale his mother had told him, who wanted to fatten up Hansel and Gretel to cook.

He frowned, feeling helpless while he tried to make the connection. He answered truthfully. 'I've signed on for a six-month lease at Pyrmont, yes.'

'And this is for some shop your friend owns.'

'It's my fiancée, and it's not "some shop" but the newest, brightest store in town . . . and we both own it,' he said. The very instant it was out, he wished he hadn't bragged. It was a dreadful mistake; that little prideful flourish was now focusing unwanted attention on the Sugar Palace and ultimately on Grace.

A sly smile now crept across the woman's ungenerous mouth, doing nothing to improve his opinion of her. 'Is that so? What's this special new store, George?'

'It's a glorified sweet shop, May.'

Alfie cut Dooley a look of hatred.

'Uh-oh, I don't think sweetie boy here takes kindly to that sort of remark, George. If looks could kill, eh? You'd be bleeding out at my feet.'

'He's doe-eyed about the girl, although being engaged is news to me. She's a smart one. Got tickets on herself. I have no idea what she sees in this petty crook. The shop seems to be doing a brisk trade – fairly minting money, they are, May.'

Alfie refused to bite, sensibly realising that nothing he said right now would help him or Grace.

'You see, Alfie,' May said, as though they were picking up the threads of a friendly conversation – it was Sabini all over again – 'we just need your help. Is that too much to ask of an old friend?'

'I don't know you,' he bleated.

'But you know George here,' she reasoned.

'Only to get beaten up by or fleeced.' He knew he shouldn't have said it, but he hated always quaking in front of Dooley. Grace wouldn't. Grace would face him head on.

May laughed, unconcerned and certainly unmoved. 'Well, you've got to be friends with George and then he won't hurt you, will you, George?'

George shook his head with a smile as cruel as hers.

Alfie sighed. He wasn't going to be able to wriggle out of this. 'Who are you?'

'I'm May Smith. Don't forget that name now. You know the other two whores up the road. You should fear me too.'

'What do I have to do?'

'Ah, I knew you'd see it our way, lad,' George said, giving him a friendly clap on the back that felt like a fresh warning.

May turned back to Alfie. 'I need you to store some gear for me.'

His heart sank. He'd promised Grace he would stay away from anything like this. 'How much?'

'About ten pounds.'

It didn't take much imagination to work out what he would be storing. Even so, he needed to hear it spoken aloud. 'And what am I looking after for you?'

'Cocaine,' May said, direct and clear. 'What else?'

'That's not much in packaging, surely you can—'

'Well, if it's not that much, then you won't have a problem tucking it away somewhere safe,' she said, her tone hardening. All pretence at friendliness was gone.

'Surely you need it here, though, to distribute. Why keep it down at Pyrmont?'

His ear sang a familiar song of pain. 'Because May wants to, that's why!' Dooley snapped.

Alfie covered his ear. He couldn't go through a burst eardrum again. 'Mr Dooley, you nearly sent me deaf the last time you beat me. I can't afford to lose my hearing.'

'George, lay off,' May ordered. 'Alfie, I need this stuff stored today.'

'What if I say no? Is Mr Dooley going to break some bones for me?'

'Among other things,' Dooley said. He cupped a hand behind his ear and said, 'May, what is that you hear?'

She threw her head back and gave a nasty chuckle. 'I think I might hear the sound of breaking glass and screaming women, George.'

Alfie didn't need to ask what they meant by that; he had always been fast to catch onto any innuendo or hidden meaning. But George Dooley decided to explain it to him anyway.

'All it takes is a brick, Alfie, and your tough-talking fiancée will shatter like the front of her store window, because, I swear to you, each time she mends it, I'll have it broken again. Or maybe I'll have the shop broken into and smashed up.'

Alfie swallowed, and it felt like he was trying to digest the shattered glass of Grace's pride and joy. He wondered what Grace might do in this situation. His inclination was simply to capitulate and save her shop, but he knew she'd find some way to fight back if she were put in his position.

'What's in it for me?' He couldn't believe he'd said it. He didn't know if he was more surprised than they were.

May laughed. 'Oh, so now you're interested?'

'No, but I'm the one taking the risk. I'm presuming that's the point, so I might as well get something out of it.' He looked from May to Dooley, despising them both for putting him in this situation.

'You're right there, lad,' May said. 'The heat's on me at the moment and I don't fancy a spell in gaol. I've avoided it so far and I plan to keep it that way. 'But they don't call me the Cocaine Queen for nothing!' Her voice was snapping now. 'So I must hide my snow somewhere safe, and your wife-to-be sounds sugary sweet . . . butter wouldn't melt . . . as innocent as the dawn. Am I right, George?'

'She's as white as your snow, May.'

That made them both laugh. Alfie didn't think it was funny – it wasn't even a clever play on words – but then George was a thug and an idiot. There was nothing sophisticated about him, but he was rat cunning, that was for sure. Alfie had to match George. He had to make sure they at least got something out of it, if only reassurance of being left alone in future.

'Once off?' Alfie asked.

'No, lad, get wise,' May said. 'There'll be another shipment next month. You do know they've made it against the law for chemist shops to sell morphine, don't you?'

Alfie nodded; that was why the barrow business had been so brisk and profitable.

'So that's just great for business for me,' May explained, sounding buoyed. 'I'll charge 'em twice as much and the silly bastards will still pay whatever I ask.'

'Or you could charge half and move twice as much,' Alfie said. 'It's all about volume, May.' He ducked before George's fist connected with him. 'If you don't mind me saying,' he said, straightening back up.

'What do you mean?' she demanded.

He shrugged. 'I don't mean to tell you how to run your business, but if your plan is to move as much cocaine as you can—'

'It is,' she stated, frowning to convey she thought him stupid. 'I've taken on rather a lot of it.'

'Well, putting up the price isn't going to achieve that. They know what they used to get their stuff for.'

'Yeah, but now they can't,' she argued.

He looked at George and back at May. 'They'll get it somewhere else.' It seemed so obvious. 'You're not the only people selling it. There are dealers all through Surry Hills, Woolloomooloo, Darlinghurst . . . the whole east. There are influential people in Sydney's underworld, shall we say, who are diversifying. Everyone knows how good the yield from cocaine is, especially if you cut it.'

Before Dooley could try to hit him again, May held up a hand. 'Go on.'

'Well, even the fellows who used to exclusively control the gee-gees and never bothered about much else – not even sly grog – are now moving into other areas that are'—Alfie rubbed his thumb and two fingers together—'lucrative,' he finished, proud to say a word Grace had taught him recently. He'd liked it when he learned what it meant. He wasn't sure they knew it, but his gesture was more than sufficient. 'I know a couple of the casino boys are already shifting cocaine. Increasing their loads is inevitable. And they're a dangerous mob.'

'I'm aware of the competition,' May murmured.

'It's better for you to undercut their prices. You're already known for solid supply, presumably, and you already have a customer base. The new people still have to set up their networks.'

'And cutting it?'

Alfie shrugged. 'That's up to you. Cut it too much, and word will get around. But if you keep it as pure as you can, that too will get around and drive customers to you faster than you can imagine. Lean towards the highest quality you can afford, at the lowest price you can let it go at. You can play with the balance down the track when you're confident you can shift enough of it.'

May was interested, he could tell. 'I hear you've done some of this buying and selling yourself right under the noses of the police.'

'That's all behind me now, May,' he said, risking using her name again and hoping it would help establish some sort of relationship. He was already so late to meet Grace. Was it only last night he'd proposed? She'd trusted him enough to say yes, and now he'd let her down within hours, already mixing with the wrong sort, now negotiating a bargain with them.

'But you'll store our stuff?'

'Do I have a choice?'

She laughed but it was Dooley who answered. 'Not if I have any say in it.'

Alfie kept his face neutral, though he wanted to scowl. 'There has to be a time limit.'

George grabbed him by the scruff of his neck. 'You don't tell us—'

'Or I'll go to the police myself,' Alfie finished, once again surprising himself. 'I don't want this in my life. I'll do it as a gesture of goodwill towards you, and because I don't want my business trashed.' He didn't even want to utter Grace's name in this place. 'But if we don't sort out a deal, then I'll take my chances. If the heat's on you now, you can be sure it's only going to get worse. The police will be watching you, shadowing you.'

'They likely already are – it's why we're talking.'

'So I'll cover you for now,' Alfie replied. 'But the shipment next month that you mentioned? You can find another stooge for that. It's not going to be me. Smash up the Sugar Palace. I'll squeal and you'll be the ones in gaol. I can repair the shop.' It was a gamble, and he sounded infinitely more confident than he felt.

Alfie watched them share a glance and May couldn't hide the nod she gave Dooley.

'All right. Here's the deal,' May said. 'George won't smash your girlfriend's storefront if you keep our stuff safe in your warehouse over the coming three weeks or so.'

'Or so?' Alfie shook his head. 'No, we have to agree now – and before Mr Dooley clouts me again,' he said, shifting himself off balance in case. 'I want to warn you that it makes no difference. I can't be bullied any further on this. You have ten days from today. Before I pay the next rent, the very last grain of that cocaine must be gone from my premises or I'll dump it.'

George's face turned purple. 'You'll do no such—'

'Mr Dooley, I'm far more scared of letting down my fiancée, or what the police will do with me, than I am of you. Be absolutely sure, both of you, I'll think nothing of tipping your snow into the harbour if you don't stick to our bargain. I don't want to see either of you again.'

May shrugged. 'All right. But I'm not giving you anything for this.'

'That's all right. The time I'll store it is now one week,' Alfie said, not showing how much terror he felt about the agreement, which was unfair at best. He tried to cast a good spin on it: it was something he could live with – just – so long as everyone kept up their end of the bargain and it didn't endanger him or Grace. But it meant ignoring the fact that storing their cocaine threatened to explode the life he had recently begun to dream he was making. They didn't care. 'Let's say it's a favour. One day I may need one in return. That's how it used to work when I was a lad in London.'

May gave a nod. 'You have a deal.'

'I'll need you to shake on that, May. I know you'll be good for it, one week from today,' he said, daring to extend a hand. He could feel the bristling anger of Dooley, who was no doubt experiencing pain at being cut out of the negotiation.

May stood from the chair where she'd been reclining, looking ridiculous in her fur coat within the scruffy Surry Hills house. She was smaller than she'd appeared, but standing didn't improve her ugly looks. She gripped his hand and shook once.

Alfie pressed his luck. It felt important to be clear, especially in this moment. 'Now, May, that means my shop and our staff are safe. My fiancée is safe. Our products are safe. Are we all agreed?'

'Yes, yes,' she said, waving her hand carelessly. She was already past any interest in him.

Alfie stayed firm. 'I need to hear it from Mr Dooley, please.'

'George, for heaven's sake. Give your bloody word now!'

'I promise,' Dooley said in a singsong voice, sneering with his hand over his heart. 'Your girlies and your shop are safe.'

'Right,' May said, bringing the strange meeting to a close. 'Now, get on with you. Mr Dooley here will bring our stuff just after midnight.'

And that was that. Alfie was escorted out of the house by Dooley and shoved into the street.

'Clear off, Sweeting. I'll see you soon.'

'Make it well after midnight, Mr Dooley. Then I can be sure that I'll be alone.'

'You're really that scared of that girl of yours, aren't you?'

'And you should be too,' Alfie said, over his shoulder. He began to hurry, eager to get away from this rat's nest and to make his apologies to Grace.

24

It took all of Alfie's powers of persuasion to convince Grace that he'd simply wanted the warehouse premises to be perfect for her, and that the workmen had held him up and he'd lost track of time. He hated lying to her, but it was the only way.

At first she didn't believe him, but when he'd promised to take her first thing the next morning, she'd calmed down slightly. Her father had weighed in as well, reminding her that he'd had to wait a week just to get a broken window fixed last year.

Alfie had spent the rest of the afternoon and evening in the warehouse, not only preparing for Grace but most importantly for George Dooley's visit. Alfie had been worried that there might still be a long way to go in terms of sprucing up the premises to be presentable to Grace, but to their credit, all of the tradesmen had been prompt in turning up and fast in their work. The carpenter was still there when he'd walked in.

'I was just off,' the man said.

'I'll pay you a bonus if you can fit that bench tonight.'

'Aw, mate, that's another hour's work. I've got to get home for my dinner.'

'I know, but listen. The owner is coming in tomorrow first thing. It will impress her no end if this work is done. Besides, apart from the bonus I'll give you . . .' Alfie took out a single pound note that he'd kept from the barrow days, all he had left from the cocaine sales after buying Grace's ring. He watched the man's eyes widen; it might buy a pair of shoes for children at home or pay for groceries for a while. It was surely irresistible. He offered it. 'Go on, mate. Just finish it.'

The man sighed. 'Right.' He took the pound note and pocketed it. 'My wife will understand when she sees that.'

Alfie rolled up his sleeves. 'I'm going to clean up. I want this place spotless for tomorrow.'

'They've all worked hard, done a good job. It looks good.'

The carpenter was surely right, but Alfie wasn't going to stand back and admire his efforts yet. He needed the warehouse and new kitchen area to impress. It was his first real job for the Sugar Palace and also his brainchild; Grace had not had anything to do with finding it or kitting it out. He wanted to show her that he had plenty to contribute to their operation.

He turned back to the man, now on his knees sanding back the bottom of a cupboard to fit. 'Er . . . can I ask a favour?'

'Another one?' The fellow sighed.

'Tom, isn't it?'

'That's right,' the man said, looking at him expectantly.

'Can you cut me a hole in the floorboards beneath that cupboard?' He pointed to one on the far side where all the storage was to be.

'What on earth for?'

Alfie didn't know what to say so he remained silent.

Tom twigged. 'A hidey hole?'

'Something like that?'

'How big?'

287

Alfie measured it for him in the air, using his hands to plot out the square. 'About yay big.'

'Not that wide. And deep?'

Again Alfie used his hands to measure about a foot's depth.

Tom rubbed his chin, then shook his head. 'No, mate. Too deep, you'll hit rock.'

Alfie sighed.

'I could do a fake cupboard, though,' Tom said.

Alfie frowned. 'What do you mean?'

'To all intents it just looks like another cupboard – and it is – but when you open it, it's shallow – there's a secret compartment behind it.'

Alfie's interest lit. 'Sounds perfect. I only need it for a week.'

'I don't want to hear any more,' Tom said, putting his hands up defensively. 'Use it as a safe. Only you'll know about it.'

'Okay, good. Can you do it in the office area you've set up instead, then?'

Tom nodded, glancing over to the partitioned area that Alfie had told him was for the store's other owner to do her paperwork, plot new menus, take phone calls, make orders and generally have a quiet place to think. Alfie knew she'd never dreamed of that luxury and he wanted to give her this.

'Easy enough,' Tom said. 'But if it's to be a hidey hole, then the office is the first place anyone might look. I'd suggest over there.' He pointed.

'Below the rack?'

Tom shrugged. 'You've already got storage space built in. It's not going to be a busy place – I mean, it's more your long-term stuff there. You wouldn't have people coming and going in and out of those cupboards, so they're unlikely to notice the fake one.'

'Got you. Okay, there then. Right at the end. It will be hidden by uniforms hung on the rack.'

'There you go. No one will bother too much with it.'

'Thanks, mate.'

'I s'pose you want that by tonight as well?'

Alfie grinned. 'It's almost as important as the bench.'

Tom finally grinned back. 'Right, leave me to get on with it all.'

———————

The next morning, Alfie followed Grace with held breath. She was silent as she walked around, touching surfaces and looking up the full height of the warehouse. He held her silence, not wishing to interrupt her, yet he was anxious that it meant she wasn't sure how to let him down gently, that this really wasn't what she had hoped for.

Grace suddenly turned on her heel, taking him by surprise. 'Alfie,' she began, her voice stretched. 'This is beyond my wildest hopes and dreams.'

He blinked in shocked delight, opening his mouth to speak, and for once words failed him, he was so thrilled.

'I love this. I can smell the paint, so I know you've had it painted all bright and white so it feels clean and fresh. I've been into these warehouses before with Dad and they're usually dark and gloomy, but this!' She turned a full circle, her expression one of awe. 'All this light and these enormous ceilings, the cupboard space and, oh Alfie, the benches! They're so huge and wonderful. I can really spread out and cook several products at once.'

He pointed to the marble slab waiting to be installed. 'I . . . er, I thought you could use the marble for tempering and cooling your chocolate.'

'It's brilliant. And not just chocolate. For toffees, for our fudge, oh . . . so many uses. I love it!' She launched at him and he could tell from the pressure of her hug and its length that he had more than fulfilled her brief.

'We can add more hobs if you need them?' he offered.

She smiled. 'I couldn't be more satisfied, Alfie, truly I couldn't. And to be honest, I didn't think I could be more excited than I was about the shop, but this . . .' She sighed. 'This is going to change everything. We can produce so much more and faster. There's enough space that I can probably have some helpers to assist with making the confectionery.'

'You must,' he said, taking her hand, feeling reassured by the engagement ring on her finger and trying not to think about the stash of cocaine Dooley had delivered that morning, together with his sneering look and menacing scar that lifted whenever he attempted a smile.

If Grace only knew, Alfie's life would be finished. His dreams shattered. He could try to explain that it wasn't his fault, that he was threatened – blackmailed – and he was just trying to keep them safe, but she would cover her ears, close her eyes to him and tell him to get out of her life.

No. She must never know.

So it was with some trepidation he said, 'One more surprise.'

'What is it?' she said, happily intrigued.

'Come with me.' Holding her hand, he guided her towards the partitioned area at what would be the quieter end of the warehouse.

When he walked her around the partition, she clasped her hands to her mouth and tears welled.

He swallowed. 'Is it all right, Grace?' His voice was tentative.

Grace sniffed. 'It's not just all right, Alfie. It's nowhere near all right. It's so very past all right . . . it's amazing. My own space.'

He smiled widely. 'All yours. You can sit quietly and dream up new products, but you can also take phone calls – I've had a phone put in. Oh, and I've been looking into one of those new calculating machines. Bit expensive right now, but I think maybe by the end of the year we could afford one, to make the accounting much faster and less laborious. So that tiny desk would be where it goes, because you can pull up a chair and sit in front of the machine, with room for till receipts or any pages from your files.'

She looked at him as though he were a walking miracle as he moved to the main desk.

'Lots of drawer space and bigger compartments for your files. We'll put a calendar here and a desk diary so you can make your appointments. And there's enough room for you to interview new staff here, and space just outside if you want to conduct some training.' He was on a roll now. 'If you look over there, I've put in some rails so you can have uniforms in various sizes ready to go for new staff.'

She came up to him and leaned a head on his shoulder. It was a gesture of such affection, a sign of their togetherness, that the fear of Queen May's stash not too far from where Grace was standing began to retreat. 'Deliveries will come in through that door.' He pointed. 'And there's oodles of storage for whatever you need.'

'I can't wait to show Holly.' She grinned. 'Thank you, Alfie. Thank you for understanding me and wanting to give me what I need.'

He smiled back at her. 'Darlin', I'd give you the moon on a silver platter if I could.'

'I'll settle for this warehouse, a fairy floss machine, and to become Mrs Alfie Sweeting.'

He kissed her. 'Done.'

———

After the day's work was finished and the tally on the till told them they'd just had their best day yet – near enough to triple what they'd taken on opening day, which Grace never thought could be topped – they all went back down to the warehouse to celebrate.

'I want all the girls to see it,' Grace said, 'and you're all going home in cabs this evening,' she added, leading them down George Street. 'Come on, Alfie's organised a treat for us.'

He was standing outside the store, a hansom cab waiting as he bowed to Grace and her staff before helping them to clamber on board. 'It's a special day, girls. We're doing it in style,' he said, leaping aboard and making Lizzie and Sarah giggle as he squashed himself in between them. 'Congratulations, all of you. What a day!'

'It seemed just steady, didn't it, Grace,' Holly admitted.

'Yes, but I was selling so much more to each customer,' Sarah said.

Alfie watched Grace lean forward with interest. 'You're right,' she said.

Holly nodded too. 'It's true. Mr Landish has been in each day for a small bag of toffees or a few pieces of fudge, but today he purchased a box of hard centres and a box of soft, plus some boiled sweets. That's probably four times his usual spend.'

'I sold eight toffee apples in one go to one customer!' Sarah added.

'Why?' Grace asked, intrigued. 'Did you find out?'

Sarah nodded happily. 'It was for a birthday party.'

Alfie grinned; he knew exactly where Grace's sharp and agile mind was swinging. He gave his fiancée a wink. 'Shall we talk about birthday party treats and specials later?' he offered archly. 'We're here. Come on, ladies. I'll go first, so I can help you out and pay the cabbie.'

He felt like his world had finally changed. He was making his own luck, making his own way and for the first time without any crooked angle to it. He kissed Grace's hand as she alighted and couldn't hide his grin, although when he looked up, Grace's expression had fallen. He followed her gaze to the warehouse door, which was open, banging raggedly in the wind coming up off the harbour.

'We locked up!' Grace said, stricken. 'I watched you do it.'

Alfie gathered his wits quickly. 'Yes, I probably didn't do it properly.'

'It's very windy down here,' Lizzie said.

'Come on, let's go in.' He hurried the girls towards the door. 'But let me check first that no one is inside.' He went in and quickly checked any hidden spots, then stepped back out. 'All clear,' he assured them, opening the door wider for the girls.

Grace held him back. 'Have we been broken into?'

'Well, let's go and check. Darlin', we haven't moved anything in here yet. It's bare bones. There's nothing of value, unless they wanted a marble slab – and good luck to anyone brave enough to try to steal that.'

She nodded. 'You're right. Of course. I'm being paranoid.'

He wasn't entirely sure what that meant but he was glad she sounded reassured.

Inside, the girls were behaving as Grace had the first time, looking up and making soft noises of awe, twirling around with wide eyes.

'This is ours?' Holly said, not prepared to believe it yet.

Grace laughed. 'Apparently,' she said. 'I felt just like this a few hours ago.'

Alfie was trying to enjoy their happiness, but he was con-centrating, casting his attention this way and that. *Had they been broken into?* He knew he'd locked that door securely that morning after showing Grace around.

Holly sidled up. 'Okay, Alfie?' she murmured, sniffing out that something might be wrong. 'What's going on?'

'Dunno, Hols.' He shrugged, trying to shake off the sense of dread that was growing by the minute. He darted a look towards the secret cupboard, but of course he couldn't tell if the drugs were still safely in place without going over.

'A burglary?' Holly whispered as they watched Grace show their girls the office area.

His heart felt as though it was pumping twice as hard; he could feel the pressure of its efforts near his ear. And it sounded like a drum, reverberating through his chest. His breathing turned shallow and even remotely, like a distant thought waving from the horizon of his mind, he knew he must have lost all colour in front of Holly.

Her worried tone told him he was right. 'Alfie?' She squeezed his arm.

'Holly . . .' He shook his head with horrified disbelief. 'The snow.'

Her forehead creased deeply. 'Snow?' she repeated in a low hiss. 'What do you mean?'

He held his belly as though he might be sick. 'Queen May's.'

'Queen—?' She stopped, but her expression told him she knew that name all too well.

'What are you two whispering about?' Grace came up smiling. 'Everything looks all right to me. Maybe you didn't secure the door properly, as you said.'

Holly recovered quickly. 'Nothing. Alfie's not feeling too well.'

'Oh?' Grace said, concerned. 'What's wrong?'

He shook his head again, following Holly's lead. 'Just came over all funny like, darlin'. I might just get some air.'

Grace reached for his arm. 'Let me—'

'No, no, don't you worry. I'm all right. I haven't eaten, that's the problem.'

'I'll go with him, Grace,' Holly said. 'You enjoy this moment. It's so wonderful.'

She took Alfie's arm, leading him towards the door where he burst out of the warehouse, all but gasping, drawing in air like a man starved of it. 'You'd better tell me what's going on.'

He knew he could tell Holly anything; she might be young, but she'd moved in the same world as him, and she was his only ally when it came to any activity of this ilk. Alfie didn't hesitate. He told her everything that had happened from the moment George Dooley had grabbed him outside the warehouse and bundled him from Pyrmont to Surry Hills for his audience with May.

'I had no say in this,' he said, staring intently into her eyes, hoping she believed him. 'I had to get out of their clutches and the only way was to strike a bargain.'

Holly gave a low whistle. 'She's bad news.'

'We have a deal, though,' he said helplessly.

His young friend nodded. 'Which, in truth, I imagine she will keep. When Tilly made a deal, shook on it, she meant it. I heard her telling that no-good husband of hers that all you've got is your word around the streets, and if that ain't worth a pinch of shit . . .' Holly said, now doing a very good impression of Tilly, 'then you got nothing, and no one will respect you and no one will fear you.'

Alfie nodded gravely. 'Holly, you have to go in and check.'

'How can I, with Grace around? I don't even know where it's supposed to be.'

'I'll tell you. And I'll keep Grace occupied. But I need to know if it's gone.'

Holly nodded, looking cornered but as though she understood that only she could help.

At that moment, Grace stepped out to check on him. 'Better?'

'Much,' he said, though he still felt like his heart was pounding. 'Whew, I felt so queasy. I think we need some food. How about we take the girls nearby for something to eat?'

'Like what?'

'Oh, some of that new raisin bread you and your parents were talking about that's now being packaged, or maybe we give them a proper meal. I know somewhere that's still doing wartime food of a meat pie sandwich. It'll be fun. I'll tell them how it's made, and they'll make groaning sounds and then they'll taste it and know how decent it is.' He faked a laugh.

Grace smiled, raising a brow. 'You were in the British Army! What do you know about Australian wartime food?'

He tapped his nose. 'Enough.' He winked at her, amazed that he could sound so light-hearted while his heart thumped a dark rhythm of fear.

'Right, well, let's do that. And then I suppose I'd better let Norman know about the door. The lock's actually broken, so I think you did close up properly and it's been a deliberate entry by vandals.'

Alfie seized the opportunity. 'Holly, we're going to see the police after we get some food. Can you wait in case someone—'

'Oh, she doesn't have to do that,' Grace began.

'No, I want to,' Holly said. 'Besides, I'm not really hungry. I'd love to take a quiet walk around. My mind is brimming with ideas.'

Grace laughed. 'Of course. All right, I'll get them to wrap up some food for you. We'll be back to get you later. There's nothing much for the police to see anyway. I guess Norman will wait for me to take a statement and do his report.'

Holly nodded, smiling. 'We'll celebrate properly when we're done with all of this. Oh, Alfie, you'd better give me the keys, just in case.'

'Ah yes,' he said, thinking, *Clever girl, Holly.* 'Here we are.' He moved back to hand her the keyring and then whispered with his back to Grace, 'Furthest right cupboard behind the rail to hang uniforms. Fake compartment.'

Holly gave a quick nod and Alfie turned, plastering on a fake smile for Grace's benefit as they waved goodbye.

25

Holly moved back inside the warehouse space. She really did want to enjoy marvelling at their new premises, but she had pressing business now that needed to be resolved. This was no light event, easily sorted and put behind them. If the stuff was gone, then Alfie's life was in danger. None of the gangster women she'd known or heard about would flinch at hurting someone who crossed them, and most would turn a blind eye to someone being snuffed out to teach others a lesson.

She owed Grace and Alfie so much for the chance for a new life among normal society, rather than its underground and more lawless side. In a way, protecting them meant protecting herself. 'I'm not going back to you, Tilly,' she murmured. 'And I'm not working for you either, May,' she said, as if saying it aloud made it a fact. Angrily, she ducked beneath the hanging pole at the far end of the warehouse and saw the new cupboard. *They'd certainly never want for storage space*, she thought sadly, aware of how hard Alfie must have pushed and cajoled the tradesmen to get this place ready for Grace.

She opened the furthest door. If the cupboard was full, you wouldn't notice that it was shallower than the others. But she spotted the concealed hatch and lifted it open. She felt around the hidden space inside, knowing it was empty, but checking all the same.

During her time with Tilly, she'd been small enough and, more to the point, inconsequential enough to go unnoticed much of the time. Tilly had always known Holly was smart, and had commented on her quick mind often enough. But she'd taken for granted that Holly's abilities would always belong to her. As a result, she'd spoken openly around her, half the time hardly knowing the youngster was there, rigidly paying attention, gathering up information and storing it.

And that knowledge haunted Holly now as she smelled the faintest aroma of ammonia, which, she knew from paying attention around Tilly, was used in the process of making cocaine. Helplessly, almost intuitively, she licked her lips and tasted the tart bitterness that she knew cocaine left behind in the mouth. She presumed some residue must have floated around the tiny space when the package was inserted, and perhaps more was released when it was disturbed.

In any case, the cocaine was gone.

She didn't look forward to telling Alfie.

Holly was alone for less than an hour before Grace and Alfie were back, this time with a sombre-looking policeman in tow. His uniform was so neat, Holly felt she should straighten her own clothes. His buttons shone and he was tall, rake thin and long-faced, but not without a certain handsomeness. It was probably the uniform, she decided.

'Holly, this is Senior Sergeant Norman Jenkins.'

Holly didn't know what she was supposed to do: shake his hand? She nodded. 'Hello, sir.'

'Norman is fine,' he said kindly, winning a smile from Grace.

Oh, of course, she thought. *This is* that *Norman.*

'Did you find anything odd, Miss, um . . .?'

Holly shook her head. 'Holly is fine,' she said, echoing his words, and he grinned back. 'Er, no I didn't, but I don't know what's to miss.'

'Well, nothing, actually, Norm. As I explained, we haven't moved in yet,' Grace said. She led Norm away to look around the warehouse.

Holly looked at Alfie, who was still grey, silent. She shook her head and watched his expression fall still further.

'It's baffling as to why anyone would break in,' she heard Grace saying to her policeman companion.

'I'm dead, Holly,' Alfie whispered.

She moved to stand next to him. 'Don't say that. Go and see May. Don't wait for her to find out.'

'And say what?'

'That her gear has been stolen.'

'Why would that make any difference to her?'

'It won't. But just looking at you, she'll be able to tell you weren't behind it. Maybe you can strike a new bargain?'

Alfie shook his head. 'Holly, it was ten pounds. I'll never pay it off.'

'You'll think of something. For now, think of Grace. Think of the shop, think of your marriage, think of me! You've got a lot to live for. Don't wait for them to come and find you.'

'They won't let me survive this.'

Holly had a thought, frowning. 'Who delivered it?'

'Dooley,' Alfie said flatly. 'Dooley seems to work for no one and everyone all at once. I thought he was in cahoots with Kate Leigh, but he certainly acted as May's messenger boy and stooge.'

'Who knew about it?'

He shrugged. 'Just me, May and Dooley were in the room. I don't know if she told anyone else.'

'And did Dooley see where you put it?'

Alfie turned to stare at Holly with an expression of horrified understanding. 'Yes. I was quite proud to show him how well it would be hidden and that I'd had a special cubby built for it.'

She looked down. 'He's done it again, Alfie. I'd put all my money on it. He's making you take the fall for his theft, and he's probably going to sell it to someone like Tilly. He wouldn't risk selling it to the public, in case the word got out to the wrong people.'

Holly was sure Alfie's lips had now lost colour. She grabbed his arm in case he staggered.

'I'll be fine,' he said, looking anything but. 'I think you're right. Who else would do it but Dooley? He wants me to go down.'

'Here's what you're going to do,' Holly said, one eye on Grace and her policeman, who was taking his leave. 'You're going to tell her.' She nodded towards Grace.

'I can't!' he bleated.

'Then I will. Maybe her friend can protect you.' Holly watched Norman raise a hand in farewell.

'I can't prove he did it,' Alfie hissed, nodding and raising a hand to the policeman. 'Thank you, Senior Sergeant Jenkins,' he called.

'Yes, you can!' Holly insisted, with one final glance at Grace, who'd likely noticed something was wrong. 'Idiot like him, he'll have left his fingerprints behind. They can check that now.'

'Norman's going to put in a report, but there's not much else that can be done at this point,' Grace said, arriving back to where they stood. She frowned. 'What's going on?'

'Alfie can tell you,' Holly said. 'Go on. Grace will help you, I promise.'

Holly looked at Grace with an expression that urged her to

find forgiveness, but Grace had already cut her gaze away from Holly to focus, with a coalescing darkness, on Alfie.

Grace listened in gathering shock. It wasn't that she didn't believe Alfie; the reason for the thickening silence and stillness about her was the notion that it didn't matter what she did, how many debts she paid off, or how much trust she invested in Alfie: he was unreliable. He'd borne out her mother's threats and he'd let her down once more. Spectacularly.

Cocaine in her new warehouse.

Grace didn't know how to respond other than with the obvious. 'May is surely no bunny,' she said. 'She'll be sending her henchmen after you.'

'She already has,' Alfie said, his tone morose and his eyes incapable, it seemed, of meeting Grace's. 'She sent in Dooley.'

Holly shook her head. 'Alfie, none of us know who he works for. I can't imagine that's her way. None of the gang leaders would behave that way. It's too dangerous. She was onto a good thing and she knew it, being able to hide her stash here.'

Grace cut him a withering look. 'What possessed you, Alfie?' The words came out strained and laced with disappointment.

'It may not feel like it, and it may not look like it, Grace, but the bargain I struck with May was to protect you.'

'Me?' she repeated, her voice higher, more stretched.

He explained what George Dooley had threatened. 'They thought it amusing that they would smash the shop's windows and then, the moment we repaired them, they'd do it again. They threatened to smash up the shop as well, spoil your ability to serve a single customer. These people don't care who they hurt, Grace. I didn't want them hurting you, or Holly and the girls.'

'But—'

'I was backed into a corner. They grabbed me outside the warehouse, bundled me off to Surry Hills, made me stand in front of May while George Dooley hit me around the head again and forced me to accept their terms or they'd start harassing you and the shop. I couldn't have it. It's an old-fashioned protection racket,' Alfie said. 'It happened in London. They offer protection to your place of business, which means no one else from rival gangs will touch it, but you have to pay them for that protection you didn't want in the first place.'

'That's extortion!' Grace snapped.

'It is. It's obviously becoming rife in Sydney now.'

Grace was horrified. 'You mean shopkeepers are paying up?'

He shrugged. 'Some do, others might risk the consequences.'

'My father hasn't—'

'That's because of Norman. Your engagement to a police officer offered a layer of protection that you and your parents probably didn't know you had.'

There was an awkward pause before Grace took control again. 'Well, I won't be a part of it,' she said.

It was Holly's turn. 'But that's just it, isn't it, Grace?' They all turned to her. 'Alfie was trying to make sure the Sugar Palace, and especially you, were never touched by these thieves.'

Grace felt her lips twist and settle into a thin line of unhappiness that she suspected looked much like her mother's in the same mood.

'Surely this isn't Alfie's fault,' Holly urged.

'Can't speak for yourself now, Alfie?' Grace asked. It was unkind but she was hurting. She sighed audibly and tried to think what they could do. 'A solicitor might argue that you were blackmailed and under grievous threat. The fact is, though, you broke the law. You could have gone to the police and—'

'But he was frightened for others—' Holly began.

Grace stalled her outburst by raising a hand. 'He has no criminal record in New South Wales . . . or anywhere else in Australia, am I right?' She looked at Alfie.

Alfie nodded. 'I don't have a criminal record anywhere in the world.'

Grace gave a shrug. 'Well, then, a good barrister might be able to argue that an innocent member of the public has been targeted by gangsters and acted in fear for his life and his family, his livelihood . . . that he had to go along with their threats. It could get you off the hook, or at the very least reduce the sentence you might get.'

'Grace, I swear on every part of me, on our future together, that I did this out of a need to protect you. I bargained with May to ensure it was a once-off. I told her if she or her stooges turned up again, I'd go to the police myself . . . and I'd chuck her cocaine in the harbour. I meant it too.'

'You should have gone to the police straight away. The police know these people, Alfie,' she said, and she knew it sounded like she was ticking off like a child. Grace knew that tone, had heard it many times from her mother. She hated hearing it in her own voice, but she was incandescent with fury, and was just glad that she could show control in front of Holly.

'How could he, though?' Holly jumped in. 'He's just told us Mr Dooley was knocking him around and May was threatening the people he loves. What was he supposed to do other than agree?'

'I think he was right to agree in the moment, Holly, but then he should have alerted the authorities and perhaps together we could have done something about it. Folk like May Smith dodge and weave, but if the police can catch them in the act, that's the way we'll finally get them behind bars. We know what people like May and Tilly do, but they cover their tracks well. This would have been an ideal opportunity.'

'Dooley watches me. I know that now,' Alfie said. 'He would have known the moment I left the warehouse to come to the shop and struck then anyway. He would certainly have known if I'd gone to the police – would have followed me when I did it – and that would have meant the shop could have been trashed out of spite.'

'You could have sent a message via someone else!' Grace said.

'Who, Grace? You?'

'Why not?'

'Because you'd react like this. Angry, hurt, let down, disappointed, ready to throw my ring back in my face.'

'I'll, er . . .' Holly looked uncomfortable, backing away from them and pointing towards the door. 'I'll see you at home.'

———

Alfie barely looked Holly's way, all of his attention on Grace.

'You *have* let me down,' Grace said, sounding choked. 'And I hear Holly's argument that you were backed into an impossible situation. I know you were damned either way, but I think it will always be like this, Alfie. I think the George Dooleys of the world will always be nearby, making some threat or another.' Tears sprang to her eyes and she blinked quickly, turning her head away.

He hated seeing her like this, but he had to stand his ground. 'That's not very fair.'

'Isn't it? You know fair is working within the law, Alfie, and somehow since the day you stepped into our grocery store, you've worked outside of it. Your whole life, although I accept you didn't necessarily choose it, has been running from the law and the type of life that the rest of us try to live within. I was raised to accept that there's no such thing as a quick dollar; it must be earned. Hard work is behind success, unless you're a lawbreaker. I have to accept that's how you got the money together so fast for your part of the Sugar Palace . . .' She opened her arms wide. 'And now this. I've

304

tried to make allowances. I've believed in you and trusted you even against my instincts, but here we are, Alfie. I am now the proud renter of the storage facility for the woman known as the Queen of Cocaine in Sydney's underworld. You've made me complicit with the activities of a gangster . . . for the second time!'

With that outburst, she surprised him by all but falling into his arms, crying on his shoulder, and he allowed his hopes to rise as he put his arms around his beloved Grace and held her close.

'I'm sorry, I'm so sorry. I just wanted to keep you safe.'

'I know,' she wept and after a brief silence she pulled away and took a difficult breath. He hoped with all of his heart it was to forgive him. 'I need some time, Alfie, to think.'

He kept his hands on her shoulders, looking at her intently. 'What do you mean?'

'I mean I won't marry you. Not yet. I have to get this all straight in my mind.'

She couldn't . . . 'Grace, I didn't—'

'I want to marry you with my heart full and feeling only love, not this . . . this despair. I wish I could just let it go in my mind, but Dooley's like dust. You can sweep it away and everything feels clean and in order, but then you look again a week or so later and it's back. He's never going to leave us alone.'

Alfie looked at her sadly. He realised this wasn't one of those occasions where he should keep talking, keep trying to manipulate the situation with his charm. Grace looked resolute, and to badger her would force her to dig herself even deeper into her decision. No, it was best to let her be, let her think it all through and find her own way back to him. 'Then I shall wait,' he said. 'I would wait forever for you anyway.'

She looked back at him with a great sadness that hurt his heart.

'And Norman, I'm sure, will look out for you. He's a good man.' Alfie added.

'He'll do his best to help you if you tell the truth,' Grace said.

'I know. I can tell. Out of his affection to you he would probably see this from my point of view rather than from a colder angle of what's right is right and what's wrong should be punished.'

'You're right, and I'm a little embarrassed. I never knew Norman to be one for shades of grey.'

Alfie took a moment so he understood her. It was back to the colour wheel again, he realised. 'Police have to be black and white, but in this case he'd be blinded by his affections. We shouldn't put him into the position of having to make that choice.'

Grace sighed. 'But knowing how Norman is, I suspect if we told him the truth he would see no benefit in taking you into the station in handcuffs. Yes, in a harsh light you've broken the law, but Norm is career-driven. He wants to catch the big fish. You're more use to him on the outside perhaps.' She sounded hopeful.

'Not interested in the tiddlers?'

'What's a tiddler?'

Alfie found a small smile. 'A really tiny fish.'

'I see. Well, no, I imagine Norman would take the attitude that if you're under the watchful eye of the police that he may have a chance of catching someone like Dooley who can lead him to the biggest of the fish.'

'Then he'd be smart,' he said, deciding not to tell Grace that while he may well help lure someone like Dooley, it wasn't going to save his neck from the likes of May Smith.

'There's nothing else you need to tell me?' Grace asked. 'Now's the time, Alfie.'

He put his hands up in a defensive stance. 'There's nothing but my love for you, and my determination that you keep enjoying this success.'

They stared at each other, both suddenly awkward and perplexed at the situation they found themselves in.

'I don't know what to say any more,' Grace said and he liked that she was not trying to hide behind kind words.

'There's nothing to say. I have to make this right with May.'

'Alfie, tell me you're not thinking of—'

'Darlin', stop worrying,' he said. 'I know how these people work. I'll smooth it over with May, and I'll help the police in any way I can.' It was a terrible lie. He had no way of smoothing anything with May, other than to offer himself up to her whim. And he had no power to help the police. If anything, their mere presence would give the likes of Dooley more reason to be rid of him. He didn't know what he was going to do, but he had to try.

26

Tilly Devine eyed Alfie with the gaze of a cat watching a fearful mouse. He'd finished what he had to say and, feeling grateful that she hadn't carried out her threat at the very sight of him, stood as still as that mouse might under her terrifying gaze of malice.

'You've a nerve coming back, you know. I nearly had Jim break your scrawny neck for you at the gate.'

Alfie said nothing, simply waited, while she toyed with him.

'So what's in it for me, Alfie boy?'

'The cocaine. It's yours – I want nothing to do with it. I would guess it's stashed at his home. He lives at Newtown. His wife is Betty Dooley.'

Tilly smiled. 'I know where he lives. But this cocaine belongs to May Smith, you tell me.'

Alfie nodded. 'It does, that's true. But May doesn't have to know that you have it.'

'Oh, Alfie, pet, you know how it works,' Tilly drawled, giving a chuckle. 'It's a small world us folk move about in. Everyone eventually knows your business. Someone, somewhere – whether it's you or someone you know, or George Dooley's barber for all

I care – will say something and it will reach the right ear until May knows that it's me who acquired her stolen cocaine haul.'

'Could you sell it back to her?'

'I could. But why would I trouble myself over that?'

Alfie shrugged. 'For the profit.'

'Not enough, Alfie. And you know it. Why would I want that sort of drama in my life? May and I give each other a wide berth. She doesn't interfere with my business, nor I with hers. If I break that agreement, it could turn into a sort of war, like I have with old Kate Leigh, the silly bitch. I don't need problems like that. No, you're asking for my help out of some strange idea that we're mates or something. I owe you nothing.'

'I know you don't.' Alfie had known this was a long shot, but he hadn't thought she'd dismiss him so quickly.

'Then why the hell are you standing in my house with that hangdog expression?'

'Because May will have me killed.'

'Why should I care? She'll have you killed anyway, pet, for stuffing her around, you know that.'

'Not if you tell her that you found the snow at Dooley's – or worse, purchased it from him.'

'Again, I don't know why I'd help you.'

'Because Dooley didn't even hesitate to steal from you, Miss Devine,' Alfie lied, remembering all too clearly that moment's pause and flicker of fear in Dooley's eyes. Even so, Dooley's greed had clearly outweighed his anxiety. 'I told him when he mugged me that the money belonged to you, not to me.' He noticed she was listening, even if she wasn't giving him her whole attention, busy adjusting the huge silken scarf she had laid across her sofa.

'Go on,' she said.

Alfie decided to work the lie. It was his only hope. 'He laughed when I said the money belonged to you.'

'What do you think he meant by that?' she asked, finally looking at him properly.

'Er, well, I took it to mean that he couldn't care less who it belonged to,' he said and, before she could reply to this, added, 'and even less when he knew it was you. *I don't give a rat's arse about Tilly Devine* were his words. And he went on to say that he doesn't rate you against May, anyway, and especially Kate Leigh,' he finished, using what he knew to be her weakness against her.

Tilly frowned, entirely focused on him now. 'Is that so? What else did he say?'

It was working. He continued to layer the lies like coats of impenetrable paint. 'Oh, that he doesn't reckon you'll be the one who survives the turf war with Miss Leigh. He says he's putting his loyalties with her. That's who he works for, and why he was happy to steal from you. He was just pretending to work for May Smith to find out more about her set-up.'

'Kate Leigh ordered the theft?'

Alfie gave an innocent shrug. Best to play dumb now. 'I pleaded with him to take my share and let me deliver what I owed you, but he just beat me harder, burst an eardrum.'

'I hope you aren't looking for sympathy, Alfie boy.'

Alfie shook his head, trying to look as innocent as he could. 'No, I'm not. I'm looking for revenge. But I don't have the ability to take it.'

'And you think I do.' It was a statement, delivered in a flat tone.

'Yes,' he said, equally direct. 'You have the muscle, you know people who can find him and, Miss Devine, I think you have a reason to. You can get Kate Leigh back for setting up against you, and you can also make money from May's cocaine by selling it back to her . . . or set up an alliance with her by returning it to her – telling her you took it off Dooley.'

Tilly gave a cruel smile. 'You've got it all worked out, haven't you?'

'If I had your clout or the network of people who work for you, I'd do it myself. It will only take a whisper from you to put out the word that you want George Dooley, and he'll probably be hauled here before you and wetting his pants before sunrise.'

She laughed, clearly liking the sound of his revenge. 'I thought he didn't fear me.'

'No, I told you what he *said*. What he truly feels is likely something else. Miss Devine, George Dooley is a bully, and like all bullies I've ever known, he's a coward. He's playing all you clever women off against each other because he thinks he's smarter. Bullies usually do.' Alfie, feeling he had momentum now and should keep it rolling, held up his hand with the stump. 'When I lost this finger, Mr Sabini didn't taunt me, didn't yell at me, didn't set out to frighten me any more than his presence already did. He simply stated the facts. He told me his problem with me, and he told me that it was important to punish me and why. He never raised his voice, he didn't laugh at me when I pissed myself, and I think deep down, he didn't like having to do what he did but, as he explained, it was necessary. And then he quickly got on with it. When it was done, he made sure my hand was bound up tight and then he had his lads drop me at a nearby hospital so I could get some help. He even congratulated me for not screaming – he said he was proud of me for taking my medicine like a man should.'

'And why are you telling me this . . . as deeply fascinating as it is?' She didn't try to hide the sarcasm.

'Because people like Mr Sabini and you, or May Smith or Kate Leigh, don't need to beat people up for pleasure. If it is done, there's a reason – it's a warning, or it's a lesson, or a demonstration to others. You're in a business – you don't have time for hurting people who you may need. Whereas someone like George Dooley hurts people because he enjoys it. He didn't have to burst my eardrum or punch me as much as he did. There were four of them, and I was no match for even one of them. So he could have just fleeced me and gone. But he needed to hurt me.' Alfie wasn't finished; he just needed to push her a little harder. 'Dooley's pretending to me he works for you and pretending to May that he works for her, while all the time working for Kate Leigh.'

'What do you mean he said he's working for me?' If Alfie had been losing her during his speech, he had her attention now.

Alfie nodded. 'He as good as said that you'd sent him that day, to steal your own money and make it look like a mugging. Then I'd owe you and be in your debt – again.'

'That filthy bastard. He said that?'

It was time to drive her into action. 'He said you were not and never had been a woman of your word and that you broke faith easily and laughed about it.' Alfie watched Tilly's whole expression change from shocked to vengeful. He drove his point home. 'I couldn't believe it at the time and, Miss Devine, I must tell you that when I was lying there on that cold laundry floor, hurting from my injuries, I knew it wasn't true because I'd been involved with the Sabini mob on its fringe, and I'd learned the ways of people who operate in the shadows, shall we say. My father worked for him and I met Sabini a number of times. I remember him telling me that in his role as the head of a gang, you just don't hurt people for fun, right? You never know when you might just need that someone to run an errand, deliver a message or carry a package – or keep your secret. He also told me that playing one gang off against another was as good as a death warrant. *Never do it, boy*, he said to me. *Loyalty is everything*.' Alfie was making it all up, but he knew it sounded good. '*Always be as good as your word*, he taught me. Whether it's keeping to a deal . . . or seeing through a threat.'

Sabini had not uttered those words, had never had anything much to do with Alfie other than the incident with his finger, but Alfie recalled Holly saying that Tilly's word was her bond. He knew he had Tilly on the hook now and he mustn't let her go. If he could lure her rage to the surface, then he might soon feel a moment's pity for George Dooley at what was coming his way.

'The thing is, Alfie, I don't want to teach Dooley any lesson. Hearing all this, he's done his dash with me. So you leave it with me now, and get on your way.'

Yes, it was just a moment's pity but nothing more that Alfie felt as he left the Woolloomooloo terrace – for the last time, he prayed. He only hoped he'd done enough.

It was taking all Grace's resolve to smile at customers and staff and to keep her tone breezy. But she was as transparent as the glass-like shards of sugar she'd made to poke into marshmallow or a pile of chocolates or lollies and clip cardboard signs to. The customers marvelled at them, wondering aloud if she could make them in different colours that they might use on cakes. She'd never thought of it and liked the idea, but right now she couldn't play with it in her imagination, or think about how she might produce and sell those shards commercially. Her mind was bruised and bleeding over Alfie. She didn't know how to help him, and she felt with every ounce of herself that Alfie's very nature precluded him from ever walking a safe line. He couldn't help himself. Danger found him and whether or not he welcomed it, he seemed to know how to court it.

Is that what you want? Grace didn't know whether the voice she heard was her mother's or Norman's . . . or perhaps her own. But the question hung in the sugar-scented air like an invisible cloud. She remembered learning at school about Margaret Clitherow, known as the 'Pearl of York'. The woman had died an agonising and torturous death in the late 1500s for refusing to admit or deny that she had harboured Catholic priests. The girls at school with Grace had all demanded their history teacher tell them the story, and she had reluctantly explained that if Margaret had made a plea, it would have taken her case to trial and then her three children might be called to testify. Determined to spare them that attention, which could go badly for them, she refused. Despite being pregnant with her fourth child, she accepted torture and a death sentence. The cruelty of her story had stuck with Grace throughout her life. She remembered listening aghast and yet avidly at how Margaret's own front door was used to crush the pregnant woman to death, as more and more bricks and boulders were laid upon her to force the plea or death – the court did not care which came first. Margaret had chosen death, aged just thirty – a few years older than Grace.

Dramatic as it was, that was how Grace felt now – as though she was being crushed by her indecision over Alfie. She wanted to be his wife so very much, and yet she didn't trust that a future as Mrs Sweeting would not bring a lot more sorrow to her life. What if they had children and Alfie was still being pursued? The darker agents in Sydney could find Alfie, and make use of his criminal instincts. What if, despite his best intentions and all of his promises, those people began to endanger their children, or her safety, or that of her staff? They might choose to burn down her store with all of them in it if they wanted to be particularly vicious.

Holly found Grace, to all intents refilling the jars of boiled sweets but lost in her thoughts, her hands still, her gaze far off.

'Grace, we could use your help at the counter. The lunchtime trade is heating up.'

'Yes, I was just getting more of these,' she replied absently.

Holly gently touched Grace's shoulder. 'Is there anything I can do?'

Grace knew what the younger woman meant. 'Oh, Holly, you're good to both of us. I know you want me to forgive him just like that,' she said, clicking her fingers. 'But I can't.'

'Why? He didn't do anything other than try and protect you.'

'I guess that's the simple way of looking at it, but we're talking about marriage. It's for life, Holly, and I don't want a future where I'm visiting my husband in gaol, or promising our children he'll be out soon and them hardly knowing their father. I don't want to live under the threat of losing him at any moment or worrying every time he's late that he might be lying in a ditch, or dying somewhere.'

Holly stared at her, saying nothing as Grace continued.

'It's horrible to think like this about someone you love with all of your heart . . . and I do love him, Holly, I do. But Alfie is trouble. He was trouble on day one and he's still giving me grief.'

Holly looked at her sadly. 'You can't find it in your love-filled heart to give him another chance?'

'Holly, you'll be saying those exact words to me next time. I'm not as young as you; I can't risk thinking in terms of black and white. Of course I could give him another chance but, you see, I already have . . . He's had a couple of very good chances already, riding on his most sincere promises of going straight. Remember, he was selling cocaine from the very barrow selling product from the Sugar Palace.'

Holly looked down, no doubt feeling guilty for being part of that situation. Grace felt bad because Holly was simply obeying the people who ruled her life, but this wasn't about her. She continued. 'I do feel so sorry for Alfie, because I know in his heart he wants to live a straight up and down life – at least for me – but I'm not convinced he's cut out for it. He's what is called an opportunist.'

Holly stared back at her, perplexed.

'What I mean is, when the chance to make quick money or easy money finds him, he's always going to want to risk it. He can convince himself it's "just this once" or "I'll stop as soon as I've made this much", but the problem is that *we* are the ones who feel the full impact of his decisions. He really should have gone straight to the police after May coerced him.' Before Holly could say the obvious she continued. 'No matter the consequences, he should have gone to the authorities. I'd rather have some broken glass or have lost a shop full of product than have Alfie in prison or beaten up again.'

'Where is he today?'

Grace shrugged. 'I don't know. I'm sort of glad I haven't seen him, to be honest, because I'm not sure what to say.'

'How did you leave it yesterday?'

'Badly. I told him I won't marry him right now.' Grace swallowed the lump in her throat. She didn't want to cry, not here.

Holly looked stricken. 'Then he's got nothing to fight for, Grace, and nothing to lose.'

'What do you mean?'

'You've left him with no choice but to go and make it right with May Smith somehow.'

Now it was Grace's turn to feel stricken. 'Why would he do that?'

'Well, you can imagine she's ropable by now with her stash gone.'

'But how can he make it right?'

'No idea.' Holly shook her head. 'What did you think would happen? People like May and Tilly don't just let things go. They don't cut their losses and say "Never mind, Alfie." You know what it took to make Tilly leave him alone – without you, he'd be dogmeat by now. They make someone pay if something's not gone according to their wishes . . . especially if they're out of pocket.'

Grace watched with increasing horror as Holly's eyes filled with tears. The youngster was making the most appalling sense. 'I didn't know.'

Holly didn't look impressed by her answer. 'We have to find him before he does something silly.'

'Like what?'

'Like offer himself up to May. He doesn't want you being hurt, but she can surely work out for herself that if she wants her stolen stash turned into money, that you're the one she'll have to come after. Alfie would sooner die than let anything happen to you.'

'All right. We get through the lunchtime trade and then we'll search for him.' Grace closed her eyes. How could she help him? Even if she wasn't sure she wanted to marry Alfie, she couldn't lose him – not like this.

27

May Smith's already plain face had taken on a purplish hue. 'That little bastard. Does Sweeting really think he can get away with this?'

Dooley shrugged. 'I always knew he was dodgy.'

'Dodgy?' she hurled at him. 'He was your idea!'

'And it was a good one. I'll be truthful now, I didn't think he'd double-cross us.'

'You're sure he's pretending that the stuff was stolen?'

'Well, his expression is as innocent-looking as the snow he was supposed to be hiding but, yes, I think he's faking the theft.'

'Who is he saying might have stolen it?'

'I daren't say,' Dooley said, touching his scar and looking concerned.

'What daren't you say?' May demanded, as Dooley shuffled awkwardly. 'You'd better bloody spill it, George!'

Dooley sighed. 'He whispered to me in confidence that he reckons you've had your own boys steal it and make him responsible.'

'He what?' A spray of saliva hit Dooley's face as May spat the words in rage.

Dooley put his hands up defensively. 'Don't kill the messenger.

I'm just telling you what he said. I want to do the right thing by you because it was my idea to use those premises, but now the police are involved.'

May looked furious. 'Who called the pigs?'

'I doubt he did – he wouldn't like the law much either. I imagine his do-gooder fiancée might have got involved. She's close to a fellow in the police.'

'And you're telling me this only now? Did you really think I'd be stupid enough to let my cocaine be stored in premises with the police lurking around?'

Dooley swallowed. 'I don't think you're stupid, May, no. And Senior Sergeant Jenkins has nothing to do with Grace Fairweather any more, from what I can tell, not since their engagement was called off. But she probably called in a friendly face once she realised her warehouse had been broken into. She wouldn't know anything about the cocaine. As far as she's concerned, it was thugs breaking in to see if there's anything of value to steal.'

May pursed her already thin lips. 'But you think Sweeting set it all up to look that way, is that it?'

'Yep. He can "lose" the cocaine, then blame us.'

'He thinks he can get away with this?'

'I don't know what he thinks. Alfie's a petty criminal. He's had some form growing up in the East End of London, but he's low-end, May, always has been. He's trying to use your shoulders to raise himself into higher circles, shall we say.' He gave a helpless shrug. He was doing a good job, he thought, of giving the air that they were equals simply discussing business.

'He's got a strange way of climbing that greasy pole. He knows I'll have to deal with him now, doesn't he?'

'Well, he certainly knows how this game works. But he has a silver tongue, that lad, and if I didn't know better, I'd think he was Irish for the good luck that follows him.'

'His luck's run out,' May said flatly. 'No one makes a fool of me.'

―――――――

George Dooley was feeling pleased with himself as he leaned against the bar of the Fortune of War Hotel down at The Rocks. It was full of the usual clientele of sailors, so it was loud and raucous. He didn't mind; he liked the noise and the anonymity while he drank. Even though he wore a suit, there was something about his scarred face that gave off just the right amount of menace that others understood he should be left alone to his thoughts.

And even though his expression might not show it, he was feeling as cheerful as he could remember feeling. He'd pulled off two impressive scams with his own so-called 'bosses' and, as a bonus, had been able to use gullible, easily frightened Alfie Sweeting as his stooge.

The perfect fall guy, he thought, smiling as he took a sip of the celebratory whiskey he'd treated himself to after he'd sunk the middy of Toohey's to quench his thirst. The meet with May had been tense. He'd had to manipulate her just right, but he'd managed it. Now, if his instincts served him right, May would be after Alfie's jugular and would likely have it slashed without blinking. That would rid him of a problem. He hadn't enjoyed how Sweeting had taken over negotiations with May, even pushing his own knowledge about selling cocaine. The little bastard had deliberately cut him out. George was the one who had come up with the idea to save May's arse in the first place. Without his cunning mind or his connection to Alfie, she wouldn't have had a safe place to park her cocaine that was well away from police eyes; even in their imagination, they wouldn't think to look in Grace Fairweather's new warehouse at Pyrmont.

But he'd shown them, hadn't he? He chuckled out loud and

took another swig of the rich amber liquid, which scorched the back of his throat as it slipped down his gullet. Yeah, he'd shown them both that he wasn't to be trifled with . . . and neither of them knew how or what had happened.

Stupid Alfie would be desperately dancing, trying to keep it quiet that something of note had been taken in the break-in – he could hardly tell his high-mannered girlfriend that he had cocaine secreted out the back. George laughed now, imagining her face if she knew. And how truly naïve was Sweeting, showing him the cunning hiding place. He'd sounded so proud and earnest that he could protect May's drugs. 'But only for the week, mind,' George murmured, imitating how scared Alfie had sounded even while negotiating. 'Stupid bastard. And now you've got nothing, you little toe-rag, and May's gonna get you.'

George's face darkened as he finished the final slug of the Scotch and gestured to the barman for another beer. His thoughts roamed. *Meanwhile, you bitch, May, you've lost your snow and you have no idea where or to whom.* He planned to sell it to Tilly for a song – she wouldn't be able to resist it.

The barman slid him another middy and George nodded as he continued his happy thoughts. *Maybe I'll take Mrs Dooley on a small holiday with the proceeds . . . clear out of Sydney for a bit while the dust settl—*

He grimaced as he was jostled on his right side, spilling his beer. 'What the hell?' he began, turning to see an unapologetic sneer from the man who had squeezed in next to him.

'G'day, Dooley.' Someone on his left spoke.

George swung around and was confronted by no less than Jim Devine. He felt his stomach lurch and the Scotch burned its way back up his throat. 'Mr Devine.'

'You led us on a merry dance, Dooley,' Big Jim said. His breath smelt of liquor, and he removed his large fedora hat.

George had never been this close to Devine and only now realised Big Jim was taller than him, more strapping. He was an ex-shearer and army bloke, George knew, and he liked to use his big fists on other men. But George wasn't due any sort of beating. He couldn't imagine why they were looking for him and said as much.

'Really? Playing innocent, eh?'

'Mr Devine, I really don't know what you mean.' George watched Jim's eyes swim slightly. The man was a known alcoholic, but it was also known on the streets never to underestimate him. He could hold a lot more liquor than the average bloke. His cheeks were flushed and his pale eyes looked smaller than ever, the pupils tiny. George wondered if he'd been smoking opium. Nevertheless, Big Jim wore a three-piece suit and his tie hung neatly from his collar; if George was being honest, the man's tidy look felt all the more intimidating. 'Can you tell me why you're here looking for me?'

'Tilly would like to see you.'

'What does she need me for?'

'She wants you to do something for her,' Jim said, smiling almost conspiratorially.

'Oh, a job. Well, why didn't you say?' George gusted, more cheerful now. 'Happy to do anything your good wife wants, Mr Devine.'

'I'm pleased to hear that, Dooley.'

'Er, does she need me now?' George asked, looking up at the clock above the bar. It was almost the six o'clock swill, and he wanted to finish the beer he'd paid for before the bar closed.

'She does.' Jim nodded. As if he could read Dooley's mind, he smiled. 'We can buy you a beer later, mate. Happy wife, happy life, eh?' He gave George a playful punch that he felt through his suit into his muscle. He could just about imagine what it might feel like if Jim put his back into it and took a swing, aiming for his jaw.

He wasn't going to ignore the request; even though it came with a smile, George could tell it lacked warmth and behind it resided the hardest of hard faces, of someone who potentially enjoyed violence even more than he did.

———————

They turned left once they'd exited the pub, both men flanking him closely.

'Mr Devine?' George asked. He didn't know the other man.

'Yes, mate?'

'Aren't we going to Woolloomooloo?'

'We are. We're going the pretty way, George.'

'The pretty way?' As far as George knew, there wasn't one of those.

'Tilly asked me to fetch something from one of her suppliers down here at the harbour.'

'Oh, right.'

'You don't mind walking with us?'

'No, no, not at all,' Dooley said, feeling a faint stirring of worry that began in a place where he felt especially vulnerable. It was as though his skin was shrivelling. 'Er, what are we picking up?' he asked, anxious to fill the increasingly tense silence.

'Never you mind, Georgie. That's Tilly's business. It's just down here.'

George knew they were in Pyrmont, not too far from Alfie and Grace's warehouse. He even recognised Ways Street, ramshackle and narrow with no pavement to speak of and a row of rundown brick houses. There wasn't a single tree that he could pick out in the darkness, but a couple of small-funnelled chimneys were smoking, suggesting there was life behind the dark windows, though you wouldn't know it; the street was silent until a lone dog barked.

'Shut up, you mongrel!' Jim's companion growled. They were the first words he'd spoken since he'd caused the beer spillage, Dooley realised. Suddenly, nothing about this moment felt friendly and he couldn't imagine that the three of them might share a Toohey's together . . . ever.

'This is it,' Jim said, leading them up to a front door, as sullen in the darkness as the rest. 'Knock on it, Georgie, would you?' he said, a match flaring as he lit his cigarette. 'There's a good fellow.'

George did as he was told. He wanted to be away from this pair as fast as he could.

He got his wish.

The door opened and a large, muscled man in a dirty white vest regarded them. A fag hung from the side of his mouth and he scratched a sizeable belly as he watched them. 'This is him?'

'Here you go, Whitey,' Jim said and gave Dooley a shove from behind. It wasn't especially hard, not enough to make him stagger, but firm enough that he felt instantly terrified.

He swung around, determined not to show it. 'Mr Devine, er, is the job Tilly wants done here? What exactly does she want me to do?'

'She wants you to die, Dooley.'

The words hung like six menacing blades between them, poised to launch, and the breath he'd taken in shock seemed to hang in concert with the imagined blades, trapped in his throat, unable to come out as a yell of panic or a bleat for mercy.

'Tilly doesn't take kindly to people who double-cross her, George, and we think you've had a lot of fun double-dipping recently.'

George felt panic shiver through him. 'I don't know what—'

'Save it, Dooley. We know you mugged that little shit Sweeting, and I have to hand it to you, it was cunning. Except you stole that money from Tilly, not him. It didn't belong to him . . . and no one steals from my wife or me and gets away with it.'

'Mr Devine, can we—?'

'No,' Big Jim said, his face as friendly as a block of old and scarred concrete. 'You're off to meet your maker, Dooley, and answer for all your sins. You know what to do, Whitey. Don't arse about either – just do it and get rid of the body.'

Dooley opened his mouth to yell his despair, but he hadn't seen that Whitey had a hammer in his hand throughout the conversation. That hammer was used now to smash George Dooley's skull. He went down like a sack of flour being unloaded from hefty shoulders at the docks, barely conscious after one blow.

'I got the boys out the back,' Whitey murmured to Big Jim as though they were discussing the weather.

'Let the fish have at him,' Big Jim said, removing an envelope from his jacket pocket. He tossed it Whitey's way. 'Bit extra in there for the lads to have a beer when it's done.'

'Thanks, Jim,' Whitey said and without any further farewell, he dragged George, moaning, by his legs deeper into the corridor and then stepped over him to close the door. The last words Dooley heard were, 'Right, let's get you finished off, mate, and on your way.'

He closed his eyes and cursed the day he'd met Alfie Sweeting.

28

Grace left Sarah and Lizzie in charge of the afternoon trade. Holly agreed to visit all the usual haunts Alfie might be found at, while Grace walked back down George Street, weaving her way into the familiar territory of The Rocks, past her parents' store, barely looking at it. She was on a mission to reach the police station she'd looked at every day of her life, never needing it.

Now she did, her jaw set in a rictus of worry. Many considered its red stone façade to be a curious conceit of its designer, James Barnet: a building with such a practical use looking like a Palladian water gate. But Grace had always considered it inspired, allowing a property of such pragmatism to have an almost folly-like appearance. She stepped beneath the pretty entrance arch, feeling the cool of the thick stone cavity. The same architect had designed the General Post Office, she thought, so why award a man with a track record of such grandeur a project if you didn't want his opulent style to shine through? She didn't know why she was thinking about James Barnet at this moment, but her mother always said the mind is a strange beast that tries to protect us when we're frightened. Grace wondered if that was what was happening now: her mind focusing her on trivia to prevent her going into full shock, to keep her functioning. Probably. Above the arch, she noted the initials of Queen Victoria sitting with a lion's head, which she knew was a symbol of British justice. The lion had a policeman's truncheon in its mouth, and she felt vaguely reassured that she was in the right place to get help. She was thankful that she knew Norm Jenkins well enough to call on him like this.

'Afternoon, miss. How can I help you?' the desk sergeant asked as she approached.

'Er, I'm wondering if Senior Sergeant Jenkins might be around?'

'He is. Who shall I say is asking?'

'Could you tell him it's Miss Fairweather?'

'Ah, Miss Fairweather,' the sergeant said with a knowing smile. Presumably all of Norman's colleagues had heard about her, and for the first time Grace realised how hard her rejection must have been on him. He would have told them all that he was engaged to be married to Hugh Fairweather's girl from the grocery store at The Rocks. It was a very small world down here, and they'd know her father and his shop. 'I'll let him know,' he said. 'Take a seat.'

Grace thanked him and turned away; she was too anxious to sit still. She gazed at the posters of wanted criminals and wrong-doers around New South Wales, and was staring closely at the names when she heard a familiar voice.

'Grace?'

She swung around. 'Norman,' she murmured with relief and then checked herself. 'Senior Sergeant Jenkins, I mean.'

He grinned kindly. 'This is a surprise – a nice one,' he added quickly. Then he appeared to sense her anxiety. 'Are you all right?'

Grace paused, not sure how to begin. 'I suppose I am.'

He frowned. 'That isn't a reassuring answer. I take it this isn't a social call?' he asked gently.

She'd never really heard that tone from him before and was both surprised and comforted by it. 'It's Alfie.'

'Ah,' he said, raising a brow knowingly. 'Shall we go in here?' He gestured towards a small room.

Grace followed him in, realising they probably interviewed law-breakers in there. There was nothing salubrious about it: a plainly painted room, no window, a table and two chairs.

He noticed her taking it in. 'Sorry, but it gives us privacy.'

'It's fine. Thank you for making time to talk to me.'

'Why wouldn't I? Grace, you can call on me anytime. I hope you know that.'

She nodded, smiling sadly. They were actually friendlier, more in tune and somehow even kinder to one another now than they ever were when they were together.

'What's happened?' he asked.

She told him her fears for Alfie.

'He stored cocaine?' he repeated, blinking. 'What's in his head?'

'He did not do so willingly. It was either that, get hurt himself and then watch me and my staff get hurt – certainly traumatised – as they threw bricks through our windows.'

Norman didn't respond, so Grace continued.

'They threatened him that they would take it out on me and the shop – deliberately choosing something they knew would hurt him – if he didn't do exactly what they asked.'

'So he did.'

'Only to a point,' Grace insisted and went on to explain how Alfie had threatened them back. 'Norman, he's trying so hard to walk the straight line and live a clean life, but these people won't leave him alone. They threaten him, use him and they know his weakness.'

'You,' Norman said flatly.

'Yes. He'd rather die than have me physically hurt.'

'I'm glad to hear it.'

'Why?'

'Because I lost you, that's why. And if I must live on with you as someone else's wife, then I want to know it's with someone who would die for you.'

'But I don't want him to die . . . and certainly not for the sake of my shop.'

'Grace, this is not about you. This is all about his life and his criminal past – it's catching up with him.'

Grace shook her head, filled with despair. 'We think he's trying to negotiate, to find a way out of this mess, but I'm scared—'

'Negotiate? Doesn't he of all people know what these criminals are like?'

'Norman,' she began again, tempering her voice. 'I agree, it would have served him better to come straight to the police. However, when you hear it from Alfie's point of view, standing there in front of May and her thug, he had to make an on-the-spot decision that kept us safe *in that moment*. It was easier to agree, especially as they promised they'd be watching him. But now that the cocaine has disappeared, I think he's in too deep. I'm terrified about what he'll do to fix this. Even Holly is convinced he's offering up his own life – certainly risking it – to save me and the girls.'

'Does he know where the cocaine is now?'

'I have no idea. But Holly suspects that it is likely with George Dooley. She says that's what Alfie will think too.'

Norman shook his head knowingly. 'That lowlife. You said he was the one with May Smith, though. It was his idea to use the Sugar Palace's warehouse.'

'Yes, it was. And Dooley has done this before.'

'I see. What happened last time?'

'I don't want to go into it, Norm,' Grace said quickly, realising she was digging a deeper hole for Alfie. 'We don't have time.

The fact is, Dooley's a creep and he plays all sides, pretending to work for someone while giving others the impression he works for them.'

'While all the time working for his own ends?'

'Yes. He masquerades as a gentleman in his suit, but he's every bit the thug. He's threatened me repeatedly.'

That got Norman's attention. 'Directly?' He frowned at her.

She nodded. 'Yes, he seems to think it's all right to walk into my life and make threats of violence. But that's not the point – there's someone worse than Dooley after Alfie. May and her people now think he's stolen her stash. There will be no forgiveness.'

He shook his head thoughtfully. 'No, there won't. These people don't deal in forgiveness, only revenge.'

'Which brings me here in my urgent need. I need your help in finding Alfie. I'm worried about what he's planning.'

'I say this respectfully, but I can't send all our men out hunting for Alfie. Many would say he's probably got what's coming to him.'

Her gaze narrowed. 'And what would you say, Norman?'

He sighed. 'I'd say I'm going to do all that I can because it's you who is asking. But I cannot take men away from their tasks to find Alfie. He'll turn up.'

Grace met his gaze, barely blinking. 'What if he turns up dead?' Her voice broke on the last word.

Norman looked back at her. 'I'll find him. Leave it with me now.'

'I appreciate anything you do but I can't leave it. I'll look for him myself with Holly.'

'Grace, do not go to May Smith, please.'

She raised her chin. 'I'm afraid I can't promise that.'

There was a knock at the door and the desk sergeant opened it. 'Sorry to interrupt, sir.'

'You're not,' Norm said. 'Miss Fairweather was just leaving.

She's reported a missing person.' He waited for the policeman to explain what he needed.

'A body has just turned up in the harbour.'

Grace gasped and the desk sergeant hesitated.

'Go on,' Norman instructed.

'It's the body of a man. They think the corpse got caught up on the ferry Koompartoo from Milson's Point.'

Norman nodded gravely. 'Did the ferry passengers see anything?'

'Not most, no. It was a passenger who was outside, at the back, who saw the body. They're taking the dead man to the morgue at the Water Police.'

Norman started ushering Grace out of the room, but she had no intention of leaving the police station before this conversation was finished. She allowed him to guide her into the main reception area, the desk sergeant following them, but refused to leave his side.

'Looks like a gang war killing, sir.' The younger man looked almost excited by the prospect.

Grace's stomach dropped, her heart racing. She tried to calm herself. *Don't jump to conclusions.*

Norman frowned. 'What makes you say that?'

'They found a wax bag of what looks to be cocaine in his mouth. His mouth had been badly stitched together so they were making some kind of point. I think he must be a snitch or something.'

Grace's voice sounded thin and stretched as she spoke, her hands shaking. 'It's Alfie.' She took a shuddering breath. 'He said they'd kill him. They were watching to see if he went to the police, Holly told me. They'd have seen you.' She knew she was babbling but couldn't help it.

'Grace! We don't know anything. This could be anyone.'

Her eyes blazed tearily at him. 'Really? What is your gut telling you, Norman? Right now, be honest. Who do you think has been pulled dead from the harbour?'

'I'm not in the business of guessing,' he said, sounding resolute. He put a hand on her shoulder. 'Now go home. Let us do our grim work and I will come by later.'

'Promise me, Norm.'

He glanced at his sergeant, embarrassed by the familiarity. 'I promise. Let me do my job. Sergeant, can you ask one of the constables to see Miss Fairweather back to The Rocks, please?'

'No, I don't need escorting.' At Norman's glance of frustration, she hardened her voice. 'I am fine, Sergeant Jenkins. I have a business to run.'

She didn't know why she said that, because suddenly nothing was more important than finding out whether Alfie was alive. She couldn't do that with a police chaperone.

As she left she heard her former fiancé giving instructions. 'Sergeant, get hold of that lout Finke. Find out the word on the streets from the gangs. I'll contact my counterpart in the east. He'll know if someone's been fingered.'

She hurried away, pleading inwardly that it wasn't Alfie, wondering what on earth she was going to do if it was.

Grace found Holly loitering around the warehouse, having looked at home and the Sugar Palace. It wasn't madly busy but steady, and the girls were handling the customers capably, assuring her they would be fine for another couple of hours until the early evening rush.

Grace was relieved; she couldn't face the cheerfulness required to serve customers right now. But she also felt helpless, because she knew she wasn't functioning at her normal level of focus.

She decided she might as well go to the warehouse in case Holly was there, and at least do something practical, like start setting up, perhaps ordering that sugar she so badly needed, although the notion of doing something as pedestrian as a sugar order while Alfie was missing, possibly dead, felt like an appalling betrayal of the man she loved.

Holly was sitting on the floor of the warehouse, her knees gathered up and her head bent to them.

'Holly?'

The girl looked up at Grace with red eyes. 'I keep hoping he's going to walk in. Have you heard about the body at the quay?'

'How do you know?' Grace asked, astonished, terrified and filled with a fresh welling of emotion all at once.

'I've been asking around. Word was whipping around this area that a man's body has washed up or something.' Holly's eyes filled with tears. 'What if it's Alfie?'

Grace told her what she knew, including the cocaine stuffed in the man's mouth. As horrible as the story was, she needed to be honest now. 'I'm worried that it's him, but we don't know that – Norman says they're looking into it and he'll come by later.'

Holly wept. 'It's a message. They think he was a snitch, so they sewed up his mouth.'

'Who, though? Who would do this? May?'

Holly threw up her hands. 'Any of them. They may be women, but they're as violent as any man. They need to be, to hold their positions. This is how it works,' she sobbed. 'When you cross people like Tilly or May, they just have you killed. The problem's gone.'

'I swear to you, Holly, if the body is Alfie's I will go to my own grave if I must to bring justice to him and watch those women go to gaol – or better still, swing from a rope.'

Holly looked up at her with surprise in her tear-filled eyes.

Grace regretted her words. 'I don't mean that. I don't like any killing. But they can rot in gaol for murder.'

'We don't know, though,' Holly said, reversing her previous stance. 'We don't know whose body it is.'

'That's right.' Grace nodded. 'That's what Norman's saying. Alfie's clever. He might not be especially strong or good with his fists but he's got so much more going on up here,' she said, tapping her temple, 'than the thugs who hunt him. You said before you thought he'd go directly to May – maybe he tried to negotiate. But if he thought his life might be on the line, he could have found another way.'

'Not with you in danger, though. That's the thing. He was more worried about your skin than his.'

'I know, I know.' Grace lifted Holly to her feet and hugged her. 'Come on. We're going to see someone.'

———

'Strike me! You're back. What now?' Tilly Devine glowered at Grace, who despised being in this room again with its heavy drapes and smoke-filled air. In fact, she hated being back in this house and even in Woolloomooloo and had told Holly as much. 'And here's your sidekick. How's life treating you, Hols?' There was nothing sincere in the question; it sounded more like a jab.

'It's treating me very well,' Holly replied.

'Ooh, very high and mighty, I must say,' Tilly said, mocking her.

'Far from it. Holly works hard,' Grace said.

'Did you bring that frock I liked – the one you had on last time?'

Grace surprised Tilly by nodding. 'It's downstairs.'

'Are you lying, girl?'

'Grace never lies,' Holly said and got a look of disdain from Tilly.

'Well, well, I didn't think you would remember, let alone follow through.'

'I offered it. I keep my word.'

'All right, Miss Fairweather. What are you after?' She rolled her eyes. 'As if I couldn't guess.'

'You know what's going on?'

'Everyone knows,' Tilly cut at her, lighting a cigarette. 'People like Alfie are small time. They really shouldn't play around with the big players. This is what happens.'

'Tilly, you and I reached a truce. We made our peace and I know neither of us would go back on that.'

Tilly flicked a bit of dandruff from her shoulder. 'Yeah, the girls enjoy your lollies.'

'Good. I'm happy to keep you supplied.'

'I hear a *but* coming.' She sneered.

'No, it's not a *but*. I am happy to keep you supplied as per our arrangement. I need a new favour, though.'

'What makes you think I'm in the favour business, pet?'

'I know you're not. I'm asking, woman to woman, if you'll help me.'

'The answer's no,' Tilly said flatly. 'I don't go in for that sister-hood stuff. I work in a man's world, love, and I have a business to run, men to satisfy,' she said, wriggling her eyebrows suggestively. 'Besides, I've already spoken to your fella a while back.'

'Alfie?'

Tilly laughed. 'Unless you've got another one on the side.'

'You spoke with him? When? What did he say?'

'Well, that's between us, pet. I don't discuss my business negotiations.'

Frustration spilled out. 'Tilly, I'm trying to find out whether Alfie is still alive, or whether one of you women have had him killed. I'm asking you first before I beg my favour.'

Tilly's cigarette holder stopped halfway to her mouth for her next draw on the nicotine. 'Why would I bother killing someone like Alfie? Are you mad?'

Grace had to steady herself against the back of a chair with relief. Holly answered for her. 'A body's been pulled out of the harbour, and they're saying there's a bag of cocaine in the person's mouth.'

Tilly laughed. 'Well, well, I'm yet to hear that news. That's a message if ever I heard one.'

'I know,' Grace said, recovering, 'so you can imagine where my thoughts went.'

'Well, I have not had your man killed.' Tilly sneered. 'That said, I can't speak for others. I can think of at least one who'd want him killed.'

'May Smith.' Grace said, nodding.

'But I have got his cocaine.' Tilly laughed.

'It was you who stole it?' Grace murmured, full of disbelief.

'No, it wasn't,' Tilly snapped. 'I have simply acquired it by a means I don't plan on explaining to the likes of you.'

'Who stole it then?' Holly asked. Grace could tell she was trying not to sound demanding but not entirely succeeding.

'Who cares?' Tilly said loftily. 'The fact is, I have it.'

Grace clenched her jaw. This was going nowhere. 'Well, that brings us to why I'm here.'

'Good. I knew there'd be a deal to be struck if you're standing in front of me. Get on with it, or I'll have Jim throw you both out of that window,' she threatened, gesturing with her cigarette.

'Give May Smith her cocaine back.'

Grace was sure Tilly's laughter could be heard throughout the house. She waited until Tilly's features lost their amusement and her eyes narrowed.

'Why would I do that? Perfectly good cocaine I can make pure profit on. What's it worth to you?'

Grace answered honestly; there was no point in hedging or believing she was in a position to negotiate. 'Everything. He's worth everything to me . . . if he's still alive. I just don't know if he is.'

'Everything, eh?'

Grace didn't hesitate. 'Yes.' Suddenly she was sure. All her reservations had fled the moment she realised it could be Alfie pulled from the harbour. She knew now that she'd do anything to reverse her decision, which had sent him scuttling to make things right somehow. 'Alfie can't be contained. That's what I've realised,' she explained. 'I've been acting like my mother, expecting him to behave as I do, think as I do, be another version of me, but that's not fair to a man who grew up with his background – the exact opposite to my upbringing. Instead of trying to mould him, I should have let him be who he was. That's what attracted me to him in the first place.'

Tilly put the cigarette holder in the corner of her mouth, clutching it with tiny, stained teeth, and gave mocking applause with a slow clap. 'Wow, that must have hurt to admit.' She laughed, but she sounded impressed. Maybe it was the honesty Tilly appreciated; Grace had surprised herself with the admission, but it was true. The dawning felt like a new morning breaking in her mind, warm and optimistic like a spring sunrise with all of its promise.

Grace nodded. 'No pain,' she said, with a wry smile. 'But certainly a medicine I needed to take. But now I'm terrified I've lost him.'

Tilly sighed. 'Well, I hate to bring it back to business after all this caring and sharing, pet, but I've got ten pounds of cocaine that I can turn into a lot of dosh and you're asking me to give it away. Doesn't make for good business.'

'No, I'm asking you to give it back to May because it might save Alfie's life.'

'Might not. He could be dead. Sounds like it's him who's been swimming with the fishies,' she said, unmoved.

Grace didn't overreact; instead she gave a sigh of frustration. 'Look, I don't know May Smith and it's a little late for me to pay her a visit and try to reason with her.'

'I can assure you it is. The contract's already out.'

A fresh chill zipped through her, forming icicles in her pounding chest. 'Contract?'

Tilly nodded with a smile as though they were discussing a nice dress. 'So I hear.' She took a drag on the glowering cigarette. 'There's a hit out on your sweetheart. You're probably too late, pet.'

Grace gulped a sob, unable to control it. She knew she needed to stay strong, but her reaction was visceral.

Holly stepped forward. 'Miss Devine, I'll come back and work for you if—'

'No!' Grace shouted, breathless. 'Absolutely not. I'm not losing you too.' She reached out to pull Holly back towards her. 'Tilly, I'm pleading with you. Maybe it's not Alfie in the harbour, and if that's the case, you can make this stop. I know you can.'

Tilly smirked. 'I can try. But I want your store in return. You said you're prepared to give anything to save your fella. Give me the Sugar Palace, and I'll see what I can do about Alfie.'

Holly spoke again, ignoring Grace's hand around her thin arm. 'You wouldn't know the first thing about running the store. You don't really want it. Don't make her give it to you just because you can.'

'All right. Maybe I have a better idea,' Tilly said, her tone casual but full of mischief.

'Say it,' Grace pleaded. 'Every minute counts.'

'My girls really like those sweets of yours. They're less troublesome when they get the treats. Jim doesn't have to deal with them . . . less bruises, you know. Maybe this is an opportunity to keep them loyal. You can throw a party for them in your store.'

'What?' Grace muttered, in shock rather than not hearing correctly.

'I don't want your bloody store, Holly's right. But every year from now on, I want you to close the store for a day and throw us a party . . . let them go mad with the lollies and take anything they want.'

'Done!' Grace agreed, breathless with relief and excitement that she actually had something to offer this woman – her confectionery, of all things. 'Set the date. Make it a Sunday and you can bring all your girls for a sugar party at the Palace. We'll wait on them – they'll have anything they like from the shelves.'

Tilly laughed. 'They're not used to that, are they, Hols?'

Holly shook her head obligingly.

'I'll treat them like royalty for a night,' Grace continued. 'I'll even make a special outfit from sugar they can try on.' She barely knew what she was saying, but she would figure it out later. Right now, she needed to get Tilly fully on her side.

At this, the brothel owner actually delivered a smile of genuine pleasure. 'Oh no, you'll make that for me. I'll wear it at the party.'

'You're on! Will you shake on this?'

'I don't have to. I keep my word. You know I do.'

Grace swallowed. 'Will you send someone to May Smith's now?'

Tilly nodded. 'But remember, pet, it may already be too late. She's put money on his head and every no-good lowlife in town would gladly hit your boy over the head and drop him in the drink for twenty-five quid.'

Grace gasped. 'Is that all he's worth?'

Tilly gave a cruel laugh, her eyes cold again. 'He's worthless to them, unless he's dead. That's what you have to understand. He's simply not important to anyone but you.'

Grace and Holly left Woolloomooloo in a state of suspended tension, unsure how to feel.

Holly summed it up. 'I don't know whether to do a dance of joy or crawl under the covers in worry.'

'I know. Did we get there in time? I still don't know who was pulled out of the harbour. I need to see if Norman has learned anything. Come on, we're taking a cab. I can't face being in this neighbourhood a moment longer.'

Once inside, travelling back towards The Rocks, their conversation continued.

'I feel so helpless,' Grace groaned.

'You're not. You've done something brave, fronting up to Tilly again. I don't know how you talked her into it, but she's helping you.'

'They might have already got to him, Holly.'

'No. We have to believe Alfie has avoided anyone who wants to hurt him. Remember what you said? He's clever. Even we don't know where he is. He's probably done that on purpose so they can't get it out of us. He's still trying to keep you safe by staying hidden, and if he can stay hidden from us, he can stay hidden from them long enough for Tilly to get that price off his head.'

Grace closed her eyes for moment. 'Can she really do it?'

Holly nodded. 'I think she quite likes the idea of having May on friendly terms . . . or at least not an enemy. She's got enough trouble with Kate Leigh.'

Grace shook her head. 'I don't want to know. I don't understand this world you were in, Holly. Thank heavens we got you out.'

29

Senior Sergeant Norman Jenkins spoke with his counterpart in Surry Hills and learned the news he hoped he wouldn't have to hear.

'The word is that Alfie Sweeting has a contract out on him,' the other policeman said.

'You're sure?'

'Yes. We've heard plenty of rumblings on the street, and all of it seems to be emanating from May Smith's gang. She's probably put a price on his head, and it's not to have him returned alive.'

Norman uttered a low curse.

'What about the corpse from the harbour . . . reckon it's your boy?'

Norman sighed. 'I don't know yet. I'm waiting to hear.'

'Sounds too much of a coincidence not to be.'

'Yep,' he said, sucking in a breath. 'I just don't want to have to make the visit to Miss Fairweather to tell her.'

It wasn't long afterwards that a phone call came through from the morgue.

'What can you tell me?' Norman asked, blunter than he would usually be.

'The body's only recently arrived, Sergeant Jenkins. I can only give you early impressions.'

'I'll take those.'

'It's a man, not long in the water. Looks like a blow to the head. I can't tell you yet if that killed him.'

'What else? I heard something about his mouth being sewn.'

'It's true. The packet inside his mouth burst, actually, on his arrival. Until then, it had managed to stay intact.'

'And is it cocaine?'

'So the rumours go.' The pathologist chuckled.

'You don't think so?'

'I deal in truth, sergeant, and until I conduct the necessary tests I won't confirm or deny anything. I told you I'd give my impressions.'

'But you sound as though you're leaning away from cocaine.'

'Only because, curiously – and this is just something I alone can attest – the bag burst when the body was shifted onto the morgue slab.'

'So?'

'Well,' the pathologist chuckled again, annoying Norman, who tempered that irritation with slow intake of breath. 'I tasted sugar on the air.'

'Sugar?' Norman repeated.

'As in sweet, yes. As in potentially confectionery sugar – you know, that they make icing with.'

Norm paused in thought and the pathologist continued.

'Curious, eh?'

Not so curious to Norman; a very strong message, he thought. 'Er, yes, indeed. I'll wait for your full report.'

'I think that's best. We haven't even removed his clothes yet or checked his pockets.'

It was after he put the phone down that Norm wished he'd

waited to hear the victim's age range, any distinguishing marks and so on, which would help determine whether it was Alfie. But it was the mention of sugar that made his heart sink.

A message from the Queen of Cocaine. Icing sugar made to look like drugs, stitched into the mouth of a so-called snitch who was planning to marry the city's queen of confectionery. It could only point to Alfie and a revenge killing from May Smith, not that she'd leave any evidence that she might be connected. No, the police would not be pinning this on the Cocaine Queen, he didn't imagine.

He wondered how he was going to tell Grace and was beginning to plan how he might start such a conversation when the phone rang again. It was an internal call.

'Jenkins,' he answered.

'Someone to see you, sir.'

His immediate thought was it would be Grace, impatient for news. 'Is it Miss Fairweather?' he asked, sounding tentative.

'No, sir, it's a gentleman.'

Guilt pulsed through him at feeling so relieved. 'Did he say what this is about? I'm rather busy with identifying this harbour corpse.'

'No, sir, he didn't. He didn't want to give me his name either, but he says it's important.'

'Important how?'

'He wouldn't say, sir. Says you know him.'

'But won't provide a name,' Norman said, sounding disgusted now. He gave a sigh. 'You'd better show him in.'

What now! he thought, standing to straighten his uniform. He moved from his desk to pour himself a glass of water.

The desk sergeant duly arrived and Senior Sergeant Norman Jenkins turned to greet the visitor, finding himself momentarily silent in astonishment.

'Hello, Mr Jenkins . . . Sergeant, er, Senior Sergeant.'

Norm found his voice and it was filled with fresh relief. 'Alfie Sweeting, you surely have the luck of the devil.'

Alfie stepped forward. 'This has to be the safest place in Sydney for me right now.'

Norman nodded slowly. 'Very smart. No one would think to look here. Are you handing yourself in, Mr Sweeting?'

Alfie gave a hopeful grin. 'Wasn't planning on it. Besides, I haven't really done much . . . why would you waste your time locking me up?'

The policeman frowned. 'I could arrest you right now. You earned money gambling and selling cocaine, not to mention getting involved with the likes of May Smith and storing drugs . . . Shall I go on?'

'Would you really do that to Grace? Do you hate us so much?'

'I don't hate her at all. And I don't know you well enough to hate you, but I hate that you contribute to the law being broken. And I hate that the girl I loved . . . love . . . can only see you as the man she wants.'

Alfie swallowed hard. 'Are you sure about that? She was so angry with me the last time we spoke, I felt there was no way back into her good books.' He paused. 'She's called off the wedding.' He hated admitting that to Grace's former fiancé of all people, but he needed Norman's help now.

'I don't know anything about that, Sweeting. All I saw was a broken woman pleading with me to help you.'

'Will you help me instead of chucking me in gaol?'

'I don't know what to do with you, to be honest. I'm damned either way. She'll definitely never forgive me if I throw you in a cell, even with good reason, but I can't think of any other way to protect you from the price on your head. You know we dragged a corpse from the harbour earlier today.'

Alfie stared at him. 'My guess is that it's George Dooley.'

'Dooley? He's at the bottom of the pecking order. Why on earth would they order an execution on him? He's not worth the money they'd pay for the hit.'

'Dooley's behind it all. The blackmail to store the cocaine on our premises, the theft of those same goods, and then ratting out to May that I'd taken it. All the while he had the cocaine, probably planning to sell it to her rivals. But that sort of behaviour soon has you running foul of the people with clout . . . They don't need a scheming, short-sighted idiot mucking up fragile relations.'

Norman nodded thoughtfully. 'Yes, I imagine that would have the gangs in quite a froth. We've been trying to get May Smith behind bars for years.'

'If I tell you everything I know about May's plans for cocaine imports, will you help me?'

'I will. But Alfie,' Norman said, finally leaning into familiarity, 'there's a target on your back. You need to stay locked up for the time being.'

Alfie hated that idea, but what else could he do? 'What if the hit is called off?'

'It could be, but there are always scavengers, out to make an easy reward or impress up the food chain. You're not important in the criminal gang scene in Sydney, so saving you is not something the gang bosses would bother themselves with. And even if the hit is called off, it might be too late to get the word out to everyone. It might take weeks before they reach all those bastards, by which time . . .'

Alfie nodded sadly. 'I'm swimming with the fishes, I get it. So I'm dead either way, whether I'm no longer breathing or sitting in a cell.'

Jenkins sighed. 'There's another way that's occurring to me.'

'What's that?' Alfie was eager for any alternative and it showed in his tone.

'You leave town.'

'Leave? As in leave Sydney?'

The policeman shook his head.

'Leave New South Wales altogether?' Alfie asked, his tone uncertain.

'No, Alfie. Leave the country. Go back to England.'

His heart sank. 'What? How would I even do that?'

'There's a P&O passenger ship sailing tonight.' Norman cocked a thumb over his shoulder. 'I have some connections through my days at the Water Police. I reckon I could get you on.'

'I have no money.' Alfie held up his palms.

Norman gave him a sideways glance of disbelief. 'No matter. You sit down now and record with me everything you know on paper and sign it, and I'll have you as a state's witness. Perhaps we can shut down some of these other cocaine importers and distributors, even if we can't catch May Smith yet. But we will, of course. She'll slip up and we'll drag her into court on some charge. In return for your information, the state will escort you off its shores and pay for your third-class passage home. That's the best offer you've got, and you know it.'

Alfie swallowed. He knew he was being thrown a lifeline. Was it really his only choice? In his gut, he knew it probably was. 'Can I see Grace to—'

'Nope. This has to happen fast and in complete secrecy. I really should be arresting you, so the fewer who know about it, the better. I have contacts higher up who favour me. I think I can get them to go along with it, but I need your decision now.' Norman looked at his wristwatch. 'If we're getting you on that ship, Alfie, you'll need to be down at the docks in the next couple

346

of hours and I need to get the wheels turning through my superiors to get you a berth.'

'I won't sign anything, but you can use my name.'

'Why not sign, then?'

'Because then I can deny it if I ever have to meet those people again.'

Norman stared at him. 'You'll never meet them again. You'll be on the other side of the world, and I suggest that's exactly where you remain.'

Alfie closed his eyes. Norman was right. 'Will you at least give a message to Grace for me?'

'No.'

'This isn't just a way to get a ring back onto her finger, is it?' Alfie demanded.

Norman gave a grim smile. 'I don't think you realise how much she loves you. Sticks in my craw to say it, to have to admit it, but I don't think there's any way back for me – in fact I know there isn't. However, I'm going to preserve your life for her sake. Frankly, you're a crook and you know it. You're better off with your own kind back in London. But I'm not having you put thoughts in her head about there being a possibility of seeing you again. A note will give her hope; a note will make her remember just how much she loves you and may push her to making some poor decisions.' He shook his head. 'No, I won't do it. If you leave, you leave cleanly. No note. Let her hate you.' He shrugged. 'I don't care how much she despises you. I just want her safe and sound.'

Alfie felt like crying. 'Just leave her, as though I don't care enough to tell her what's going on?'

'Look what you've already done to her, mate. Is that a loving fiancé?'

Alfie squirmed under the man's judgement.

347

'Run away back to your kind, Sweeting. Let Grace rebuild her life. She can. She's still young enough and with her store, she'll be highly sought after by every mother with a son she's trying to marry well.'

Alfie shook his head. 'I can't do that to her.'

'You can. You're bent and she doesn't need that.'

'I'm straight now,' Alfie protested. 'My crooked days are over.'

'So are your Sydney ones, one way or another.'

'You can't stop me coming back.'

'No. But if you do, I will arrest you. I'm giving you a way out to help Grace. She seemed broken today.'

That made Alfie swallow and drop his head. He was cornered in every direction. 'For Grace's sake then,' he finally said. 'Tell me what I have to do.'

30

The Fairweathers and Holly gathered in the grocery shop, which they'd closed early. No one felt like being upstairs, where it would mean confronting domestic life. At least down here, Grace's parents could pretend to be busy, except no one was focused on anything other than the alarm that the body in the harbour was Alfie.

'Look, love, no amount of you worrying is going to change anything,' her father tried. It wasn't helpful.

Her mother's words were worse. 'I told you that boy would bring nothing but trouble,' she said, pointing a finger, then wringing her hands.

Grace had the presence of mind to know her parents were as worried as she was, not just about her but for Alfie too, and so she forgave her mother's sharp tongue.

Holly looked worn out. Neither she nor Grace had slept. They'd tried to rest to keep their strength up, but ended up sipping cocoa in the kitchen talking about Alfie, with Grace ultimately blaming herself for much of what had gone wrong.

'He'll be all right,' Holly had tried to reassure her. 'Alfie's too smart to let himself get trapped.'

'He is trapped, though. If he's not already dead, he might soon be. We have to prepare ourselves for the worst.' Grace groaned, placing her head in her hands. She was tired of thinking about Alfie's final day; she kept imagining him trying to argue for his life, all the pain that the gangsters might have inflicted upon him, and his fear, knowing it was no longer possible to wriggle out of the hole he'd dug for himself. Did he ask them to be remembered to her? Or maybe, even in those final, traumatic moments, he didn't so much as utter her name for fear of focusing their attention on her.

And then she had helplessly imagined what it would have been like when he was tossed into the cold, dark water of the harbour. Had he been conscious? Hopefully not. If he had been, he'd have sunk quickly, probably holding his breath for as long as his lungs could hold up against the pressure. Then, still sinking, because they would have weighted his pockets or perhaps tied cement blocks to his feet, he would have gasped into the chilling, black depths, once, twice, maybe a final time as his lungs filled with salty water, screaming her name far beneath the surface, yelling his apology for—

'Grace!'

'What?' she shrieked, her nerves stretched from having lived and relived this scene of death and despair in her mind despite her best efforts.

'Norman's here,' her mother murmured, glancing towards the door where Grace's former fiancé stood.

It was not yet six, Grace realised, glancing at her watch, but it could have been midnight for all she knew; she had lost track of time while waiting for news. Night had indeed closed in and given how cold the hours were once the sun went down and the breeze blew in over the sea, few people were out and about. Norman wore a sheepish expression. She couldn't tell whether he was bringing the worst possible news or something only marginally better;

he certainly was not giving the impression that he was the bearer of any glad tidings.

Grace braced herself and felt the reassuring grip of Holly's hand suddenly clasping hers. 'He'll be alive,' she heard Holly whisper before Norman cleared his throat.

'Hugh.' He nodded. 'Mary.' They nodded back but didn't say anything. 'I'm, er, I'm here to speak with Grace.'

'Everyone knows everything, Norm. You can speak freely,' Grace said, surprised by how steady her voice sounded. 'What have you come to tell us?'

He looked around, as if mildly surprised that he wasn't going to be invited upstairs to sit down; Grace could almost read his mind as he seemed to sense this was not a time for formalities but to get on with it.

'Here, let me take your coat,' Hugh offered.

The air was expectant. Curiously, cutting through her thick desperation and everyone's anticipation, Grace could smell the sack of coffee beans that her father had cut open just before they had closed, ready for the week's trading. She recalled how, as a child, she had always loved putting her face close to the open bag and inhaling. The smell of roasted coffee beans had become a familiar and addictive aroma of childhood, and as Norman seemed to take an age to remove his outdoor clothes and time seemed to slow down, she decided she would make a coffee-flavoured fudge and a coffee-flavoured toffee that she would enrobe in dark chocolate. And then, as if Holly too had been struck by the same distraction, she whispered, 'I wonder if a chocolate-coated coffee bean might work?'

Grace turned to her in disbelief and awe; surely Holly had been gifted to her by the angels as a muse but also as a defence against all things dire, including the imminent bad news. 'What a brilliant inspiration,' she whispered back, knowing immediately that such a novelty would work.

She watched Norman settle himself, turn to them all and take a breath. *Go on, Norman, say it*, she said in her mind. *Tell me it's Alfie's body at the morgue and let me grieve, let my family get on with its life.*

'Grace,' he began, and she swallowed imperceptibly. 'I can confirm that the body that was pulled out of the harbour earlier today is not that of Alfie Sweeting.'

Her jaw released its fierce clamp and everyone sighed out a gasp of relief. Grace wondered if she'd misheard, but the relaxing of the tension in her father's shoulders and the way her mother's tightly pursed lips became slack was confirmation that she'd heard right. She was sure that Norman could sense they'd all believed Alfie to be dead, despite all their spoken reassurances to each other these past few hours.

Norman smiled quickly. 'I know that must be a great relief,' he said, echoing the obvious.

'So do you know who it is?' Grace wondered aloud. She didn't mean to sound curious, because not only did it not concern her, but privately she didn't care. All she cared about was that it was not Alfie.

Norm nodded. 'We do. It's George Dooley.'

Grace gasped alongside Holly. Grace hated the man, but it didn't change her shock. 'What happened?'

'Who knows.' Norm shrugged. 'He moved outside of the law, and I suppose got what was coming to him. Dooley was a slippery character by all accounts, and no one knew who he actually worked for.'

'Himself,' Holly snarled. There was no shock or sympathy in her voice. 'He was a horrible man. He never cared who he hurt.'

'That may be,' Norm agreed, 'but he was still murdered, so we have to treat him as we would any victim.'

'And Alfie?' It was Mary who cut around all the other questions to the only one that truly mattered to their quartet.

Grace took a deep silent breath.

Norman Jenkins gave a soft shrug. 'He's gone.'

'Gone?' Her mother asked for her, sending a glance towards Grace. 'What do you mean *gone*?'

Norman lifted both hands slightly. 'Alfie came to see me earlier.'

'What?' Grace breathed, her voice thin and stretched. 'When?'

'Um, a few hours ago, after you left the police station.'

'I don't believe that. Why wouldn't he come here?'

'It was too dangerous. I'd like to say too dangerous for him, but I think he was more concerned that he might steer those thugs your way.'

Hugh nodded. 'Very wise.'

'Anyway, he was smart enough to go to the one place in Sydney that the people who wanted him dead would not think to look . . . my office.'

Grace couldn't believe what she was hearing. 'What did he say?'

'He made a deal. Information in exchange for his freedom,' Norm said.

'All right . . . but where is he?'

'He's gone, as I said. No longer on Australian shores.'

'What are you talking about?' Grace said, exasperated. 'Would you please tell me where my fiancé is?'

'He left on a ship this evening bound for London.'

His statement was met with a silence leaden with fresh shock.

'I don't believe you,' Holly said, looking anxiously at Grace. 'He wouldn't have left without seeing us.'

'Well, he did,' Norman said, and Grace wondered if there was just a slight whiff of triumph about his statement.

'Norm, tell me exactly what happened between you and Alfie,' Grace demanded.

Norm obliged, filling them in on the conversation he'd had with Alfie at the police station.

'He struck a deal to give you information about May Smith?' she asked. 'And agreed to leave without seeing me?'

Norman nodded. 'I suppose one can't blame him. Alfie was eager to escape the people who wanted him dead, Grace.'

'Yes, but . . .' She didn't know what to say. Her shock was now complete. Had Alfie been a liar all along? Had he romanced her simply because a better life beckoned alongside her? She helplessly looked to her mother, who was just as helplessly wearing an I-told-you-so grimace. Her father couldn't meet her gaze.

Holly could, though. She rounded on Grace, stepping between her and Norman so their stares met. 'You can't possibly believe that. He wouldn't just agree to that.'

'I . . . I don't know what to believe,' Grace admitted.

'He departed on this ship,' Norm said, handing her a piece of paper. 'I helped him to get on board quietly, invisibly, through my contacts.'

'But he left without saying anything? Not even a message?' Grace repeated weakly. It came out as a question again.

'He did ask me to say, "Tell Grace I'm sorry." I'm sure he wanted to say more, but there wasn't much time.' Norm sounded deeply apologetic.

'No!' Holly raged. 'That's absolute rubbish, Grace, and you know it. Do you really think Alfie would walk away from you?'

She looked down sadly. 'I don't know what to believe any more.'

Her father walked over to put his arm around her. 'Come on, Grace, the good news is that he's safe. That's what you wanted to hear, and now you need some rest – we all do.'

'No, wait.' It was Holly again. 'He left no note?' she hurled at Norm.

Norm shook his head, lips firmly closed. 'I'm sorry, no.'

'That doesn't even make sense,' Holly persisted, turning to Grace and forcing her to meet her gaze. 'You know that makes no sense, Grace. He loved you more than anything. He wouldn't leave without at least trying to see you, and he definitely wouldn't go without a letter or note of some sort.'

'But even as you say that, Holly, he's on a ship to London – running away from his responsibilities,' Mary said, sounding resigned.

'That's unfair, love,' Hugh said. 'He was running away from being murdered and potentially from bringing more troubles for Grace. It's quite a different situation. Would you rather he was the fellow pulled from the water?'

Even in her despair, Grace felt vaguely impressed by her father's gentle reprimand.

'That's not what I mean, Hugh.'

Norm cleared his throat. 'I'm very sorry, Grace. He didn't have time to think. He simply had to react.'

Holly frowned. 'So how come you let him go? How come you helped him?'

Grace was surprised that Norm troubled himself to answer; she suspected Norm saw the young woman as a child.

'Because he helped the police,' Norm said. 'We're not that interested in the little fish, miss. We want to land the big ones. Alfie gave us some information we desperately wanted in exchange for leaving the country.'

'And was that your idea, Norm?' Grace asked.

'Pardon?'

'I asked if it was your idea for Alfie to leave on that ship.'

He looked trapped. 'Well, we discussed his options,' he began. 'I did suggest if he got out of the country, he would be safe and that I'd help him to do that.'

She nodded; this was starting to make sense. 'Well, thank you, Norm. Thank you for helping him.'

Norm looked around, realising that was probably Grace's way of bringing this conversation to a close. 'I guess I'll be on my way, then. There shouldn't be any more trouble now Alfie's gone, but you know where to find me.'

Hugh moved towards the hat and coat stand just inside the store door. 'I'll see you out, Norm. In fact, we might walk out with you. Coming, Mary?' her father said, reaching for Norman's coat.

'Yes, I could use some air,' her mother admitted. 'Grace, would you like—?'

'No. I think I'd like to be alone.'

'Are you going to be all right?' Her mother sounded worried.

Grace looked at her. 'What choice do I have? There's nothing I can do to bring him back.'

'Very pragmatic of you,' her mother said, still concerned, watching her.

'I don't know what else to say,' Grace replied, not ready to admit that all she wanted to do was go upstairs and cry for days. Maybe she would do just that. Right now, she wanted everyone to stop watching her. 'I think I need to be alone.'

Hugh sighed. 'You'd better come with us then, Holly.'

Holly looked at Grace, unsure.

Grace gave her an attempt at a smile. 'I'll be fine. I really would like just a few minutes alone.'

'We shan't be long. Can you lock up after us? We'll come in through the back door.'

'Yes,' Grace said and before her mother could add the inevitable, she added, 'And I'll switch off all the lights.'

Grace heard her father thanking Norm as they left the shop. 'Our family is very grateful . . .'

Grace turned away in case Norm looked back. She didn't want him to see her eyes glazed with tears. She duly bolted the door, top and bottom, before checking that the sign facing her read "Open". She peered out into the night and could just see the retreating figures of her parents, Norm in the lead with his long stride. She watched Holly look back towards the shop, knowing she would not be able to make out anything beyond the low glimmer of light that the streetlamps cast out in a small pool. The shop was plunged into darkness, herself included. It was what she needed.

Grace sighed, grateful to be alone, and leaned her head against the cool of the glass for a few heartbeats. She could count each one, so aware of time passing as she was. Would it be like this from now on? Was all that expectation for her new life since Alfie had arrived into it now reduced to a dark silence where she would be aware of her own breathing? She needed to let it go. Accept her loss and, in doing so, hopefully find a way forward into a different life. And so she allowed her heart to leak its pain.

Slow at first, it began to pound its hurt until she felt the reverberation of that agony through her whole body. He was gone. They'd all been right. They'd all won. She had been wrong all along in trusting Alfie. Oh, she knew he was a rascal from the moment she'd met him, and then that almost innocent, scallywag way of his had given way to a cunning streak. Not a villainous one, but a side to Alfie that could look the other way, that could convince himself that bending the law here or breaking the law there wasn't truly wicked. He wasn't hurting anyone, she imagined he had told himself, he was just getting on, finding loopholes and tiny corners in life that others hadn't noticed where he could operate outside of the law. Yes, that was how he would have regarded it: he was operating outside of set laws rather than breaking them. Every petty thief and thug probably thought like that. They'd never see themselves as genuine criminals – that title was for the big earners . . . the bullies . . . the kind of people who could order a death.

She stifled a sob. Even if she could forgive his misdemeanours or his stupidity at believing that people like Dooley would keep their word, she couldn't forgive cowardice.

There! She'd let her true pain into her mind like a poison. Alfie had chosen safety over her, he had chosen freedom over her, and he had chosen a life without her. That toxic realisation and acceptance would now corrode all the love she had invested so quickly in him. He was gone. He'd run, like one of those deserters they talked about during the war.

She lifted her head, knowing she had to face her despair to push through it, until perhaps she could almost hate Alfie. She took a deep breath, trying to calm her racing pulse. It was only then, her sight having adjusted to the darkness, that she saw a silhouette standing in front of the counter. She gasped; his shape was unmistakable and his footsteps through the shop's back entrance had been silent.

'Evenin', darlin', Alfie murmured. 'You know I could never leave you, certainly not without a kiss goodbye.'

With helpless tears running down her cheeks, Grace crossed the shop floor and fell into his welcome arms.

'I knew you wouldn't just leave me! I couldn't believe what I was hearing from Norm,' she said, her face buried into his shoulder.

'He was trying to help,' he admitted. 'I even got on the ship.' He gave a slightly choked laugh. 'And then I had to work out how to jump ship,' he said. 'I don't know what I was thinking getting on board. I just had to get back to you.'

She looked up from his embrace with wonderment. 'I'm so glad you did. But Norm will be furious.' She chuckled through tears.

'Yes, he will. This bad penny keeps turning up to ruin his chances with you.'

She'd wondered if that had anything to do with Norm's willingness to let Alfie go. 'Do you think that's why—'

'Not intentionally, darlin', no, but it didn't hurt to be rid of me, did it, while feeling good about helping you, keeping you safe?'

She leaned back, her arms around his neck. 'Thank you for being brave and coming back to me.'

'A very scary man once told me that I have to be prepared to pay my dues and only then can I hold my head high. I want to hold my head high around you, Grace. I want to be the man you need me to be.'

'So what will you do?' she said, wiping tears from her cheeks.

'I'm going to hand myself back into the police and give them all that they want.'

———

Seated at the kitchen table, Alfie held Grace's hands.

'You're sure?' she asked, having listened to all of his reasons for turning himself in. She had to be certain he understood what he was giving up in order to stay, for them to eventually be together.

'I have to, sweetheart. It's the only way.'

'Yes, it is,' she agreed. 'It's also right, Alfie.'

He nodded.

'As much as it grieves me, it also makes me proud.' She turned one of his palms over, kissing it softly.

'Proud,' he scoffed lightly. 'What's to be proud about being behind bars?'

'Well, there's dignity in facing up to your actions, taking responsibility for them. Holly won't see it that way, of course,' she said, but then added hurriedly, 'Look, I don't mean to sound holier-than-thou, but if we get the right legal help and your situation is fully explained, I'm sure your time in gaol can be minimised. But at least you will have done your time. Many can respect you for that. I can respect you for that.'

Alfie nodded thoughtfully. 'I'll explain to Holly that I don't want to run any more. I've been running all my life, and I don't want to lose my favourite girls.' He squeezed her hands. 'I want a future with you, Grace, to have a family of my own, to help in the business – I have so many new ideas. If I had taken Norm's advice and run away to England, I know I couldn't have lived with myself. I would have felt like I had abandoned you and nothing on this earth could make me feel all right about that. And you're right, I may go to prison but not for long, darlin', I promise.'

She felt her heart let go of all of its darkness, pounding now with a strange sense of urgent joy. This was surely Alfie's moment of epiphany, turning a corner and understanding what it meant to be a good man, a good husband.

'So let's agree. I'll turn myself in, face the consequences?'

'Yes,' Grace said, nodding emphatically. 'It's brave and right. It will clear your conscience and, dare I say, mine. If anyone wants to point the finger, I can put my hand on my heart and say Alfie is doing his time.' She looked deeply into his eyes. 'Will you manage?'

He adopted his familiar cocky air. 'Oh, I'll be fine. I've been in tighter scrapes. You just be waiting for me on the day they let me out for a celebration party,' he said, leaning in to kiss her cheek and make her smile.

She did smile but cried at the same time. Alfie pulled her close.

'You'll be all right. You and Hols will look after each other.'

Grace nodded through her fresh tears. 'Do you have more to offer the police? Something that will help reduce your sentence?' Grace asked, her mind already scrambling towards practicalities.

'I've already given them May Smith for the illegal importation and dealing of cocaine – and I've owned up to hiding that cocaine. That's what I'll go to prison for. However, I have a list of names of fellas who are not only involved in illegal gambling and race fixing, but are beginning to get mixed up in importing cocaine. That could be a real help to the authorities.'

'Won't that get you into bother being a . . . what do they call it? A squealer?'

He laughed at her term and shook his head. 'No, I'm not too worried about that. I'm hopeful the police will help by allowing blame to fall on Dooley, who can't defend himself – everyone knows he had no loyalties. He didn't live by the code that other crims do. They'll believe that he spilled his guts to police to try and save himself before he was bumped off.'

'You're certain of that?' Grace insisted.

Alfie grinned. 'Of course. I'm far too small fry to even be considered capable of doing much more than what I'm told.'

'What about the contract out on you?'

Alfie shook his head. 'That's over now May's about to be busted. She will know it was Dooley.'

'I can make sure of that,' Grace promised. 'Believe it or not, Tilly Devine and I have reached an . . . understanding, shall we say.'

They heard her parents and Holly arriving into the alley downstairs; they'd be through the back door in moments.

Alfie stood, still holding Grace's hand and kissed it. 'Will you wait for me, darlin'?'

She nodded. 'However long it takes.'

'Will you visit me?'

'No. I couldn't bear seeing you there, but I'll write to you. It will make our reunion much sweeter,' she whispered.

He seemed to accept her reluctance to have anything to do with prisons, nodding sadly. 'Will you still marry me?'

She smiled, tears in her eyes. 'The moment you are released.'

Alfie nodded. 'Do you forgive me?'

She didn't hesitate. Not only because she felt no need to pause and think, but because she knew he needed this reassurance more than any other. 'I do. I forgive you. And I trust you, Alfie, to have a clean slate and a new trustworthy approach from now on. I know when you return to me it will be as a free man – not just free from a prison cell, but free from your past . . . free to make a good life out of honest endeavour. I can't wait for our life together.'

He held her close and kissed her. It was slow and gentle, as though he was savouring every moment. Grace knew she was; she didn't know how long it would be until they'd see each other again.

They pulled away reluctantly as her parents arrived upstairs, looking shocked.

'Alfie!' they gasped.

Holly hurled herself at him, hugging Alfie close. 'I knew it! I knew you wouldn't leave us.'

'We thought—' Hugh began.

'I know,' Alfie said, pausing for a second to kiss Holly's bent head. 'I thought so too . . . but only for a moment, Mr Fairweather. I couldn't leave your daughter behind. My heart would hurt too much knowing I couldn't see her.'

'You'd rather go to gaol?' her mother asked, astonished.

'I think I would die for her, Mrs Fairweather,' he said, matter-of-factly.

'You nearly did,' Holly said, looking up to him with shining eyes.

Later, at the police station, a stunned Senior Sergeant Norman Jenkins read Alfie his rights, all the while looking at Grace with an expression that was somewhere between disbelief and apprehension.

'You had your chance, Sweeting,' he said as a constable arrived to handcuff Alfie. 'I'm confused as to why you didn't take it and escape.' He didn't allow Alfie to answer, deciding instead to press the point. 'You won't dodge prison, you know that.'

'I know, Norman,' he said, cheekily familiar. 'But you see, I've got something very sweet waiting for me.' He glanced over and winked at Grace as the handcuffs locked into place.

'Is that really necessary?' Grace asked, nodding at his wrists.

'It's protocol, miss,' the policeman said, looking at Norman, who nodded.

Alfie was gently turned and led towards the door. He looked back at Grace and Holly and grinned. 'See you soon, beautiful girls.'

EPILOGUE

November 1925

It seemed impossible, and yet the noise and speed of the work on the Sydney Harbour Bridge had intensified. The sound of metal being hammered, sparks flying above, was loud and at times exciting, other times exhausting.

'It might be finished by the time we get back,' Holly remarked.

This had made the Fairweathers and Norman Jenkins laugh. 'I doubt that very much, young Holly,' the newly appointed detective replied.

Grace had thought Norman looked rather good in his new dark suit and hat, which had replaced his sergeant's uniform. He now worked uptown at the police headquarters. The information Alfie had provided had helped him to crack open a cocaine syndicate linked to two gambling rings, setting him up for the promotion. She felt proud of Norman and had told him as much, when her parents were out of earshot looking at something on the harbour with Holly.

'I have your Alfie to thank for it,' Norm said, without embarrassment or rancour. 'I'm still shocked he defied me, but he also gave me something that was astonishing in its power.'

Grace nodded. 'Alfie showed himself to be brave in facing up to his failings.'

He smiled knowingly. 'His failings don't change anything for you, though, do they?'

She had laughed, knowing exactly what he meant. 'It's hard to stop loving someone, Norm.'

'You stopped loving me,' he said in an arch tone, and she could see he regretted the remark.

'Were we really in love, or we were in love with the idea of being a couple, being married, having a family?' she asked. 'I know you enjoy being around my parents . . . but that's because you didn't have the happiest of childhoods. Do you mind me observing that perhaps you were in love with that notion of a happy family?'

He looked thoughtful. 'I don't mind you observing it, no. But I want you to know, I was highly aware of how I felt about you but I clearly didn't convey that fully. I can see now that I didn't reveal my feelings sufficiently, occupying myself instead with the practicalities. I was too . . .'

'Bossy?' she finished for him, even though she knew that was not the word he searched for. 'A woman needs wooing, Norm. Remember that for next time. She likes a strong man but not one who wants to rule her.' She had smiled again and squeezed his arm. 'And there will be a next time for you. You're far too handsome and eligible now; women will be falling for you left, right and centre.'

He smiled, then looked down. 'But not you.'

'No. Not me. We're friends . . . true friends, Norm. You helped me when I most needed it. And I know it ran against your inclinations, that helping Alfie was potentially detrimental to your career, but you did it anyway, because you wanted to help me.'

'It was only for you.'

'And I'll be forever grateful.' She'd decided never to reveal her understanding that he had probably harboured an ulterior motive – albeit small, even unconscious – for his help.

'And so now you have an eighteen-month wait for him.'

She shrugged. 'Six months have already passed. I have a year left. It will go fast enough, and Alfie wrote to say that the solicitor has recently mentioned that he might even get out earlier.'

'He might, yes. They reward good behaviour, and I imagine Alfie is a popular and model prisoner.'

'I warned him not to get cocky and to start some innocent lark in prison that could get him noticed as a con artist.' She laughed.

'They say a leopard can't change its spots, Grace,' Norm cautioned her.

'Yes, but a leopard can be tamed. I plan to tame the wildness in Alfie, because I know he's yearning for domesticity.' She smiled. 'I have to trust my instincts.'

'And you're sure about going off to Europe for months on end?'

'Of course I am. I'm excited.'

'Not as excited as Holly,' he said.

She laughed. 'No, I've forbidden her any sugar for a week. She can barely contain herself. I'm going to have sleepless nights because there's no way she's closing her eyes.'

Norm smiled. 'It's very exciting for someone so young to be doing this grand trip. It's further than I've ever been – perhaps ever will.'

'She'll come back feeling changed in every way, I'm sure, and with new skills, new confidence and a new outlook on life. It's what I want for her.'

'You're good to people, Grace. I hear you've taken on more staff.'

She gave an embarrassed shrug. 'Lizzie and Sarah are like old hands now, and they could run the shop with one or two extra, but I decided to take on four new staff and get them trained up. Lizzie is a very good taskmaster, as it turns out – she's got real spine and won't put up with any nonsense, but she's also kind and perceptive. Mum and Dad will keep an eye on things while I'm gone. Between us, I think Mum is rather looking forward to sweeping in daily with her eagle eye and making sure it's all running to clockwork.'

'You're in a very different mood to six months ago.'

She nodded. 'It wasn't easy. But I picked myself up, focused on the shop.'

'I was worried for you. I thought losing Alfie might break you.'

'No. I knew he wouldn't escape prison time. And I'll be honest, learning that George Dooley was out of my life helped. I don't wish pain on anyone, Norm, but he liked to inflict it on others. I won't say he got what he deserved, but he certainly paid the price for his decisions.'

'He did. We've not caught his killers yet, but my gut tells me that while May Smith might have put a price on Alfie's head, I don't think she had Dooley killed.'

'The icing sugar was chilling, though. Surely that was directed at me . . . or at least the business.'

He gave a look of indecision. 'I'm fifty-fifty on that, Grace.'

'But it's sugar. How much more pertinent could it be?'

'It could simply be about money. Everything in the whole underbelly of Sydney is about money, you know that. Just about every crime. Even the violence we see in homes from time to time is often because that couple is struggling over money and their ability to cope is stretched too thin.'

'What's your point?'

'My point is that cocaine has a very high value and they're not going to waste what would have been the equivalent of perhaps many hundreds of pounds to deliver a message in the mouth of a corpse. But icing sugar mimics cocaine well enough, and the message is still there to those who understand. I think there's a chance you're reading the message personally and making the wrong connection . . . although you could be forgiven for doing so, given Dooley's attention to you.'

'Which I never wanted,' she groaned.

'No, but it had nothing to do with you or the Sugar Palace and was simply about Dooley himself. He wasn't exactly a loyal man. He was an opportunist . . . a thug for hire.'

'So if not May, who killed him, do you think?'

Norm shrugged. 'He'd managed to offend just about everyone, so take your pick.'

Grace gave a shudder. 'We'll never know and, frankly, I don't care, although I do care about his widow.'

'One of your new staff, I gather.' Norm shook his head with disbelief.

'Do you know everything, Norm?'

'Oh, I keep my ear to the ground. That was generous of you.'

'Well, she came into the shop, wanting to apologise that her husband's behaviour had threatened my livelihood. I think it was very decent of her. And it wasn't her fault that she was married to a monster. We got talking, as women do, and I decided she is a lovely person – and now suddenly impoverished. Without her husband's income, albeit a dodgy one, she must earn a living. I don't know what possessed her to marry him, but she loves working at the Sugar Palace, earning her own way, and she's got some great ideas for recipes. Besides, I understand her loneliness.'

Norm nodded. 'That makes sense. I never wanted to cause you pain, Grace. I thought you'd be angry with me for forcing Alfie out of the country, but it was the only way I could think of to save his life.'

'It was a safe way, anyway.'

Norm shifted his weight. 'I know there's no chance for us, but I do like this.'

'This?' she queried.

'Our friendship.'

She nodded; she liked this new relationship too.

'But I'll be honest,' he added. 'I doubt I shall ever stop loving you. Allowing Alfie to live under threat of death would have killed you as much as him. Offering him a way to safety was my selfish way of looking after you.'

She'd accept that. It made everything feel easier . . . neat.

Holly interrupted them. 'Passengers are boarding!' she said in a tight voice, just short of a squeal.

Grace looked at Norman with a look that conveyed an amused *Time to go*. 'You'll keep an eye on them, won't you?' she pressed, glancing over at her parents. They suddenly looked older, smaller, in her mind.

'I promise,' he said. 'If you promise to come back safe and sound.'

'Come on!' Holly said, now in an all-out shout.

'They won't leave without us, Holly,' Grace said, rolling her eyes with amusement. She looked back at Norm. 'Thank you.'

He shrugged as if there was nothing to thank him for.

'No, really. You've become the very best friend a girl could have.'

'The best kind of ex-fiancé is no claim to fame,' he said, but his tone was light and his gaze amused.

'I'd better begin the teary goodbye with Mum and Dad. Mum looks so tightly stretched, I'm frightened she'll catapult off this quay.'

'She'll miss you more than you give credit for,' he said softly. 'It must be wonderful to be loved so much.'

Grace and Holly were out on the middle deck with a host of other passengers bound for Europe. First-class passengers, she noted, were on the top deck, but she and Holly were happy with their cosy cabin with twin beds and porthole in second class. It was all very compact but easy to live in for the next five weeks at sea.

They were sailing towards the heads. The ship's horn blasted and brought her out of her thoughts of leaving Australia.

'That's the ship thanking the pilot,' Grace explained to Holly, who had been waving at every craft they passed from ferries to a lovely old wooden barquentine that was being towed into port.

'The pilot?'

Grace explained that this referred to the tiny tugboat and the man she saw boarding it with confidence from the big ship just moments ago, which had guided them safely out of the harbour and into open water.

'But we can see where the sea is, surely?'

Grace laughed. 'Yes, I'm sure the captain and crew are well aware, but they could be English or European and don't know these waters close to the harbour well enough. A maritime pilot navigates them into and out of a harbour safely. It happens all over the world.'

'I think I love being at sea.' Holly sighed.

'We've barely begun,' Grace said, laughing, 'but I agree. It's very exciting.'

'My life is exciting! I can't believe I'm really here, Grace.' Holly made a point of pretending to pinch herself. 'And it's all because of you, taking pity on a girl who didn't think she should ever dream of a better life.'

Grace grew a little more serious, smoothing down the sleeve of Holly's dress. In her new clothes, she looked every inch the proper miss. 'It's Alfie you should thank. He was the one who noticed you and told me about you. Tilly might have thought she was sending in her spy to keep an eye on him and his barrow, but it was Alfie who encouraged her to send you. He was determined to get you away from that ghastly life.' She shrugged. 'I wouldn't have known you without Alfie.'

Holly looked down. 'I miss him.'

Grace nodded and gave a sad smile. 'I do too. But you know, Holly, when we're all reunited, I believe we shall all be different for our experiences. Alfie will never want to be put behind bars again. And Europe is going to change us. Do you know that Mr Brunner in Switzerland is going to teach me how to conch chocolate to its uniformly rich and creamy state, and Mr Perkins in London has agreed to show me how to encapsulate fruit into a lightly scented cream, where both remain luscious within their capsule of chocolate? I am thinking about a new line of sophisticated, adult chocolates that use liqueurs, while I want you to learn how to make superb fruit jellies that we can preserve easily within their dusting of sugar. There is so much to learn. We're going to grow, expand our business, and by the time Alfie comes out, you and I are going to find new sites to open our second store in Sydney and our first store in Melbourne.'

Holly's eyes were shining. 'Grace! That's scary.'

'No, it's ambitious, and you're going to be very important to the success of our business. Do you know why?'

Her young companion shrugged.

'Because while I have a lot of ambition, I can't wait much longer to start a family. If I leave it much longer, it may pass me by. So I'm going to get busy having babies and I need you to be me. Be my arms and legs for a while.'

'Grace, I'm not sure I can be—'

'Of course you can. I'm so certain of it. Holly, I want to make you a partner as soon as you turn eighteen. You, me and Alfie will own the Sugar Palace equally. You're young, you're smart and you're as excited as I am by confectionery.'

Holly looked as though she might faint from all this extra excitement.

'My aim is to make the Sugar Palace one of the most recognisable, loved and successful operations in Australia, but I need you to help me achieve that, because I also want to be a good wife and a good mother through our busy years.'

Holly hugged her. 'Thank you, Grace. I would be grateful just to have you for my family, but . . .' She couldn't finish because tears welled and her throat caught. 'Happy tears,' she choked out as Grace put an arm around her.

'Holly!' a young woman called out, waving. Grace had seen Holly talking with her earlier. She was travelling with her parents and three sisters to Southampton in England. Around eighteen, she was the youngest by far; her sisters looked to be in their late twenties and Grace had noted how Holly's eyes had lit to see a passenger not too far off her own age. 'Come and see this.' She pointed away from the cluster of passengers.

'Go on,' Grace encouraged Holly. 'Nice to make new friends. It's a long voyage.'

'Back in a sec,' Holly said, and Grace noted the wind had already dried her friend's eyes. She watched her leave and then turned back to lean over the deck, enjoying the opportunity to be alone with her own thoughts.

She folded her arms against the wind that was picking up and closed her eyes briefly while she allowed herself to accept that while life had taken a few surprise turns, everything had turned out for the best. There was so much to look forward to and plenty to be grateful for, not the least of which was her healthy bank account and the ability as an independent woman to take herself off as she was now to explore life, the world – even herself. Yes, she too would grow through this journey. She had already changed even in this last year: no longer working in the family store or living above it. For the past five months, she'd rented a two-bedroom flat for herself and Holly and given that up now to travel.

When they got back to Sydney, she'd think about more long-term lodgings, perhaps a shop site that had accommodation above. Leaving the grocery store properly had allowed her to stop feeling like a child, which she presumed working alongside parents so often unhappily promoted. Working for herself gave her a sense of identity and power; decisions, good or bad, were hers to make now. She'd come a long way in a short time, and although she knew many would consider Alfie a poor decision – a mistake, even – she didn't view it that way. Alfie had broadened her, broken her out of her sheltered existence and allowed her to glimpse a larger life. She didn't love all of it, of course; his actions had created so much angst, but she'd grown through those challenges and was somehow tougher, more worldly for it.

She'd never expected to throw a party for a group of working girls, for example. As promised to Tilly, Grace had opened the shop on a Sunday during winter, when her idea of creating sculptures from chocolate that the girls could admire before smashing would not suffer from the heat. She'd kept her promise to make Tilly a dress that was a fabulous confection of licorice, spun sugar and boiled lollies to serve as jewels. She'd laid all the edible elements against a waxed paper form and, after helping Tilly into the dress, the madam caused a sensation among her workers, dropping glittering sugar wherever she moved. She even let them pull off bits of the confectionery to enjoy. Holly had the great idea to make fascinators from spun sugar, which the women adored, and even some hats from licorice straps wound together. Grace and her team had filled the store to brimming with a new line of cakes they wanted to trial as well as candy floss with the new machine. When the party finally ended, the women looked like they all needed a good sleep so the vast amounts of sugar they'd consumed could be quietly dealt with by their exhausted bodies. Even Tilly looked like she never wanted to see another piece of fudge. 'Well done, pet. We had a very good time. We'll see you next year for the same.'

That was about as much praise as Tilly might heap on anyone, Grace was sure, and the two women shook hands: not friends, but no longer enemies. As she made to leave, Tilly had tapped Grace on the cheek. 'He'll be back before you know it. That Alfie will talk his way out of prison long before his sentence ends.'

The Sugar Palace would not have happened as fast without him and his ideas. And it had its own momentum now. Her notion of opening new sites was not out of reach, and she would make that a reality once Alfie was back in her life. She touched the affectionate and amusing letter he'd recently sent, which she kept in her pocket. She took it out now to read it again, reminding herself that she would make it her business to teach him to write for himself in the future.

Hello darlin',

I've got a mate writing this for me. His name is Albert and we share a prison cell. They call us 'The Two Als' here, and I must say I feel lucky that I share my life with Big Al. He's a good sort and has taken me under his wing, teaching me the ropes. We're not connected to any gangs in here and we keep ourselves to ourselves, but we have set up a little game of two-up that we play once a week. We can't make much but Albert likes the tobacco he wins and I like that it keeps my mind busy. I'm like Holly . . . I like to count and play with numbers in my head. And that brings me to an idea I had, darlin', to make big sugar numbers that people can use for birthday celebrations, or even small ones on sticks that they could prod into cakes. Anyway, it's a thought you can play with when you're in one of your imaginative moods.

Life isn't so bad, but I know it's going to be so much better when I'm out and I will never, never come back here, I swear it on my life. But for now I am doing all right, all things considered. Each night I kiss the photo you sent me and while I know you and Holly will be making tracks for my old country by the time this reaches you, I hope that you can feel me kissing you each night wherever you are. Albert had a suggestion. We can see the moon from our cell and he said I should tell you to look at the moon at the same time each evening, knowing I'll be looking at it too.

Shall we try it? Let's say around nine o'clock each evening, even if she's behind clouds, and I'm going to blow a kiss to the moon and you can catch it. I'll kiss you at nine o'clock every night, no matter where you are in the world, and I shall send my love with it and my promise that we shall be together as soon as I can get out of here.

Oh, by the way, the solicitor has told me that if I keep up my good behaviour and polite ways, I might be able to get out earlier . . . maybe even in time for your next party with Tilly. Albert read me your letter and I laughed at the descriptions you gave of Tilly in her sugar dress and all the girls drunk on sweets and chocolates. That must have been some party. Well done to you and Holly.

Well, my darlin', I am proud of how brave you're being, sailing off to a new land, and I hope it is everything you wish it to be. I know you and Holly will return with lots of new recipes and new ideas for the Sugar Palace. I'm sure by the time I hold you again you'll be telling me about a new shop somewhere, and my chest will swell out more than you can imagine at my girl and how clever and brilliant she is.

Nobody believes me that you're my fiancée when I show them your picture. So I need to hurry up and get out of here

375

so I can put a ring on your finger and show them all that Alfie Sweeting is a winner and his wife is even more impressive. Hug Holly for me. Catch my kisses, and know I want only the best for you. I look forward to hearing about your adventures.

x Alfie

Grace sighed. It was indeed an adventure ahead . . . England, Switzerland, France and Belgium. Three months of travel and enrichment in the business of chocolate and confectionery. She felt a fresh thrum of excitement just thinking about everything they'd get to experience.

Grace looked at the sun bouncing off the sparkling Sydney waters, creating a kaleidoscope of reflections like thousands of diamonds as the ship heaved itself slowly away from the city's backdrop. She moistened her lips against the drying breeze as it whipped at her hair and tried to find a way to lift the shawl she'd wrapped around her shoulders.

And as she did so, she tasted salt and helplessly began to think about combining it with sugar . . . a looser, chewy caramel, perhaps, sprinkled with tiny salt flakes. Maybe even a liquid caramel, salted and offered as a topping for ice cream or to layer in cakes. She could call it their marine range, or the Sugar Palace seaside range, and add chewy jelly gums in the shape of starfish, whales and little boats, and boiled sweets that looked like multi-coloured fish. A range of ice cream could be part of it – she'd never offered ice cream in the store and it would require rethinking the layout and setting up refrigeration, but ice cream was a logical new line for a specialty sweet store. Everyone loved an ice cream at the seaside, didn't they?

Yes. The Sugar Palace didn't need to constrain itself. Anything that involved a sweet treat should be hers to play with, and then there was that birthday-party line that she hadn't yet begun to think through . . .

Grace remembered how the same thought had hit Alfie in the same moment. She smiled. It was a sign of their bond and how in tune with each other they truly were. She would wait for him, and they would plan that new range together.

The ship gave another blast, a last farewell to Sydney as they sailed through the famous heads that all ships passed through, either arriving into the safe harbour or leaving it. Grace inhaled, holding the breath that contained her last tie to Australia, and then let it out slowly, smiling at the notion of exhaling her last gulp of Sydney air.

They were out into open sea, and it felt like a release from regrets. Home was behind her. Life was in front of her.

ACKNOWLEDGEMENTS

I'm not sure why it's taken me so long to write a story about confectionery. I've been obsessed with sweets since the mid-1960s when I was old enough to be given pocket money. I remember a silver sixpence each Friday, given specifically to take to the local sweetshop in Hove, Sussex.

I can conjure the smell of that shop this moment. First, opening the huge wooden door and the bell sounding above us children trooping in. The owner was a woman who looked one hundred years old to me, but now that I think about her, she was simply steely-haired. She was tall, dressed immaculately with a pixie haircut, red lips and a voice that sounded like she was either a smoker or she gargled with gin and gravel. It was an old-fashioned newsagency and tobacconist that sold everything from all the daily newspapers to every incarnation of cigarettes and tobacco and, most importantly, the glorious confectionery.

Huge jars of sweets lined the shop. I can smell them in my imagination . . . pear drops, mint imperials, sherbet pips, spaceships, toffees, jellies and a host of others I won't become tedious naming, so many of them glistening with a dusting of sugar crystals to slash the roof of my greedy mouth.

Then there were the boxes of chocolates. In England, it was the norm to give a proper selection of boxed chocolates and they came in so many sizes, including one box that was so huge it could blot out a desk. It usually had a scene of a cottage and countryside on it and no doubt where we have derived the expression of 'as pretty as a chocolate box'. Don't get me started on Easter time in that shop.

But the very best part was below the counter; at a five-year-old's height were low shelves laden with open boxes of sweets: black jacks, fruit salad, liquorice straps, sherbet fountains, gob-stoppers, lollipops, musk sticks, violet sweets, bubble gum . . . on and on. These were all four for a penny, so with six pennies to burn, that's where I lurked. I could spend at least ten minutes – a lifetime when you're small – carefully curating my choice for that weekend. Those sweets didn't have to be shared either.

I wish I could remember the owner's name. She would carefully count out our sweets into little white paper bags that she would twist at the corner, so we could be assured we were getting what we wanted. She would then count out our money, ensuring we learned how to add up our own purchases to get it exactly to sixpence in my case. This was very kind of her to take time out of her day to attend to children and not expect our mothers to do this. I learned from her for my character of Grace about taking an interest in the children who would drive the booming sales in her sweets.

Those sorts of everyday English sweetshops are lost now, dis-appearing through the 1970s and 1980s as supermarkets took over. Now you still get the tourist version, but the memory is as indelible in my imagination as it probably is for Aussies who are nostalgic about the local milk bars from that same time period.

Sweets still remain very important in my life. And as a baker I reach for sugar in all of its incarnations most weeks to pull together something delicious. I think I would go into full-blown panic if my pantry didn't have caster sugar and soft brown sugar at the ready at any time, and I still like to take a little sugar in my tea and coffee. I always have chocolate stashed away in corners for a moment of need, plus I have sweets all over the place – the glovebox and door of my car, in pockets, in handbags, in drawers. Nothing thrills me more than discovering a sherbet lemon at the bottom of a handbag I haven't used in a while. I eat it immediately.

I just never grew up from that little girl in the sweetshop, and although this story is set in Australia, it feels as real and nostalgic to me as it felt when I was crafting *The Chocolate Tin* and I went wild in my imagination for chocolate, one of the great loves of my life.

Anyway, there are people to thank who have made it possible for me to bring this book into being. I would like to acknowledge Heather Garnsey, a local historian, for her unwavering and generous help with Sydney's social history when I was struggling to find what I needed. To Fiorella and her colleagues at The Rocks Walking Tours: being taken around with a guide who was as excited about the walk as I was became intoxicating and together we pulled together a skeleton of Grace Fairweather's life down at The Rocks in the early 1920s.

The Fullerton Hotel's guide, Vicki, who gave me all the lovely history surrounding the old GPO that is now a five-star hotel. And to Jess in marketing for a magnificent book about the history of the old GPO and its new purpose. My thanks to Natalie Cody, one of the fabulous guides from the Queen Victoria Building in Sydney where I chose to base *The Sugar Palace*. She got into the excitement of the tale and came up with old photos and ideas. Thanks to Dr Nicola Teffer, who did her best to help me with Quong Tart Tea House, which I desperately wanted to use in the story. Sadly my tale is set in the wrong era but I loved the research.

The Police and Justice Museum down at Circular Quay is so worth a look – please visit – and support these fabulous presentations of the city's history. I learned so much that has gone into this story about the razor gangs and brothel owners.

Sadly, Charlotte Street down at The Rocks, which I was desperate to see, was all closed up due to Covid. In fact, I had to make a separate journey back to Sydney one weekend simply to get into the Police and Justice Museum, which only opened on Saturdays during the restrictions. Despite it all, I managed to find enough through those tricky times to write this story for you, which I hope you enjoy.

It's meant to be fun. I hope you can taste sugar on your lips as you read and that it makes you want to reach for candy floss or marshmallow each time you close the cover on another chapter!

Thanks to my publishing team for all their enthusiasm for this project, especially Ali Watts, Amanda Martin, Heidi Camilleri, Hannah Ludbrook, Jo Baker, Chris Ebbs, Janine Brown and Holly Toohey, and Louisa Maggio for the achingly sweet and pretty cover. On and on my thanks go to the Penguin team around Australia for their support. That of course extends to all the booksellers around Australia and New Zealand – support them, everyone – and thank you for always stocking my books. Libraries – thank you for having my books on your shelves, available for audio and digital too, for when people in your communities come looking.

And to my readers. Can't miss out on a big *mwah* to all of you for looking forward to another of my books. Thank you for joining me on a nostalgic journey with this one into a sweet tale with a sour underbelly.

Finally, my family . . . love and sweet thanks for the laughter and constant support. Fx

Book Club Notes

1. The Sugar Palace sounds like a delightful destination. Which of Grace's creations would be most irresistible to you? Were any of your childhood favourites mentioned?

2. Grace's parents expect her to marry Norman. In what ways would such a union have changed the course of Grace's life? Do you think he was ever really a likely suitor?

3. 'What's life without some risk?' Grace asks her mother after being warned that Alfie is a dreamer. Do you think Alfie's wins are worth the risks when he is gambling with others' futures?

4. When Grace discovers what Alfie has really been up to under the cover of her sweets business, she is furious but she gives him another chance. Do you think she made the right decision?

5. Alfie is determined to make sure Holly doesn't have to work in the brothel as she's destined to. Does Alfie have any other qualities that you admire?

6. In what ways do Grace and Alfie make such a successful team in business, and in life?

7. How do the characters of Grace and Alfie change throughout the course of the novel?

8. Do you think George Dooley made his own destiny?

9. Tilly Devine and May Smith were formidable true characters from the era. Discuss the ways in which women's lives and choices back then were different to today.

10. Who would you cast in the roles of Grace, Alfie, Holly and Tilly in a screen adaptation of *The Sugar Palace*?

11. Did you spot a character from one of Fiona's other novels visiting the Sugar Palace?

12. Have you ever visited any of the real-life settings from one of Fiona McIntosh's novels?

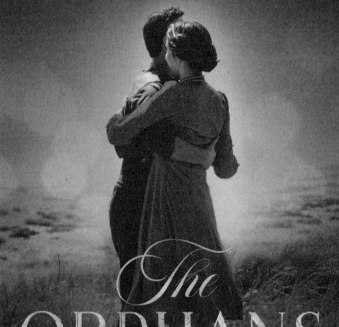

MILLION COPY BESTSELLING AUTHOR

FIONA McINTOSH

The ORPHANS

Orphan Fleur Appleby is adopted by a loving undertaker and his wife and she quickly develops a special gift for helping bereaved families. Her ambition to be the first female mortician in the country is fuelled by her plan to bring more women into the male dominated funeral industry.

Raised in the outback of South Australia's Flinders Ranges, Tom Catchlove is faced with a life-changing tragedy as a young boy. He works hard but dreams big, striving for a future as a wool classer.

A chance encounter between the two children will change the course of their lives.

By adulthood Fleur finds herself fighting for the survival of the family's business, while her widowed father drinks away generations of prosperity and a new, conniving stepmother wants Fleur gone. When Tom emerges from the isolation of the desert to find new work at the port woolstores, his path crosses with Fleur's again – only to be caught up in a murder investigation, in which they can only trust each other.

At once tragic and triumphant, *The Orphans* is an unforgettable story about a unique bond between two children that will echo down the years, and teach them both about the real meaning of life, of loss, and of love.

'Flawless.' *Australian Women's Weekly*

INTERNATIONAL BESTSELLING AUTHOR

FIONA McINTOSH

The

SPY'S WIFE

Evie, a widow and stationmaster's daughter, can't help but look out for the weekly visit of the handsome man she and her sister call the Southerner on their train platform in the wilds of northern England. When polite salutations shift to friendly conversations, they become captivated by each other. After so much sorrow, the childless Evie can't believe love and the chance for her own family have come into her life again.

With rumours coming out of Germany that Hitler may be stirring up war, local English authorities have warned against spies. Even Evie becomes suspicious of her new suitor, Roger. But all is not what it seems.

When Roger is arrested, Evie comes up with an audacious plan to prove his innocence that means moving to Germany and working as a British counter-spy. Wearing the disguise of dutiful, naïve wife, Evie must charm the Nazi Party's dangerous officials to bring home hard evidence of war mongering on the Führer's part.

But in this game of cat and mouse, it seems everyone has an ulterior motive, and Evie finds it impossible to know who to trust. With lives on the line, ultimate sacrifices will be made as she wrestles between her patriotism and saving the man she loves.

From the windswept moors of the Yorkshire dales to the noisy beer halls of Munich and grand country estates in the picture-book Bavarian mountains, this is a lively and high-stakes thriller that will keep you second-guessing until the very end.

MILLION COPY BESTSELLING AUTHOR

FIONA McINTOSH

FOUL PLAY

A NEW JACK HAWKSWORTH NOVEL

The heart-stopping new crime thriller in the Detective Jack Hawksworth series by blockbuster author Fiona McIntosh.

Superstar footballer Luca Bruni is being blackmailed for a night of lust he swears he didn't participate in . . . except the ransom photo denies that. A media darling on and off the field, he has powerful charisma, a perfect home life he'll do anything to protect, and more money than he knows what to do with. He's determined to defy the extortion racket.

When Detective Superintendent Jack Hawksworth learns that the cunning mastermind behind this crime has already swindled a dozen of the world's most highly prized male athletes, he is instructed to keep the situation from escalating and prevent a media frenzy.

Intrigued by the creativity of the crime and the shockwaves it is creating through the global sporting fraternity, Jack begins a journey into a case that has tentacles far more wide-reaching that he ever imagined – and far more deadly.

The explosive new blockbuster from an internationally bestselling author.

Powered by Penguin

Looking for more great reads, exclusive content and book giveaways?

Subscribe to our weekly newsletter.

Scan the QR code or visit penguin.com.au/signup